Hunting Hannah

by

C. B. Clark

Dedication

To my awesome editor, ELF. It's been a long and wonderful journey.

Chapter 1

Hannah Marchand slid the dust-coated plastic blind aside and peeked through the apartment lobby window. She blew out a shaky breath. The big black truck with the dark-tinted windows was nowhere in sight.

She heaved the heavy duffel up and slung the nylon strap over her shoulder, pushed open the door, slipped through to the sidewalk, and bolted to her car parked fifty meters down the street. Chest heaving, she unlocked the car and wrenched open the back door. She tossed in the bag and slammed the door closed.

The rumble of a vehicle's powerful motor shattered the morning quiet, and she jerked to a standstill, her heart pounding.

Not now. Please, not now.

She ducked, crouching beside her car, and peeked over the small car's hood.

A large black SUV pulled out of a cross street and cruised down the road toward her.

The female driver stared ahead, focused on steering the large vehicle between the parked vehicles lining both sides of the residential street.

Hannah's breath whooshed out in an explosion of air.

Not him! Not this time.

The SUV continued down the street and turned the corner.

Her knees shook as she stood and glanced around, hoping no one had witnessed her cowering in fear.

She froze.

A small white sheet of paper was stuck under her windshield wiper, a ragged corner flapping in the morning breeze.

A trill of unease rippled along her spine, and she whipped around and once again studied her surroundings.

Nothing.

No suspicious idling vehicle, no dark figure lurking in a doorway. The street was deserted.

The paper was probably a flyer announcing a local garage sale or a fundraiser. She leaned over the hood, lifted the wiper blade, and tugged out the sheet. Unfolding it, she gasped.

Written in bold red marker were the words, *True love never dies.*

The paper dropped from her nerveless fingers and fluttered to her feet. A gust of wind caught it, and the ominous note blew into the street, landing in a puddle left over from the previous night's rain.

She sagged against the car's fender.

Derek! It was him. He'd left the note. How many times had he quoted that same phrase?

She tugged her phone from her pocket. Time to call the cops. This had to stop. Stalking was a serious crime. She pressed the number nine on the digital keypad but stopped before hitting the next two numbers. What was she doing? If her boss at the magazine heard Hannah was possibly in danger, Marilyn would clamp down like a mother hen and demand Hannah cease all field assignments and work from the safety of the office.

That restriction would be a death knell to her budding career. She couldn't do her job if she were hiding, and Marilyn wouldn't trust her to handle future challenging assignments. She'd be stuck reporting on trivial topics like the paint color of the year or a new diet fad.

She stared at the soggy paper. The red ink had blurred, the threatening words dissolving in a red haze that resembled blood. But she didn't need to see them. The words were branded on her brain.

True love never dies.

She shuddered and stuffed the phone back into her pocket. If she wanted to be an investigative journalist like she'd always dreamed of, she had to handle this nightmare herself. She didn't want anyone, especially her senior editor, thinking she was soft.

Traffic was picking up as people began their morning commute, but there was still no sign of a black four-by-four pickup truck. She could escape like she'd planned. Once she was out of Vancouver, Derek wouldn't have any idea where she'd gone, and she could focus on her assignment.

But she had to play it smart. He could be lurking somewhere nearby, watching, waiting for her to leave so he could follow. He'd done that before. She'd left home, thinking she was alone, but then there he was…standing in the dairy aisle of the grocery store, mingling with her fellow office workers in the crowded lobby at work, or lurking on the street across from her hairdresser's shop, or— She shuddered and scanned the street again.

No sign of her stalker.

Now was her chance to get away. At least for a couple of weeks. By the time she returned, he'd hopefully have lost interest, and the harassment would end. But she wasn't out of the city yet. She had to assume he was there, waiting to confront her and profess his undying love, demanding she give him a second chance.

She'd lain awake all night, thinking about how she was going to slip out of town without him finding out. As the dawn's cold light filtered through her bedroom window, she'd come up with a plan. It wasn't fancy, but she hoped the simplicity of her evasion would catch Derek off guard.

She scurried around the hood of her car and flung open the driver's door. Jumping in, she settled behind the wheel, strapped on her seatbelt, and adjusted the rearview mirror. Inhaling a deep breath, she gripped the steering wheel.

Here we go.

She started the car and signaled as she entered the line of traffic. No point being evasive. Not yet. Not until she was certain he was tailing her. He knew what vehicle she drove and where she lived. If he was watching, she wanted to lure him into the open.

And then, God willing, she'd lose him in the heavy rush-hour traffic filling the streets. If she made it out of Vancouver without him following, she'd be free of her constant weight of fear and the terrible certainty that he was escalating and her life was in danger. The two weeks away would give her time to recuperate and think, to plan what she'd do next and how she'd stop him.

She studied the street.

Still no sign of him or his truck.

Maybe this would be easy.

As if conjured by the power of her thoughts, an all-too-familiar black truck roared past the car trailing her and squeezed into the space behind her vehicle.

Her heart lodged in her throat.

The gleaming chrome grill of the massive truck filled her rearview mirror. The darkened windshield hid the driver's face, but she knew it was him. How many nights had she spotted the large black truck parked on the street outside her apartment?

She shot another glance in the rearview mirror.

The jacked-up truck was tailgating, its lights blinding, its monstrous front bumper almost on top of her small car.

Anger replaced her fear. Tightening her grip on the steering wheel, she wrenched the wheel hard to the right. The car squealed around the corner into a narrow alley, missing a dumpster by centimeters. Her heart rate kicked up a notch.

The thunderous roar of the pursuing truck's powerful motor echoed off the brick walls like a ferocious charging beast.

Muttering a prayer, she jammed her foot on the gas pedal, and the little car sped down the narrow lane, bouncing from one rain-filled pothole to another. The graffiti-painted walls were a blur as she navigated past garbage cans, stacks of weathered wood pallets, and an old mattress. Bursting into the cross street, she held her breath as she squeezed the car between an SUV and a sedan and blended into the flow of traffic.

A blare of horns erupted behind her.

She glanced in the rearview mirror.

No one was letting the big vehicle merge into the lane.

The black truck was blocked.

She fist pumped the air. Yes!

Turning left at the next intersection, then taking a sharp right and another right, she flew up the on-ramp leading to the four-lane freeway, her car's engine screaming in protest. The highway was jammed bumper-to-bumper with commuters heading into downtown Vancouver from the suburbs.

Her gaze swung between the rearview mirror and the double lane of vehicles ahead. She sped past a red sedan and swerved into the right lane, grazing the rear bumper of a blue car. The impact jolted her car, and for a heart-stopping second, she lost control.

The driver behind her braked, narrowly avoiding a major collision. He blasted his horn and scowled his displeasure.

Heat flared up her neck, but she raced on.

Another quick glance in the rearview mirror.

No sign of a black truck.

Not yet.

She gunned the motor, weaving in and out of traffic, earning more angry horn blasts. Another four kilometers, and without signaling her intention, she whipped across two lanes of traffic and exited the freeway onto a secondary road. She backtracked three blocks and reentered the freeway, going in the opposite direction.

Traffic was light heading out of the city, and she zipped down the road. Euphoria swamped her. Her plan worked. She'd lost him!

For now.

The thought of him following her to Renton Falls made her stomach heave. She rolled her shoulders to ease the tightness in her back and neck. Derek didn't know she was leaving town or where she was going. For the next fourteen days, she was safe.

The stress of the past months was wearing. She couldn't sleep, hardly ate, and was afraid to leave her apartment. Every time her cell phone rang or signaled an incoming text, her heart raced, and her stomach clenched. After she got over her initial disappointment about the small-scale article, she'd jumped at this assignment. Renton Falls, a small lumber town in northern British Columbia, wasn't the usual locale for her writing assignments, but it was hundreds of kilometers from Vancouver. Hundreds of kilometers from Derek.

She studied the line of traffic behind her in the mirror again.

Still no black truck.

Accelerating, she passed the car ahead, slipped into the right lane, and set the car on cruise control. She wiped the dampness from her brow with the back of her hand and settled behind the wheel.

He wasn't following her anymore, and there was no way he'd find her. Not where she was going. For the next two weeks, she'd be free of the constant worry and unease that had drained her soul.

She exhaled a deep breath, switched on the radio, and relaxed for the first time in months as the throbbing beat of rock and roll filled the car.

Chapter 2

She squinted in the glare of the noonday sun as it blazed in the rearview mirror. The road behind was empty of vehicles. Like the previous time she checked. And the time before that and the time before that. There hadn't been another car, pickup truck, or semitrailer behind her since she'd pulled out of the gas station in the last town.

She smiled her first real smile in weeks. Derek was hundreds of kilometers away in Vancouver, sitting in his big truck outside her apartment, twiddling his thumbs and wondering where she was.

She'd driven straight through, only stopping for bathroom and snack breaks. The car's air conditioning shut down the previous afternoon, and she had to drive with the windows open. She grimaced. Never a good idea when travelling on gravel roads. A layer of dust caked her once-shiny gray car, and the windshield was chipped and starred from flying rocks.

The long hours of driving, the endless dust, and the bone-deep achiness from the rough roads were worth the discomfort. She was as far from home as possible without getting on a plane.

As if.

Flying was out of the question. Derek would be watching the airports. She shuddered. He'd know if she hopped on a plane, and, with his connections, it wouldn't take him long to find out where she was going.

She gripped the wheel and steered the car out of a deep bone-jarring rut and onto smoother gravel. It would be a miracle if the springs on her little car survived.

When Marilyn Reynolds, the managing editor at *Aspire,* called Hannah into her office the previous week and assigned her the story on archaeological excavations in northern British Columbia, Hannah's ego had burst like a balloon. Another puff piece. Another article no one would read. Most readers didn't care about archaeology unless gold bullion or priceless diamonds and rubies were discovered. The days starring a dashing archaeologist fighting off evil villains and discovering ancient relics were over. People were interested in current world events, not ancient history.

In the three years she'd worked at *Aspire,* not one of her stories had run as the lead article. Marilyn assigned her items on fashion, trendy restaurants, and minor celebrities, while Hannah wanted to investigate political scandals and climate change or report on the latest financial crises. Those stories sold magazines and garnered a journalist a coveted feature article, a front-page headline, and awards.

Her first reaction was to refuse the assignment, but when she had time to think, she changed her mind. Researching the story would get her out of town. *Way* out of town. And right now, she desperately wanted to disappear for a few weeks. Somewhere no one would find her. More specifically, a place *Derek* wouldn't find her. All the better if she was getting paid for her disappearing act.

As it turned out, her older brother, Peter, was a friend of an archaeologist who was leading an excavation in northern British Columbia, and had agreed to take her to the remote site and make the necessary introductions.

It would be great to see Peter. He and his wife had recently split up after three years of marriage, and he was struggling. She hoped to offer him a shoulder to cry on and a sympathetic ear.

A sign at the top of the hill indicated Renton Falls was less than an hour away. The small town was located on the shores of Sturgeon Lake, off the Alaska Highway in northern British Columbia. Logging was the main industry, which wasn't a surprise, considering the acres of towering coniferous trees lining the sides of the road and stretching into the distance.

Shifting her bottom on the seat, trying to find a comfortable position, she bit back a yawn. She was ready to get out of the car. More than ready. It had been a long two days.

Bang!

The car pitched, the tires skidding on the loose gravel.

Her tiredness vanished, and her heart rate shot through the stratosphere. She clamped hard on the steering wheel, struggling to control the vehicle, swerving close to the trees at eighty kilometers an hour. Steering into the skid, she eased off the gas, gently touching the brake.

The car swerved, spewing gravel from the rear tires.

A steep ravine, lined by sharp rocks and stubby pines, rushed toward her. Holding her breath, she braced for the impact.

Incredibly, the tires gripped the road and the car slowed, skidding to a stop centimeters from the weed-filled shoulder and deep ditch.

Easing her cramped sweaty fingers from the steering wheel, she switched off the engine. Dust settled over the car in a choking cloud. Her heart thundered in the sudden silence, and she sucked in a lungful of dusty air. She unclasped the seat-belt strap and laid her head against the steering wheel. Oh man. That could've been bad. Real bad.

A sharp rapping sounded on the window beside her.

She jumped and let out a shriek.

A face loomed in the driver's-side window.

Before she could react and hit the lock control, the door swung open and cool air rushed in.

A man, his features shadowed by the glare of the late afternoon sun, stood in the door opening. "Are you all right?"

She scrambled across the seat, digging into her purse, searching for her cell phone. Tugging it free, she wielded the small phone as if it were a weapon.

He held his hands out, palms up, before him. "Hey, take it easy, lady. I'm not going to hurt you."

Who was this guy? Did it matter? He was a stranger, and after the stress of the past months, her nerves were raw. She didn't trust anyone, especially a man. She lived in the city. She knew the stakes...a woman alone on a deserted road in the middle of nowhere. Her fingers trembled as she punched 911 into her phone.

Chapter 3

"Good luck with that." He nodded at the phone clenched in her hand. "There's no cell service out here."

"What?"

"Go ahead. Check it out. You'll see what I mean."

She studied the screen. No signal bars. Stuffing the useless phone into her pocket, she edged closer to the passenger side door. "Who are you?" She swallowed. "What do you want?"

"Your car was swerving all over the road. You're lucky you didn't go over the bank." Tilting his head, he stepped closer, and his dark gaze settled on her. "I stopped to make sure you're okay. Are you?"

"I-I don't know what happened. I heard a bang, and the next thing I knew, the car was out of control. I-I almost hit the ditch."

"Come on out of there, and let's make sure you're not hurt." As if aware of her nervousness, he stepped back, giving her space to climb out.

As soon as she stood on the gravel road, her legs wobbled, and she sagged and would've fallen if he hadn't caught her around the waist.

"Careful. You're probably in shock." Keeping his arm around her, he led her to the side of the road and helped her sit on a large flat-topped boulder. He released her and backed up a few paces.

She squinted, getting her first clear look at her

rescuer. Something other than fear fluttered in her stomach. With his shoulder-length dark hair and rugged face, he was leading-man-meets-heartthrob handsome. The rest of him wasn't bad either. Tall, with a body worth weeping over, from his broad shoulders down to his muscular thighs encased in faded denim. Her gaze returned to his face.

The glint in his dark eyes made it clear he was aware of her examination.

She flushed, and heat surged up her neck and onto her cheeks. But then she remembered where she was—on a deserted road in the middle of nowhere. His good looks didn't mean a thing. She, of all people, should know that. "Thanks for stopping, but I'm fine now."

His warm smile transformed his rugged features from handsome to seriously high-decibel hot. Silver lights sparked in the depths of his ebony eyes. "I'm harmless, I promise. I'm from around here, and when we see someone in trouble, we stop to offer help. It's the code of the North."

His husky voice washed over her like a warm bath, and she opened her mouth to thank him again, but her tongue refused to cooperate, as if she were caught in a spell, held captive by nothing but the power of his gaze.

Slow down, girl.

She didn't know this guy. He could be an axe murderer, or a rapist, or— She shook her head and rubbed her hands over her face. Or a decent person who saw someone in trouble and stopped to help.

He pointed at her car. "Looks like you've got a flat. Do you have a spare?"

"Wh-what?"

He puckered his brow. "Are you sure you're okay?

You didn't hit your head or anything?"

"I-I don't think so."

"You blew a tire. You're lucky you were able to stop the car before you went over the bank. There was a guy a few years ago whose car went into the ditch. He wasn't found for weeks."

"My car has a flat tire?"

"Looks like it." He turned toward the car. "Where's your spare tire and jack? In the trunk?"

"No, it's okay. Thanks, but I can take it from here." She pushed to her feet. Her father had been a mechanic, and he'd made sure her brother and she knew their way around a car. He'd taught them how to change a tire, do an oil change, and even change the spark plugs.

He ignored her protest and strode to her car, leaned into the driver's side of the vehicle, and flipped the switch to open the trunk hatch. Strolling to the open trunk, he fished inside and withdrew the jack and lifted out the spare tire. The muscles in his arms bulged as he slid the jack under the bumper and pumped the handle until he raised the car.

"No, really." She hurried to his side. "I can do that." As considerate as it was for this friendly stranger to offer her help, she could look after herself.

"I'm sure you can, but this time you don't have to." He pried off the hubcap and spun the lug nuts loose with the tire iron. "You rest while I finish this up."

She opened her mouth to argue but stopped when his black T-shirt stretched taut across the muscles in his back and shoulders and the faded jeans molded to his lean hips. She prided herself on her independence, but maybe this one time she could sit back and enjoy the view. Besides, he seemed friendly enough. She shouldn't judge all men by Derek. There were lots of nice guys out there. Look at her brother. Peter was a nice guy. If he saw someone with car trouble on the side of the road, he'd stop and help.

"Where're you headed?"

She tore her gaze from his enticing rear. "Renton Falls." She regretted her answer the second the words left her mouth. She shouldn't have told him her destination. The less information she shared with this stranger, the better.

He wiped a hand over his brow, leaving a streak of grease across his sweaty forehead that somehow made him even more attractive. "Renton Falls isn't exactly a tourist destination. What're your plans in town?" He loosened the bolts, wrenched off the flattened tire, and tossed it aside.

"I'm meeting my brother."

"Really?" He stood and wiped his hands on his jeans. "I know most everyone in town. Who's your brother?"

His scent, a mixture of fresh-washed cotton on a warm spring day and engine grease, wafted in the air between them. "My—" She swallowed and glanced at her watch. "—my brother's waiting for me. I told him I'd meet him at three o'clock. He'll be worried if I'm late, and..." Again, the butterflies fluttered deep in her belly, and she lost track of what she was saying as she stared into his coal-black eyes.

The blare of a horn rent the air, and she jerked.

A white, rusted pickup truck blasted past, its powerful diesel engine rumbling. The male passenger smirked and gave a thumbs-up. The truck's rear tires sprayed a cloud of thick road dust that hung in the air.

She sneezed and waved away dust. "Do you know that guy?"

"He lives in Renton Falls." Two bright spots of red stained her rescuer's rugged cheeks. "I'll finish up here, and you can get on your way." He swung back to the car.

The truck's noisy interruption had cleared the cobwebs out of her brain and jerked her back to reality. *What was she thinking?* Even if the guy fixing her flat tire was a serious hottie, that was no excuse for gaping like a teenage girl. She didn't know him. She'd never met him before. She knew better, especially after the nightmare of the past months.

The old saw about not trusting a book by its cover was all too true when it came to men. Derek, with his wavy auburn hair, hazel eyes, chiseled chin, and tight abs was drop-dead handsome. At least, she used to think he was, until she saw through his good looks and into the man beneath the easy charm.

"You don't read this garbage, do you?"

She blinked at the harshness in his voice. "What?"

"This!" He held up a magazine, his dark brows drawn together, his mouth curled in a sneer. "Tell me you don't read this crap."

She blinked again, shifted gears, and focused. "What are you talking about?"

"This rag." He waved the magazine in the air like a flag. "That's what I'm talking about."

She wrinkled her brow.

The guy was holding the most recent edition of *Aspire.*

She'd brought a few copies in case one of the people she interviewed for her story wanted to read her past articles. "What's wrong with that magazine?"

Anger blazed in his dark eyes, turning them a deep black. "Wrong? Everything's wrong with this garbage." He tossed the magazine into the trunk of her car.

Her confusion transformed to irritation. What was his problem? The magazine was well respected. Both the online and print editions sold well, and its circulation was growing. Sure, there were articles on fashion, food trends, and celebrity gossip, but the magazine also featured probing, informative stories on current politics and environmental issues. "Have you read it?"

"Why should I?" He snorted. "It's a gossip rag."

She stared, nonplused. His disgust was way out of proportion. Now *she* was furious. She planted her hands on her hips. "You have no idea what you're talking about." The heated words rushed out. "If you'd taken the time to read an issue, you'd find *Aspire* delves deep into matters that are important, topics that concern everyone."

"Wait." His eyes narrowed. "Why are you defending that rag?" He retrieved the magazine from the trunk and flipped through the pages. The furrow between his brows deepened, and his jaw tightened until his features looked as if they'd been carved from granite. "Are you a journalist? Do *you* work for *Aspire*? Did you write one of these articles?"

She studied the miles of unbroken green forest and the empty stretch of gravel road and shivered and backed away. She was alone on this desolate stretch of road with a man who was possibly unhinged. "Of course not." Her lie filled the space separating them. Something about *Aspire* infuriated him. Now wasn't the time to admit she was one of their journalists. "I like to read the magazine. That's all."

His mouth curved in a sheepish smile. "Sorry. I guess I overreacted." He tossed the magazine back into the trunk, heaved in the flat tire and jack, and slammed down the lid. "Your tire's fixed, and you're good to go."

She pushed back her irritation. "Thanks for your help."

"Maybe I'll see you around."

Not if I can help it. She pasted a smile on her face. "Maybe."

He nodded and strode toward his dusty red truck and climbed behind the wheel. The engine started with a loud rumble. He waved and steered the truck away from the shoulder and headed down the road, vanishing in a cloud of dust and gravel.

She smoothed her shaking hand over her long braid. Jeez. What was his problem? In a matter of seconds, he'd gone from charming and helpful to a block of ice. No, not ice—a volcano ready to erupt.

He wasn't a fan of *Aspire*; that much was certain. She shook her head. Just her luck the most attractive man she'd met in ages turned out to be an opinionated, raving maniac. When it came to men who were losers, she was batting a thousand these days.

Chapter 4

An hour later, she drove over a rickety one-lane wooden bridge past several large industrial warehouses and a card-lock gas station, and entered bustling downtown Renton Falls.

Ramshackle houses, painted bright shades of turquoise, pink, and blue, lined the narrow gravel road. Mangy-looking dogs, chained to metal stakes in the weed-choked front yards, snarled and barked as she drove past.

She followed the directions Peter had given her and drove along the main street and past a gas station to the central business section.

A barbershop with an old-fashioned red-and-white striped pole on the sidewalk in front, a hardware store, a café advertising a daily special of fried liver and onions, and a grocery store with metal bars covering the front windows lined the dusty street.

Drivers in four-wheel-drive pickup trucks—mostly bearded men sporting sweat-stained caps—greeted each other with short toots of vehicle horns and a casual wave.

She couldn't help searching for a dust-covered red truck, even though the last thing she wanted was to run into her good Samaritan.

Turning off the main street, she parked in front of a white three-story building bearing a sign inscribed with the words *Renton Falls Hotel est. 1929*. Peter had asked her to meet him in the bar in the ancient hotel, where he was staying the night. He'd booked her a room there as well.

She was looking forward to seeing him. They had a lot to talk about—or not talk about. She hadn't decided if she was going to tell him about Derek. Peter had enough on his plate. He didn't need her problems.

Entering the rustic building through the main door into the lobby, she followed a sign to a pair of old-fashioned wooden saloon doors. Pushing through the doors, she blinked in the dim light. A heavy musty smell—redolent of stale cigarette smoke, spilled beer, and what she feared was a gut-churning combination of urine and vomit—swamped her. She wrinkled her nose. Peter had told her the locals called the bar the Zoo.

Fitting.

The bar looked like it was stuck in a 1980's time warp. Despite the *No Smoking* signs posted on the dingy walls, many of the beer-drinking patrons, laughing and talking in loud voices that drowned out the twang of the honkytonk music playing over the loudspeakers, were smoking.

She hadn't taken more than ten steps into the noisy packed room when she was jostled from behind. Icy moisture seeped through her sweater, and a powerful, yeasty beer smell wafted in the air.

"Shiiiit!" A burly bearded man, a foolish grin on his grizzled face, held two brimming jugs of frothy, amber-colored beer in his meaty hands. "Sorry, lady." Spittle sprayed from his wet lips. His eyes were red-veined, his face flushed. He shoved past her and staggered across the room, beer sloshing out of the jugs and spilling over his hands and his camouflage-colored baggy cargo pants. He collapsed onto a chair, nearly upsetting the jugs of beer he'd set on the small, round table.

His friends cheered.

He grinned, beaming like he'd won an Olympic gold medal, and raised his arms in a victory salute.

She wiped the large wet splotch on her favorite pink sweater. Great. Now she stank like a brewery. She eyed the raucous crowd. Trust Peter to pick a dive for their reunion.

Her brother was an anthropologist, and he always said he learned more about human nature from the characters he met in bars than anything he read in books.

She shook her head. She could imagine what an alien would think of the human species if one were to observe the chaos of the Zoo.

"Hannah, you made it!"

She peered through the haze of smoke.

Peter grinned from across the room and jumped to his feet and rushed toward her.

A lump formed in her throat.

At first glance, he hadn't changed. His shiny cap of thick blond curls tumbled to his shoulders and hung in his eyes, but beneath his unruly dark-blond beard, his face was gaunt. New creases bracketed his wide mouth, and shadows clouded the light-blue depths of his eyes, turning them a smoky gray.

He clasped her in a hug and swung her off her feet, squeezing so tightly she feared her ribs would crack.

"It's great to see you, Stick."

She grimaced at the childhood nickname.

Peter had coined the name because she was so skinny when she was a kid. He knew she hated the nickname, but over the years, his use of the pet name had become an indication of their closeness.

She kissed him on his beard-roughened cheek. "You too, Peter. It's been too long."

He loosened his embrace and studied her with an assessing scrutiny. A frown furrowed his brow. "Is something wrong?"

"Nope. I'm fine." She faked a smile.

"You know you're a horrible liar." He hugged her again. "Now tell me what's going on."

"It's nothing. I had a flat tire on the road outside of town. That's all." She should've known she couldn't hide anything from him. Peter was older by two years, but they'd stayed close even though they were both consumed by their careers.

"A flat tire?" His eyes narrowed. "Are you all right?"

"I'm fine. The guy who stopped to help didn't think much of *Aspire*. That's all." Better he thought she was upset by a stranger who didn't like journalists than the reality of being stalked.

"Are you serious? Has the man no taste?" He opened his mouth wide in feigned shock.

"Obviously not." She smiled at his teasing, and her irritation at the roadside encounter faded. What did she care what the handsome stranger thought? She'd never see the guy again, and never have to face his disdain.

"Do you want me to track him down and teach him a lesson?"

Her smile widened at the image of her teddy bear of a big brother facing off against the tall dark-haired stranger with the bulging muscles. Peter wouldn't stand a chance unless it was a battle of brains. Her brother was the smartest person she knew.

He'd always come to her rescue when they were children. That's why she hadn't told him about Derek. Derek was dangerous. If Peter went after him, Derek would attack like a raging pit bull. She couldn't live with herself if Peter was injured because of her. Besides, she was a grown woman. She'd figure the situation out herself.

Right. And that's why you ran away?

She ignored the snarky inner voice, determined to put the unpleasantness out of her mind and focus on why she was in Renton Falls. Time was ticking. She had a deadline. Marilyn had given her two weeks to research the story, write the article, and submit it. Even if the assignment wasn't going to be the lead story, Hannah cared about her job, and she was determined to write the best article possible.

"You sure you're okay? You seem—" He narrowed his eyes. "—unsettled."

"It's you I'm concerned about." The signs of heartbreak were all too visible on his haggard face. "I'm so sorry about you and Marissa. Are you going to tell me what happened?"

His shoulders drooped as if he were exhausted, and he scrubbed his hand over his bloodshot eyes. "That's a long and dreary story. I'll tell you another time." He brightened. "Come on." He grabbed her hand. "Let me tell you about our canoe trip."

"Canoe trip? What are you talking about?" She let him lead her to a table.

He raised his hand and ordered her a beer and another one for himself. "Our canoe trip down the Sturgeon River. How else did you think we were getting to Keyoh?"

The waitress set two frosty mugs of beer on the table.

"Thanks, Rhonda." Peter grabbed a mug and held it up. "Here's to our adventure."

"Wait a minute." She frowned. "Are you telling me we have to canoe to the archaeological site?"

He nodded. "It's a two-day trip."

"Really?" She'd been so consumed with her worry about Derek she hadn't had time to conduct her usual research into the assignment. Peter had said he'd take her to an interesting archaeological site and introduce her to the head archaeologist, and she'd left the arrangements to him. She knew the place would be remote, and she'd figured they'd have to drive a couple of hours, but a two-day paddle down a river? Where the heck was this Keyoh?

"There aren't any roads. Going by boat's the only practical way to reach the site unless your editor's willing to spring for a helicopter." He chuckled.

Not likely. The assignment was definitely low budget. But still…a two-day paddle down a river…

"Come on, Stick. You used to love canoeing." He swallowed a gulp of beer and swiped his hand over his mouth. "It'll be like a mini holiday. We could both use the break."

She wiped beads of moisture off her beer mug. Why not? Peter was right. She did love canoeing. And Derek couldn't follow her down the river. An image of that folded note with the threatening words slashed in red marker stuck under her windshield wiper rose before her, and she shivered.

"Come on. This trip'll be like old times. We haven't spent much time together. Not since—" His voice broke.

A lump thickened her throat, and tears pricked her eyes. The canoe trip would give her time. Time for him to tell her about the pain of his marriage breakup. Time for her to offer a sympathetic ear and support. "I guess I don't have a choice. It sounds good. Let's do this."

"Great!" He rubbed his hands together. "I borrowed a canoe and paddles from a friend. He's always wanted to paddle the Sturgeon River, and he's jealous he's not going, but I explained you were here on an assignment, and this trip was work."

"You told your friend about me and why I'm in Renton Falls?" After the unsettling events of the past few months, she'd grown secretive. The fewer people who knew her whereabouts, the better.

"Chill, Stick. I only told Joe. Besides, what's the big deal? You're a famous journalist on a big assignment. You should be proud of that."

She shook off the shiver of unease that iced her gut. Peter had no idea about Derek, no idea why she wanted her whereabouts kept secret. She forced a smile and faked fanning her face. "Stop. You're making me blush."

"I'm proud of you, Sis. I really am."

Tears moistened her eyes. "Thanks, Bro. But you do know this assignment isn't that big of a deal, right? The story'll probably be buried in the back pages of the magazine where no one'll read it."

"I have faith in you." His smile grew, and he raised his mug. "Come on. Drink up."

She laid her hand on his arm, stopping him. "I'm here for you. Any time you want to talk. I'm a good listener. You know that, right?"

His ragged gaze met hers. "I remember. But don't worry. We have two long days on the river and an even longer night ahead of us. Once I have you trapped in a canoe, I'll fill you in on all the boring details."

She smiled at his weak attempt at humor and lifted the heavy mug and bumped her glass against his.

Chapter 5

Hannah laid the wooden paddle across the bow of the red fiberglass canoe and stretched the kinks out of her back. They'd launched from the Renton Falls dock early that morning in the brilliant August sunshine and had been paddling down the Sturgeon River for the past three hours. Her muscles complained at the unfamiliar exertion. Her parents had taught her to paddle when she was a young girl, but between her focus on her career and living in the city, she hadn't been in a canoe in years.

She brushed away a blackfly droning past her ear and picked up her paddle and dipped it into the milky, green water. A lot was riding on this trip, but if Peter's friend was as knowledgeable as he said, and Keyoh was as interesting an archaeological site as he'd indicated, she'd have the background for an intriguing story. She hoped the narrative would show the depth, richness, and complexity of the traditional culture of one of Canada's Indigenous nations.

Her editor would be happy, but not everyone was a fan of *Aspire*. An image of the man who'd fixed her flat tire rose before her—the flush of anger darkening his rugged face when he discovered the stack of magazines in the box in her trunk, his heated words—

"Having fun yet?" Peter shouted over the splash of fast-flowing water. Like they had when they were younger, he sat on the bench seat in the stern and manipulated his paddle to steer the sleek canoe.

From her position in the bow, she guided him through the fast-flowing water. "This river's beautiful." She plunged her paddle into the water and inhaled, relishing the fresh scents of fish and algae-covered rocks basking in the warm August sun. The tense muscles in her shoulders and neck relaxed, and the stress of the past months eased.

The Sturgeon River watershed was remote, rugged wilderness with little evidence of the passage of man. The river was wide, and the aquamarine-colored glacial-melt silty water emitted a faint scratching noise as the canoe passed through the fast-moving current. A thick, impenetrable forest of pine, Douglas fir, spruce, and aspen trees lined the banks.

She tilted her head back.

A bald eagle soared high overhead in the azure-blue sky.

Another screeched from atop a tall fir tree.

A loud splash drew her attention, and she glanced to her right.

The red humped back of a sockeye salmon broke the water as the huge fish fought its way up the river to its spawning grounds.

Around the next bend, a young black-bear cub stood on the gravel bank, drinking from the river. The bear glanced at the approaching canoe and crashed into the bush.

It felt good to be outdoors in the fresh air after the past months of being afraid to leave her apartment, hiding behind locked doors and windows, and jumping at shadows.

Stop!

She bit down hard on her bottom lip. She wouldn't think about Derek. Not now. Not until she was back in Vancouver. He'd ruined enough of her life. She refused to let him destroy the simple pleasure of this beautiful canoe trip.

"Hannah?"

She jerked, her paddle slipped, and she rushed to grab it before it fell into the river. "What?"

"You've been awfully quiet, and Lord knows, that's not like you. You usually talk my ear off."

"Yeah, well, consider yourself lucky."

"Let's stop for lunch." He rubbed his left shoulder. "I don't know about you, but I could do with a break."

They edged the canoe into the shore beside a small mossy clearing. She climbed out of the boat and stretched her stiff back.

"I figured you needed a rest." He grinned as he hauled the canoe up on shore. "There had to be a reason you sloughed off on your paddling. For the last half hour, I was doing all the work while you were off in la-la land."

"Really? *You* were doing all the work?" She thrust out her hands. "Do you see these blisters?"

"Ouch." His smile faded. He slipped off his lifejacket, grabbed a backpack, rifled through the contents, and yanked out a small red pouch with a white cross emblazoned on the front. "You'd better put some bandages on those blisters. We have more paddling ahead."

"I'll be okay. It's my own fault. I should've worn gloves."

He set down the first aid kit and patted her on the shoulder. "I'm glad you're here, Stick."

Her heart clenched. "Yeah. Me too." He was her big

brother, the one person she could count on to have her back no matter what.

He dug once again in the backpack and tossed her a paper bag and grabbed one for himself. "Come on, let's eat. I'm starving." Eying her up and down, he frowned. "You could do with some more meat on your bones. You've lost weight since I last saw you, and Lord knows, you didn't have any to spare."

She forced a smile. "Well, you know what they say? A girl can't be too rich or too thin."

And just like that, the emotional moment ended, and they were back to their usual brother-sister teasing.

They settled on the grassy bank overlooking the river and dug into the bag lunches provided by the hotel where they'd stayed the previous night.

Peter swallowed a bite of his ham-and-cheese sandwich, picked up a flat pebble, and chucked it into the swirling eddies. The small rock skipped across the water and landed with a splash. "Do you want to tell me what's bothering you?"

She shot him a glance.

His piercing blue-eyed gaze studied her.

"Me?" She swallowed a bite of sandwich. "You're the one with the broken heart, remember?"

"True, but I spent the past three hours regaling you with the tragic tale of my sorry life." He tossed more stones into the river. "I'm worried about you. Something's going on. Don't tell me it isn't."

She wasn't surprised he was so intuitive. As a child, she'd run to him whenever she was hurt or upset. He'd dried her tears and listened to her secrets. She trusted him. Completely. But she hadn't told anyone—not her friends, nor her coworkers at *Aspire,* and especially not

Marilyn—about Derek.

She'd considered going to the police, but Derek came from money, and his family was heavily involved in provincial and local politics. He was a successful architect. His firm designed multi-million-dollar, award-winning buildings.

Her family was blue collar, and she was a struggling journalist. If she went to the cops, it would be a classic case of he said, she said. His word against hers.

Maybe she was overreacting, and Derek wasn't stalking her. He had friends who lived in the area, and that was why he was always parked outside her house.

Maybe.

But that didn't explain him showing up at her work, or the countless other places she'd spotted him in the past months.

"Come on, Sis. Spill. I'm waiting." The furrow between Peter's blond brows deepened. "You know I'll pry it out of you sooner or later. I always do."

She chewed the inside of her cheek. Maybe it was time to tell someone. Sharing her burden would be a relief. Marilyn suspected something was bothering Hannah. The managing editor was an astute observer of human nature. That was one of the reasons she'd achieved so much success. No matter how important or how business savvy the person she interviewed was, Marilyn always managed to ferret out the truth.

But not this time.

Somehow, despite Marilyn's probing questions, Hannah had managed to keep Derek's harassment a secret.

"Hannah?"

She studied Peter's face.

Love and concern shone in his blue eyes.

He was her brother. If she couldn't trust him, who could she trust? She licked her lips. "Promise you won't do anything crazy."

"Me?" He smirked. "When have I ever done anything crazy?"

"This is serious, Peter. Promise you'll listen with an open mind."

"Pinkie swear." He crossed the small finger of his right hand with hers.

She couldn't help but smile, and she gave him a little shove. "I mean it."

His expression turned solemn. "So do I, Hannah."

"Okay." She sucked in a steadying breath. "I think I'm being stalked." Once she started the sordid tale, it was like a dam burst, and the shocking words spilled out. She told him about meeting Derek, how they'd dated for a few months, how everything seemed perfect.

Until it wasn't.

He'd asked her to go away with him for a weekend to a cabin in the mountains.

She'd made plans to get together with friends, and she told him she couldn't go. Besides, they hadn't been dating long, and she wasn't sure about her feelings. She liked him and was attracted to him. What woman wouldn't be? He was the perfect package…handsome, successful, and fun to be around. But there was something she couldn't put her finger on, something he was lacking.

At first, he tried to convince her to change her plans. He even confessed he was planning on proposing at the romantic cabin he'd rented, and he showed her the diamond ring he'd bought.

She couldn't hide her shock, and that's when she made a fatal mistake. She told him the truth—they hardly knew each other, and she wasn't ready to marry him. Not then. Maybe not ever.

His usual calm and easygoing demeanor evaporated, and his face had flushed red with fury. He called her terrible names, the slurs spewing like poison between his spittle-flecked lips.

His unexpected rage and vitriol were shocking, but that wasn't the worst. She looked into his eyes, and it was like his mask had slipped. The rage vanished, replaced by an icy abyss, the absence of anything warm or familiar, anything human. Frightened, she ordered him out of her apartment.

He stormed out, but not before he uttered a final menacing threat and vowed she'd regret her decision.

"I hoped that would be the end, and I'd never see him again." She shuddered and rubbed the goose bumps on her arms. "He showed up at my door a few days later carrying a massive bouquet of red roses and begged me to forgive him, saying that he loved me and wanted to marry me and that we were destined to be together. His eyes…" She struggled to swallow over the lump clogging her throat. "I hardly recognized him as the man I'd been dating.

"When-when I refused to accept the flowers, he lost it and slammed his fist into the wall and repeated his threats." She squeezed her eyes shut to erase the image of Derek's rage-infused face. "One…one of my neighbors peeked out her door and asked if she should call the cops. That's the only reason he left. He tossed the flowers on the floor and stomped down the hall.

"After that, he called me at all hours of the day and

night. I stopped answering the phone, but then the texts and emails started. He showed up at my apartment, demanding I let him in, so we could talk." She shuddered, and the tiny hairs on her arms prickled. "When I wouldn't let him inside, he punched the insert in the lobby door and smashed the glass."

"Tell me you called the police." Peter's voice was ice.

She shook her head. "I just wanted him to go away and leave me alone."

He tightened his hands into fists, clenching and unclenching. "What else has he done? And don't tell me nothing because I see the fear in your eyes."

"I'm pretty sure he's been following me. Whenever I go anywhere, I have this feeling he's close by and watching. His truck's been parked on the street outside my apartment building and across from the magazine office." She blinked, fighting off tears. "I-I can't prove anything, but I think he was in my apartment when I wasn't home."

"What?" Peter surged to his feet.

"I-I came home from work last week, and the door to my apartment was unlocked." She sucked in a breath. "I always lock the door. You know I'm careful." Another shaky inhalation. "I checked, and nothing had been taken, so I thought I was mistaken. I've been under a lot of stress, and it's possible I left the door unlocked. But the apartment felt different." She shivered. "I can't put my finger on anything specific, but I know someone had been in there."

His jaw clenched and a vein throbbed in his neck. "What else happened?"

"The day I left for Renton Falls, I found a note under

the windshield wiper. I...I..." Her voice hitched in her throat.

He rubbed her arm. "Breathe. Just breathe."

She wiped the back of her hand over her mouth. "Someone had written, *True love never dies* in red marker on the paper. I-I know it was him. He'd read the phrase in a book somewhere, and he often said that same thing to me when we dated."

Peter's eyes blazed fire. "What the hell, Hannah? Why am I just now hearing this?" He rubbed his hand over his beard. "Tell me you called the police, and they arrested this loser."

She shook her head. "His family has connections, and it would be his word against mine. Don't you see that? No one will believe me."

He heaved an explosive breath and kicked a fallen branch, sending it flying across the narrow gravel beach. "This is the #MeToo era, not the 1970s. The police have to take you seriously."

"That's not the only reason I haven't reported him." Tears streamed down her face. "I agreed to take this assignment because it took me away from Vancouver and away from Derek. If my senior editor knew about Derek and what he's been doing, she'd cancel the assignment and put me on desk duty. My job's important to me. I don't want Marilyn to think I can't handle myself in tough situations."

She grabbed a tissue and mopped her wet face. "I need time to think, to figure out what I'm going to do, how I'm going to handle this." She didn't mention her wild drive out of Vancouver. If he knew the extent to which Derek was prepared to go to follow her, her brother would go ballistic.

"Okay. Here's the plan." He planted his hands on his hips. "When we get back to Renton Falls, you're going to talk to the police. This harassment must end."

He was right. Derek had to be stopped. She knew that better than anyone. The unrelenting fear of what he'd do next was affecting her work and her life. "Thanks, but I'm a big girl. I can figure this out on my own. This trip is what I need right now. Derek's far away, and for the first time in a long time, I feel safe." She picked up a twig and twirled it around her fingers. "Let's not talk about this anymore. Not for the next few days. Okay? I'm here on assignment. I want to focus on that."

He didn't respond.

When she couldn't stand his silence a second more, she tossed the stick into the river and faced him. "Well?"

He shoved his hair off his forehead and nodded. "As long as you promise you'll talk to the police after this trip's over. You won't be alone. I'll be by your side every step of the way. Together, we'll shut this jerk down."

Fresh tears filled her eyes. She hadn't realized how much she needed to hear his unconditional support. Maybe, with his help, there was a way out of the nightmare. "Do you mean it? You'll help me?"

"Of course." He nodded, and an unruly blond curl fell over his broad forehead, nearly obscuring his eyes. "No one messes with my baby sister. No one."

She slipped a handful of tissues from her pants pocket and mopped the tears from her face. "Thank you for listening."

"What's a big brother for?" He wiped his damp eyes with the tail of his T-shirt and smiled. "On a lighter note—your story on Keyoh's going to be awesome.

Everyone's gonna want to read it. One day, before too long, I'll hear about you receiving a Pulitzer Prize."

His joking tone eased the tension, and for the first time since she started telling him the frightening truth about Derek, her body relaxed, and her breathing returned to normal. "You're piling it on a bit thick, don't you think?" She narrowed her eyes. "Wait a minute. You want something, don't you?"

"You know me too well." He chuckled. "I'm buttering you up, so you'll make me look good in your article. You know—" He flipped his shoulder-length blond hair. "—a handsome, dashing anthropologist and his adventurous life. I'll be the new Indiana Jones. Heck, I'll have to beat off the ladies."

Picking up the paper lunch bag, she crumpled it into a ball and tossed it, missing him by centimeters. "You'll be famous all right, but only because you're the brother of a nationally renowned journalist."

Peter beamed. "Atta girl."

Chapter 6

Roman Patrick unzipped his sleeping bag, tossed back the wool blanket, and sat up.

Shas, his Newfoundland-cross rescue dog, snored on his quilted pad on the tent floor at the end of Roman's cot. His legs twitched in the throes of a dream in which he was probably chasing squirrels, grouse, rabbits…or a ball.

A gentle breeze stirred outside, and the branches of the surrounding lodgepole pines brushed against the walls of the large canvas tent. An owl hooted in the distance, night creatures rustled in the tall grass in the clearing outside, and the river splashed against the rocks in the rapids below the cliff.

Usually, the familiar sounds were comforting, but not tonight, nor the previous night. He'd been uneasy since he returned from buying supplies in Fort Cutter. The encounter with the woman on the road outside Renton Falls had set him on edge.

She was gorgeous in a girl-next-door kind of way. Her long ash-blonde hair, tied in a single thick braid that reached halfway down her slim back, swung with every graceful movement. To say nothing of her sky-blue eyes and kiss-me mouth. After he stopped drooling, he'd fumbled through changing her flat tire.

But then he found that stack of magazines in the trunk of her car. The glossy covers with the smiling cover-girl models dressed in flashy overpriced barely there clothing, and the all-too-familiar gold logo, stabbed like a spike to his gut.

He threaded his fingers through his sleep-tangled hair. Discovering the *Aspire* magazines ripped off the bandage of the old wound and exposed the raw hurt and anger. He'd exploded and made a fool of himself.

Who could blame him? The article *Aspire* magazine had published about him was biased and condemning, filled with half-truths and outright lies, devoid of any veracity. It took him years to rebuild his reputation, years before people forgot about the scandal, years longer before he was assigned an excavation of his own. All because of that magazine.

His eyes burned from lack of sleep, and he rubbed his hands over his beard-stubbled cheeks. He'd lain in his down sleeping bag, tossing and turning, the old anger smoldering for hours. A hundred thoughts thundered through his brain—what he could've done when the article was first published, how he should've sued the magazine and the hack who wrote the misleading story…should haves, would haves, could haves.

Instead, he'd let shock and self-pity take control, and he'd rolled over and played dead, hoping no one would read the article.

A crucial error in judgment.

In the first weeks after its publication, he couldn't go into the grocery store without seeing the magazine on the rack at the checkout counter. It wasn't long before the students and faculty at the university read the article.

He heard the whispers, saw the sly looks, but he still didn't speak up and defend himself. Why should he? The article was wrong. Anyone who knew him would know that. A month after the *Aspire* issue came out, his faculty advisor recommended Roman take a six-month sabbatical and let the scandal die down.

He'd agreed and slunk away with his tail between his legs as if admitting to his guilt.

Another mistake.

His absence from academia and his continued silence added fuel to the fire. The gossips had a field day. His reputation was shredded, his career in tatters, but like a fool, he lay low and licked his wounds. The injustice of that dark time in his life still rankled five years later.

He forced his hands to unclench and inhaled three steadying breaths. Lying there regretting the past wouldn't change anything. He shoved aside the sleeping bag and climbed off the camp cot. If he couldn't sleep, he might as well check the camp. This was his first major excavation since *The Incident*, and he was responsible for the crew and the equipment as well as the integrity of the site.

He yanked on a faded pair of jeans, tugged a black T-shirt over his head, and shoved his feet into his boots and tied the laces. Wincing, he rolled his shoulders that were tightened by hours of painstaking digging centimeter by centimeter in the soil under the warm summer sun. He grabbed the flashlight from the floor beside the cot, lifted the tent flap, and stepped outside.

Shas woofed and followed at his heels.

The moon was nearly full, and its cold pale light illuminated the camp. Excavating the Keyoh village site was a lifelong dream. Ever since he was a little boy— and his grandfather told him the tale of how two hundred seventy years ago, in 1745, a group of Ts'ilhqot'in warriors traveled hundreds of kilometers north by canoe to Keyoh and attacked the sleeping Dakelh inhabitants, massacring nearly every man, woman, and child—the site had drawn him.

After the massacre, the few remaining survivors moved away, never to return. Over the ensuing centuries, the site returned to nature. Trees, brambles, and shrubs took over and covered the burned house-pit mounds and fire-pit rings, until no trace of the once-bustling fishing community remained.

Little information, other than the oral stories passed down from generation to generation and told by the elders, existed about Keyoh. There was a brief mention of the tragedy in the journals of Father Morice, an oblate missionary who traveled through the area long after the massacre, but nothing else was recorded.

When Roman received his doctorate in archaeology, he'd been hired by the archaeology department at McKenzie University as a researcher and lecturer. He'd requested funding to undertake an archaeological investigation of Keyoh, but securing permission to excavate the ancient site hadn't been easy. Many Dakelh, including his grandfather, considered Keyoh a sacred home to the spirits of the souls who'd died in the massacre. They didn't want the dead disturbed.

Both the department chair and the university board of trustees thought the excavation was too expensive and the site too isolated. They doubted anything of consequence lay beneath Keyoh's sandy soil. The doubters were convinced the university's limited research resources would be better spent on high-profile projects that garnered favorable publicity—and therefore raised more money from benefactors.

The third, and perhaps the highest hurdle, was the

blowback from the *Aspire* article. Even though years had passed, the stench of the lies in the so-called exposé clung like a bad smell.

He'd refused to give up. Excavating Keyoh was a project he was compelled to undertake. His gut told him he'd find groundbreaking artifacts at Keyoh that would reveal valuable insight into the Dakelh, and specifically the Saik'uz culture before European contact.

His persistence paid off, and six months ago, he was granted permission to run a limited excavation of the village site for one summer season. He was ecstatic, but under no illusions. There was a price to pay. Every action he undertook at the site had to be reported to the director at the university, every purchase approved, every second he spent at Keyoh accounted for. Any mistake or error in judgment would be the project's death knell.

And the end of his career. Permanently, this time.

He was also under a time crunch. This far north, the archaeology field season was short, and he had six weeks to find something of significance. Forty-two days to undertake a project that should take years to conduct a thorough investigation. Not good enough, but his one chance to save his career and establish his place in the field of British Columbia archaeology.

He hoped.

If he messed up, he'd never be given the opportunity to run another excavation. Hell, he'd never work at a credible institution. He'd be relegated to the bowels of some small rural college in the hinterland, editing other archaeologists' research, stagnating in obscurity and boredom.

And that was why the project couldn't fail.

So far, he and his team of four university

undergraduate students had uncovered the usual assortment of stone projectile points, lithic scatters, charred animal bones, remnants of fire pits, and posthole impressions in the remains of the thirteen large house pits. Interesting, but not earth-shattering. In the morning, he planned to dig the first of a series of test pits in a new section of the site. He had a good feeling about the proposed excavations.

Circling behind the row of four nylon pup tents, he tugged the bear banger out of his pants pocket and headed to the tarp-covered cook shelter.

Last week a bear had wandered into the camp, attracted by the scent of food.

Roman had blasted the bear banger and scared away the hungry beast. A smile tugged at his lips as he recalled the loud bang and bright flash of light that lit the camp like high noon, followed by the terrified bear scrambling into the forest.

The crew stumbled out of their tents, most wearing just their underwear and T-shirts, rubbing their sleep-filled eyes, wondering what the heck was going on. Once he explained about the bear, they'd headed back to bed, and in minutes, the camp was quiet.

He yawned. No bear tonight. The cooking area was undisturbed, and as far as he could tell, he was the only person in the camp awake, but he couldn't shake the feeling he was being watched. He'd had the same prickling sensation since he returned after picking up supplies in Fort Cutter.

He'd noticed things…nothing he could pin his finger on…minor things…a piece of equipment moved from where he'd left it, food items missing, the constant primal sense of being watched.

He shook off his unease. He was tired, strung out from the pressure of leading the excavation, and his desperate desire to dig up an artifact culturally and historically significant—an artifact so unexpected, the find would restore his credibility in the academic world.

Yawning again, he rubbed his chin, and the rasp of whiskers was loud in the silent night. He had a long day tomorrow, and he needed his sleep. He motioned to Shas. "Come on, boy. Let's go back to bed."

A light glimmered through the stand of fir trees on the far side of the clearing.

A quick glance at Shas revealed the dog hadn't alerted to anything. He was busy investigating some sort of intriguing scent beside a clump of juniper bushes.

But a light that shouldn't be there was definitely glowing. Keeping his gaze trained on the flickering pinpoint of light, Roman slipped through the tall grass, careful not to dislodge a rock or make a sound. Keyoh was isolated and too far off the beaten track to attract visitors. Besides, the site was a registered historic site and was off limits to campers.

A low murmuring resonated through the cool night air.

He released the breath he hadn't been aware he was holding and broke through the stand of trees, halting outside the circle of light cast by a small campfire.

An old man sat cross-legged on the ground in front of the glowing flames. The firelight revealed the deep hollows beneath the man's prominent cheekbones and outlined the hawk-like ridge of his nose and the river of lines etched into his weathered skin. His shoulder-length silver hair was slicked back from his broad forehead. "Join me, Roman."

Roman sat on the ground before the fire and crossed his legs. Silence ensued as he stared into the dancing flames. He didn't bother to ask the old man why he was sitting in the grassy meadow in the middle of the night. He knew his grandfather. Ever since Roman's parents were killed in a car accident when he was eight years old, his grandfather, Nathaniel Patrick, had raised him.

He loved the old man, but at times, like now, he drove Roman crazy. Nathaniel should've stayed at home in Renton Falls. He shouldn't have followed Roman to Keyoh. He was too old to canoe down the river on his own and camp out in the wilderness. But he was one stubborn man, and he'd gone to all that trouble to try and convince his grandson not to excavate Keyoh.

When he was a young boy, Roman idolized his grandfather and loved listening to the colorful stories he told of their people's past. As he grew older, he watched as many of his friends were driven to alcohol and drug abuse in a bid to escape the brutal reality of their lives on the reservation.

He, too, could've followed that destructive path. He'd been tempted…many times, but his love of archaeology and his determination to uncover hard evidence of the complex culture of the Dakelh and instill pride in his community's heritage, kept him focused. If he found proof of the rich cultural traditions practiced by his Indigenous ancestors and shared that with his people, maybe his findings would help heal the deep scars left by colonization and residential schools.

"I see the guilt of desecrating your ancestors is keeping you awake."

His grandfather's rough voice drew Roman out of his thoughts. He heaved a weary sigh. How many times did they have to go through this? He'd explained to Nathaniel that he wasn't excavating Keyoh out of disrespect. His purpose in researching the site was the complete opposite.

His faith in his culture and his people was why he was there, why he'd fought so hard to lead the excavation. "I'm sorry you don't agree with me. I really am, but—" He stopped. What was the point? He was too tired to rehash the old argument. "It's late. You should be in bed. So should I."

Nathaniel picked up a broken branch from a stack and set it on the fire. Sparks crackled as the hungry flames devoured the dry wood. "I'm concerned about you, Roman."

Roman kneaded the knot tightening the back of his neck. "Come on, Grandfather. Not this again." He heaved a sigh. "Can we not agree to disagree? You showing up here, camping out in the forest, and criticizing everything I do isn't helping." Another heavy breath. "Let me have one of the students take you back to Renton Falls tomorrow. Please?"

The second the words were out, he regretted them. His tiredness wasn't an adequate excuse for hurting the old man's feelings. "Look, I'm sorry. It's been a long day. You're welcome to stay as long as you'd like." He rose to his feet. "I'm going back to bed."

"Roman?"

He paused. "What?"

"Keyoh is sacred. The ashes of your ancestors lie beneath this soil." Nathaniel scooped a handful of dark-gray dirt in his hand. "Don't you care about that?" He opened his hand, and the dirt sprinkled to the ground. "No true Dakelh would think of disturbing the spirits who rest here."

A long silence ensued as the fire crackled and popped in the quiet night. From across the river, a wolf howled, its cry hollow and lonely. A cool breeze wafted, heavy with the rich earthy scents of fish, night dew, and the flowing river.

A lump formed in Roman's throat. No matter how much they argued, no matter their differences of opinion, nothing would change the fact he loved the old man, and it killed him that he was disappointing him. "I'm sorry. I can't do this. Not tonight."

The stars had faded, and the deep darkness of night was surrendering as the sky transitioned to charcoal. The surrounding trees were silhouetted against the rosy pink and sandy yellow of dawn.

He opened his mouth to tell his grandfather once again he should get some rest, but one look at the stubborn set of the old man's jaw told Roman he wouldn't listen. With a resigned sigh, he made his way back to his tent. He unzipped the tent flap. "Shas?" The big dog who was his constant companion wasn't there. He glanced back at the flickering fire on the far side of the clearing.

Shas sat beside Nathaniel like a dark sentinel against the lightening sky.

"Shas, get over here, boy!" His voice rebounded off the wall of trees.

Shas raised his massive head and emitted a low plaintive whine that carried across the clearing, but he didn't move.

"All right, then." Roman snorted. "Stay there, you traitor, but remember who feeds you." He ducked through the tent door, closed the flap, and flopped onto his cot. At times it seemed the whole world was against him and this excavation. It was bad enough his grandfather opposed the project. Now Roman's dog, the puppy he'd rescued from an animal shelter, the pet he fed expensive dog chow twice a day, the dog for whom he bought raw beef bones from the butcher in Renton Falls, had chosen sides.

Roman wouldn't let anything, or anyone, ruin this chance to prove himself. No matter what he had to do, even if it meant disappointing his grandfather—and his dog—he was going to do his damnedest to ensure the excavation was a success.

Chapter 7

A man's face loomed over her, his mouth open in a cruel snarl, his teeth bared.

She reeled back from the rage flashing in his hazel eyes.

He lifted his arm. The blade clenched in his hand gleamed in the light cast by the streetlamp.

Run! The command blazed through her, but her limbs were frozen and refused to obey.

He thrust the knife in a downward sweep, slashing deep.

She screamed.

"Hannah! Wake up."

She opened her eyes and squinted in the blinding glare of light. Her heart thundered in her chest. Sweat beaded her brow. She blinked to clear her vision and saw Peter's familiar bearded face, his blue eyes shadowed with concern. "Peter?"

"Take it easy, Sis. You were dreaming. Looked like you were having a bad nightmare." He patted her shoulder. "You're safe now."

Inhaling deep, shuddering breaths, she sat up. Blue nylon walls, a sleeping bag tangled around her legs, the lantern light... A hint of woodsmoke from their earlier campfire hung in the air. Relief washed over her. She was in the tent she and Peter had set up on the bank above the Sturgeon River after their long day of paddling.

"Are you okay?" Peter's thick blond brows drew together.

"What…?"

"You were having a bad dream, and from the looks of it, it was a doozy."

She wiped her damp face with the sleeve of her long-sleeved cotton T-shirt and swallowed, though her mouth was desert dry. A dream? Everything was so real, as if she were there, standing on that deserted dark street as the man approached. He wore a baseball cap pulled low over his eyes, but she knew him, knew what he was capable of.

She'd braced to run, to escape his fury, but before her legs acted on her brain's urgent command, he raised the knife and— She rubbed her chest, feeling the remnants of agony as the blade plunged deep. "It was awful…I—" Her voice broke on a ragged sob.

"You were dreaming about that guy, weren't you? The creep who's been following you." Peter threaded his fingers through his tangled curls.

"He-he had a knife." She shuddered and smoothed her braid through her shaking fingers.

"Don't you see? This proves you need help, Stick. You can't handle this alone." Peter's deep voice cracked. "I'll be there with you every step of the way, but we're going to the police. This jerk has gone too far."

She sniffled. "You're right, but—" She placed her hand over her heart to still its furious beating. "—but you don't know him. His family has money and power, and he'll deny everything. No one will believe me."

"*I* believe you. And if I do, others will as well." He smoothed a damp curl from her forehead. "Okay?"

She nodded. The grip of terror the dream evoked

eased at his kind words and soothing voice. His unconditional support meant the world. It always had. Always would.

"In the meantime, I have something that might help." He rustled in a nylon sack lying at the end of his sleeping bag and produced a bottle of whisky. "Just what the doctor ordered."

"You brought alcohol?"

"I know. A Wilderness Camping 101 faux pas." A sheepish grin wreathed his scruffy face. "It's not a good idea to keep food items in the tent when you're in bear country, but I thought this might come in handy. Besides, a bear would have to be crazy to come within a hundred kilometers of us with you carrying on."

"Me?" She forced a smile. "What about your snoring?"

He chuckled and filled two plastic cups with amber liquid and handed her one. "Drink up. I guarantee this stuff'll make you feel better."

She raised the cup to her trembling lips. The pungent aroma of hard liquor burned her nostrils. She sipped, relishing the searing heat as the whisky slid down her throat, shooting tendrils of warmth throughout her chilled body. Draining her drink, she handed him the empty cup, tugged up her sleeping bag, and slumped back onto the rolled sweater she was using as a pillow.

"Hannah?" He lifted the whisky bottle and refilled his glass. "Do you want to talk about your dream?"

She shook her head.

"Are you sure?"

She nodded.

"Okay. I'll leave it for now." He drained his glass and stuffed the cups and bottle back in the knapsack.

"You're my sister and I love you. Remember that. Together, we'll figure this out."

She swallowed back another bout of tears. "Thanks, Peter." She rolled onto her side facing away from him. "Let's get some sleep."

He switched off the lantern, and darkness settled over the tiny tent. Rustling in his sleeping bag, he heaved a deep breath, another, and then lay still. In minutes, a deep rumbling snore filled the tent.

She rubbed her tired eyes. Her brother never had a problem falling asleep. Not her. According to her mother, Hannah had been a fussy baby and woke every hour. Her sleep didn't improve when she was an older child, and she'd suffered from nightmares. Even as an adult, sleep often eluded her. Tonight would be the same. She wouldn't be getting any more shut-eye, not when the vestiges of the horrifying dream clung to her like sticky tentacles.

The distant *whoot-whoot* of an owl and the soothing splash of the river didn't ease her into sleep. She flipped over to her other side and back again, unable to lie still, her mind in turmoil. What was she going to do about Derek? He was stubborn and arrogant, and he refused to accept her rejection. Even if Peter was right, and the police believed her, they wouldn't be able to do much. Derek was too devious and his family too powerful. He'd hire the best legal team in Vancouver, and she'd be made to look like she was delusional, jumping at shadows and seeing things that weren't there.

No. She knew him. He wouldn't stop harassing her. Not until she made him stop.

And how was she supposed to do that? Peter's advice that she go to the police and file a report was sensible, but if she did that, Marilyn, with her sources in the force, would find out. She'd think Hannah couldn't handle difficult situations and would lose faith in her abilities to work on challenging assignments. No way did Hannah want that to happen. She already had a tough time convincing Marilyn to let her cover hard-hitting stories.

She yawned. Tomorrow was another day. One day farther from the city and away from Derek. She and Peter planned to spend five days at Keyoh.

Five days of freedom from fear.

Five days to figure out her next step.

Chapter 8

Hannah dug her paddle into the roiling water, and the canoe sailed into a narrow canyon, shooting past steep eroding sand banks. Exhilaration coursed through her as she and Peter navigated the raging rapids, and the canoe hurtled through the vee of water between dark ominous boulders.

Another large rock loomed ahead, water frothing white over its surface.

The bow of the small vessel sank into the swell, and icy water sprayed her face. She paddled harder, digging deeper into the churning river, ignoring the strain in her shoulders.

The canoe blasted out of the wave and scooted past the rock, missing it by centimeters.

"Hang in there, Sis. One more set of rapids before we reach Keyoh," Peter shouted.

The thunderous crash of water splashing against immovable rock filled the air and echoed off the canyon walls.

She slipped off the seat and braced on her knees in the bottom of the canoe and shoved her paddle deep into the churning water. "Here we go." Her voice vanished in the rising clamor.

They flew through the rapids, plummeting into the swells with a whump and splash of spray, and shot over a rock ledge.

A hundred meters farther, and the current slowed.

Peter steered them into an eddy of calmer water and lodged the canoe against a gravel bank. "Yes! We did it!"

Releasing the breath she'd been holding, she sank back onto the canoe seat, eased her grip on the paddle, and flexed her stiff fingers. Her aching knees protested as she clambered out of the canoe onto the shore. She held the craft steady while Peter joined her.

"Great job, Stick." He grinned and high-fived her. "That was stellar."

She removed her life jacket and scanned the rocky shore and pointed at the towering cliff.

Tiny circular holes peppered the cliff wall, and dozens of swallows swooped and dove in the air, upset at the intrusion into their territory.

"Don't tell me the village site's up there."

"The trail's over that way." Peter pointed farther along the shoreline where, partially hidden by thick bush, rough steps were carved into the steep bank.

"The people who lived here must've been in good shape if they had to climb up and down that bank to fetch water every day."

He chuckled. "I expect the inconvenience was worth it. From the top, they'd have a clear view up and down the river. Any invaders had to scale the cliff and would be easily picked off from above."

"How do you explain the massacre? The attackers climbed the cliff, didn't they?"

"I don't know all the details. Roman will, and I'm sure he'll be thrilled to fill you in." He smiled. "He has a thing for this place. Ever since I've known him, he's wanted to lead an excavation here."

He reached into the canoe and hauled out a large duffel bag and plopped it onto the rocky shore. Another bag followed and then another. "Before we head up, there's something I should tell you. Something you should know." He looked everywhere but at her.

Unease settled like a lump of concrete in her stomach. "What is it?"

"Roman's a great guy, but, well, he's…" He tugged at the silver chain around his neck. "He's a little, um, prickly. Especially after what happened."

"*How* prickly?"

"You'd better hope he doesn't find out what magazine you work for."

"What does *Aspire* have to do with anything?"

"He doesn't like reporters in general, but he despises that magazine. I mean, like he *really* hates it." He flicked lint off his plaid flannel shirt. "I don't know the full story, but years ago, before I met him, a journalist who worked for *Aspire* wrote an exposé about Roman's work ethic on a dig. The journalist as good as accused him of mishandling an important artifact.

"Not that any of it was true, of course. But the story damaged his reputation." He pointed at the cliff top. "Keyoh's the first excavation he's been in charge of since then."

"Are you kidding me?" She rubbed her temples, hoping to ease the dull throbbing. "Why didn't you tell me that before we paddled all this way?"

"I don't know. I guess I wanted us to spend some time alone away from our cell phones and work." He held his hands out in a placating gesture. "Look, I'm sorry, but we don't spend time together anymore. We're both so busy."

Her first reaction was to strangle him, but her anger fizzled at the love shining in his blue eyes. So this Roman character didn't like *Aspire*. No big deal. Not everyone did. Look at the hunk who'd stopped to help her with her flat tire. He hadn't hidden his dislike of the magazine.

"Well, then, I guess I won't tell him what magazine I'm writing the article for. Hopefully, he won't ask." She slipped a strand of hair behind her ear. "I'll tell him I'm a freelance journalist, and I'm hoping to sell the article to a magazine or newspaper. I won't say which one."

"Sounds like a plan. I knew you'd figure it out." The furrows on his brow smoothed. "Let's start packing our gear to the top." Hefting the duffel bag over his shoulder, he grabbed the strap of a small backpack and turned to the trail leading to the cliff top.

"Not so fast, big brother."

He paused. "What is it?"

"You'd better hope this friend of yours falls for our little deception. If he finds out the truth, he'll probably toss me off the cliff." She sharpened her glare. "If that happens, you'll be going over the bank before me. You can count on that."

He smiled a sheepish grin. "I did say I was sorry, right?"

"You did." She scanned the empty shoreline. "Where do your friend and his students leave their boats?"

"Roman told me there's an inlet around the next bend. The crew drags the boats up the mouth of a shallow creek. The creek bank's not as steep as the cliff, and it's better for hauling gear."

"So why'd we land here? Why didn't we take the easy route?"

"My bad." He grinned. "I wanted you to experience the site as a visitor two hundred seventy years ago would have." He set his free hand on his hip. "What's wrong? You too out of shape to make the trek? I thought you told me you worked out."

She read the challenge in his blue eyes. Two could play his game. She hauled her pack out of the canoe, settled it on her back, and straightened the nylon straps over her shoulders. Striding past him, she patted his stomach. "Let's see who's in the best shape." With a wave and a cheeky grin, she ran, slipping and sliding on the loose gravel, toward the trail. "See you at the top."

"Hey. Not fair. You've got a head start."

Chapter 9

Her heart pounded like a jackhammer in her chest, and her breath was sawing in and out of her burning lungs by the time she staggered to the top of the bluff. She shrugged off her pack, dumped it on the ground, and wiped her damp brow with the back of her hand.

Peter clambered over the edge. "Man, am I out of shape." He tossed off the duffel bag and knapsack and collapsed onto the grass.

"Guess I'm the winner." She didn't even try to suppress her gloating. "If you didn't drink so much beer, you'd be better off."

"That's sacrilege." He gasped out the words between heaving breaths. "There's a reason ale and lager have been around for four thousand years. Beer's the elixir of life."

She chuckled.

Her brother loved a frosty mug of beer. He'd even written his master's thesis on the historical development of the amber ale.

She swiped loose strands of sweat-dampened hair off her forehead and studied the clearing.

Rippling waves of knee-high wild grasses, interspersed with tall lodgepole pine trees and circular patches of low-growing juniper bushes, stretched for several hundred meters along the edge of the cliff. Four tiny multi-colored nylon pup tents, and a large green canvas-sided tent had been erected under the shade of a stand of mature coniferous trees.

A large orange plastic tarp covered what looked like a kitchen area with two plastic picnic tables and a wooden shelf with a camp stove. Pots and pans hung on nails driven into tree trunks. Canvas camp chairs circled a fire pit ringed by fire-blackened stones. Firewood was stacked in a neat pile between the trunks of two trees. Towels and assorted clothing hung from a rope strung between two aspens.

On the far side of the large clearing, almost hidden by tall grass, wild rose bushes, and a grove of stunted pine trees, a group of people were crouched, studying the ground.

A dog barked, and the biggest dog she'd ever seen broke from the group and pelted toward them.

Alarm rattled through her.

The creature was monstrous, with a massive head and large powerful body covered in black shaggy fur.

If she hadn't heard the animal bark, she'd have been certain the dog was a charging bear.

The beast, jaw gaping, revealing sharp canines, bayed deep booming woofs as it raced toward them.

Peter sat up, put his fingers between his lips, and whistled. "Shas! Here, boy."

The dog sped past her and leaped onto Peter's chest, licking her brother's bearded face with a long pink tongue, yipping and yapping in excitement.

"Good boy." Peter chuckled when the dog rolled onto its back. He rubbed the animal's hairy belly and glanced up at Hannah. "Shas is Roman's dog. He looks ferocious, but he's a marshmallow, though don't tell Roman. He thinks his pet's a fierce guard dog."

"Don't tell Roman what?"

Her breath rushed out in a gasp, and she staggered as if she'd been struck by lightning.

"Roman!" Peter shoved the dog off, clambered to his feet, and shook the man's hand. "Good to see you, man."

Struggling to stay on her feet, Hannah couldn't stop staring. The man her brother called Roman was familiar.

Too familiar.

She'd never forget his tall muscular physique, or the shining dark fall of hair framing his rugged face. "*You're* Peter's friend?"

The man's friendly smile morphed into a scowl.

"Hey, do you two know each other?"

Peter's voice broke through her shock. She stared at Roman for another long second.

"We don't know each other." Roman and she uttered the words in unison.

Peter's brow furrowed, and he shot her a questioning look.

Heat flared up her neck and settled on her face. She didn't want to lie to her brother, but if he knew of his friend's rudeness, he'd leap to her defense, and that would cause a rift. She was already there under false pretenses.

She knew why she'd denied knowing Roman, but why hadn't he acknowledged their previous meeting? Why had he joined the conspiracy? Was he embarrassed by his over-the-top reaction to the *Aspire* magazines he'd found in her trunk? His dark eyes revealed no emotion, and it was impossible to know what he was thinking. She held out her hand. "Hello, I...I'm Hannah Marchand, Peter's sister."

"Roman Patrick." He extended his hand, clasped hers, and they shook.

A shock of awareness jolted through her at the touch of his warm callused palm. She swallowed hard and jerked her hand free.

His pupils dilated, and the irises turned as dark as obsidian.

"Hannah? Is everything okay?" Peter said.

She nodded, but she wasn't certain she was indicating the truth. Her heart raced like the fist-sized organ was fighting to break free of her chest. A cold wet nose brushed her hand, jolting her out of her confusion, and she petted the massive dog, burying her hands in his long silky coat.

Shas jumped up, his large paws smacking her square in the chest, knocking her backwards.

She stumbled, barely managing to stay upright.

The big dog licked her face with long laps of his wet tongue.

"Down, Shas!" Roman said.

The dog dropped onto his four paws and nudged her hand with his massive head as if asking her forgiveness.

"That's a good boy." She tickled behind his ears. "You're a sweetie, aren't you?"

The furrows in Roman's brow deepened. "I'm surprised he's letting you pet him. Shas doesn't usually take to strangers."

She shrugged. "I like dogs."

Shas barked, his tail wagging.

Peter's strained laugh filled the uneasy silence. "Hannah has a knack with animals. Our family always had a dog and two or three cats when we were kids. They followed her around all over the place. It was so cute.

She'd dress the dog in doll clothes, and—"

"I don't think your friend wants to hear our family history." For the first time since she arrived in Keyoh, she smiled, though she feared it was more of a grimace than a real smile. She patted Shas under his hairy chin. "Shas likes me. I guess your dog has good taste."

Peter laughed, but his laughter faltered when Roman pinned a searing glare on first him and then Hannah. He cleared his throat. "I've told you my baby sister's a journalist, right?"

Roman's eyes narrowed. "Really? I don't remember."

"She works freelance, and she's always looking for ideas for a good story." He cleared his throat again. "When I told her about your work here at Keyoh, she was interested. She wants to do a story on the site…you know, the natural beauty of the area, the tragic history, the artifacts you've uncovered—"

"No."

Peter's face fell. "No? Come on, Roman. You don't mean that. I know you've been burned by a journalist in the past, but this is my sister we're talking about. Any article she writes is going to be fair and honest." The words spilled out in a stream as if he were trying to get them out before Roman cut him off again. "Besides, think about it. If her story gets published, the publicity will be a good thing. Your research'll get noticed. That could mean more grants in the future so you can conduct a thorough investigation of the site like you've wanted."

Hannah slid a glance at Roman.

His mouth was set in a stubborn line, and his eyes were cold, making it clear he wasn't buying what Peter was selling.

"Never mind, Peter." She jerked her thumb at the glowering archaeologist. "This isn't going to work out. I'll leave as soon as I can."

Roman directed a pointed glare at Peter. "We'll talk about this later. In the meantime, you two can set up camp beside my tent." Roman pointed at the large green canvas tent at the end of the row of smaller nylon-sided tents. "Now, if you'll excuse me, I have work to do." Patting his thigh, he said, "Shas, come." He stomped off.

Shas barked and, tail wagging, trotted after his master.

An uneasy silence settled in the wake of the grumpy archaeologist's abrupt departure.

Peter frowned. "Are you gonna come clean, Sis?"

"About what?"

He arched his blond brows.

She flushed. She didn't like keeping him in the dark, but how could she explain the fiery roadside encounter? How could she tell him of her unexpected attraction to the handsome archaeologist, an attraction that transformed to shock when faced with his blatant dislike of *Aspire*?

Besides, it wasn't a lie, more of an omission. Sure, she and Roman had met once, but she hadn't known his name until a few minutes ago, and she certainly hadn't realized the man she and Peter had paddled two days to meet was the one person—other than Derek—she'd have gone out of her way and done everything in her power to avoid.

She doubted she'd be at Keyoh long. Once Roman figured out who her real employer was and where the article about him and his precious archaeological site would be published, she'd be in the first canoe out of there. "Come on." She lifted her backpack. "Let's set up our tents."

"Not so fast, Stick."

She pasted an innocent expression on her face. "What's the problem?"

He studied her, his gaze probing. "Something's going on with you and Roman. Don't think I didn't notice." His eyes narrowed, and his lips curved in a smile. "I'll figure it out. You can count on that."

And he would. That was for sure. Eventually, he'd ferret out the story of their unsettling roadside encounter. But by then, hopefully she'd have figured out why the handsome moody archaeologist set her off-balance.

Oh man.

And she'd thought her time at Keyoh was going to be a welcome respite from the stress of her life.

Go figure.

Chapter 10

Hannah swung a small hammer and pounded the tent pegs into the sandy soil. Less than a meter separated her miniscule nylon pup tent from Roman's spacious canvas-sided wall tent. He'd better not snore. She smashed down on the thin metal peg, driving the spike deep into the ground.

"Hey, what's that peg ever done to you?" A lopsided grin wreathed Peter's face, and his eyes were alight with avid curiosity.

"Just making sure my tent doesn't fall down on top of me." He opened his mouth to speak, but she cut him off. "Don't ask, Peter. Just this once, let it go. Please?"

His gaze met hers, the hurt all too evident in his robin's-egg-blue eyes. "I guess it's a good thing we brought two tents." He grabbed his gear and turned towards his tent. "Talk to you later. I have stuff to unpack."

She didn't like shutting him out, but she didn't want to talk about Roman. This trip was supposed to be a break from the unnerving events in Vancouver. She had to figure out how she was going to handle the Derek situation, not stress over an awkward connection with the head archaeologist.

She pounded in the final stake, slung the strap of her backpack over her shoulder, flipped open the tent flap, and crawled inside. As she laid out the self-inflating mattress and unrolled her down sleeping bag, she determined to focus on her assignment. Her career was too important to allow hurt feelings or bruised pride to interfere.

The sun was setting when she joined the group of four tired dusty grad students around a crackling campfire. She introduced herself and explained why she was there, omitting the name of her employer.

They were young, friendly, and welcoming—and excited about the article. They jumped at the chance to be interviewed.

Roman was the exception. Muttering he had reports to write, he vanished into his tent.

Frowning, she scratched a bug bite on her arm. She was going to have to employ some of that famous Marchand charm if she hoped to convince him to open up for her story. Peter said Roman was the best in his field and knew more than anyone about the archaeological prehistory of Northern B.C. If so, she'd put up with his rudeness. Dealing with difficult people was part of the job.

Her reporter's instincts kicked in, and she couldn't help wondering about his past. What made Roman Patrick tick? What was in that article in *Aspire* that upset him? Peter had hinted at some sort of problem with an artifact but swore he didn't know the whole story. The article must've been published before she started working at the magazine because she'd never heard anything about it. As soon as she had access to cell service, she'd call Marilyn and check Roman out.

He was shocked when he recognized her. Shocked? That was an understatement. His face hardened, and his eyes narrowed to slits. Such a contrast to the man who'd stopped to help her on the side of the road, the man who smiled so appealingly and had a teasing gleam in his dark eyes. At least, he'd been charming until he opened her car trunk and spotted the magazines.

"Hey, Roman. Glad you could join us, man."

Peter's warm greeting broke through her thoughts.

Roman sauntered toward the group and stood near the flickering fire.

Their gazes met, a brief unsettling contact before he shifted away.

"Tell Hannah about the artifacts we've uncovered, Roman." Sam, one of the archaeology students, tossed a log onto the fire and swept back his long red hair from his freckled face. "It's exciting, isn't it? She wants to focus her article on Keyoh." He grinned. "Who knows, she might sell the story to a major magazine, and we'll be famous."

Roman's mouth twisted like he'd eaten something sour. "I wouldn't count on that."

She stiffened, ready to do battle, but Peter charged to her rescue.

"Hannah's sold articles to some of the best-selling magazines out there," he enthused. "I'm proud of her. She won a huge journalism award a few months ago."

She winced at his exaggeration. Her article on Korean restaurants in Vancouver had earned her a certificate of merit. No big deal.

Roman snorted, and his derision pushed her over the edge. Peter opened his mouth to say something, but she'd had enough of his protecting her, and she cut him off. "Forget it, Peter. Your friend obviously doesn't think much of my work or journalists in general."

"How could I, when you people bend the truth so

you can sell your lies?" Roman's sharp retort sliced through the night.

An awkward silence settled over the group.

Her face flamed, but she refused to back down. The last time he'd criticized her profession, she'd been too startled to defend her work. Not this time. She unleashed the full force of her fury. "I can't speak for all journalists, but *my* stories are solid, backed by hours of intensive interviews and research." Desperate to escape the strained silence, she shot to her feet. "I need some fresh air."

"Hannah?" Peter called after her.

Ignoring him and the concern thickening his voice, she escaped, stumbling toward darkness and freedom from prying eyes.

Away from the warm glow cast by the fire, the night was pitch-black. The moon hadn't risen over the surrounding hills, and the sole lights shone from the stars twinkling in the clear night sky and the distant campfire.

She swiped her hand over her long braid, smoothing back the loose strands. She'd lost her temper…in front of everyone. Not cool. Not cool at all.

She breathed in the fresh night air, fighting to rein in her anger. Roman's ridicule hurt, but why did she care what he thought? She could do the story without him. The excavation's crew members were more than willing to be interviewed, and Peter would help. He wasn't an expert in northern archaeology, but he knew a lot.

She slowed her pace over the uneven ground, not knowing where she was going, and not caring. With each step, her anger abated, leaving an unnerving restlessness.

A coyote yipped and barked, its haunting cry mixing with the musical splash of water from the river below.

The heady scents of evergreens, dusty soil, and sun-warmed plants filled the still night air.

"You shouldn't be wandering around in the dark. You don't know the area, and it's too easy to sprain an ankle."

She let out a sharp cry. Roman loomed out of the darkness, as if conjured by the power of her thoughts.

"Come on. I'll walk you back to your tent." Dressed in a black T-shirt and jeans, and with his long dark hair, he was a dusky fathomless shape blending in with the dark ground and night sky.

"No, thanks. I just want to be alone." Did he think she forgave him? Just like that? She'd rather stay out in the dark all night than walk with him back to camp.

He didn't take her not-so-subtle hint. Instead, he tilted his head back and stared up at the sky. "It's a pretty night, isn't it? Won't be long before we'll be able to see the Perseids meteor shower." His mouth curved in a smile. "On a clear night, you can witness hundreds of bright streaks of meteors flashing across the sky."

"It sounds beautiful."

His gaze met hers. "It is."

Damn him. Why was he being so…normal…charming…nice? Why didn't he leave her alone to stew in her irritation? He was the last person with whom she wanted to spend any time.

The very last person.

Chapter 11

Roman gave his head a mental shake. What was he doing? She didn't want to chat. Her body language made her feelings more than clear. She wanted him to leave her alone. Well, too bad. Keyoh was *his* site, *his* excavation, and it was *his* responsibility to make sure she was safe. He'd be damned if he'd let her chase him off.

He pressed his lips together, pushing back his irritation. Peter had wanted to go after Hannah, but Roman stopped him and promised Peter he'd find his sister and see her safely to her tent. It was the least he could do after his harsh words. He and Peter had been friends since the other man earned his master's degree in anthropology. He was a great guy, fun and easygoing.

Different from his sister.

His *reporter* sister.

The moon rose over the hill, illuminating her face, and her skin glowed like a pearl in the cold light. Her blonde hair, bound in a single thick braid, hung down her back, caressing her narrow waist. Her faded jeans and simple T-shirt did little to hide her feminine curves.

He gave himself a mental slap to the head. He'd never felt such an instant attraction for a woman. Any woman. And she was definitely the wrong woman to be lusting after. She represented everything he despised—the one cataclysmic event that had almost destroyed his career. He blew out a breath. But, oh man, was she pretty.

"Is it always so, so…unnerving here?" She shivered and crossed her arms over her chest.

"Look. This isn't the city. You're in the wilderness surrounded by wild animals. If you're going to stick around, you'd better get used to it." The second the callous words were out of his mouth, he regretted them. He wasn't usually so cranky and ill at ease, but something about her unsettled him. It wasn't just the fact she was a journalist. More was at play, and he acted like a damn fool whenever she was near.

"I can't shake the feeling someone's watching me. I've felt it from the moment I arrived." Another shudder shook her slight body.

An icy tingling rippled along his spine. Over the past two days, he'd had the same disturbing sensation. His unease worsened at night. In the dark, the sense of being observed was overpowering. But he wasn't about to tell her that. "It's probably just your overactive imagination. Keyoh has a tragic history. A lot of people died here."

She rubbed her arms. "Peter told me the story. Nearly everyone in the village was killed in an attack, and the site's been deserted for all these years." She visibly trembled. "No wonder I'm spooked."

He started to say something glib, but he met her gaze, and an arc of awareness flashed between them. Mesmerized, held by the certainty the entire universe was contained in the cerulean pools of her eyes, he stopped breathing. The moment stretched into an eternity, until a large, hairy body rubbed against his leg, jarring him back to reality, and he tore his gaze away and threaded his fingers through Shas's luxuriant coat.

Saved by man's best friend.

"It's late. I'm going to bed." She whipped around

and bolted toward the distant lights of camp as if she were running from something frightening.

He watched her vanish into the darkness and rolled his shoulders. She was trouble, no question. He didn't need the complication of her nosing around, prying, and digging up the past. Especially now, when everything he'd worked for rested on the success of this excavation.

Shas growled, staring into the nearby forest, the hackles on the back of his neck raised.

"What is it, boy?"

The dog growled again.

Roman peered into the dark shadows. The group campfire had burned down to coals, and the crew had gone to their tents. It wasn't his grandfather. Shas was used to Nathaniel's nighttime wanderings, and he wouldn't growl at the old man.

So, what was it? A bear? A coyote?

The night was quiet, but he couldn't shake the sensation someone was out there watching.

He shivered and patted Shas's furry head, scratching behind his ears. "It's okay, boy. Nothing to worry about."

The dog wasn't soothed by Roman's calming words, and he growled again, low and menacing.

Roman didn't blame Shas. He wasn't sure he believed his reassurances either.

Chapter 12

Hannah wiped the beads of perspiration from her brow and raised the water bottle to her lips and gulped. The cool liquid eased her parched throat. The sun was high in the cloudless blue sky, the late-August afternoon heat penetrating the thick canopy of leafy green branches.

After an early breakfast, Peter, Roman, and the team of students immersed themselves in the new excavation project.

She had different plans. It was a beautiful day, perfect to check out the ancient village site and the surrounding area. She wanted to get a sense of the place, and maybe take a few pictures. Besides, the awkward tension between her and Roman needed time and space to cool down before she began her interviews.

She followed a narrow game trail, passing towering lodgepole pines and prickly wild rose and thimbleberry bushes, low-lying junipers, and soft lime-green mossy humps. Entering a small shaded clearing carpeted in a thin layer of dry pine needles, she paused and admired the natural beauty.

Wildflowers added bright spots of color to the thick green mat of clover, wild strawberry, and dandelion plants. An army of industrious bees buzzed the white and yellow petals.

Ripe blueberries hung from drooping branches, and

she picked a handful and popped the succulent fruit into her mouth. The flood of sweet, rich juice brought back memories of childhood summers spent berry picking with her family in the hills near their home.

The melodic twittering of birds, high atop the trees, stopped, and the woods grew quiet.

Too quiet.

She stilled. Weeks of being on constant alert had honed her awareness of her surroundings. The pounding of her heart was loud in the sudden silence. She peered into the dense stand of trees, searching the shadows for… a bear…a deer…a person? Anything to explain her sudden unease. "Peter? Is that you?" It would be just like her brother to have followed her and sneak up on her like he'd done countless times when they were children. "Come on, Peter. This isn't funny."

No response.

A squirrel skittered through the forest litter, scampered up a tree, and stopped on a branch, scolding her.

She swallowed the mouthful of blueberries and wiped her purple-stained fingers on her pants. Ever since she'd arrived at Keyoh, she'd been on edge, jumping at every creak of a tree or rustle of leaves. She was overreacting. There wasn't anything to worry about. Derek was hundreds of kilometers away in Vancouver. He didn't know where she was, and even if he did, it would be impossible for him to follow her. Keyoh was too isolated.

She picked another handful of berries.

"I see you enjoy *yalhtsul*. They're delicious, aren't they?"

She yelped and spun around. Her fingers tightened

around the blueberries, squishing them into a pulpy mash.

"I'm sorry. I didn't mean to frighten you." An elderly man, his long gray hair tied back from his weathered face, stood in the shadows of the trees. "I thought you saw me." An apologetic smile wreathed his leathery face as he strode into the clearing. He nodded at the fruit-laden bushes. "I asked you about the blueberries you're eating. My people call them *yalhtsul*. We've had lots of sun and heat this summer, and the berries are particularly sweet and delicious."

Where had the old man come from? As far as she knew, no one lived near Keyoh. The light bulb went on. *Of course!* "You're Roman's grandfather." Peter had told her the Dakelh elder was at the site, though she hadn't seen him. "Hello." She held out her hand in greeting.

The corners of his mouth twitched, and he arched his bushy gray eyebrows and stared pointedly at her hand.

"Oops. Sorry." Dropping the crushed berries, she scrubbed her palm on her pant leg, and extended her hand again. "Let's try that again."

He smiled and shook her hand, his grip firm for a man of his advanced years. "I'm Nathaniel Patrick, and you're correct. I'm Roman's grandfather. You're the reporter I've heard so much about."

She grimaced. People often referred to her as a reporter, but she preferred the term journalist. She didn't just report the news. A great deal of research and in-depth investigation went into her articles, but she didn't bother to correct him in case he held the same dislike of her profession as his grandson. "I'm Hannah Marchand.

I'm hoping to write a story about what Roman and his team uncover here."

His knee joints popped as he sat on a stump and extracted a small leather pouch. "I hope you don't mind." He pinched a clump of what looked like dried herbs between two fingers and tucked the leaves into his mouth. His lower lip bulged. "Chewing tobacco's a disgusting habit. My grandson tells me I'll get mouth cancer one day if I don't stop." He shrugged. "He's probably right, but old habits are hard to break." He spit a stream of dark juice on the ground and studied her for a long minute. "Roman's not a fan of the media."

She bit back a snort at his understatement. "I'm hoping to change his mind."

"Good luck with that." He chuckled as if he found something amusing.

In the ensuing silence, the sounds of the forest intensified. Bees buzzed, birds chirped, and a pinecone dropped from high above landed on the forest floor with a soft thud. A raucous croak shattered the stillness.

She shivered at the eerie sound. "What was that?"

"Don't worry." He spit out another stream of juice. "That's just *Datchancho* having fun."

"*Datchancho*?" Her brow furrowed. "I'm sorry, I don't understand."

"*Datchancho* is the Saik'uz word for raven." He chuckled and pointed at a treetop. "*Datchancho*'s a trickster, and he enjoys creating mischief."

She eyed the large black bird with intelligent brown eyes sitting atop a swaying branch and imagined the bird was smirking. "I'm afraid I don't know a lot about the Dakelh."

He nodded. "That's something you must correct. If

you're going to write your story, you should learn more about Keyoh and the Saik'uz people. The Dakelh have lived in this area for countless generations. Our culture and our language are rich and vibrant, even today in these challenging times."

"Would you be willing to answer some questions? Not now, of course, but when you have time. I'd like to get your perspective on the excavation as a local Indigenous elder."

His good humor vanished, replaced by a cool remoteness. He pursed his lips and spit. "I don't agree with my grandson. Keyoh should not be disturbed. This land is sacred and should be left as it is. Digging up the remains of our people is wrong." He stuffed his tobacco pouch into his coat pocket and rose. His sharp gaze zeroed in on her. "I've enjoyed our little chat. We'll speak again when you've learned more." He strode to the edge of the trees and vanished into the forest, leaving as silently as he'd arrived.

A cloud passed in front of the sun, blocking its warmth.

The raven croaked again, and the hairs on her arms prickled with the unsettling sensation of being watched. Shivering, she untied her sweatshirt from around her waist and pulled it on to cover her T-shirt, providing another barrier against prying eyes.

She fled the clearing, retracing her steps from the morning, hurrying to return to camp.

Chapter 13

By the time she arrived at the excavation site, her heart rate had slowed, and she smiled at her foolishness. No one was lurking in the forest spying on her. This wasn't the city. She was safe. Safe from Derek.

Roman's grandfather was a nice old man, but he and Roman were at odds. Nathaniel was against the project. Roman's life-long dream was to excavate Keyoh. Nathaniel was a Dakelh elder, and his pride in his people's cultural heritage was evident.

Roman was also a Dakelh, and from what she'd seen, he also respected and cared about his cultural roots. But he was a scientist, first and foremost. He wanted to find hard physical evidence that proved the depth and sophistication of his ancestors' way of life. The rift between him and his grandfather must be painful…for both men, but their opposing viewpoints would lend an interesting angle to her story. A twinge of excitement rippled through her. She'd found the hook for the article.

She strode into camp. No one was around, but in the distance, she spotted the crew and Peter and Roman clustered around what looked like a hole in the ground. Their excited voices reached across the clearing. She should go over and see what was going on, but she wanted time alone to plan out her next steps.

Someone had made a plate of ham-and-cheese sandwiches, and set them, covered with protective plastic wrap, on the picnic table.

Her stomach growled, so she grabbed a sandwich and sat by the smoldering fire, her brain buzzing with ideas for her article. She nibbled at the tasty sandwich, chewing and staring into the glowing coals.

"Would you like some water?" Roman stood before her, holding a plastic water bottle.

She jumped and choked on a piece of bread caught in her throat. Coughing, her eyes watering, she grabbed the bottle, twisted off the cap, and drank. "Thanks," she sputtered when her choking fit ended. She wiped her streaming eyes. How did he do that? She hadn't heard him approach. Just like his grandfather.

He sat in a canvas chair facing her.

Shas, his ever-faithful companion, stretched out on the ground beside him and rested his big head on his front paws. His soft brown eyes watched her.

"I heard you met my grandfather."

She gulped water, coughed, and swallowed. "He's...ah...he's an interesting man."

"What did you two talk about?" His dark gaze, so like his grandfather's, pierced her like a knife. He held up his hand stopping her before she could answer. "No. Let me guess. He told you he's opposed to this excavation. Right?"

"He mentioned something about that."

"Of course he did."

She detected a note of bitterness in his voice, and the investigative journalist in her took over. "You and your grandfather don't agree on the progress of this project. That must be hard. How are you feeling about that? Are you willing to go ahead with the excavation despite his opposition?"

His eyes narrowed. "Why are you asking such personal questions? Are you trying to dig up dirt for your article? Is that what this is about?"

"No, I—"

"Do you want to pry into my personal life, or do you want to hear about what we just found?"

"I'm sorry, I—" She started to apologize but thought better of it. He was right. She was prying, but that was her job. But maybe she was moving too fast. "Please tell me what you found."

"Up to this point, we've focused on excavating the lodge sites." He pointed to thirteen large circular depressions in the grassy meadow. "We've found postholes, cracked fire rocks, and projectile points. The usual detritus of a northern interior Indigenous site from the era. Interesting, but not earth-shattering."

"But?" The gleam in his eyes made clear he had more to tell.

"I had the students dig a series of test pits in a new area of the site." His face broke into a boyish grin, and his dark eyes gleamed. "Today, one of those pits revealed a remarkable artifact."

She sat forward in her chair, sandwich forgotten. "Really? What did you find?"

"Something quite amazing. Not the sort of artifact you'd expect to unearth in a precontact Dakelh site." His grin widened. "At one of the lower levels of the excavation, in a layer of charcoal and what we think are fragments of charred human bones, we uncovered a copper Chinese coin. Judging by its shape and size, and the Chinese characters incised into the metal, I'm certain the coin dates from the Northern Song Dynasty. That's 1100 CE!"

"A coin? From China? Here at Keyoh?"

He nodded, and a lock of glossy dark hair fell over his forehead. "I know. It's incredible. The thought of an ancient coin finding its way from China, across the Pacific Ocean, and over half a continent, at a time when historians believed the Indigenous tribes of the interior of North America had little, if any contact, with non-Indigenous groups, is astounding."

"So that's what all the excitement's about."

"The coin could be the find of the year. Heck, it could be the discovery of the decade."

"Wow!"

"Yeah, wow!" He grinned, and a matching set of dimples popped out in his lean cheeks. "We're expanding the test pit in the hopes other unusual artifacts turn up."

She gaped, caught under the power of his devastating smile. This was the side of him she'd seen when he stopped to help her with her flat tire, a side she liked very much, one she found irresistible. She forced her mouth closed. "That's exciting. Thank you for telling me."

"I thought you'd want to know. Well, I must get back to the dig." He jumped up. "Come on by when you're finished your lunch, and you can photograph the coin." He turned and strode off, a bounce in his step.

Shas rose and followed at his master's heels.

She watched the excited archaeologist and his faithful dog cross the clearing and rejoin the crew and shook her head. Wow! Just wow! And she wasn't thinking about the discovery of the Chinese coin. She drained the water bottle and tossed it into the recycling bin.

"Hey, Sis. How's it going?" Peter sank onto the chair recently vacated by Roman.

The difference between the two men couldn't have been more striking. Peter's fair hair and blue eyes were a stark contrast to Roman's dark locks and impenetrable ebony depths.

"Stick?"

"I'm sorry." She shook her head. "What did you say?"

"No wonder you didn't hear me. You were daydreaming, weren't you?" The creases beside his eyes deepened, and his eyes twinkled. "About a certain archaeologist, I'll bet."

"What? Are you talking about Roman?" Heat flared up her neck, burning her cheeks.

"Who else?"

"You can't be serious. Roman's the last man I'd be interested in."

A smirk lifted the corners of his mouth. "Whatever you say."

She shot to her feet. "I told you, I'm not interested, and believe me, he's not the least interested in me."

He held his hands in front of his bearded face as if warding off blows. "Okay, okay. I'm sorry. I was just joking." He didn't bother to hide his grin.

She glared again, and he wisely changed the subject.

He gestured at the grassy clearing. "Come on. Let's go for a walk."

She wanted to refuse, but after all these years, she was used to his relentless teasing, and she loved him. "Sure." She followed him to the edge of the cliff overlooking the river.

The distant tree-covered hills gleamed in the warm

summer sunshine, and the river sparkled and frothed below.

"Thanks for bringing me here."

"It's pretty, isn't it?" He smiled. "I knew you'd love it."

"Roman just told me about the Chinese coin you guys found. That's so exciting."

He grinned and tapped a light punch on her upper arm. "See. I was right. With the finding of the Chinese coin, this excavation has everything you need for a terrific article—a tragic history, violence, beautiful scenery, exciting archaeological finds, and a dashing anthropologist. Your editor will love it. And so will your readers." He chuckled. "Now, come on. Grab your camera. I'll show you the coin. You'll want to take pictures for sure."

He was wrong about her and Roman being attracted to each other, but he was right about Keyoh. Coming there was a good choice. If the coin turned out to be as stunning a discovery as Roman and Peter said, Marilyn would be ecstatic. The senior editor might even place the article as the feature story in the next issue.

Maybe even the cover story.

Chapter 14

A cool evening breeze wafted over her, and she shivered and leaned closer to the dancing flames, mesmerized by the vibrant blues, greens, and oranges flickering in the fire's heat. Overhead, the stars twinkled like tiny diamonds in the clear velvet night sky. The ethereal glow of the full moon shone through the branches of the tall fir trees and streamed across the meadow.

Around her, the young archaeology students sprawled in collapsible chairs, sipping coffee and reliving the excitement of the previous day's discovery of the Chinese coin.

She bit back a yawn. It was late, and she was tired from traipsing all over the extensive site and interviewing the students, but she didn't want to go to bed. She was enjoying the easy camaraderie between the crew and the peaceful beauty of the night.

She sipped from her cup of chamomile tea, relishing the subtle apple flavor. She couldn't remember the last time she'd relaxed. Weeks? Months? There was no reason to dread a ringing phone or the ping of an incoming text. She didn't have to constantly look over her shoulder, fearing she was being followed. She breathed in the air, inhaling the scents of wood smoke, pine needles, and garlic from the lasagna Sam had cooked for supper.

"Well, well, well. Look who's decided to join us."

Peter's good-natured voice broke through her serenity.

The atmosphere shifted, charged with a new vibrant energy.

Roman ambled closer to the fire and held his hands over the flames.

His appearance at the nightly fire was unexpected. Since her arrival, he'd spent his evenings in his tent, working on reports on the day's finds. From the comments of the crew, she'd learned that wasn't his usual behavior, and she suspected he was avoiding her.

They hadn't spoken since their conversation by the fire the previous day when he'd told her about his discovery of the coin. Even though he'd shared his excitement, he hadn't hidden his distrust of her as a journalist.

An awkward tension sizzled in the air between them, and as if by a prearranged agreement, they were careful never to be alone together. When it was inevitable that they'd be in the same place at the same time—like mealtimes—they didn't speak to each other and avoided eye contact. If anyone in the camp was aware of the strain between them, no one said anything.

Peter was also silent on the matter. Other than a few teasing comments, he'd remained uncharacteristically reserved. His apparent lack of interest in her love life was probably due to his excitement about the discovery of the Chinese coin. It had long been his dream to be involved in a groundbreaking archaeological excavation.

Roman settled into a canvas chair across from her. The firelight played across the planes of his face, accenting his chiseled cheekbones, strong chin, full lips, and long sloping nose. His hair gleamed like a raven's glossy feathers.

Datchancho.

That was the Saik'uz word Nathaniel had used to describe a raven. A trickster. But Roman didn't seem like the sort of man to play games.

As if aware of her gaze, he turned, and his dark eyes pinned her to her chair.

And just like that, she was caught up in his spell. She couldn't look away, couldn't move, couldn't breathe.

One of the student crewmembers asked him a question, and the invisible tie bonding them vaporized when Roman shifted to answer.

She inhaled a deep breath of cool night air, fighting to regain her equilibrium. What was it about him that unsettled her? One glance, and she was swooning.

Howls of laughter shattered the night's quiet.

She blinked. And blinked again.

The harsh planes of Roman's face softened, and two dimples danced in his lean cheeks. His deep rumbling chuckle was genuine and full of warmth.

The students seated around the glowing fire guffawed and chortled at some joke she'd missed.

She shook her head at the taciturn archaeologist's transformation, though she wasn't surprised. He was friendly and warm with the crew and Peter, always ready with a smile or a kind word. He handled the team of young students with competence and compassion, settling their minor disputes, and listening to their suggestions.

The students respected and liked him.

Peter liked him too. They were friends, and her brother was a good judge of character.

Why was it just with her Roman was cold and remote as if a barrier existed between them? Was it solely because of his dislike of journalists? Or was there something more?

Again, as if summoned by her thoughts, he rose from his chair and moved to the empty seat beside her. "What's that you're drinking?" He nodded at her mug.

She squirmed on her chair, and heat flooded her face. "Tea."

"*Chamomile* tea?" He leaned closer and sniffed the steam rising from her mug. "Smells like chamomile tea."

"I…er…um…" How to explain she'd found his secret stash of expensive organic loose-leaf flower-head chamomile tea in the cooler, wrapped in a cloth bag, and hidden under the sandwich meat?

Jillian, one of the student crew members, had joked that Roman loved his Egyptian chamomile tea, and ordered the leaves from a specialty shop in Victoria. When she told Hannah where the tea was hidden, Hannah couldn't resist sneaking a scoop to see what was so special about the tea. Now she knew. The chamomile tea was delicious, and she was enjoying her drink.

Until she was caught.

The creases beside his eyes deepened, and a smile tugged at his mouth. His dimples flashed. "If you're wondering, I hide the tea because—" He nodded at the group of students. "—those yahoos would drink it all up in one night."

"I-I'm sorry. I should have asked you before I used it."

"No problem. You're welcome to help yourself any time you'd like. I don't mind sharing with you." His eyes twinkled. "If you can find it, that is. I'm going to have to find a better hiding spot."

She chuckled and ducked her head, hoping to hide the red that must be staining her cheeks.

The fire crackled and popped, and the rumble of conversation and laughter filled the night.

He cleared his throat. "How's your article coming along?" His dark irises radiated warmth.

"Good. Really good so far. I've interviewed the crew, and I've taken lots of photos of the site and the Chinese coin and the other artifacts you've dug up." This was the first time since she'd arrived that he'd shown an interest in her article. "I'd like to ask you a few questions when you have some time."

His smile faded. "Let me think about that."

"Okay." He hadn't outright refused. That was progress. Her first attempts to interview him had failed miserably. She'd asked him probing questions about the site and his reasons for undertaking the excavation, and he'd either ignored her question, or responded with a one-word answer. Frustrating, but she wasn't ready to give up. She'd handled challenging interviews in the past.

She tried another angle. "You're fortunate to live in this area. The countryside's remote, but beautiful."

"I like it. There's no traffic, no blaring horns or car alarms, and no crowds of people. Just the river, the trees, the wildlife, and the land."

"I take it you don't enjoy living in the city?" She leaned closer, enthralled by the golden specks in his dark eyes. Her inner alarm bells rang, warning her she was heading for trouble, but she couldn't resist falling under his spell. Not when he studied her with those dark fathomless eyes as if he really saw her and liked what he saw. She wanted to learn more about this complicated man and try and understand what made him tick. And not just for her article.

"There was a time I would've done anything to escape the reservation and move to a big city." He smoothed his palm over his long hair.

She fought to focus on his words and not fantasize about tangling her fingers in his glossy curls. "But not now?"

"It didn't take long for the attractions of urban life to wear thin. I spend part of the year in Vancouver at the university, teaching and researching." He shrugged. "But this is my home, and I love this land. I guess my grandfather influenced me more than I thought."

"Your grandfather raised you?"

He hefted a log from a pile of split firewood and tossed it onto the fire. Sparks flared, and the flames soared, lighting up the night. He stared into the crackling fire. "After my parents were killed in a car accident, Nathaniel took me in. I was eight."

A lump thickened her throat. "I'm sorry for your loss. You were so young."

"I was lucky. I had my grandfather." He picked up a stick that was leaning against a chair and poked the fire, adjusting the burning wood. "He welcomed me into his home without complaint and did his best." He rubbed his chin, the rasp of beard loud. "I haven't done much to repay him."

"He knows you love him."

"Yeah." His voice was a deep murmur. "I suppose he does, but I've been a disappointment."

"A disappointment? Look at what you've achieved." She motioned toward the ancient village site.

"You earned your doctorate in archaeology, and you're in charge of this excavation. He must be proud of you."

"I'm not so sure about that."

The flickering flames softened the hard ridges of his rugged face, creating intriguing shadows and hollows. A log shifted on the fire, and in the flare of light, he looked young and vulnerable.

The walls around her heart softened. "You and your grandfather have different perspectives on this excavation. I'd like to talk to both of you about that, but I haven't seen him around camp. Where does he stay?"

His eyes shuttered, and his body stiffened, and he shut down as if a door had been slammed closed. "He likes to keep to himself. He has a camp in the woods." He tossed aside the stick and stood. "I have work to do." He barked a goodnight to the crew and Peter and strode to his tent.

She stared into her cup. The tea was cold, and she tossed the expensive dregs into the bush. That didn't go well. Her attempt at digging out the details of the rift between Roman and his grandfather had flopped, but she was persistent and wouldn't give up. She'd try again in the morning. Maybe he'd be in a more receptive mood.

Or maybe not.

Chapter 15

Roman loaded gear into an ancient twenty-foot flat-bottomed wooden boat. Paint peeled from the battered hull, and a jagged piece of broken wood jutted from the stern. Rough wooden slats served as makeshift seats. The motor looked even older. Its rusted, oil-spattered cover was cracked and held together with strips of silver duct tape. Two wooden oars floated in a pool of slimy water in the bottom of the boat.

"Why aren't we taking the other boat?" Hannah pointed at a modern-looking sleek sixteen-foot aluminum motorboat pulled up on shore.

"This one's better." He patted the side of the old boat as if he were petting Shas. "She doesn't look like much, but I've taken this boat up and down the river a dozen times. Nothing like her to get us through the rapids."

"Wait…rapids? In *this* boat?"

"Grade three plus." There was a blaze of challenge in his dark eyes.

"Really?" She swallowed.

He nodded. "You don't need to worry. We'll be fine."

"I'm not worried."

"Right." He nodded, making it all too clear he saw through her lie, and dragged the heavy boat into the creek. Tossing her an orange life vest, he shrugged into his own. "Zip up. It's going to be a wild ride."

She couldn't stop the gasp escaping her mouth.

He touched her arm, a brief reassuring graze. "You'll be okay. Besides, you and Peter navigated the Keyoh Rapids on your way downriver. Peter said you enjoyed that. These rapids aren't any worse."

"Yeah, but that was in a canoe." She pointed at the battered boat. "This looks like an old clunker."

"Trust me?"

Trust him? Did she? She didn't know him. But there was something about the confident way he handled the boat and his steady gaze that reassured her. "Okay. Let's do this." She clambered into the boat and settled on the bench seat in the bow.

He sat in the stern, his hand on the tiller, his gaze fixed ahead as he steered the craft down the creek and into the river. He directed the boat through a maze of boulders and whitewater, navigating the rapids with practiced skill. They made slow but steady headway, running with the strong current.

For the first fifteen minutes, she gripped the sides of the wooden seat and hung on tight, fearing they'd sink, but other than the oily puddle sloshing over her shoes, the boat didn't take on any more water.

She relaxed and sat back and enjoyed the passing scenery. The hills stood silent and majestic in the background as the river curved through dense evergreen forest and between steep, clay banks lined with tall cottonwoods and bowed willows.

A family of ducks swimming upriver flapped into the reeds as the boat thundered past.

The darting shapes of salmon flashed red in the rippling water.

The afternoon sun gleamed on Roman's shoulder-length black hair and highlighted his rugged face with its sharp cheekbones, strong nose, and square chin covered with the dark stubble of a beard. He was a handsome man by any definition, but his appeal wasn't just his good looks.

Of course not. She wasn't *that* superficial.

Her mouth twisted in a secret smile. Okay. Maybe she was a little shallow. She certainly appreciated his deep penetrating eyes and his tall leanly muscled body. But there was something about him that drew her, something visceral. His enthusiasm for his career, his integrity, the respect he showed his crew of students, his love of the land and the people who lived there—all combined in an intriguing package.

The craft bounced and bucked in the roiling water, and she hung on. The motor's high-pitched whine filled the air. A blue cloud of exhaust settled over her, and she wrinkled her nose and coughed. It was hard to believe she was there.

With Roman.

Just the two of them.

Alone…together.

When Peter told her Roman was planning on heading downriver to an old abandoned settlement to conduct survey work, she wanted to go. Maybe away from Keyoh and the pressures of leading the project, Roman would relax. If she could break through the barriers surrounding him, she could flesh out the details for her article.

She was even more determined to accompany Roman on his adventure when her brother told her the story of Libertas Bay.

In the late nineteen sixties, hundreds of young American men hoping to evade the Vietnam War draft, fled the United States for the backwoods of British Columbia where they hoped to live off the grid and on the land.

A group of six American draft dodgers had paddled down the Sturgeon River looking for land where they could squat. They stopped in a small bay where a creek flowed into the river, cleared the property, and built homes and outbuildings. Eventually, other like-minded people joined them, and at its peak, Libertas Bay was a successful self-sufficient community of twenty-five people.

Life in the remote commune was harsh, especially in winter when temperatures sank to thirty below, and the river clogged with ice. When the Vietnam War ended, the settlers and their families drifted back to civilization and returned to the United States. Peter told her that no one had lived at Libertas Bay since the early 1980's.

It would be fascinating to check out the homestead and see what remained of the once-thriving community. She could work the story of the now-deserted settlement into a future article.

It sounded like a great plan, but it wasn't going to happen. There was no way Roman would agree to take her.

She hadn't counted on Peter and his irrepressible charm.

Maybe the thrill of finding the Chinese coin had softened the prickly archaeologist, or her brother caught him at a weak moment, or he'd challenged him to an arm-wrestling match and Roman lost. Whatever. Peter convinced Roman to include her on the trip, and before he changed his mind, she grabbed her camera and notebook and met him at the creek.

"Hold on tight." Roman's voice was lost in the roar of the motor and the furious crash of water against immovable rocks. "This next section's going to be rough." His face was a study in fierce concentration.

The boat plunged into a hole and shot through the rapids, bucking like a wild bronco.

She yelped and grabbed for the side gunnels. Icy water sprayed her face, and she closed her eyes and hung on, fighting to stay upright on the narrow seat.

"You can look now. We're through."

She opened her eyes.

The river had widened and slowed its frantic pace.

Drawing in a breath, she relaxed her death grip on the gunnels and wiped droplets of water off her face. "You're a pretty good navigator. Those rapids were fierce."

"I told you we'd be fine." He patted the side of the boat. "This old girl's awesome." Their gazes met and held.

The world stilled, the sounds of moving water silenced, and she forgot to breathe.

He glanced away, severing the contact, and focused on steering the craft toward the shore and into a small bay. A narrow creek flowed into the river, and he pointed the boat up the creek. When the hull bumped against the grassy shore, he jumped onto the bank and held the boat steady while she climbed out. He unloaded his gear and directed her to a clearing overlooking the river.

She shrugged out of her life jacket, draped it on the side of the boat to dry, and strapped her camera over her shoulder.

A large two-story house stood on a rise overlooking the river. The faded white-painted walls sagged, and holes gaped in the roof. The windows were dirty and cracked or missing the glass entirely. The wooden front porch had collapsed into a heap of rotting boards, and the door hung open.

She climbed the bank and waded through knee-high grass and wildflowers to the rear of the house.

Two small log buildings, their roofs covered in sod, sagged under the weight of the passing years, almost hidden in the tall grass. One shed contained a rusted hand plow, rakes, and other farm equipment. Another building held lopsided stacks of rotting firewood.

Broken chunks of colorful pottery lay strewn across the dirt floor of the third hut. In the corner was an old kiln.

What must've been a chicken house lay in ruins, its walls and wire fencing a jumbled mess.

An old yellow snow machine sat in the weed-clogged yard, its windshield cracked, the leather seat torn, the stuffing puffing out in white clumps.

A rusted child's tricycle lay on its side, the front tire bent at an angle.

"It's quite the place, isn't it? It's like a time capsule." Roman strode up beside her. "The people who lived here cleared the land by hand and built the houses and outbuildings using the trees they cut down and planed in a homemade mill. Most of the houses have collapsed. This is the only one still standing."

He stuffed his hands into his pants pockets. "They didn't know what they were getting into. Living here would've been hard, especially with the cold and snow in the winter and the swarms of bugs in the summer. It's amazing the settlement lasted as long as it did."

She studied the overgrown grassy pasture, the surrounding forested hills, and the river sweeping below. "Life would've been challenging, but there's beauty here, too." She inhaled a deep breath, breathing in the rich scents of wildflowers and ripening hay. A weight lifted off her shoulders, and she relaxed. For the first time since she'd paddled down the river to Keyoh she didn't have the disturbing sensation she was being watched.

She held up her camera and snapped photos of the scenery, the collapsing buildings, and the house with the long strips of white paint peeling from the weathered walls. "Can we go inside?"

"Sure." He led the way up the creaking stairs and into the dim interior. "Be careful where you step, some of the floorboards are rotten."

She plugged her nose against the sour smell of damp rot and long-dead creatures.

Light filtered through the grime-encrusted broken windows, revealing the spiderwebs strung across the ceiling, draped like delicate lace over a dust-covered gaslight fixture.

A rusted antique wood stove was set against one unpainted wall, and a wooden chair with a broken leg lay on the floor. Her feet crunched mouse and packrat droppings scattered in a thick layer across the peeling linoleum.

He pointed to a small pile of crushed aluminum beer and soda cans and empty plastic water bottles. "No one's lived here for years, but people traveling the river spend the night sometimes if the weather's bad. Some of them don't take their garbage when they leave." His voice echoed hollowly in the large empty space.

He stood close behind her, his warm breath brushing the back of her neck, and his scent—soap, fresh air, and sweat—wafted over her. The urge to lean back against the firm muscles of his chest was overwhelming, and she swayed as if a flower drawn to the sun's heat.

"Let's check out the other rooms."

His voice cut through the spell holding her in thrall, and she prayed the light was too dim for him to notice the heat flooding up her neck and her face. Her knees shook as she followed him out of the kitchen and down a short hallway to what must've been the living room.

Large gaps revealed where stained floorboards were broken or missing. Shards of broken glass sparkled in the light streaming through the large picture window overlooking the river.

They wandered down another short hallway and stopped at a small bedroom. The door hung open by a single rusty hinge, revealing a narrow bed with a ripped and stained mattress spilling white stuffing.

A teddy bear lay on the floor in the corner, and she moved into the room, picked it up, and wiped off a layer of dust and mouse droppings. The stuffed bear was missing an arm and one button eye. Tears stung her eyes. "Binkly."

"Binkly?"

Her face flamed. Had she spoken the name aloud?

"Was Binkly your teddy bear's name when you were a child?" His mouth curved in a soft smile. "I called mine Mister Jones."

She set the bear on the bed. "I wonder what this one's name was?"

"I don't know, but a child loved him." He pointed to

the faded blue ribbon around the teddy bear's neck.

A comfortable silence settled over them.

She'd lost her beloved Binkly when her parents divorced when she was six, and her mother moved her and Peter across the country. Hannah had cried for days over the loss.

His fingers brushed her arm. "Come on. Let's check out the rest of the house." His voice was rough with emotion. "We can't stay long. I have work to do back at Keyoh." He stepped back and stuffed his hands into his pants pockets again.

Already missing the warmth of his touch, she followed him through the rest of the house. She stopped at the foot of a steep set of stairs that led upstairs. "Are the stairs safe? Can we go up and check out the second floor?"

"Let me go first." He stepped onto the first step. The old wood creaked but didn't collapse. Moving slowly, one step at a time, he made his way up the stairs until he reached the landing. "Come on up. It's safe."

She hesitated. The stairs looked sketchy.

"If those stairs supported a big guy like me, you'll be fine."

Holding tight to the wooden railing, she climbed up the creaking and groaning staircase.

He was waiting for her at the top, a grin wreathing his face, his dimples dancing in his cheeks. "That wasn't so bad, was it? I told you that you could trust me."

Her breath hitched in her throat, and a rush of heat assailed her. She met his dark gaze, unable to look away, acutely aware of the rapid rise and fall of his chest.

His smile faded, and his mouth softened. The deep obsidian of his eyes transformed to a warm chocolate brown.

An expectant hush filled the air, and an arc of awareness sizzled between them.

Chapter 16

Roman's throat worked as he struggled to swallow. She was so close he felt the warmth of her body, got a whiff of her hair—morning sunshine. He couldn't look away from her mouth, desperate to kiss her, to taste those lips and see if they were as sweet as he imagined.

One simple kiss.

What would a kiss hurt?

One kiss, and then maybe he could move on and focus on his excavation.

"We-we should—" The tip of her pink tongue poked out, and she licked her lips. "We should look around up here."

He bit back a groan.

"Wha-what's that?"

Lost in a haze of desire, he strained to hear her over the frantic beating of his heart. "What?"

"There. Something! It's moving." She pointed behind him.

He turned.

A shifting in the dark.

Pulling out his cell phone, he flicked on the flashlight, and shone the tiny beam of light ahead.

High-pitched chirping and the fluttering of wings filled the air. Bats, hundreds of the furry mammals, hung upside down from the ceiling.

"Are those b-bats?"

He swung the beam of light, sweeping the shifting mass, and the squeaking increased. "We should leave them alone. They—"

Before he finished speaking, she whipped around and ran down the stairs.

He switched off his phone and followed, focused on two things—his desire to kiss her, and his relief he hadn't acted on the impulse.

Relief?

Or regret?

Kissing her was wrong in every sense of the word, but she was different from what he expected of a journalist...softer, kinder, more intriguing. And off-limits. If the fact she was a reporter wasn't enough, she was his friend's sister. Now wasn't the time or place to pursue a complicated relationship. The excavation was too important.

By the time he reached the kitchen, he spotted her from the window. She was fighting a path through the tall grass, running toward the river as if she were fleeing. The uneasy feeling that she wasn't just running from the bats cooled his desire.

His steps were heavy and slow as he crossed the weedy field and clambered down the slope. The trip to Libertas Bay wasn't a pleasure trip or an opportunity to be alone with Hannah. He'd come there to work.

He unhooked the small pack from his back and dug out a camera, a measuring tape, and his field journal. Striding across the clearing above the river, he stopped and studied three unnaturally shaped ground depressions.

Before the American draft dodgers arrived and built

their commune, the local Indigenous people called the small bay in the river Tl'o Yedinli. The Saik'uz had used the site for thousands of years as a summer fishing-and-berry-picking camp.

Nathaniel had told him about the unusual depressions, and Roman wanted to record them in case they were archaeologically significant. Maybe one day, he'd get the chance to lead an excavation there.

He laid out the measuring tape and measured the length and width of each depression and recorded the dimensions in his journal. Holding his camera, he snapped photos from different angles. He also noted the vegetation growing in the depressions.

"Roman. Come look at this."

He stuffed his gear into his pack and followed the sound of her voice down to the creek and a short way upstream to a grassy knoll. "What is it?"

"Look." She pointed at a tall leafy deciduous tree. The tree's bark was rough and scabbed, its branches drooping from the weight of dozens of tiny red apples.

"Apple trees aren't endemic to this area. The people who lived here must have planted this tree." Picking two apples, he rubbed them on his shirt until their skins shone. He bit into an apple and chewed. Juicy sweet tartness flooded his mouth. "Try one. They're delicious." He handed her an apple.

She accepted the small fruit, but before she could bite into it, she stopped and pointed. "What's that under the tree?"

He tossed the apple core into the weeds and crouched on the ground. Brushing grass and forest litter aside, he studied the small erect, square stone block. "It looks like a grave marker." He dug his pocketknife out of his pocket and gently scraped the moss-covered, weathered gray stone.

"Something's etched on the stone." Her voice was filled with excitement "Can you read what it says?"

He sat back on his heels. The letters were worn by the passage of time and harsh weather, but he could make out the words. He read the inscription aloud. *"Willow Harmony Fleishman. At rest in the Sturgeon River woods. 1971-1977."*

"How tragic! She was just a little girl. The poor thing was only six years old when she died." Her eyes brimmed with tears. "Her parents must've been devastated."

"Nathaniel told me that one of the families who homesteaded here lost a child. That was the reason they left."

She sniffled. "How did it happen? Do you know?"

He rose and placed his arm around her shoulder and drew her close, offering her comfort. "If I remember correctly, she drowned in the creek."

A single tear slipped down her face and hung on her chin like a jewel.

He touched the glistening teardrop, and the urge to kiss her struck like a punch to the gut. He edged closer, breathing her in—

"I wonder what happened to the family. I mean, after they left. When I get back to the city, I'm going to see if I can track them down." She waved her hand at the old settlement. "To travel all the way from the States to what must've seemed like the middle of nowhere… The hard physical labor to clear the land, build houses and outbuildings, and plant gardens and raise their own food…for the dream of a better life. And then to lose a child and have to leave her behind. It's heartbreaking, but it would make a great story."

Desire vanished, and he stumbled back, his anger flaring. For a moment, he'd forgotten she was a reporter. "The family's probably still grieving. The last thing they'd want is a nosey reporter showing up at their door and rehashing painful events from the past." He huffed out a breath. "I thought you were different, but you're not, are you? You reporters are all the same. You don't care whose feelings you tromp on. All you care about is selling your stories." As soon as the words spewed out, he wanted to snatch them back.

"A *nosey* reporter? Is that what you think of me?" Her blue eyes sparked fire.

He opened his mouth to apologize but stopped. He'd been open with her from the start. He didn't like reporters. End of story.

But you like her.

You like her a lot.

He frowned at the voice whispering in his brain. "It's getting late. We should head back." He strode down the bank. Now, who was the one fleeing?

"Roman, wait."

He didn't want to stop, but he did. Just like he didn't want to turn and face her, to witness the hurt caused by his cruel words. But he did. Her blue-eyed gaze drilled into him, and he flinched.

"If you dislike journalists so much, why did you allow me to stay at Keyoh and research my article? Why didn't you insist I leave?"

How could he answer when he didn't know the reason himself? Maybe he'd let her stay because she was Peter's sister. Or because she seemed different from other reporters. Or because she was so damned beautiful, his knees turned to water every time he saw her. Whatever the reason, the damage was done. "I don't know. Maybe I made a mistake."

Before she asked him another hard-hitting question, he strode along the bank to the boat, tossed in his gear, and shoved the heavy craft into the stream. Keeping his gaze fixed on the mouth of the creek and away from her, he shrugged into a lifejacket. "Come on. Let's go." He heard the rustle as she donned her life vest, but he still didn't look.

She scrambled into the boat and perched on the bench seat in the bow. "I hope someday you'll trust me enough to tell me what happened to make you dislike journalists so much."

He pushed the boat out into the water, jumped into the stern, and steered the boat into the river. "Maybe I will. One day." *What the hell?* He didn't talk about the *Aspire* article. Not ever.

He slid her a glance.

Instead of the anger he expected to see on her pretty face, a raw look of compassion shadowed her blue eyes.

Chapter 17

"Hey, Stick, you home?"

"Peter?" She lifted her head from the pillow and rubbed the sleep from her eyes.

He unzipped the tent flap and poked his head through. "You awake?"

She yawned and peered at her watch. "Are you kidding me? It's six o'clock in the morning. What the heck do you want?"

The corners of his eyes crinkled, and he grinned. "Come on, get up. Roman's going fishing, and he wants to take you."

"What?" She frowned. "I don't want to go fishing." And she certainly didn't want to go fishing with Roman. Not after his disparaging remarks the previous day. *Nosey reporter, indeed!*

"I already told him you're going." He crawled into the tent and tossed her the pants and shirt she'd worn the previous day. "Get dressed."

"I don't believe you." No way would the moody archaeologist want to spend time alone with her.

Peter's face flushed. "I might have twisted his arm a bit."

A bit? Peter must've held Roman down by knife point to coerce him into taking her fishing. "I'm not going."

"Come on." He smiled the smile he used when he

wanted to get his own way, the one he'd employed so successfully with their mother, his teachers, and basically any female over the age of five. "Think about it. Fishing at Keyoh will add color to your story, give it some depth." He pushed out his lower lip in a fake pout. "Please, Stick. For me?"

She swallowed a groan. She never could resist him. "Okay, I'll go, but if I don't make it back by lunch, come looking for me."

He pumped his fist in the air. "Yes!"

She tossed her shoe. "Now get out of here so I can get dressed."

His smile faded. "You haven't seen my journal, have you?"

"Your journal?" Peter started writing his thoughts in a journal when he was ten, after their parents divorced. He'd kept up the habit, and every evening on the trip, he wrote in the little red book. "It's missing?"

He threaded his fingers through his hair. "I can't find it anywhere."

"Did you look in your duffel or your day pack?"

He nodded and then shrugged. "I'll look again. It has to be around somewhere." He backed out of the tent. "Hurry up. You've got ten minutes to get ready."

She resisted the urge to throw the other shoe. She didn't want to be alone with Roman. Not. One. Bit. But a part of her—a teeny tiny part deep inside—was excited at the prospect. She dragged on her pants and tugged her sweater over her head. Not bothering to look in the hand mirror, she finger-combed her hair and plaited it into a single braid and crawled out of the tent.

Peter was waiting, his gaze fixed on his wristwatch. "Nine minutes. You're cutting it close."

She bit back a snarky retort.

"Come on. He's waiting." He gestured for her to follow.

Roman stood by the woodpile, his back to them, Shas at his side. He held two fly-fishing rods in one hand, and a plastic tackle box in the other.

"Hey, Roman." Peter strode up and clapped his friend on his shoulder. "All set?"

Roman turned. His gaze settled on Hannah, and his smile faded, replaced by a frown. "What's this? I thought just you and I were going fishing?"

A flush settled on Peter's face. "Well…um…ah…" He grimaced theatrically and rubbed his temples. "I have this bad headache." More furious rubbing. "It just came on, and there's no way I'm up to fishing." He brightened. "But Hannah will go with you." His gaze shifted. "Right, Hannah? You always said you wanted to try fly-fishing."

She bit back a curse. Damn Peter. He'd backed her into a corner. She slid a glance at Roman.

He was frowning, his displeasure clear.

"You don't mind taking Hannah, do you? I'd really appreciate it. I want her to get the full northern experience while she's here," Peter said.

A tiny pulse beat a rapid pace in Roman's rigid jaw.

Shas barked, his tail whipping back and forth. He too looked pleadingly at Roman.

Roman heaved a resigned sigh and grunted.

Shas barked again as if in approval.

"Thanks, buddy. That's awesome." Peter grinned like a shark. "You're a great friend, my man."

Roman's mouth twisted like he'd tasted something sour, but he gestured to Hannah. "Let's go."

Peter's smile covered his whole face, and he no

longer rubbed his temples, his *headache* miraculously cured.

She shot him a fiery glare that should've caused him to burst into flames, and with her heart skipping beats, followed Roman across the clearing and down a trail to the mouth of the creek.

He didn't say a word as they strode along the rocky shore beneath towering cottonwood trees to a deep clear pool of water shaded by leafy tree branches.

Shas raced to the creek's edge and lapped water with his long pink tongue.

Roman set the rods and tackle box on the rocky shore. "Have you done much fly-fishing?"

She shook her head. "No, but I've always wanted to learn."

He rigged one of the fishing rods with fly-fishing line and attached a fly. His motions were skilled and sure, and it was obvious he knew what he was doing.

"How long have you been fly-fishing?"

"Since I was a little boy. Nathaniel taught me." He attached line to the second rod. "What type of fly do you want to use?" He gestured at the colorful collection of flies in the tackle box.

"They all look so pretty. Which one do *you* think I should use?"

"Pretty, huh?" His mouth curved in a smile.

She ducked her head to hide the red searing her cheeks.

"We're fishing for rainbow trout, so—" He selected a dark furry fly with a wisp of a tail. "This is a woolly bugger. It's supposed to resemble a dragonfly larva. Trout love those."

"Woolly bugger?" She shook her head. "Really?

That's what it's called?"

He grinned. "That's its name." He pointed to another hook. "This one's a black ghost, and this one's a royal coachman." He picked up a tiny bright-green fly. "This little beauty's a green weenie."

She chuckled. "Where did you get them?"

"I made them."

"*You* made them?"

His cheeks pinked. "It's a hobby of mine. Something I do in the winter. I use wire and feathers and even strands of Shas's hair."

"Wow." She could only imagine the hours of work it took to create the realistic looking flies. "You're a talented man." *He's probably a talented kisser too.* The unexpected thought coming out of left field was like a bomb detonating, and her breath whooshed out.

Seemingly oblivious to the havoc raging through her, he finished tying on the fly and handed her a rod. He smiled, the matching dimples in his cheeks flashed, and the tiny lines beside his eyes deepened. "Okay. Let's catch some breakfast." His smile faltered. "Hannah? Are you ready?"

She shook herself out of her daze. "Er…sure…yes." She eyed the rod. It was longer and more flexible than the casting rod she was used to, and the line was thicker. "What do I do? How do I start?" She'd watched people fly-fish, and the sport looked graceful and elegant, but she was all thumbs holding the two-and-a-half-meter-long rod.

"Hold the rod with your thumb on top of the grip." He grasped his own pole so she could see where to place her fingers. "Don't squeeze too tightly."

She copied his handhold. "Like this?"

"That's great. Now, stand with your feet shoulder width apart and make a forward stroke like you're hammering a nail into a wall." He cast his rod, and the line sailed out over the still pool in a graceful arc. His movements were easy and fluid, like an elegant dance. The fly landed with a soft plop in the water. "Your turn."

She released a loop of line like he'd done and cast. The line ran out less than a meter, and the fly landed in the gravel on the shoreline. "Oops."

"Here." He set down his rod and moved behind her. "Let me show you." His hand covered hers, and he adjusted her fingers on the fishing pole.

She shivered at the warmth of his breath fanning the back of her neck, his callused hand on hers, his body brushing hers... She struggled to breathe, to concentrate on his instructions. Standing this close, she was all too aware of their height difference. The top of her head met his chin. An impulse to lean back against him overwhelmed her. What would be his reaction? Would he pull away?

"Now, start slowly, accelerate smoothly through the stroke, and stop abruptly." His actions followed his words as he helped her with the cast. The line released and soared over the creek, and the fly settled on the pool of water.

"Yes!" She hooted and giggled like a schoolgirl.

His deep chuckle rumbled through his chest. "Good job." He lifted his hand from hers and stepped back. "Try it again."

Her hand tingled from his touch, and her heart skipped beats. It took all her concentration to focus on what she was doing and not on the riot of sensations rocketing through her. "Okay. Here goes." She swung her arm in a short curved stroke, aiming at the pool of water. The line propelled forward, and the fly hit the water.

"You've got it." A boyish grin wreathed his rugged face. "Keep that up, and you'll hook a fish."

She lost herself in his warm, approving gaze.

A shiver of something, something she'd never felt before, rippled in the air between them.

His pupils dilated, and his gaze shifted to her mouth.

She wasn't the only one thinking of kissing. Gulping, she licked her lips. A sharp tug on her line, and she yelped and fumbled to hold onto the rod. "I think I caught one!" Another tug dragged the line under the water. "I did. I have a fish. What do I do now?"

"Keep your rod tip high. You want to keep pressure on the fish, so it can't shake off the hook." His dark eyes sparkled. "That's right. Now slowly reel in your line but keep up the pressure."

Her hand cramped from turning the reel, and the muscles in her forearm complained. The rod bowed, and beneath the water, she caught a glimpse of the silver back of a fish. "Help me. Please."

"You're doing great. You can do it."

She reeled and reeled, but the fish was still in the water. How much line had she let out?

"It's a good size. Keep reeling." He was as excited as if he were the one catching the fish.

Her heart warmed at the light in his eyes and the dimples dancing in his lean cheeks.

Striding to the water's edge, he grasped the line and tugged the squirming fish out of the water and held the trout aloft for her inspection. "It's a beauty." He lifted her in his arms and swung her in a circle.

Shas barked in excitement and pranced, tangling at their feet.

She wasn't looking at the fish or Shas. She only had eyes for Roman. The warmth of his embrace and the comforting weight of his strong arms seeped through her shirt.

Their gazes met, lingered.

Her knees wobbled, heat surged through her body, and with it, a rush of desire.

He lowered his head and pressed his mouth to hers.

The world spun out of control, and she sank deeper into the kiss, relishing the dizzying sensation of his lips on hers.

Far too soon, he released her and stepped back. Clearing his throat, he displayed the fish again. "Nice job."

She blinked. Right. The fish.

The beautiful silver fish with the horizontal pink and green stripes on its sides. Its gills flapped, and its mouth gaped as it struggled for air.

The thrill of desire faded. "Can we let it go?"

"You want to release this fish?"

She nodded. "I-It's so pretty."

He chuckled. "You have a soft heart." He pried open the fish's mouth and gently removed the hook. Crouching, he set the wriggling fish in the water, and holding it horizontally, he moved the animal back and forth a few times, and then let it go.

The trout's tail fin flicked, swishing from side to side, and then the fish darted away into the deep shadows.

She smiled. "Thank you."

"You're the one who's going to have to explain to

your brother and the rest of the crew why there's only porridge for breakfast."

His laughter washed over her like warm honey, and she couldn't help but laugh too.

Once again, their gazes locked.

Her laughter stilled at the heat glowing in his eyes, turning them the color of melted dark chocolate. Unable to turn away, pinned beneath the net of attraction flaring between them, her blood heated. Her pulse throbbed.

An eagle screeched, breaking the spell, and she tore her gaze from Roman's and stared up at the sky.

The big bird swooped over the tops of the trees lining the creek, sailing lower and lower as it flew over the water. A big splash, and the bird pulled up, a wriggling fish caught in its talons. The eagle flapped to a tall tree overlooking the creek and landed in a branch with its catch.

"There goes your fish. It wasn't his lucky day, I guess. I'm sorry." His voice was rough.

Tears burned her eyes. "Poor fish."

"Hey. Don't cry. That's nature. The eagle needs to eat too." He brushed her tears with the back of his hand.

She shivered. Oh man! She was in trouble. Big trouble. The man was her kryptonite, and she couldn't resist him. When he was near, all she thought of was how much she wanted him to kiss her.

Again.

But she was there under false pretenses. What would happen when she revealed who she worked for and in what magazine the Keyoh article would be published? She wasn't good at subterfuge, and she hated lying. Better to come clean now, and then they could explore whatever was happening between them. She smoothed the wrinkles from her shirt and opened her mouth to reveal the truth.

"Hey, you two. How goes the fishing?" Peter loped down the bank, a grin wreathing his hairy face. "I'm starving. How many fish have you caught?" He stuttered to a stop, and his gaze shifted from Roman to Hannah. "Am I interrupting something?"

"No." Both Roman and Hannah spoke at once.

Roman grabbed the fishing rods and tackle box, and with an apologetic look at Hannah, he strode down the creek to the trail leading to camp.

"Um, sorry, Stick. I didn't know..." Peter's voice trailed off.

She spun around and scrambled over the rocks in the opposite direction, heading up the creek.

"Was it something I said?" Peter called after her.

She ignored him and kept walking.

Chapter 18

The sun was low in the sky, and the day shed heat in layers. A welcome breeze off the river cooled the August air. A tang of smoke from the ever-present campfire mixed with the buttery aroma of onions frying in the pan on the propane cook stove.

Hannah sat at the picnic table, peeling carrots. The students took turns preparing the meals, and tonight was Zack's turn. Desperate for a distraction from her unexpected feelings toward Roman, she'd offered to help.

Her plan flopped. It turned out, peeling carrots left plenty of brain function to think. After spending the previous afternoon with Roman at the old settlement downriver, and that morning fly-fishing, she was even more confused. She'd enjoyed their time together. The animosity between them eased, and he was relaxed and fun, as if once away from the responsibilities of running the archaeological excavation, he was free to be himself.

When he stood close, she wanted him closer. When he touched her, she ached for his caress. And when he kissed her— Oh my!

After Peter interrupted them at the creek, she'd gone for a long walk, hoping the solace of nature would clear her mind and help her wrap her brain around what had happened. Unfortunately, the nature bath hadn't cleared her fog. She was more confused than she'd been when

Peter dragged her out of bed that morning.

Roman had kissed her. A brief but unforgettable kiss. The press of his mouth on hers had left her body aching and wanting so much more.

So, what now? Where did they go from there? She had to confess the truth. The longer she put off telling him who her employer was, the harder coming clean was going to be. She tossed a peeled carrot onto the cutting board and grabbed another carrot from the two-kilogram sack.

She was a good actor, and her fake smiles and forced laughter passed without comment. Other than a few teasing remarks and sly looks, Peter remained uncharacteristically silent. His lack of interest in her love life was probably because he still hadn't found his journal.

He made light of the loss, but she knew it distressed him. He relied on expressing his innermost feelings in the journal when he was stressed, and right now he was dealing with a broken heart. The breakup with his wife had devastated him.

No matter how hard he tried to hide his hurt, it was evident in his forced laughter and the hollow look of sadness that filled his face when he thought no one was looking.

She'd been wrapped up in her confusing feelings about Roman, but after supper, she'd help her brother search for his journal.

She set the peeled carrot beside the pile of others and reached for another one.

The crew couldn't stop talking about the Chinese coin they'd unearthed. No wonder.

Even with a dull-green coating of oxidation from

being buried in the ground for hundreds of years, the round copper coin with a flower hole in the middle and the four Chinese characters engraved into the soft metal, was an impressive artifact, and she'd taken dozens of photos.

According to Roman, the coin had probably been a present from the Chinese emperor who ruled during the later stages of the Song dynasty. The lucky recipient had passed a thin rope through the flower hole and tied smaller coins onto strings, displaying his wealth and prestige.

"What the heck?" Sam's excited shout broke through her thoughts.

The peeler slipped, and she cursed under her breath at a sharp pain. A tiny bead of blood seeped from where the blade had sliced into her skin.

"Look what I found." Sam was digging something out of the coals in the fire with a stick. Slipping a protective pad over his hand, he picked up a small object and set it on a stump.

"What is it?" Peter stood and moved closer to Sam. "Is that a ring?"

"Yeah."

"What's it doing in the fire?" Peter grabbed his headlamp and shone the narrow beam of light on the ring. "It looks expensive."

The other students crowded around. Their exclamations of surprise filled the night.

"Let me see that." Roman extended his hand.

Sam placed the now-cooled ring on Roman's palm.

"*This* was in the fire?" Roman asked.

Sam nodded. "I saw a glint in the hot coals. The ring couldn't have been in there long, or the band would've melted. I'm pretty sure the metal's gold."

"How did it end up in the fire?" Peter asked. "Did anyone here lose a ring?"

The crew members shook their heads.

Hannah's gut tightened. She wiped a smear of blood on her pants. "Can…can I see it?" Something about the gold band raised alarm bells.

Roman crossed to the table and held out the ring.

Peter shone his headlamp on the narrow gold band with its single princess-cut diamond.

The blood drained from her head, a wave of dizziness washed over her, and she swayed.

"Hannah? What is it? What's wrong?"

Peter's frantic voice was lost in the clamorous roar filling her brain. She peered at the ring again.

The gold band with the large solitaire diamond glittered in the flickering firelight.

An ice ball formed behind her sternum. She clutched the table as her mind spun with the nightmare possibilities.

"Help me! She's going to pass out."

Peter's frantic voice echoed through the din. The remaining strength drained out of her, and she sagged.

Strong arms grabbed her as she spiraled into a dark abyss.

Chapter 19

Roman caught her before she slipped from the picnic table bench and fell onto the hard ground.

Chaos erupted as everyone panicked, crowding around, trying to help.

His heart thundered in his chest, but he thrust back his fear. He had to keep a cool head. Keyoh was his project, and he was responsible for everyone at the site. "Clear a space."

Rafferty shoved carrots, a cutting board, and cooking pots off the table. They landed with a crash on the ground.

Roman laid her limp body gently on the picnic table. "Shine some light on her. Bring a bottle of water and a blanket." He barked the orders, and the crew rushed to comply.

"Let me look. I have industrial first-aid training." Peter elbowed through the hovering students and lifted Hannah's hand. His face was ghostly white, but his movements were calm and steady as he measured her pulse and conducted a brief examination.

Hannah's skin was ashen, her eyes closed, her body limp and unmoving.

Peter wiped his gleaming forehead with the back of his hand and met Roman's gaze. "Her heart rate's a bit fast, but her vitals are good. I think she fainted."

"Wi-will she be okay?" Roman asked, shocked at

the stammer in his voice.

Peter nodded. "She should be fine after she gets some rest."

A surge of relief gusted over him. His legs wobbled, and he gripped the table for support.

"Why did she pass out?" Sam asked, his voice hushed.

"I don't know." Peter shrugged. "Maybe she didn't drink enough water today, or she's exhausted from walking all over the site researching her article in the hot sun, or she has the flu. It could be anything." He swiped back a lock of hair from his forehead. "Let's give her some space. She'll be okay."

Peter's words of reassurance calmed the crew, but Roman wasn't fooled. His friend was doing a good job hiding his concern, but he was freaking out. He pulled Peter aside. "Help me carry her into my tent."

"Your tent? Why?"

"It's larger than hers, and I have a camp cot. She'll be more comfortable there, and you and I can keep an eye on her." He didn't wait to see if Peter agreed. He wrapped his arms around her shoulders and lifted.

Peter grabbed her legs.

Together they carried her past the concerned students and into Roman's tent. They settled her on the cot and covered her with a warm blanket.

Peter knelt on the floor beside the cot and clasped Hannah's hand. "Stick, wake up." When she didn't respond, he tapped the back of her wrist. "Come on. Wake up." His voice cracked with worry.

Roman stood back, watching Peter's frantic efforts. A lump thickened in his throat. His friend was a good brother, and he really cared about his sister. Roman didn't have any siblings, but he did have Nathaniel. His grandfather loved him. He'd never doubted that. Despite their current disagreement, he knew he could count on him. He laid a hand on Peter's shoulder. "Let her rest."

Peter glanced up, anguish shining in his eyes. "But she—"

"You said yourself that her heart's beating normally, and her breathing's good. Right?"

Peter nodded. "I think she fainted, but I don't understand why she passed out, and why she isn't waking up."

Roman tugged the ring from his pocket. "Do you think the sight of this caused her to faint?"

Peter sat back on his heels. "I don't know."

"Have you seen the ring before?"

Peter shook his head. "Never."

Roman examined the ring. The diamond was huge, possibly two carats, and the ring looked expensive. "Any idea as to how this ended up at Keyoh and in our fire pit?"

Again, Peter shook his head. "No idea."

Roman's thoughts pinged off the tent walls like scatter shot from a shotgun. The ring's sudden appearance was ominous. He felt the menace deep in his bones, as well as a desperate urge to protect the woman who lay unconscious on the camp cot.

Her dark-blonde hair had escaped the single braid and fanned across the pillow. Her long eyelashes swept her pale cheeks. Beneath her eyelids, her eyes shifted back and forth as if she were seeing something frightening. Her mouth opened, and a low moan escaped.

The sight of the ring had upset her. *Upset* her? The second she looked at it, her face drained of color, and she passed out.

"I guess we'll have to wait until she wakes up to find our answers."

Peter stood and smoothed the palm of his hand over his unruly curls. "Keep an eye on her, will you? I'm going to run to my tent and get my sleeping pad and bag." He adjusted the blanket covering his sister. "Looks like I'm going to be spending the night in here." He crossed to the opening and slipped through.

Roman dragged a camp stool close to the cot and sat. He couldn't take his gaze off her. What was it about her? Something—her fragile beauty, her strength of character, her dedication to her work—flustered him. Flustered? Hell, just being near her threw his entire world off-kilter.

Since she'd arrived at Keyoh, he'd made it his mission to keep his distance. Easy enough to do when he was busy directing the excavation of the test pits and ensuring the correct protocols were in place for the recovered artifacts.

But Peter, employing the full force of his legendary charm, convinced Roman to invite her to join him on his trip to Libertas Bay. If that wasn't bad enough, he was tricked into taking her fly-fishing the next morning. Peter's attempts at playing Cupid were more than obvious, but Roman agreed to take her anyway. Look where those choices led him—kissing her, embracing her… All wrong in countless ways.

He didn't blame Peter. It wasn't his friend's fault Roman couldn't stop thinking about her. When the sun set, every fiber of his being prickled with the awareness she slept a mere meter away. The thin canvas wall of his tent and even thinner nylon fabric of her pup tent were all that separated them. He lay awake, tossing on his narrow cot, wondering what she wore to bed—fuzzy pajamas, a T-shirt and cozy flannelette pants, or nothing at all?

Tonight was a perfect example. He hadn't wanted to join the group for the pre-supper gathering, and he wasn't in the mood for idle chitchat. What he needed to do was stay away from Hannah until he understood what the heck was going on and why he couldn't stop thinking about her.

He'd had the intention of working in his tent, as he'd done every evening since she arrived, but then he poked his head out of his tent and saw her sitting at the table preparing supper. Her blonde hair, freed from its usual thick braid, flowed like liquid gold in rippling waves down her narrow back. His brain froze, and other parts of his body took over. The next thing he knew, he was stepping through his tent flap and marching over to her like a salmon returning to its spawning grounds.

Her feminine fragrance had wafted on the night breeze, fanning over him, igniting an inner fire. Watching her peel carrots wasn't sexy or alluring in any way, but his blood heated, and it was all he could do to keep his hands off. Somehow, over the past two days, she'd breached the walls he'd erected around his heart, and before he knew what was happening, he was taking her on a river trip, teaching her to fly-fish, and spilling his guts, telling her about his childhood and his rocky relationship with his grandfather.

Before he had a chance to make a total fool of himself by drooling, Sam found the ring. After that, all hell broke loose.

He picked up the ring from the plastic camp table.

What was it about the diamond ring that shocked her so much she fainted? He drew the lantern closer and held the ring under the spill of bright light. Faint markings were etched into the inside of the band. He surged to his feet and strode to a large plastic tub. Ripping off the lid, he dug through the jumbled equipment, and grabbed a small magnifying glass. He returned to his chair and held the ring under the glass.

The markings sharpened, and the tiny letters became visible.

True love never dies.

He'd never given a ring to a woman, never loved anyone enough to make that sort of commitment. But he'd seen his friends' engagement rings, and read the romantic inscriptions etched into the metal bands. No question. This was someone's engagement ring.

He examined the ring again. There was another marking on the narrow band. He adjusted the lens.

A tiny heart. Inside the heart were the initials *HM & DP*.

His scalp prickled. H.M.? Hannah Marchand? Was that possible? Was this her ring? Was she engaged? Neither she nor Peter had mentioned that detail.

He sat back and rubbed his temples. Who was D.P.? And how had Hannah's ring ended up in the fire?

The tent flap flipped open, and Peter bustled in, his arms loaded. "Any change? Has she woken up yet?"

Roman shook his head.

"Damn." Peter dropped his supplies on the ground. "She's been out a long time."

"Who's D.P.?"

Peter blinked. "What?"

Roman held out the ring and magnifying glass.

"Take a look at the inside of the band."

Peter's brow furrowed, but he took the ring and lens and shifted closer to the light. He met Roman's gaze, his eyes wide. "H.M. are Hannah's initials." He gasped and his hand went to his chest. "Oh my God. D.P.! I can't believe this."

"What?"

Peter studied the ring again, his forehead grooved.

Roman wanted to shake his friend and force him to speak, but he stuffed his hands into his pockets and calmed his voice. "Tell me what you know."

"On the canoe trip here, Hannah told me she's being stalked. Some guy she dated didn't like it when she rejected him. He's been making threatening phone calls and following her. He even left her a weird note on her car." He scratched his scruffy beard. "I convinced her to talk to the cops when we get to Fort Cutter."

Roman's anger erupted and found a target in Peter. "Are you kidding me? You knew this jerk was stalking her, and you didn't tell me?" He'd read stories of women who were stalked by their exes, men who wouldn't take no for an answer. They broke into their victim's homes and left threatening notes or gifts, so the women knew their safe space had been violated. Some of those men resorted to violence. The thought of Hannah facing that harassment stabbed like a knife to the gut.

Peter extended his hands in a placating gesture. "The extreme isolation of this place is one of the reasons she's here. Keyoh's a hell of a long ways from Vancouver. No way could this loser have followed her."

Roman gritted his teeth, wanting to argue, but Peter's logic was solid. Access to Keyoh was challenging. Other than by helicopter, the only ways to reach the remote site were by boat or an arduous four-day hike from Verity.

Besides, he'd know if someone uninvited was lurking in the forest. Nathaniel wandered the site at all hours of the day and night. He'd have noticed if a stranger was in the area. "What's this guy's name? D.P. Are those his initials?"

"I only know his first name. Derek."

D.P.!

Of course. The *D* stood for Derek.

Maybe.

Or was it a coincidence the initials inscribed on the ring were the same as Hannah's and the letter of the first name of the man who was stalking her? What were the odds? How had the ring ended up in the fire? Had Hannah thrown it into the flames? But if so, why was she shocked when Sam found it?

Those were the million-dollar questions.

He strode to the entrance.

"Where are you going?"

He ignored Peter's question and ducked through the tent flaps.

Chapter 20

Hannah opened her eyes and squinted in the light. Her head throbbed, and her brain felt as if it were stuffed with cotton. The sense something was wrong was overwhelming. She lifted her head off the pillow and studied her surroundings.

She was lying on a bed.

No. That wasn't right.

She was on a camp cot, covered by a soft gray wool blanket. The glow from a lantern on a nearby plastic folding table revealed green canvas walls.

Her eyes widened.

She was in Roman's tent!

She shoved off the blanket and sat up, swinging her legs off the cot.

A hand on her shoulder stopped her. "Take it easy, Stick."

"Peter?" She blinked, fighting to clear her brain. "What happened? What am I doing in Roman's tent?"

"You don't remember?" His brow furrowed.

She shook her head. But was that true? There was something…she couldn't put her finger on exactly what, but the certainty something had happened, something bad, settled like a block of ice in her stomach. "Tell me."

"You were helping Zack with the dinner prep, and the next thing I knew, you fainted." He threaded his fingers through his shaggy blond curls. "Roman and I carried you in here."

The ferocious pounding in her head amped up a notch. "I passed out?" Her mouth was parched and her voice raspy. "Why did I faint? What happened?" He handed her a plastic water bottle, and she unscrewed the cap and gulped. The cool liquid slid down her throat, easing the painful tightness.

"You really don't remember?"

She shook her head.

"Like I said, we were sitting around the fire, and you were at the picnic table peeling carrots. Zack was frying onions, and we were all talking about finding the Chinese coin. Everyone's excited. It's a stunning find, and—"

"Stop." She held up her hand, halting his nervous rambling. There was something he was afraid to tell her. "What happened?"

"Sam found a diamond ring in the campfire. When Roman showed you the ring, you turned pale as a sheet and fainted. Good thing he caught you before you hit the ground."

Her brain froze on a single word. *Ring!*

Panic set in, and her heart bounced in her chest as if it were fighting to break free. Memories of the previous night crashed over her like a tsunami. Sam found a ring in the fire. When she saw it, she couldn't breathe, and then the darkness.

She shuddered and tugged the blanket around her. It couldn't be the same ring. How was that even possible? Diamond rings all looked similar. Didn't they?

There was no way the ring Derek wanted to give her—the one she refused to accept that last night they were together—ended up in a fire pit at Keyoh. But she'd seen the engraving on the inside of the gold band. Or had she? She wasn't sure. Not about anything.

She rubbed her forehead. The stress of the past months was wearing, and she was seeing boogeymen around every corner, jumping at every sound, afraid of her shadow.

"Hannah, are you feeling okay? Do you want a doctor? Should I use the camp satellite phone and call for a medivac?"

She swiped a lose strand of hair off her face. "Where's the ring?" But then she saw it on the camp table. She bit down hard on her bottom lip, hoping the pain would fend off the disabling fear. "Can…can I see it?"

Peter's gaze delved deep. "Are you sure you want to do that?"

She held out her hand. "Show me."

He picked up the ring and set it on her palm.

The gold band with the princess-cut solitaire diamond looked like the ring Derek had bought. But how was that possible?

"Is it Derek's?"

"It can't be."

"There's an inscription on the inside of the band and two sets of initials." He handed her a magnifying glass. "Have a look."

She didn't want to look. She knew what the engraving said. Derek had shown her the inscriptions he'd had etched on the inside of the narrow gold band. But what if she was wrong, and this was a different ring? One of the students, or Roman, could have bought the same style of ring and brought it to camp.

But what if she was right, and it *was* Derek's ring?

Her hand shook as she lifted the magnifying glass.

HM & DP.

She gasped and dropped the ring like it burned. It fell onto the canvas floor and rolled under the cot.

True love never dies. HM & DP.

Hannah Marchand and Derek Pasternak.

She met Peter's anxious gaze. "I-I don't understand. How did that ring end up here?"

"Is it possible you had it in your pocket, and it fell out when you were setting a log on the fire?" His gaze shifted around the tent, looking anywhere but at her. He didn't believe his desperate theory any more than she did.

"I never had the ring." She smoothed her trembling hands over the blanket. "Derek showed it to me the last night we were together. He planned to ask me to marry him, but I wouldn't accept the ring. It was too soon. We'd only been dating a few months."

She chewed on the inside of her cheek, tasting blood. "He was so angry when I rejected him." Angry? That was an understatement. She shuddered as she recalled Derek's rage-flushed face. "The last I saw of the ring was when he stuffed it into his coat pocket and stormed out of my apartment. I never saw the ring again…until tonight." Her voice broke on a sob.

His mouth tightened into a grim line. "Don't worry. We'll figure this out." He patted her on the shoulder and stood. "You should try and get some sleep." He pointed at a sleeping bag laid out on an inflatable pad on the floor. "You'll be safe. I promise. I'll be right here all night."

"What about Roman?" She gestured at the canvas walls. "This is his tent. Where's he going to sleep?"

He shrugged. "In here, I guess."

Her heart skipped a beat. Even with her worry over the ring's shocking appearance, the thought of sleeping mere centimeters from Roman sent a thrill sparking through her.

A thrill?

Or panic?

She lay back on the pillow—Roman's pillow, Roman's bed, Roman's sleeping bag—and tugged Roman's blanket to her chin. A familiar scent wafted in the air—a musky mix of wood smoke and soap. Roman's scent. "The next time I pass out, I don't want to wake up in Roman's bed. Okay?" She fought to keep her voice light.

"I'll be sure and pass that on." He tugged off his boots and crawled into his sleeping bag. "Now, try and get some sleep. Don't worry about the ring. We'll figure it out tomorrow."

The ring!

Here.

At Keyoh.

Impossible. Yet, there it was. Under the cot, out of sight, but the ring might as well have a neon sign glaring over it. Her mind buzzed with a thousand frightening scenarios. Was Derek skulking in the forest watching, waiting for an opportunity to strike? A stinging chill slithered down her spine.

She was letting her imagination run wild. Derek wasn't at Keyoh. How could he be? He didn't know where she was. She'd lost him in the Vancouver morning rush-hour traffic. No way could he have followed her.

She rolled onto her side and drew her knees to her chest. Maybe Peter's wild theory was right. In her university classes, she'd learned about Occam's razor, which stated the simplest solution was usually the correct one.

Simple solution—Derek slipped the ring into her coat pocket without her knowledge, and she'd had it all this time. She often wore the same sweater. The pink fleece, zip-up jacket was her favorite. Had she been wearing it the night he'd shown her the diamond ring? She couldn't remember.

But that's what must have happened. It explained everything.

But what if she was wrong? What if the impossible were true, and Derek had followed her to Keyoh? A bone-shaking shudder wracked her body.

What if, indeed?

Chapter 21

The glowing silver orb of the full moon dipped low in the predawn sky. Moonbeams stretched across the ground, illuminating the rough steps carved into the sandy hillside.

Skidding and sliding on the loose earth, Roman bounded down the steps to the gravel beach.

The Sturgeon River flashed white as it splashed and churned over the sharp black rocks of the Keyoh Rapids. The remains of an old fishing weir, once used by the Saik'uz to trap salmon, peeked out of the water.

Untying his laces, he tugged off his leather hiking boots and tossed them on the gravel bank. His T-shirt and jeans followed. When he was naked, he plunged into the river, gasping at the shock of the frigid water. He ducked his head under again and again, desperate to clear his mind.

When he returned to his tent earlier after checking the site was secure, Peter met him outside. Hannah was asleep, and her brother didn't want to wake her. His voice was hushed when he explained her reaction when she wakened from her faint. He'd shown her the ring, and she confirmed it was the diamond ring the jerk who was harassing her had tried to give her. She didn't have any idea how the ring ended up at Keyoh.

Peter fired off a dozen frantic questions. How did the ring get to Keyoh? Why was the ring in the fire? Who put it there? Was Hannah in danger? The questions went on and on in an endless reel, but Roman didn't have the answers.

Witnessing the raw fear on his friend's face gutted him. The past few months had been difficult for Peter. First, he and his wife had split up, and now his sister was being stalked.

Hoping to ease Peter's apprehension, Roman offered platitudes that even as he spoke, he knew he couldn't guarantee. Keyoh was his excavation, and he wouldn't let anything happen to Hannah or anyone else on his watch; the site was isolated, and there was no way Hannah's stalker could have followed her there; he wasn't hiding in the forest, or someone would have seen him.

A sour taste filled his mouth, but his reassurances calmed Peter, and Roman urged him to get some sleep. They'd talk more in the morning. Roman would have the crew conduct a thorough search of the area, just to be sure this Derek Pasternak character hadn't pulled off a miracle and followed Hannah all the way from Vancouver.

The river rippled around his waist, and water streamed off his hair and face. He shivered in the predawn chill. Unlike Peter and Hannah, and everyone else at camp, he hadn't followed his own advice. Sleep wasn't in the cards. Not for him. He and Shas had wandered the meadow for hours, checking and rechecking the camp was secure.

Shas hadn't growled or barked or alerted to anything other than wagging his tail and sniffing at an intriguing scent on a rotten stump.

Even Nathaniel was tucked away in his sleeping bag

at his campsite. Roman had checked.

All was safe.

But that knowledge didn't help him sleep. His tent was off limits. How could he sleep in there when Hannah was in his bed? He could crawl into her tent and set up a sleeping bag, but he wouldn't be able to relax with the scent of her surrounding him.

He'd decided a dip in the river was what he needed to focus his thoughts. He shivered and almost smiled. He'd read about cold water immersion therapy. The theory was that bathing in icy water offered immeasurable health benefits. He smoothed the palm of his hand over his sodden hair. Wasn't he the New Age guy?

He waded to shore and climbed onto a large rock, letting the cool air dry his hair and body, ignoring the goosebumps riddling his skin. His teeth chattered, but he clenched his jaw.

The stars had faded, and gray and pink streaks lightened the charcoal sky. The dark-green humps of the distant forested hills were visible.

The *kik-kik-kik* of a kingfisher's call broke the dawn's stillness.

He inhaled, relishing the heady sweetness of the late-blooming wild roses lining the bank, but neither the beauty of the dawn, the immersion in frigid water, nor the fresh air eased his turmoil.

Even before the discovery of the diamond ring, Hannah's presence at Keyoh rattled him. He didn't know what to say or how to act around her. One minute he felt an immediate and strong connection. The next, he remembered she was a journalist, and his walls went up, and he shut down.

The kiss by the creek was everything he'd imagined and so much more, but one kiss wasn't enough. All he could think about was how much he wanted to kiss her again. Hell, he wanted to do a lot more than kiss her.

But a relationship could destroy his career. He was the project leader, and he was under a microscope. One misstep and he'd never run another excavation. He couldn't allow himself to be distracted. Besides, once she finished her research for her article, she'd be in the first canoe out of there and on to her next story.

Peter's revelation that Hannah was being stalked shocked and angered him. His friend should have told him. How could Roman protect her if he didn't know what he was facing? He wanted to hit someone. No. Not *someone*. Derek. He ached to smash his fist into the bastard's face and give him a taste of what it was like to be afraid.

Breathing deep, he struggled to suppress the all-consuming rage firing through him. He had to keep a clear head. Hannah could be in danger. Real danger. If there was even a possibility her stalker was in the area, Roman would do whatever he could to keep her safe.

He climbed off the rock, grabbed his clothes, and struggled into them. Sliding his feet into his boots, he tied the leather laces. He threaded his fingers through his tangled wet hair.

Now to find Nathaniel. His grandfather would know what to do. He always did.

Chapter 22

"What are you doing up?"

Hannah flinched, jumped to her feet, and wiped cold ashes from her hands. She'd been so immersed in her thoughts and searching the fire pit she hadn't heard Roman approach. The early-morning sun was behind him, and its warm golden rays surrounded his tall form with a nimbus of light.

It was impossible to see his features clearly, but his ruggedly handsome face was imprinted on her soul, and what her eye couldn't see, her mind filled in—dark, piercing eyes framed by strong black brows, sharp cheekbones, broad forehead, and aquiline nose. And those devastating dimples that flashed when he smiled.

Unless he was thinking of kissing her, then his face softened, his eyes warmed, and his dark irises sparkled with golden lights.

"Hannah? Did you hear me? Why are you up? You should be resting." He scanned the row of tents. "Where's Peter?"

"He's still asleep." She tucked a loose strand of hair behind her ear. "I-I couldn't sleep. After last night, I…" Even though her brother slept less than a meter away, she'd startled at every sound, her heart racing, her pulse pounding. Finally, she'd given up and climbed off the cot and snuck outside, careful not to wake him.

Roman studied his wristwatch. "No one'll be up for

a couple of hours. You shouldn't be out here alone." He motioned at her ash-covered hands. "What are you doing, anyway?"

She rubbed her dirty hands together. "I was searching the fire pit." Her face heated at his continued scrutiny. "I-I wanted to see if there was anything in the ashes."

"Did you find something?"

She shook her head. "I don't understand. How did that ring get in the fire?" The question raged through her brain on an endless rewind. Along with the even more terrifying thought that Derek had followed her to the remote archaeological site and was at Keyoh. An icy chill drilled into her bones, making it impossible to get warm, and she shivered and rubbed her arms.

"Here, take this." He shrugged off his faded navy-blue sweatshirt, the one he often wore in the mornings and evenings when it was cool. The letters UNBC, the university where he'd told her he'd earned his undergrad degree, were embroidered in forest green across the front.

"I-I-I'm o-ok-kay." Her teeth chattered, and she struggled to push out the words.

"You're freezing! Come on." Ignoring her protests, he laid the sweatshirt over her shoulders, and like he was dressing a small child, he helped her stuff her arms into the sleeves, and then he zipped up the front. "This'll keep you warm."

The shirt was too big, and the sleeves hung below the tips of her fingers, but the welcome warmth washed over her, and she snuggled into the soft cotton. The heavy sweatshirt smelled like him—woodsmoke, fresh air, and pine. "Thank you."

He nodded, and for the first time she noticed his long hair was dripping. "Your hair's wet. Were you in the river?"

"Just a quick dip, but I wouldn't recommend it. The water's glacial." He grabbed a gray hooded sweatshirt off the clothesline and shrugged into it. "I suppose I can't convince you to go back to bed."

She arched her eyebrows.

"I'll take that as a no." He heaved a resigned sigh. "I'm not leaving you here alone, so I guess you're coming with me." He clasped her hand in his. "Come on."

She held firm, resisting his tugging. "Where are we going?"

"To talk to Nathaniel."

"Nathaniel?"

"My grandfather. Remember?" The crinkles at the corners of his eyes deepened.

Of course she remembered. She'd been meaning to talk to Nathaniel, to get more background for her story, but she hadn't seen the old man since she'd met him in the forest on her first day at Keyoh.

"Will you go with me?" Roman tightened his fingers around hers. "Please? I want to ask Nathaniel if he's seen anyone lurking around."

She glanced at the deserted camp and shivered. "Yes. Sure. That…that's a great idea."

He led her past the row of colorful pup tents with their sleeping occupants snuggled inside. They crossed the clearing, and he paused at a recent excavation site. A meter-wide square of earth was flagged and taped off. He released her hand and crouched beside the hole and pointed. "This is where we found the Chinese coin."

She inspected the small square trench. "Are you going to extend the excavation and see if you can find more artifacts like the coin?"

"That would be ideal, but the grant I received from the university won't cover the cost of an extensive dig. With the tight timeline we're under, test pits are all we can manage."

"Are you kidding? You and your crew dug up something incredible. Who knows what else you'll find?"

He rose to his feet. "That's the nature of this business. The big money for field research goes to the more visible projects." He gestured at the expanse of grassy meadow. "No one in the archaeology arena cares about Keyoh. Not really. The site's too remote." He kicked a pebble, and the small stone flew across the grass. "Unfortunately, the clock's ticking. Most of the pine trees in this area were killed by the pine beetle epidemic that swept the province in the late 90's. All those dead trees mean there're thousands of hectares of land ripe for forest fires. If a fire happens here, any artifacts will be buried under a thick layer of ash and debris. Keyoh will be much more challenging to excavate."

"But the artifacts you and your crew have found are important. Surely that counts for something."

He shrugged. "I was lucky to secure a grant for six weeks." Moving to another pit, he knelt on the ground and pointed at a scattering of dirt-encrusted cream-colored flakes lying on the surface of the soil in the bottom layer. "These are human bone fragments that have been fully calcined." He must have sensed her confusion, because he added, "The bones were burned by a very hot fire."

"*Those* are human bones?"

He nodded.

"But there're so many." Dozens of tiny, off-white bone fragments lay scattered on the dark soil.

"When Chief Khadintal, the *detsah*—"

She interrupted. "Hold on. What's a *detsah*?" This was important to him, and because of that, it was important to her. He didn't share his thoughts often, and she wanted to make sure she understood.

"The *detsah* was an elder, and the leader of the extended families that camped in an area. Khadintal was Keyoh's *detsah*. He and his men returned to the village from a hunting expedition, and they found the pit houses burned, and the bodies of their loved ones butchered. The Tsilhqot'in attackers killed almost everyone that day."

He swiped the back of his hand over his mouth. "The fragments of human bones we've recovered are mixed in with a layer of ash and charcoal. As part of Dakelh tradition, the survivors stacked the bodies in piles and cremated them." He gestured at the site. "We've found calcined bone in almost every test pit."

The peaceful meadow glowed in the early morning light.

Birds flitted in the branches of the tall fir trees rimming the clearing.

A vee-shaped flock of Canada geese flew overhead, their loud honking breaking the silence.

A tragedy of unimaginable proportions had occurred there. Hundreds of people lost their lives in a violent altercation, their bodies cremated by the survivors, their charred bones left amongst the ashes to turn to dust.

A lump thickened her throat. "That's so sad."

He stared at his dirt-smudged hands and wiped them on his jeans. "The bone fragments we uncover will be collected and reinterred with an appropriate Dakelh ceremony when we're finished."

"The excavation of this site means a lot to you, doesn't it?"

His chest rose and fell as he inhaled and exhaled. "It's been a long-held dream of mine to lead an excavation at Keyoh. I want people to learn about the rich and complex culture of the Dakelh. Our traditions and stories go back long before European contact.

"Much of our culture was lost when the Indigenous population was decimated by disease, and we were forced out of our traditional territory. Residential schools and the Sixties Scoop didn't help. My people, especially the youth, need to learn our cultural roots so they'll take pride in their Indigenous heritage." His dark eyes shone with his fervor.

"Maybe my article will make a difference. If it's published in a prominent magazine—" *like* Aspire "—people will take an interest. They'll care what happened here and will want to know more. That'll garner your project increased funding, and maybe you'll be granted permission to conduct a more thorough investigation."

"Maybe." He rose and brushed dirt from the knees of his pants. "Come on. We'd better get going. I want to catch my grandfather before he heads out fishing." He pivoted and in a few long strides, he'd crossed the clearing and strode into the gloom and shadows of the forest.

Hurrying after him, she ducked under low-hanging branches and skirted fallen trees. She stumbled, tripping over a hidden root, and would have fallen if he hadn't caught her around the waist. The warmth of his arm branded her skin through the thick cotton sweatshirt.

Their eyes met, the planet stopped spinning, and time stood still. The wind died, and the branches of the towering fir trees stopped swaying and creaking.

Caught in the spell of his intense gaze, she licked her dry lips. Her heart fluttered.

His pupils dilated, his eyes transforming from obsidian to dark chocolate, as his gaze fixed on her mouth. He lowered his head.

Her mouth parted.

A raven's raucous croak echoed from high atop a tree.

The searing heat in Roman's gaze vanished, and he dropped his arm from around her waist and stepped back.

A chill set in where his arm had rested.

The raven cawed again, its unblinking brown eyes watching. The trickster opened its beak and squawked in a hideous imitation of a laugh.

Datchancho.

She shuddered and wrapped her arms across her chest.

Roman cleared his throat. "Let's find Nathaniel." He turned and started down a narrow, winding trail.

Reeling from a riot of inexplicable emotions, she forced her wobbly legs to move and stumbled after him. What the heck just happened? Or…*almost* happened. He was going to kiss her. She'd read the desire in his eyes. And she'd wanted him to kiss her. Very much. Her heart fluttered, and she tripped over another root and let out a shriek. Grabbing onto his arm, she stayed on her feet.

Focus!

The order rang through her addled brain.

Inhaling a deep breath, she picked her way over the uneven ground, hurrying her steps, matching his long stride.

Chapter 23

They stepped into a small clearing hidden by trees. A tattered sleeping bag lay on the ground atop a pile of fresh-cut spruce boughs. Thin tendrils of smoke rose from the smoldering ashes in a fire pit ringed by fire-scorched rocks in the center of the clearing. A metal grill was set over the fire, and a soot-blackened pot filled with simmering water heated.

"Nathaniel?" Roman's brow furrowed. He called again. And again. "Nathaniel, where are you?"

"He hasn't been gone long. The fire's still hot." She rubbed a scratch on her cheek where a branch had poked her. "He must be nearby."

"I hope so." Roman sank onto a stump beside the fire pit and clasped his hands between his knees. "We need to talk to him and find out what he knows."

Her heart skipped a beat, and she peered into the dense forest. Evergreen branches swayed in the gentle breeze, and shadows danced under the canopy. Her skin tingled with the uneasy sensation they were being observed, the same feeling she'd had since she arrived at Keyoh. "Do-do you think someone else is here?"

"I don't know. I doubt it." He scraped his hand over the dark stubble sprinkling his chin. "Nathaniel's always out walking the trails, harvesting berries and medicinal plants, or fishing. He'd know if a stranger's lurking about."

From somewhere deep in the forest, a branch snapped, the sound cracking like a gun shot.

She jumped and slapped her hand over her mouth to stop a scream. "What was that?"

"Maybe Nathaniel or a deer or a branch breaking in the wind. I'm sure it's nothing to worry about." But his body tensed, and his eyes narrowed as he stared into the trees. "Nathaniel? Is that you?"

The wind picked up, and a distant ominous rumble filled the air.

He blew out a breath and stood. "Looks like a storm's coming. We'd better head back to camp."

Dark menacing clouds rolled in and covered the sun, lowering the temperature by a dozen degrees.

She shivered and huddled deeper into the heavy cotton sweatshirt. "What about Nathaniel?" She had to shout to be heard over the rising wind. "He's out in the storm. He doesn't have a tent to protect him from the rain. He'll get soaked."

Another rumble filled the air.

"Don't worry about him. He'll be fine. He's a tough old guy." A warm light suffused his dark eyes. "I'll come check on him later."

His husky voice flowed over her like a slow dance, and once again, she was drawn under his spell. She forgot the impending storm, forgot her concern for Nathaniel, forgot everything but the tall man standing before her. As if drawn to a life force, she leaned closer, wanting, needing, aching—

A bolt of lightning ripped the air, followed by a booming crack of thunder that reverberated off the surrounding hills and rattled her bones. The dark clouds opened, and rain poured down in heavy sheets.

And just like that, the moment was lost.

"Come on. Let's get out of this storm." He grasped her hand, and together they raced through the pelting rain and frigid wind gusts.

She concentrated on not stumbling over the slick roots and loose rocks, but part of her brain was distracted by the comforting warmth of his hand.

Trees creaked and swayed, their branches whipping in the howling wind. A flash of light lit the dark sky like fireworks, followed by a thunderous crash that shook the ground.

He veered off the overgrown deer trail and thrust through tangled willows and prickly wild rose bushes and halted in front of a towering rock wall.

"Wh-wh-why are we stopping here?" Her teeth chattered, and shivers wracked her body.

"You'll see." He released her hand and brushed aside a curtain of overhanging roots and tangled bushes, revealing a narrow gap in the rock face.

"Is that a cave?" Rainwater sluiced off her sodden hair and dripped in her eyes. She wiped her sleeve over her face.

"You bet." He grinned, his eyes sparkling despite the heavy downpour. "Come on. Let's get out of this storm." Crouching, he crawled on his hands and knees, squeezing his tall muscular body through the small opening.

She peered at the dark cavity. Did he expect her to crawl into that tiny hole? What if a bear was in there, or the roof collapsed? No one from camp knew where they were. They could be trapped in there forever.

He motioned for her to climb through.

She shook her head. No way. Small dark spaces

made her nervous, and she avoided them wherever possible.

"Come on." He beckoned again. "It's nice and dry in here."

Another bright flash of light and a rolling boom. The icy rain poured down.

She was shivering so hard, her knees knocked together. The storm wasn't letting up anytime soon. If she stayed out there in the downpour, she risked hypothermia.

Tottering on shaky legs, she approached the opening and sank onto her hands and knees, landing in a mud puddle where rainwater dripped off the rocky outcropping and pooled on the sodden ground. She cursed under her breath and shoved up the sleeves of her borrowed sweatshirt. Grabbing the rock edge, she pulled herself up to the opening.

Her heart beating a rapid tattoo in her chest, she crawled into the narrow, dark fissure. Sharp rocks gouged her knees and the palms of her hands as she inched into the stygian darkness. She glanced over her shoulder at the dim light filtering through the tangled roots and shrubs into the opening behind. Facing forward, she gritted her teeth and shuffled ahead.

A hand brushed her arm, and she squealed.

"Hey, it's just me. It's okay. You can stand up now." Roman gripped her elbow and helped her stand.

The air in the cave was cool and thick with humidity. She wrinkled her nose at the musty, earthy smell and wrapped her arms over her chest and shivered.

"I know it's cold in here, but it'll warm up once I start a fire." His husky tones were magnified in the confined space.

A match flared, and she blinked in the bright light. "You brought matches?"

"Of course. Did you think I was going to rub two sticks together?" He set the burning match to a pile of dry moss and twigs he'd gathered. In minutes, the fire crackled cheerfully.

She scooted closer and held her hands over the flames, reveling in the warmth.

The firelight flickered on sparkling veins of white quartz and mica embedded in the rock walls, creating intriguing designs. The flames crackled and sparked, and a thin tendril of smoke spiraled on an air current, funneling like a chimney into the cave's arched roof high above her head. The floor was littered with rocks, dried leaves, branches, and twigs. From somewhere back in the depths of the cave, the steady drip, drip, drip of water echoed.

Rain pattered on the ground outside the cave, and the wind shrieked. Thunder rumbled.

The cave walls enveloped her like a womb within the earth, a sanctuary from the storm. The warmth of the fire filled the small space, and safe from the elements and the worry of prying eyes, she relaxed.

Roman sat cross-legged on the ground in front of the fire. Wiping his hands on his soaked jeans, he tugged a cell phone from his pants pocket.

"You brought your phone? There's no cell service here, is there?"

He chuckled. "No. Even if there was service at Keyoh, we wouldn't get any bars in this cave. The rock walls would block reception." Fiddling with the phone, he tapped the screen. "Nathaniel showed me this cave when we visited Keyoh when I was a kid. I found my first arrowhead in here. That's when I was bitten by the archaeology bug and determined that someday I'd excavate Keyoh."

"Lucky for us you remembered where the entrance was." She grabbed a branch from the dwindling pile, snapped it in two, and tossed both pieces into the fire.

Holding up the phone, he pointed it at the glistening rock wall. A bright light flashed. "Since we're here, I figure I should take a few photos. They'll go in my report, along with a request to conduct another project here next season."

"Do you think that'll happen? Will the university let you do that?"

He shrugged. "Who knows? It depends on how well this summer's excavation goes."

"You found the Chinese coin. That'll help."

"I hope so, but this project's under a microscope. I can't afford to make any mistakes."

Her heart melted at the worry in his dark eyes. "Peter told me that he thinks you're doing a great job."

"Your brother's a good friend." His mouth twisted. "Unfortunately, the director at the university doesn't hold me in the same high regard."

She'd never seen his vulnerable side, and she liked it. She *really* liked it, but before she could delve deeper, he changed the subject.

"How long have you been a journalist?"

"Three years or so."

"Did you always want to be a reporter?"

"I've wanted to be a journalist since I was a kid." She stared at the flickering flames. "I didn't want to just report the news, I wanted to uncover the story behind the headlines and help people understand why world events

153

went down the way they did. That's why I studied journalism in university." She picked up a twig and twirled it in her fingers. "I guess I was naïve, but I wanted to make a difference. I still do."

"Like Bob Woodward and Carl Bernstein." A soft smile played across his lips.

"You know about them?"

"Of course. They're the journalists who exposed the Watergate scandal." The corners of his mouth twitched. "I don't always have my nose buried in an excavation pit."

The cozy confines of the cave and the flickering firelight loosened her tongue, and she leaned closer. "They're the reason I wanted to be an investigative journalist. Their investigation led to the resignation of a crooked president."

"I saw the movie." He grinned. "I even read the book."

She chuckled. "Did you, now?"

As if a switch were thrown, his face hardened. "Too bad all reporters don't have their integrity."

"Why do you dislike journalists?" *And why do you hate* Aspire? But she was a coward and didn't speak the final words aloud.

"Most reporters can't be trusted. All they care about is selling a story. They don't care if the facts are true or who their words hurt."

"Do you want to tell me what happened? I'd really like to know."

"Why? So you can write about it in your article?" His body bristled, anger radiating off him in visible waves. "I've been screwed over once. I don't plan to let it happen again."

154

She reeled back. "I asked because I thought we were friends, and I want to understand. That's all. Anything you tell me will stay between us. I promise you that."

He picked up a stick and stirred the glowing coals. "I told you, I don't trust reporters."

"Even me?"

He met her gaze.

The steady drip of water in the back of the cave was loud.

A clap of thunder rumbled.

"I don't know yet." He stood and brushed off his jeans. "We're running low on firewood. I'll get some more."

"I'll get it." Desperate to hide the hurt his words caused, she jumped to her feet and hurried deeper into the cave. The dirt floor was littered with the accumulation of years of debris, and in no time, she gathered an armful of wood. She turned to head back to the fire but stopped. The wood fell from her arms and landed on the ground with a loud clatter. "Roman, come look at this."

"What is it?" He rushed to her side.

"Look." She pointed into the dark. "Someone's been in here."

He switched on the flashlight app on his phone, and a blinding beam of light brightened the small cave, illuminating a two-liter plastic water bottle half full of water. His shoulder brushed hers as he swept the beam of light around the cave, revealing a sleeping pad with a down sleeping bag on top, a battery-operated camping lantern, and a large nylon backpack set against the rock wall. "Hold this." He handed her his cell phone. "Shine the light on the backpack."

The light wavered, bouncing off the walls and floor as her hand shook. Something about the camping equipment filled her with trepidation.

He squatted and untied the strings holding the backpack closed and rifled through the contents. His face was grim, his mouth a thin line as he pulled out a folded piece of paper and held it up to the light.

"What is it?" Her voice was a thin squeak.

The furrow between his dark brows deepened. "It's a map of Renton Falls and the Sturgeon River."

"What?" She leaned closer and studied the map.

Keyoh was circled with red ink.

Her breath whooshed out, and she dropped the cell phone. "He's here, isn't he? Derek's here."

Chapter 24

As soon as the storm let up, they crawled out of the cave and headed back to camp. Roman attempted to hide his concern, but the furrows lining his brow and the flat light in his eyes revealed the truth.

She heaved a relieved breath when they arrived at camp with its string of colorful pup tents.

The kitchen area was bustling with activity as the crew ate a late breakfast and prepared for the day ahead.

Roman, his face grim, gestured to Peter, and the two men disappeared into Roman's tent.

She fled to her own tent and huddled on her sleeping mat. Curling her knees to her chest, she wrapped her arms around her legs, and drew her sleeping bag closer. The sight of the camping equipment she and Roman discovered in the cave endlessly replayed through her mind. None of the items had dust covering them, so the equipment hadn't been in the cave long.

Even now, safe in her tent, surrounded by the archaeology students and Peter and Roman, a heavy weight of fear filled her soul.

"Hannah?" Peter zipped open the tent flap and crawled inside. "Hey, are you okay?" Concern etched his bearded face.

She blinked back the sting of tears. "I guess you heard."

"Roman told me what you guys found." His face

was haggard and new lines furrowed his brow. He tugged a small metal flask out of his coat pocket. Removing two plastic glasses from his other pocket, he filled the cups with amber liquid and handed her a glass. "Here. This might help."

"Where've you been hiding that?" Roman ran a dry camp, and alcohol wasn't allowed. Shortly after their arrival, Peter had reluctantly poured out the remains of his whisky bottle to comply with Roman's rules.

"I kept this hidden, thinking it might come in handy."

"And you think this is the day and the time to drink it?" She glanced at her watch. "It's still morning."

"Doctor's orders. Drink up." He raised his glass, guzzled, and leaned against her pillow. "I don't blame you for being concerned. I'm worried too."

Hoping to stop the impending flood of tears, she sipped her drink. The potent liquor burned down her throat, and she coughed. "Wha-what is this?" Her eyes streamed, and she coughed again.

"Over-proof rum."

"Are you nuts? This stuff'll kill a person."

"Maybe." He smirked and slurped another long drink. "But you'll die happy."

Despite her unease, she chuckled. He'd always been good at making her laugh. She sipped again, and the liquor slid down her throat like silk, spreading warmth from her belly through all the cells in her body. The suffocating fear gripping her heart eased.

"You know, there's a simple explanation for that stuff you guys found in the cave. It was probably left by a camper who stopped here for the night. Lots of people canoe the Sturgeon River to Fort Cutter. I did it last summer with a group of friends. It's a great trip."

"Come on, Peter. You don't believe a canoeist camped in that cave, do you? Keyoh is a protected historic site. Camping is prohibited."

He shrugged. "Maybe someone was caught in a rainstorm and stayed the night in the cave where it's dry. Like you and Roman did." He studied the amber liquid in his glass. "Or maybe a couple of the archaeology students have been sneaking out of camp and hooking up there." He shrugged. "Any one of those scenarios is more believable than Derek following you to Renton Falls and canoeing down the river to Keyoh."

"It's him, Peter. I know it."

"How would he get here? He'd have to have some mad river skills, and from what you've told me, Derek's a city boy. Even if by some miracle, he made his way to Keyoh, how could he survive in the forest undetected?"

She sipped her drink, welcoming the comforting warmth and the drowsy haziness that dulled her apprehension. "Derek could've hired someone with a motorboat. A local who knows the river."

He shook his head. "We'd have heard the boat."

"Maybe everyone was away from camp when he arrived. Or he hired someone to fly him in by helicopter. You said that's what would happen if there was an emergency." He opened his mouth to speak, but she held up her hand, stopping him. "I know—the noise again. But he could have had the pilot set him down a few kilometers from Keyoh and walked the rest of the way." She sat forward. "Didn't Roman mention there were old Indigenous trading trails in the area? Derek could've hiked in from Verity."

"You're giving the guy too much credit. Besides,

how come no one's seen him?"

"I don't know, but I'm not imagining this, Peter. Derek's here." She placed her hand over her chest. "I know it. I feel it here."

He looked unconvinced. "I don't know, Stick. Everything you're saying is possible, but I don't see it."

"How do you explain the stuff in the cave? Why would a random camper leave his gear behind? And what about the ring? How did that end up in the campfire?"

"I don't know. I haven't figured that out. Not yet." He scrubbed his beard. "Roman's having a meeting with the crew right now. He'll find out if any of the students have been using that cave."

She nodded, though she doubted Roman would find the answers he wanted. A crew member wasn't using the cave. Neither had a stranded paddler sought refuge within its rock walls. Derek was at Keyoh. Somehow, he'd made it to the remote site and slipped in without anyone noticing. He was using the cave as his hideout and creeping through the forest watching her, biding his time until—

"Roman was pretty shaken up when you guys got back to camp."

Peter's voice broke through her rising panic. "He-he was?" Her hand trembled as she raised her glass for another sip of the fiery liquor. She blinked. The glass was empty. When had that happened?

"I've never seen him so upset."

His words, and the liquor, warmed her insides. The thought of Roman being concerned for her well-being pleased her.

Peter refilled her cup. "Drink up, Sis. You need this more than I do."

She clasped the plastic cup in both hands and sipped again. A fuzzy fog filled her vision, and the intense foreboding that tightened her gut into knots eased.

"Hannah?"

She blinked, fighting to focus. Why was he swaying? She opened her mouth to tell him to sit still, but speaking was too much effort, and she sagged back on the sleeping bag and yawned.

He chuckled. "I see you still can't handle your liquor." Taking her cup from her limp hand, he covered her with a blanket. "Rest well, Stick. I'll see you later, and we'll talk some more."

His voice echoed as if from a great distance, rising and falling in waves of sound, fading until there was nothing but darkness.

Chapter 25

Roman jammed his hands into the front pockets of his pants. He didn't want to do this, but Peter had insisted.

The guy had been worried about his sister after the ring was found, but the finding of the camping gear in the cave pushed his concern to the limit.

Roman didn't blame him. Hell, he was alarmed as well, but he didn't feel good standing before his crew giving them the third degree. But he was the excavation director, and the integrity of the site and his crew were his responsibility. Hannah's safety was at risk, and he'd do anything to protect her, even if it made him uncomfortable.

He studied the group of young people seated in a semicircle, facing him, on lawn chairs and stumps. Was anyone hiding something? He didn't think so. They'd all been students in his archaeology seminars for the past two terms. He'd chosen them because of their dedication to archaeology, their respect for Indigenous people's cultures, and their enthusiasm. He considered each one of them a friend. "Just so we're clear, no one knows anything about the ring Sam found in the fire last night?"

They shook their heads in denial.

"Okay. And none of you has been in that cave on the east side of the site?"

Again, they shook their heads.

He let the silence drag on. His gaze lit on Sam.

The undergrad, with his patchy red beard and tangled long auburn hair, bounced his knees up and down and toyed with a braided leather string wrapped around his wrist.

The kid was holding back. "Is there something you're not telling me, Sam?"

Sam's face beneath the beard flushed red. "It's probably nothing, but my hoodie's missing. You know, the one with my favorite band's logo on the front? I bought it last year at Schmoo Fest." He shrugged. "I washed it in the river two days ago and hung it on the line to dry. I looked for it this morning, but it's gone." He shrugged. "Maybe it blew off the line in that storm this morning, but I can't find it anywhere."

Roman nodded. "Anyone else notice anything missing?"

Jillian, the sole female member of the group, chewed on her bottom lip. Her waist-length light-brown hair was tightly braided in a style she'd told him was called micro-braids. "I can't find my package of Swiss chocolates. I hid them in my backpack, so you guys wouldn't find them and eat them. They were gone when I looked yesterday."

"So that's why you've been scowling at me all day," Sam said.

"I figured you took them. I know how much you like chocolate."

"If I'd known you had Swiss chocolates hidden in your pack, I might've looked for them, but I'm not the one who took your candy. Ask the rest of the crew. They like chocolate too."

The students all proclaimed their innocence.

Roman held up his hands until they quieted, and once again, their attention was on him. "Okay, so far Sam's hoodie and Jillian's chocolates are missing. Anything else?"

"I'm on kitchen duty today, and I was planning on making grilled cheese sandwiches for lunch." Rafferty's sweat-stained canvas safari hat was tugged low over his forehead, shadowing his eyes. Only his scruffy dark beard was visible. "I know there was a block of cheddar in the cooler this morning, but it's not there now."

"Anyone else missing anything?" Roman asked again.

Peter, who'd been standing at the back, cleared his throat. "Have any of you seen a book—" He made a square shape with his hands. "—about this size with a red leather cover? I can't find my journal, and I've been looking for it for the past couple of days."

Again, the group shook their heads.

Zack, the tallest of the undergrads, stood. He wore his usual attire of a black cap covering his buzzed scalp, a black T-shirt emblazoned with an indie rock band's logo, a black baggy jeans, and black scuffed boots. "I-I'm also missing something. I…" His Adam's apple bobbed in his thin throat.

Roman nodded for him to continue.

"I brought a bottle of vodka to camp." He met Roman's gaze. "I know it's against your rules, but I didn't think it would hurt anything. It's just that sometimes I need something to help me sleep." His nostrils flared as he breathed in and out. "It's missing, too."

Roman's first reaction was to fire Zack on the spot. The kid knew the rules when he'd agreed to join the excavation, and he knew the consequences of breaking those rules. Roman had been clear on that. But now wasn't the time. Items were missing from camp, too many items. His tingle of unease ramped up to a full-out storm assault.

"Are we done here, Roman?" Sam asked. "We've told you everything we know."

"Yeah." Rafferty pushed his hat back. "Can we get back to the site? I was scraping a layer of ash and calcined bone that looked promising."

Zack nodded. "We should get back to work. You know we need to, Roman. We only have three more weeks."

They were right. Time was a factor. In three weeks, they were expected to have completed their work and restored the site to its original state, leaving no trace of their excavations or their camp. A week after that, he was required to present a report on his findings to the director and the board members at the university.

He studied the grassy meadow shining under the warm late-morning sunshine. So much area to cover and so little time. The sandy soil beneath the tall swaying grasses and junipers held more artifacts that would change the scientific community's perception of precontact Dakelh society. The ancient Chinese coin was a stunning discovery. Other artifacts just as impressive as the coin would remain hidden forever unless he and his crew excavated them.

But what about the diamond ring in the fire and the camping supplies in the cave? He ground down on his back molars. The stuff in the cave could be explained by a passing camper seeking shelter. The sleeping bag and backpack could've been left there months ago or even last summer. He cringed at the holes in his theory. A camper would've taken his equipment when he departed.

A plausible explanation could be made for the ring. Hannah's ex-boyfriend slipped the ring into her pocket without her knowledge, and it remained there until it fell out when she was tending the fire.

And the missing items? The crew members were young. They had other things on their minds. They could be mistaken about the clothes and food.

All possible scenarios.

Maybe.

But maybe not.

What if Hannah's stalker had somehow followed her, and he was there at Keyoh, hiding out, stealing supplies, and spying on them? Roman shoved his unease aside. He had a job to do, one he'd dreamed of undertaking his whole life. He nodded at the crew. "Okay. Get back to work, but if you see or hear anything, and I mean *anything* unusual, I want to hear about it. Are we clear?"

Relief flooded their youthful faces, and they all nodded. In seconds, they were laughing and joking with their usual camaraderie as they hurried across the meadow to their stations.

He threaded his fingers through his hair. Apprehension settled in his gut like a heavy stone. He'd keep a close eye on the camp, and an even closer watch on Hannah. Despite her poor career choice, the thought of her filled him with happiness. The more time he spent with her, the more time he wanted to spend. Her blue eyes sparkled like diamonds when she laughed, and her creamy skin flushed pink, her—

He gave himself a mental boot in the ass. *Stop*

daydreaming about the pretty girl and get back to work. But first, he'd stop by her tent and check on her. His concern wasn't personal. He was just doing his job. As the chief archaeologist in charge of the project, he was responsible for all personnel, visitors included.

Yeah, right. His inner voice chuckled snidely. *And that's the only reason you want to see her. You're just doing your job. What a guy.*

He tapped on the side of her tent. "Hannah? It's me, Roman." He waited, but she didn't answer. "Hannah?" Still no answer. Maybe she was sleeping. He should leave her alone, but what if she wasn't in her tent? What if she'd gone for a walk? On her own? He had to make sure she was safe. It would only take a second to check, and then he could relax.

Unzipping her tent door, he crouched and peered inside.

She lay on her side wrapped in her sleeping bag. Her eyes were closed, and her breathing was deep and steady in sleep.

Peter had said she was having a nap. Nap? His nose wrinkled at the strong alcohol smell permeating the tent. More like she'd passed out. Trust Peter to have snuck a bottle of his favorite over-proof rum into camp. But could he blame his buddy? Hannah had been in shock after they found the camping gear in the cave. If the rum helped soothe her panic and provided her a respite from her fear, he'd keep his mouth shut.

She moaned and turned onto her back. Her blonde hair, freed from its usual braid, spread beneath her head like a golden cloud, her mouth opened, and her breathing deepened.

He shook himself out of his daze. What was he

C. B. Clark

doing? Watching her while she slept was wrong, if not a bit creepy. He backed out of the tent, zipped the door closed, and stood.

Okay. He'd ensured she was safe. There were no more excuses to linger. Back to the excavation.

Chapter 26

Hannah adjusted her bottom on the hard boulder, trying to find a comfortable position. She tossed a pebble into the swirling water, enjoying the soothing gurgle and splash of the river washing against the rocks, and the melodic chirping of birds. The sky was azure blue, and a few puffy white clouds floated on the horizon. A thin, wispy vapor trail streamed behind a jet high in the sky.

The sun was a warm caress on her shoulders, the gentle breeze teasing wisps of hair that had come loose from her braid. She closed her eyes and inhaled the rich earthy scents of fresh water, wildflowers, and ripening wild grass.

A mosquito whined by her ear, disturbing her peace. She slapped at the pesky insect, wishing she could swat her worries away as easily. Surprisingly, she'd slept the previous afternoon and all through the night, helped by the half-bottle of rum Peter had poured into her glass.

She woke that morning with a headache and a queasy stomach, probably from the rum. The liquor had numbed her brain, but with the light of morning, her worries returned full force. Searching for a quiet spot—away from the others—to think, she'd descended the dirt steps carved into the hillside to the riverbank.

The red canoe she and Peter had paddled from Renton Falls rested on the gravel bottom-side up so the hull didn't fill with rainwater. The lifejackets and paddles were tucked under the gunnels out of the rain.

Hard to believe they'd arrived at Keyoh only five days ago. So much had happened…good and bad. On the positive side of the ledger were the crew's find of the Chinese coin, the progress on her research for her article, reconnecting with Peter, and her growing feelings for Roman.

But ever since Sam found the ring in the fire, she'd been on edge. On edge? She scowled. More like a steady state of panic. Peter's explanation that Derek had slipped the ring into her pocket, and she'd unknowingly brought it to Keyoh, and the ring somehow fell out of her pocket and into the fire was possible—if you believed in miracles.

The equipment she and Roman found in the cave was solid evidence someone had camped there. When had the camping gear been left? Last summer? Last week? Was it still being used?

She slapped her arm, swatting at another mosquito. Even with all the items missing from camp, no one else was convinced there was anything to worry about, but her inner alarm bells were blaring. Was Derek at Keyoh? Was that even possible? Or was she overreacting and panicking for no reason? But what if she wasn't? What if, at this very moment, he was close by? She shuddered and studied her surroundings, but she couldn't detect anything disturbing.

She scratched a bug bite on her arm and pushed her worries aside. Her thoughts led back to Roman. As they so often did. She was falling for him. Hard. The more he revealed about himself and his passion for archaeology and his Indigenous heritage, the deeper her feelings. His intense dislike of journalists, and of *Aspire* magazine, complicated the situation. She needed to tell him the truth. Sooner rather than later.

"I see you're enjoying the sunshine on this beautiful day."

She let out a squeak. "Nathaniel. I-I didn't hear you arrive."

"I apologize. This is the second time I've startled you." He smiled, displaying a mouth filled with perfect gleaming-white teeth. "I'm used to hunting in the woods, and I've learned to tread silently so as not to disturb game." Crossing to a log that had washed up on shore, he sat and set the fishing rod he carried on the ground. He rested his heavily veined hands on his lap. "I understand you and my grandson came to my camp to visit on the day of the storm. I'm sorry I missed you. I was out checking my traps."

She shivered as she recalled that day. Nathaniel's empty camp, the sudden storm, the cave where she and Roman had sought shelter, the camping items in the back of the cave…

"I see your fear. The strain's visible in your eyes."

His voice cut through her disturbing memories, and she met his gaze.

No film of cataracts dimmed the penetrating brightness of his dark eyes.

She shook her head. "I'm sorry. I don't understand." Oh, but she did. He was perceptive. She was afraid, very afraid. "I guess you heard about the ring Sam found in the campfire?"

"Roman told me that one of the students found a diamond ring in the camp's fire pit."

"Did he also tell you about the equipment he and I found in the cave?"

"He mentioned it."

"And the clothing and food that's missing?"

He nodded, his gaze solemn.

"What…what do you think? Is someone here? Someone we don't know?"

He rubbed the palms of his hands on his faded jeans. "I haven't seen anyone, but you're wise to be cautious."

Her heart skittered. "You don't think I'm overreacting?"

"Trust your instincts. If you feel uneasy, there's a reason."

She liked and respected the old man, and it felt good he didn't try and explain away her fears.

"How's your article coming along?"

"Thank you for answering my questions earlier. Your insight and knowledge are invaluable additions to the story." The research for her article was almost complete. The interviews with the crew and Nathaniel had gone well, and she'd even managed to squeeze a few words out of Roman.

She had lots of great photos of artifacts, pit-house depressions, and the excavation sites. The star attraction was the ancient Chinese coin, and she'd shot several closeups of the artifact. The unusual find would be the focus of her story. Readers would love learning of the discovery of the coin and the mystery surrounding it.

"You work for *Aspire,* don't you?"

She lurched and teetered, almost falling off the boulder. "How…how do you know that?"

"I may be getting on in years, but I keep up. I've even been known to watch television a time or two." His chuckle floated on the warm air. "I read your article on logging old growth forests in British Columbia. You did an excellent job presenting both sides of the issue with fairness and impartiality. You're a talented journalist."

She flushed. "I'm sorry. I should have—"

"Don't worry. I won't say anything." He flashed his dentures again. "You'll tell Roman when the time's right."

She studied the sunlight sparkling on the water. "What happened? Why does he distrust journalists so much? And can you tell me why he hates *Aspire*?"

"That's not my story to tell. You need to ask Roman." He studied the sky and pointed a gnarled finger at a bald eagle soaring high on the afternoon's warm air currents.

The large brown bird with its distinctive white head and tail circled lower and lower until it was a few meters over their heads, and the swish of its powerful wings filled the air. The raptor opened its hooked yellow beak and emitted a high-pitched piercing whistle.

She stared at the riveting sight.

The eagle swooped past, centimeters above the flowing water, its feet extended, talons out. Unlike the other day when the eagle snatched the trout from the pond, this time the bird missed its prey. It emitted another haunting screech as if disappointed and sailed above the treetops. Soon it was a mere dark speck in the vivid blue sky.

"You're fortunate. *Tsebalyan* seeks you out."

"*Tsebalyan*?" Despite the day's warmth, a chill swept her.

"*Tsebalyan* is the Dakelh name for a bald eagle. *Tsebalyan* is an important symbol in my culture. The bird represents strength." He studied her for a long moment. "You're going through a difficult time, but you're strong like the eagle." He tapped his hand over his heart. "In here where it counts. *Tsebalyan* recognizes that."

Glancing at the now-empty sky, she shuddered. She didn't feel strong, not with the frightening possibility Derek was at Keyoh. She shook off that unsettling thought and focused on her story. Nathaniel was relaxed and open. Now was the time to ask him the question that had been burning in her mind since she arrived, the one she'd been reluctant to ask when she'd interviewed him earlier. "Why don't you want Roman to excavate Keyoh?" When she first discovered the rift between the two men, she'd planned to use it as the focal point for her story. The situation was more complicated now that she'd grown to care about Roman, but she still wanted to know.

The furrows lining Nathaniel's brow and the grooves beside his mouth deepened. For the first time since she met him, he looked his age. "Roman means well, but we don't need to dig up the bones of our ancestors to learn about ourselves."

"The artifacts he and his crew uncover will help the Dakelh people who are alive today. He believes that the more he discovers of his early cultural traditions, the better. He wants his people, especially the youth, to be proud of their heritage. Don't you see that?" She sat back, hoping to see the light of understanding in his dark eyes, hoping her words healed the rift between grandfather and grandson.

"*Tsebalyan* was right to choose you. You have a good heart." Picking up his fishing rod, he stood and smiled. "I've enjoyed our conversation very much, but now I have fish to catch. I'll see you at supper." He strode along the riverbank, his back ramrod straight, moving like a man half his age.

She watched his ascent up the cliff. He loved his grandson, but a chasm separated them. If only they could see that they wanted the same thing—for their people to take pride in their heritage. They were just going about it in different ways.

It was time she told Roman the truth. She pursed her lips. That revelation would explode like a keg of dynamite, but if Nathaniel knew she worked for *Aspire,* others might figure it out as well. Far better if Roman heard the truth from her than someone else.

She glanced at the sky, searching for the eagle.

The bird sat atop a tall fir tree overlooking the river, ruffling its wings, scouting for fish.

Nathaniel had said she was strong. She hoped he was right. She'd have to dig deep for every bit of courage she possessed if she were going to confess. Standing, she brushed off the seat of her shorts and followed the path up the steep bank to the bluff.

She was puffing when she reached the last step.

An eagle's sharp screech echoed across the river valley.

She jumped and stumbled over an exposed root, falling and landing with a thump on her knees. Cursing, she wiped off the dirt and tiny pebbles embedded in her skin. She pushed to her feet but stopped and studied the ground.

The sun's rays glistened on a shiny rock partially buried in the sandy soil.

She knelt and brushed the dirt and grass aside, revealing the tip of what looked like an agate. A thrill rippled through her. Ever since she was a little girl, she'd collected agates. The shores of Lake Wakasu, near her childhood home, were littered with the pretty glass-like stones.

An irresistible urge to hold the stone and caress its sleek surface overwhelmed her, and she dug her fingers into the soft dirt and freed the agate. It was about six centimeters in length, shaped like a perfect teardrop, and possessed a translucent amber color. An indentation circled the narrow end of the agate, as if someone had etched the line into the rock's hard exterior.

"Everything okay, Hannah?"

She jerked at the sound of Roman's voice, and the agate fell from her fingers, bounced on the dirt, and skittered down the steep slope. "Oh no!" She lunged after it, sliding on the loose scree, dislodging rocks and clumps of earth that bounced down the hill, landing with a splash in the river. A cloud of dust filled the air.

A hand grabbed her arm, stopping her rapid descent. "What the hell, Hannah? What are you doing?"

She wiped her damp forehead and met Roman's questioning gaze. "I dropped something." Spotting the agate lodged against an old juniper root, she tugged her arm free of his grip. She slid another few feet and scooped up the agate.

"What's that? A rock?" The tiny lines at the edges of his eyes crinkled, and he smiled. "You slid down this cliff for a *rock*?" He chuckled. "Must be some rock. May I see it?"

She opened her fingers and held out her hand.

The tear-drop-shaped agate glowed in the sun.

"It's an unusual shape and a pretty color." He moved closer. "Wait. Is that etching around the narrow end?"

"I found it up there." She pointed to the hilltop. "I know I shouldn't have dug the stone out, but I love agates, and—"

"Hey. It's okay." His warm gaze settled on her, and his lips curled in a smile. "You're not in trouble."

She could feel the heat of his body, and she swayed, bending closer, aching for his touch.

"You're different from what I expected." His voice was a quiet rumble.

She swallowed. "I-I am?"

He nodded. "You're not like other reporters I've encountered."

"I-I'm not?"

"No." Still holding eye contact, he brushed a lock of her hair behind her ear. His fingers lingered, caressing her cheek with a feathery touch.

She shivered.

His gaze shifted to her mouth, and he lowered his head.

Her heart pounded with the certainty he was going to kiss her, and her eyes drifted closed.

A dog's bark rent the air, and her eyes flew open. She jerked back.

Shas bounded down the hill, his tail wagging.

Roman cleared his throat. "Show me where you found the agate."

Chapter 27

Roman studied the disturbed ground where Hannah had removed the agate, but his thoughts weren't on the intriguing rock she'd discovered. His fingers tingled from where they'd brushed the satiny skin on her cheek, and the silky sweep of her blonde hair. He'd wanted to taste her lips again to see if they were as sweet as he remembered, and he almost had until Shas showed up, and the moment ended.

As if he knew Roman was thinking of him, Shas whined and pawed Roman's leg.

Roman rubbed him behind his ears, and Shas's tail whipped up a small cloud of dust as it swept the ground.

"Do you think it's an artifact?"

He turned and faced her, the first time he'd looked directly at her since the almost kiss. "It could be." Holding up the agate, he pointed at the etched line. "I've seen similar markings on stones before. This line may have been cut into the surface so a rawhide string could be wrapped around it." He set the agate on the ground. "It was probably worn around the neck as ornamentation."

"Really?" Her eyes sparkled. "So, hundreds of years ago, an inhabitant of Keyoh wore this agate? How cool is that?"

He couldn't help but smile at her enthusiasm. "Pretty cool."

A frown furrowed her forehead. "I shouldn't have dug it out, should I? I'm sorry."

The archaeologist in him wanted to tell her the truth, that she'd destroyed the integrity of the artifact, but the man in him couldn't squash her excitement, couldn't bear to see the light dim in her pretty blue eyes. "No. It's okay. You haven't ruined anything." The lie slid off his lips, but his chest swelled at the smile that lit her face.

"Really?"

He nodded, mesmerized by her deep summer-blue eyes. But then he remembered where he was, and who he was, and the very real possibility that anyone could see them. He tore his gaze away. "I'll get my tools and check this out."

"Can I watch?"

He risked a glance. The smart answer should be no. He couldn't afford the distraction. "Sure."

She beamed. "Great. Thanks."

He grinned like a hero receiving a medal. Or a fool destroying his career. He strode across the clearing to the supply tent, jerked an excavation kit, a bucket, and a digital camera from the shelf, and returned to the top of the bluff.

She was still there, sitting on the ground, studying the agate.

Shas sat beside her, his pink tongue lolling, an adoring expression on his hairy face.

Roman shook his head. He wasn't the only one falling under the beautiful journalist's spell. Kneeling beside her, he set the bucket and camera on the ground, and dug out a trowel, two brushes, and a dental pick.

She tugged out her cell phone. "Do you mind if I take pictures for the article?"

He shrugged. "Go ahead." Gripping the pointed trowel in his hand, he scraped a millimeter of soil from the ground where the agate had been. Working carefully, he removed the dirt, layer by layer. With each layer, he scooped up the dirt and sifted it through a portable shaker screen.

All too aware that mere centimeters separated their two bodies, he struggled to keep his focus on the work. If he leaned a little to the left, his arm would brush hers. Her feminine scent wafted over him. The sun beat down on the back of his head, and beads of sweat popped out on his brow. He didn't dare look, but he felt her gaze on him like a warm caress.

The only sounds were birds tweeting, the splash of the river, and Shas's panting.

He hit a layer of darker soil mixed with tiny pieces of charcoal. Sitting back, he used the tail of his shirt and wiped the sweat off his brow. He picked up the camera and snapped a picture of the stained soil.

Hannah leaned closer, and her arm grazed his shoulder. "What is it? Did you find something?"

A jolt of awareness shook him, and his stomach did a triple gainer. "This area has an interesting soil profile." Fighting to rein in his overwhelming desire to kiss her, he pointed at the excavation. "See this layer of ash and charcoal?"

She nodded.

He gestured to a large circular depression a meter away. "That's the site of a pit house. We recorded it when we conducted our initial site survey. My guess is that the lodge was burned, probably when the Tsilhqot'in attacked, and this charcoal detritus is from that fire."

"You mean this agate—" She picked up the glossy

rock, and tears pooled in her eyes. "—was worn by someone who died in the massacre?"

"It's certainly possible." A lump thickened his throat. A vivid image of a Dakelh woman wearing the teardrop agate on a leather thong around her neck rose before him, and as he often had before, he imagined the morning of the attack.

Smoke billowing in a choking cloud, gray ash floating in the air like snowflakes, terror-filled screams echoing off the thick stands of coniferous trees.

A woman stumbling through the knee-high late-summer wild grasses, her eyes wide with fear, tears running down her cheeks, blood dripping from a gash in her forehead.

A man, his face painted a frightening mask of red-and-black stripes, a stone ax clutched in his raised fist, racing behind.

The woman staggering and falling to the ground. Sparks from a nearby burning pit house falling around her, igniting tiny flames in the dry summer grass.

Before she scrambles to her feet, the pursuing man grasps her long, dark hair in one hand and drags her to her knees. He rips off her rawhide thong with the tear-shaped amber agate and tosses it aside. Raising his weapon, he smashes it with a sickening thud on her forehead.

She collapses in a lifeless heap.

"Roman?"

He blinked back tears, fighting to break free of the nightmare tragedy of the past. The woman he'd envisioned was his ancestor. She'd died a brutal, violent death.

"You really care about what happened here, don't

you?"

"Of course I do." He refused to meet her gaze, not wanting her to see his visceral reaction. "Keyoh's an important archaeological site. The 1745 massacre of the village inhabitants by the Tsilhqot'in changed the course of Saik'uz history. The events here should be studied and recorded."

His voice was robotic as if he were lecturing his students, but he couldn't stop. He had to distance himself from the emotional gut punch of the past tragedy. He jammed his hands into his pants pockets. "Excavating this site and studying the artifacts and human and animal bones uncovered provides us with the opportunity to learn more of what life was like in precontact Dakelh society."

He slid a glance at her, expecting to see boredom written across her pretty face.

"No wonder you fought so hard to gain permission to excavate this site. The people who lived here were your ancestors, and you don't want them or the tragedy that happened to be forgotten." Her eyes were wide, her pupils dilated with interest. "That's what drives you, isn't it?"

His heart froze for a nanosecond, and then pounded, the blood pulsing through his veins. She got him! She totally got him. He opened his mouth to tell her how much her understanding meant, but she spoke again, and all thought of camaraderie vanished.

"What happened to make you dislike journalists? What was in the *Aspire* article that upset you? Will you tell me?"

Her blue eyes were filled with compassion, and for the first time in years, he was tempted to tell someone about the magazine article that almost ruined his career. But something held him back. He couldn't forget she was a journalist, and her job was to empathize with the people she interviewed—so they'd open up, bare their souls, and reveal their deepest secrets.

He tightened his grip on the trowel, turned back to the excavation, and scraped another layer of dirt, focusing on the task at hand.

Her unanswered question hung in the air, and tension built until he thought he'd break. She didn't take the hint and leave like he so desperately wanted. When he couldn't stand her silent presence a second longer, he tossed the trowel on the ground and jumped to his feet. Hands braced on his hips, he faced her. "Look. We're not friends, okay? I don't want to talk about my personal life." He winced at the harshness of his voice. "Why don't you see if your brother's learned anything new about that ring Sam found in the fire? The last thing I need here is trouble from your ex-boyfriend."

Her gasp was loud, but he fixed his gaze on the tree line. A bitter taste filled his mouth. *We're not friends.* Way to go. Really? What were they, then?

The sound of sobs and the thud of her footsteps as she ran through the knee-high summer grass struck him like a hail of bullets.

Oh yeah. He was a jerk all right.

Chapter 28

Roman sighed and headed to his tent. One of the downsides of overseeing the project was the reams of paperwork and forms that needed to be filled out...often in triplicate. He'd finish the mind-numbing administrative part of his job and get back into the field. There was a new test-pit site that looked promising, and he wanted to be the one to excavate it.

He'd been pushing himself hard—up at first light and working until dark—struggling to fill his mind with the project, so he'd avoid thinking of Hannah and the hurt dulling her blue eyes after his cruel words.

He unzipped the tent door, stepped through the canvas flaps, and froze.

What the hell?

Papers were strewn across the canvas floor. The lantern lay on its side, the glass shattered. His cot was tipped over, and his sleeping bag had been slashed. Feathers floated in a gust of air. The backpack in which he stored his clothes was slit open, pants, shirts, and underwear strewn in a heap. A plastic storage tub was upside down, its contents of trowels, brushes, and an assortment of tiny dental picks, scattered.

His first reaction was shock.

His second, fury. Who the hell had done this? Not one of his crew. And not Peter or Hannah. So...who did that leave? Nathaniel? He discounted the thought as soon as it entered his mind. No matter how much his grandfather opposed the excavation of Keyoh, the honorable old man wouldn't resort to vandalism.

Anger burned deep in his gut, and the overwhelming urge to hit someone, to smash his fist into the face of the jerk who trashed his tent and belongings blasted through him. He squeezed his hands until his nails dug into the skin of his palms.

The coin!

Heart lurching, he crossed the tent in two strides. The metal strongbox was in the corner under a pile of clothes that had been tossed. Fishing in his pants pocket, he dug out a tiny key and picked up the small rectangular case. One side of the box was dented, and deep gouges scored the metal key slot where someone had pried open the lid. His hands shook as he lifted the top.

The box was empty.

He squeezed his eyes closed and gritted his teeth until they ached. Opening his eyes, he looked again.

The nightmare was real. The coin was gone.

Cursing, he threw the lockbox against the wall. It bounced against the canvas and fell to the floor. He jammed his hands into his front pockets to stop from smashing something. He'd been so damn careful and followed protocol to the nth degree. After the ancient coin was discovered, he'd photographed it in situ in the layer of soil where it was found. He'd excavated the coin from the dirt and immersed it in distilled water to remove remnants of soil and ash. Then he'd wrapped the coin in specialized packaging and placed it in a small wooden container and set the container in the sturdy metal strongbox. He'd stored the box in his tent to ensure its safety. Each step followed the most stringent archaeological practices.

He kicked the empty box and winced at the jolt of pain in his toe from the impact. Someone had intruded into his tent, vandalized his possessions, and stolen the coin. Sinking onto his knees, he buried his face in his hands. This was his worst nightmare. A similar scenario five years ago had destroyed his career.

The past rolled over him like a bulldozer. Chimney Inlet was his first assignment as a director of a field excavation, and he was responsible for a crew of two dozen archaeologists and technicians. It was a major excavation, and his team was tasked with mapping, recording, and excavating the ancient marine site.

They uncovered the remains of an old hearth, charcoal flakes, a bone fishhook, and a cache of stone tools. Carbon dating showed the site dated from the last ice age, twelve thousand years ago.

The age of the find and the complexity of the tools uncovered created a stir in the archaeology community, and media outlets picked up the story.

Roman was the belle of the archaeological ball, and a reporter from *Aspire* magazine contacted him and requested an in-depth interview. Flattered by the attention, Roman had agreed.

But then the shit hit the fan. The bone fishhook arrived at the museum in a dozen tiny pieces. Somehow, the artifact had been shattered in transit.

A curator from the provincial museum accused Roman of mishandling the important artifact.

Roman had personally overseen the cleaning and packaging of the fishhook. The artifact had been in one piece when it left Chimney Inlet, but the rumors spread like wildfire.

The reporter from *Aspire* pounced on the story, and the next thing Roman knew, he was on the front cover of the gossip rag, his reputation in tatters, his career at a dead end. It took him five years to convince the university to give him another chance to lead a project.

That's why he was strict about following protocol at Keyoh. He couldn't risk another fiasco. He was careful with the coin. He'd followed the best practices of artifact preservation to the letter and beyond. The other more common artifacts they'd uncovered—stone points, glass trade beads, bone fragments—were labeled, wrapped in special tissue paper, placed in wooden crates, and stored in the supply tent. He kept the strongbox in his tent because he didn't want it out of his sight.

A thought intruded into his dismay…the ring!

The diamond ring Sam found in the fire was gone.

He'd stored it in the lockbox along with the teardrop agate Hannah had found. Now they were both gone. What the hell was going on?

"Roman? Are you in there?"

He didn't look up, didn't move, but he heard the swish of the flap as Nathaniel entered the tent.

"Oh, my! What happened?"

"Someone trashed my tent and stole the Chinese coin." Roman swallowed, barely managing to speak the shocking words aloud.

"What?"

Roman met his grandfather's stunned gaze. "Whoever vandalized my stuff stole the coin. They also took the diamond ring Sam found in the fire pit and the amber agate Hannah discovered." His voice was wooden.

Nathaniel righted the camp cot and sank down,

187

setting a plastic bag beside him. "Do you have any idea who did this?"

Roman shook his head. "It must've happened when the crew was working on the test pits on the east side of the site. Hannah was down at the river, and Peter was helping me map a new section of the site. No one was in camp all afternoon."

The lines on Nathaniel's face deepened. "There's someone here."

Roman glanced at the tent opening expecting to hear voices, but the camp was quiet, the crew busy at their excavating. "I don't hear anyone."

"I've seen him, Roman. He's here."

"*Who's* here?" Roman scrubbed the stubble on his cheek. "Come on, Grandfather. I don't have time for this. Not now. *Who* are you talking about?"

Nathaniel rubbed his hands together. "There's someone at Keyoh who's not part of your crew."

"What?" Roman jolted to his feet, his mind whirling, his worst fear confirmed. "Are you sure? Have you seen him?"

"When I returned from fishing after lunch, I saw a man. He was by the crew boats near the mouth of the creek."

Roman bit back a shudder. "Go on."

Nathaniel leaned forward. "I followed the man and watched as he entered the cave on the east side of the site. You know, the one where you and Hannah found the camping gear."

Roman nodded and gestured for Nathaniel to continue.

"At first, I thought he was a tourist looking for shelter for the night, but then I spotted his rifle."

Roman sucked in a sharp breath. "Tell me about this man."

"He looked furtive, and I knew he was up to no good." Nathaniel rubbed the tops of his thighs as if he were pressing out the wrinkles in his baggy jeans. "I watched the cave until he left, and then I entered and searched his gear." He lifted the plastic bag and set it on his lap. "I found these items stuffed in the bottom of the sleeping bag." Rummaging inside the small plastic bag, he pulled out two scraps of fabric and a small, leather-covered red book.

"What's all that?"

He handed the bits of fabric to Roman.

Roman's mouth dropped open. "You found panties inside the sleeping bag in the cave?" There were two pair, one white and one black—lacy, skimpy, silky. Women's underwear. "I don't understand."

"I also found this." Nathaniel's face was set in grim lines. He held out the red book.

"What's this?" Roman studied the book. He opened the cover. Familiar writing filled the page. "It's Peter's journal! He's been looking everywhere for it." He rubbed at the sudden ache in his head. "I don't get it. Why would this stranger have Peter's journal?"

"There's more." Nathaniel held out a small square card.

Roman stared at the card, but he didn't reach for it. His mind was buzzing with a thousand scenarios. He didn't know if he could handle any more shocking revelations.

Nathaniel placed the card in Roman's hand. "Look at it."

He didn't want to look, but he did. "What the hell?

What's Hannah's library card doing in that cave?"

"Look at the back."

He turned the card over. *CM & DP. True love never dies* was scrawled in red letters. The floor dropped out from under him, and the card slipped from his fingers and fluttered to the ground.

Her stalker! Derek. D.P. The sick bastard had stolen her personal possessions and brought them with him—as what? Souvenirs? The thought of the stalker fondling her underwear made him gag, and it was all he could do not to vomit.

Roman eyed his ravaged tent. The stalker had upped his game. He was no longer being subtle. He wanted them to know he was there, wanted them to know he could get at them any time he wanted, wanted them scared. A headache started behind his eyes, stabbing into his brain.

"I've searched Keyoh, but I can't find the man with the rifle. He's good. He covers his tracks and moves quietly through the forest. I waited at the cave, but he never returned. He must have found another hideout." Nathaniel gestured at the torn sleeping bag, ripped backpack, and upended tub with its contents scattered across the dirt floor. "Did he do this?"

"Who else?" Roman threaded his fingers through his hair. He grabbed a pump-action short-barreled shotgun from the floor and headed for the tent opening.

"Where are you going with that?"

He slowed but didn't stop. "I'm getting the crew together, and we're going to find that jerk."

"Roman, wait. Please."

He wanted to shut out his grandfather's pleas, wanted to charge out of the tent and start searching. But he'd been taught to respect elders. He stopped and faced Nathaniel. "What is it?"

"I understand your anger, but you should think this through. This man followed Hannah to Keyoh. That wouldn't have been easy. Not for anyone. He's determined, and if you track him down, he'll be as dangerous as a cornered bear." Nathaniel rose to his full height and pinned Roman with a penetrating gaze. "Don't tell Hannah what I found. She's strong, but—" He nodded at the underwear and card on the floor. "—that will destroy her."

"I won't tell anyone." Especially not Peter. His friend would go ballistic if he knew Derek was packing around his sister's underwear like some sick trophy. And he definitely wouldn't like that the creep was reading the private thoughts in his journal.

"You must keep her safe. This man will stop at nothing to get what he wants. And he wants her."

"I'll protect her." He hefted the shotgun in his arm. "That's what this is for." He turned back to the opening.

"Where are you going?" Nathaniel asked again.

"To find Hannah. That pervert's not getting anywhere near her. Not as long as I'm here."

His grandfather nodded approvingly. "You must protect your woman. It's what a man does."

Roman sucked in a breath.

Your woman.

His woman.

"I'll look after her. No worries about that." He gripped the shotgun tighter, turned, and stormed out of the tent.

Chapter 29

Hannah's gut lurched at the sight of the cold congealed eggs. She nibbled a bite of toast, hoping it would settle her stomach, but the bread stuck in her throat. Grabbing her cup, she drained the cold coffee, washing down the lump of food.

Some of the crew members sat drinking coffee at the picnic table. Others lounged in chairs around the smoldering fire. No one spoke, and the only sounds that broke the strained silence were the crackling of the flames and the chink of cutlery.

They were exhausted. They'd been up most of the night searching, using flashlights to spear the darkness as they looked for the intruder.

She shuddered. Intruder? Not just any intruder. Nathaniel had seen him. His description of the man he'd followed matched that of Derek. Somehow, her stalker had tracked her to Keyoh and landed at the site without anyone hearing or seeing him.

Since his arrival, he'd been sneaking around the camp causing havoc. He'd taken food and clothing. To make sure she got the message he was close, he dropped the diamond ring into the campfire. When that didn't stop the project, he ransacked Roman's tent and stole the Chinese coin. Now, he was somewhere in the woods, hiding, watching, waiting…

Waiting for what? What did he plan next?

She shuddered and gave up the pretense of eating. Rising from the table, she tossed the contents of her plate into the garbage bin and set her dirty dish in the wash basin. She wheeled around and bumped into a solid wall of hard muscle. Losing her balance, she yelped and stumbled back a step.

Roman caught her by the arms, holding her steady. "Easy there, Hannah. Are you okay?"

His touch seared her skin. Their gazes met, and for a heartbeat, she stopped breathing. But then reality intruded, and her reaction switched from desire to irritation.

He meant well, but his overprotectiveness was driving her nuts. Ever since he'd charged into the meadow where she was snapping photos of the new excavation test pits, his dark eyes flashing fire, his face set in rigid lines, a shotgun cradled in his arms, he hadn't let her out of his sight.

He'd gathered the crew and Peter and told them about the intruder and the theft of the coin.

Everyone was shocked and rushed to their tents to see if Derek had stolen or destroyed their possessions.

She and Peter had done the same, but nothing else was damaged. For some reason, Derek had inflicted his anger on Roman and Roman alone.

Roman organized the group into pairs and laid out the parameters of a search grid. But even though they scoured the crew camp, searched the cave, the area by the creek, Nathaniel's camp, and the surrounding forest, Derek eluded them.

"Hannah?" Roman stood back, his brow furrowed. "Are you sure you're okay? You're pale."

"I'm fine." The lie slipped off her tongue. She was

anything but okay, but she didn't want or need his constant vigilance. She was tired of being a victim, tired of the crew's pitying looks. Their sympathy and Roman's protectiveness were pushing her over the edge.

His fingers brushed her arm. "Look, we'll find Derek. Until then, stay in camp and you'll be safe."

"It's been a long day. I'm going to rest in my tent." Without waiting for his response, she about-faced and fled.

When he didn't follow, she heaved a deep breath, part disappointment and part relief. She craved space, room to breathe without the physical attraction percolating between them. This wasn't the time to be falling for a man. Her life was too complicated, but she couldn't help herself. Roman was tall, dark, and handsome—the epitome of every romance movie's dreamy hero. Who didn't love a brooding Heathcliff-type man with a secret past?

Despite their off-the-scale attraction for each other, any chance of a relationship was doomed. He didn't know she worked for *Aspire,* and the lie hung like a specter in the air. Until she fessed up, and Derek was no longer harassing her, she needed to keep her distance. Easier said than done. The more time she spent with Roman, the harder it was to suppress her growing feelings.

"Stick! Wait up."

For a heartbeat, she thought of ignoring Peter and continuing her escape to the refuge of her tent. The concern in his voice stopped her. "What is it now?"

He held up his hands. "Hey, don't bite my head off."

"I'm sorry." She grimaced. "It's all this stuff that's going on. It-it's too much."

"You'll be okay. Roman won't let anything happen to you. You know that, right? He's got this." He toyed with his silver chain. "He's a good dude, and he really likes you."

Her mouth dropped open. "What are you talking about?"

"Come on, Sis. A blind person could see the vibes between you two." A smile curved his lips. "Poor sap. He has it bad."

Was that true? Roman liked her?

Butterflies danced in her stomach. But then she remembered Derek and the alarming events of the past two days, and her bubble of happiness burst. A wave of exhaustion overwhelmed her, and her shoulders sagged. "I'm sorry, Peter, but I'm tired. I want to go to my tent and rest. We can talk later. Okay?"

He studied her, his blue eyes delving deep. "Sure. Get some sleep. I'll keep an eye on camp while you're resting. Try not to worry."

Tears burned her eyes. He was the best big brother. "Thanks, Peter." She turned and trudged to her tent. Unzipping the opening, she crawled inside, rezipped the closure, and collapsed onto her sleeping mat.

****

She rolled over and opened her eyes. The afternoon sunlight had dimmed, and the tiny tent was filled with shadows. How long had she slept? She checked her watch and frowned. That long? She hadn't planned on napping, hadn't thought she could silence the alarming thoughts firing through her brain enough to sleep. The time alone was supposed to be her chance to figure out her tumultuous thoughts—the frightening certainty Derek had followed her to Keyoh, and how she was going to confess she'd lied to Roman about her employer.

Instead, she'd fallen asleep.

She yawned and smoothed loose strands of her hair off her forehead. The camp was quiet, without the usual buzz of conversation, chopping of firewood, or rattling of dishes as the next meal was prepared. The crew must be out searching for Derek, or they'd returned to their excavations.

She rose from the sleeping mat, grabbed her kit bag, fished out her brush, and retied her long hair into the single braid that hung down her back. Smoothing her sleep-wrinkled shirt and pants, she unzipped the flap and crawled out of the tent.

A square white piece of paper lay on the ground, a rock weighing down one corner.

She stared at the folded paper, and then she scanned the area. Late-afternoon shadows stretched across the grassy meadow, but no one was around. Her scalp prickled, and her stomach quivered. She removed the rock and picked up the paper and unfolded it.

The note was from Roman. He wanted her to meet him at Nathaniel's camp. Apparently, he and Nathaniel had something important to tell her.

Why had he left the note without awakening her? Couldn't they talk at the crew camp? Maybe Nathaniel had told him she worked for *Aspire,* and Roman was going to order her to leave Keyoh, and he didn't want to break the news in front of the crew.

She reread the message. Whatever he wanted, his request sounded urgent. She smoothed her hand over her hair and down her long braid. He'd told her not to leave camp, and now he was asking her to do that very thing.

She studied the clearing and the encroaching forest of tall trees and dense undergrowth. If he wanted her to meet him elsewhere, he must feel she'd be safe going there. Besides, she wouldn't go alone. She'd ask Peter to go. Tucking the note into her pocket, she set off to find her brother.

He was sitting slouched by the smoking campfire. His head drooped forward, and his chin rested on his chest. His eyes were closed, and a cacophony of snores erupted from his open mouth.

So much for her protector. Should she wake him? She tugged out Roman's note and read it again. Leaving the safety of the camp was foolish, especially alone. She looked at her brother. Dark circles rimmed his eyes, and new lines furrowed his brow. He was exhausted. He'd been up the previous night searching for Derek.

Torn between her overriding curiosity and common sense, she chose the risky move. She refused to live her life in constant fear. Not anymore. Hadn't Nathaniel told her she was strong like the bald eagle?

She'd go to Nathaniel's camp and hear what the two men had to say. But she'd be careful. Rooting in the box on the picnic table, she dug out a large cannister of bear spray. The powerful pepper spray was supposed to deter a charging bear, so it should take out a man.

She'd be back before Peter woke up, but just in case, she grabbed a scrap of paper from a cardboard box filled with papers used to start the fire. Picking up a pencil from the picnic table, she wrote a note explaining where she was going and why. She set the note on the table, and gripping the bear spray, she headed across the meadow toward the trail that led to Nathaniel's campsite.

Jillian was hunched over a test pit, and Sam was

close by, shaking dirt through a sifter screen. They were focused on their work and didn't look up when Hannah passed.

In the distance, Zack was taping off a square of ground, while Rafferty stood nearby writing in a notebook.

Roman must've put the search for Derek on hold so the crew could continue their explorations of the site.

She didn't blame him. Their time at Keyoh was limited, and the team had to make the most of every minute.

She stepped into the thick stand of trees and followed the narrow winding trail. After a few hundred meters, tall leafy birch and alder trees replaced the old-growth stands of towering Douglas firs.

The afternoon sun filtered through the branches, dappling a small pond rimmed with cattails and water lilies. The steady hum of insects filled the still air. A dragonfly flitted over the murky water, its iridescent-blue wings flashing. A narrow creek flowed out of the pond, the crystalline waters rippling over pebbles and around fallen trees and humps of lush emerald-green moss.

Nathaniel's camp was only two hundred meters ahead, but she couldn't resist the meadow's peaceful beauty. A few minutes to refresh and prepare for whatever Roman was so determined to tell her wouldn't hurt. Kneeling on the soft moss before the clear pool, she set the bear spray on the ground, cupped her hands, and filled them with cool water, and splashed her face.

Heaven.

She dried her skin with the sleeve of her shirt and glanced at the clear pool. The surface was smooth like a mirror and reflected her visage and the puffy white clouds floating in the soft blue sky behind.

A man's face appeared in the reflection. Thick wavy auburn hair framed his beard-stubbled cheeks.

She screamed and fell back on her heels, her heart thundering in her chest.

"Hello, Hannah. It's been a while."

Fumbling for the bear spray, she gripped the can and raised it, slipped back the plastic guard, and pointed the nozzle.

His smile transformed to a scowl. "You don't want to do that."

"Oh, but I do." She pressed the trigger with her thumb. An orange cloud shot out and blasted him.

He yelped and stumbled back, his hands covering his face.

Her eyes burned and tears flowed as tiny droplets of spray wafted in the slight breeze, but she kept her thumb depressed on the trigger.

He fell to his knees and scooped handfuls of pond water and splashed his face. "What the hell, Hannah?" He scrubbed at his red irritated skin. Tears streamed from his puffy eyes. "You'll pay for this, you bitch. You'll see." His voice was a hoarse screech filled with venom. He turned and stumbled into the forest. "I'm not finished with you. You can count on that."

The empty can fell from her nerveless hand, and she collapsed on the ground, drew her knees to her chest, and curled into a ball.

Chapter 30

Roman froze.

A scream. A woman's scream! Somewhere close.

"Hannah." His bellow echoed off the trees. In the next heartbeat, he took off running across the uneven ground, his arms pumping, driving his legs to dig deeper and push harder. Sprinting down the trail, he leaped over exposed roots and shoved branches out of his way.

Shas barked and raced behind.

Roman's heart pounded, and his chest heaved as he fought for breath. He hadn't heard another scream, but his gut knotted with the certainty Hannah was in trouble. Bursting through a stand of old growth firs and into a small meadow, he stumbled to a stop.

She sat on the mossy bank of a narrow creek, her face buried in her hands.

"Hannah." He hurried to her side and fell onto his knees. "What is it? What's wrong?"

She dropped her hands. "Roman. Thank God."

His heart lurched at the sight of her pale tearstained face. Her eyes were red and swollen. Fear radiated off her in visible waves. He gathered her in his arms and embraced her trembling body, smoothing his hands over her back and murmuring soothing words. "It's okay. You're safe. I'm here."

Her tears dampened his shirt.

He scanned the clearing searching for the cause of

her distress. A bear? A wolf? Derek?

The meadow basked in the warm August sunshine, and a steady drone of insects filled the air. Birds chirped and flitted amidst the reeds and cattails. The creek splashed as it trickled out of the pond.

Nothing to fear. Not now. Not anymore, but something had frightened her.

He tightened his arms. Her head rested against his chest; her soft body molded to his, her slim, curvy form fitting him like a glove.

Her sobs eased, and the trembling stopped as her body relaxed, and she sank into his embrace.

Smoothing the palm of his hand over her golden hair, he slid the thick silky braid through his fingers, unwilling to release her, wanting the moment to last forever. He breathed in her scent—wildflowers, sunshine, and— His nostrils stung, and something caustic caught in the back of his throat. He coughed. And coughed again.

He loosened his embrace and pulled back. His eyes burned and watered. He spotted the cannister lying on the ground. "What happened? Why did you need to use the bear spray? Was it a bear? Did it charge you?"

She wiped her damp face with the back of her hand and sniffled. "He was here! Derek. I saw him."

His heart stilled. "What?"

Her body trembled like a leaf in the wind. "I-I found your note, and I was heading to Nathaniel's to meet you like you asked, but then I saw this meadow, and it was so pretty, I couldn't resist stopping, and—"

"What? Wait a minute. Are you telling me Derek was here? Just now?"

Her lower lip trembled, and fresh tears glistened in

her eyes. She nodded.

Shas whined and circled her, tapping his front paw on her leg, begging for a pat.

Sinking onto the ground, she threaded her fingers through the dog's thick black hair.

Shas settled beside her, resting his head on her lap, offering comfort.

Roman wiped his streaming eyes and studied the surrounding forest. Where was the bastard? Roman had spent all the previous night and most of the morning scouring the area for Derek, but he hadn't found him. And now he showed up here and confronted Hannah? He rubbed the back of his neck, fighting to think through the red mist of rage.

It would be easy for someone to hide in the dense undergrowth. Derek could be crouched in the woods watching them at that very moment, waiting to strike. Nothing moved—no shadows shifted in the depths, no cracking of branches, no furtive footsteps.

Not wanting to frighten her more than she already was, he gentled his voice and sat down beside her. "Okay. Start at the beginning. Tell me what happened."

"I-I found your note outside my tent and—"

"Wait a minute. What note? I didn't leave you a note."

She tugged a piece of paper from her pocket and handed it to him. "I-I thought it was from you."

He studied the note. His gut clenched. Derek had been in the camp right outside her tent. If he made it that far undetected, he could have— He shut down the list of horrifying possibilities. He had to focus on what was happening now, not what could have happened. "I didn't write this." Crumpling the note in his fist, he tossed it aside.

"You didn't? I should have known it wasn't from you." She hiccupped a sob. "I should've stayed in camp like you told me, but—" Her voice broke.

He ground down on his back molars and tightened his hands into fists. Derek wrote the note to lure her into the woods and away from the others. His pulse pounded, the pain in his jaw from clenching his teeth a throbbing ache. "What—" He inhaled a steadying breath and tried again. "What did Derek do? Did he hurt you?" He'd kill the jerk if he'd touched her. He scanned her face and body, but other than the tears streaming down her face and her puffy red eyes, he couldn't see any visible marks or bruises.

Fresh tears brimmed in her blue eyes. "I saw his reflection in the pond. He-he was standing right behind me, and I screamed." She nodded at the cannister of bear spray. "I-I was terrified, and I sprayed him. He…he got mad and threatened me, but then he-he left. He must've heard you coming."

Typical of a bully. The coward had run away, but he couldn't have gone far. Again, Roman scanned the forest, and again he saw nothing disturbing. He should gather the crew and go after the sick creep. Now. Before he found another place to hide.

His gaze lit on Hannah's wan tear-streaked face. No, not now. He couldn't leave her, not when she was upset. He coughed again. Besides, they both needed a shower to wash off the remnants of the bear spray. But after that, he'd start searching. Damn right he would.

Derek couldn't hide forever. He'd find him, and when he did… The throbbing in his jaw ramped up, and he breathed in through his nose for four counts, held the breath for seven, and breathed out through his mouth for a count of eight. Like the counselor had taught him when he'd sought help for his anxiety after the damning article in *Aspire.* He repeated the coherent breathing until his heart rate slowed, his overpowering rage eased, and he felt more in control.

"Come on." He stood and grasped Hannah's hand and helped her to her feet. "Let's go back to camp and get cleaned up. You'll be safe there." He winced at the blatant lie. How could he guarantee her safety? Just yesterday, Derek had waltzed into camp, vandalized Roman's tent, and stolen artifacts. He'd snuck in a second time that afternoon and left Hannah the note, and no one had stopped him.

Wait a minute!

Roman faced her. "Where's your brother? Why didn't he come with you?"

She wouldn't meet his gaze. "Um…er…he's sleeping."

"What?" He'd left Peter on guard duty. His friend had promised he'd keep a close eye on his sister. "What do you mean he's sleeping?"

"Please don't blame him. He was up all night searching, and he's exhausted." Fresh tears filled her eyes, and she held out her hands in a pleading gesture. "This is *my* fault. I shouldn't have left camp."

He bit back his anger. She was upset enough; she didn't need him coming down hard. But he'd have a word with his friend. You could count on that.

Shas barked and raced to the bank of trees where a figure stood in the shadows.

Roman's heart rate kicked up, and he braced, ready to fight. He'd do anything to protect Hannah.

Anything.

Chapter 31

Shas barked again, but the sound was a happy, welcoming sound, not one of fear.

"Hey, you two." Nathaniel strode into the clearing, holding a string of three rainbow trout. "I—" He stopped and dropped the fish on the ground. "Something's happened." His gaze shifted from Hannah to Roman and back again. "Tell me."

"Derek was here. He confronted Hannah. She sprayed him with bear spray, and when he heard me coming, he ran off."

Nathaniel's eyes opened wide. "That's terrible. I'm so sorry, Hannah. Are you all right?"

"I am now, but I was terrified. He was so angry—" A fresh sheen of tears shone in her eyes, and a single drop slid down her cheek and dripped off her chin.

Nathaniel placed his hand on her shoulder. "Remember *Tsebalyan*. You're strong like the eagle. You fought back, and the bad man ran away."

Roman met his grandfather's gaze. "Did you see any sign of him in the forest just now?"

Nathaniel shook his head. "I was down at the creek fishing." He patted Hannah's arm. "Keyoh has many places where a man can hide without discovery, but my grandson will find him. You trust Roman to keep you safe, don't you?"

More tears streamed down her face, and she sniffled.

"Of-of course I do."

A rush of warmth flooded Roman, and he felt ten feet tall—strong and powerful, willing to slay dragons to save his woman. But he couldn't do it on his own. "When we get back to camp, I'm calling the authorities. It's time we let them know what's going on."

"I'll come with you." Nathaniel picked up the string of fish. "These will be a nice addition to the evening meal."

Refusing to let her out of his sight, Roman clasped Hannah's hand, and together they headed out of the clearing.

Oblivious to the tension thickening the air, Shas raced ahead, chasing squirrels and sniffing tree trunks.

Nathaniel brought up the rear.

Unable to shake the feeling they were being followed, Roman kept looking over his shoulder, scanning the forest shadows.

A branch snapped.

Shas stiffened and the hairs on the back of his neck rose. He raced back to Roman and pressed his big body against Roman's legs.

Moving Hannah behind him, protecting her with his body, Roman slipped his pocketknife out of his pants pocket, wishing he'd brought the shotgun.

"What is it?" Hannah's frantic whisper broke the strained silence.

"I don't know, but Shas is afraid of something."

As if to prove his point, the dog whimpered, his gaze fixed on the trees.

"You go and check, Roman," said Nathaniel. "I'll stay with Hannah."

Roman hesitated. He didn't trust anyone else to

protect her, not even his grandfather.

"Go on. I'll keep her safe." Nathaniel nudged him.

Roman clicked the knife open, and the sharp ten-centimeter blade unfolded with a soft snick. Not much of a weapon, but it would do serious damage in close quarters. Edging into the trees, he braced for an attack.

Another crack of a dry branch and the rustle of bushes.

Adrenaline coursed through his body, and his heart rate sped into the stratosphere. Controlling his breathing, trying to remember everything Nathaniel had taught him about tracking prey, he crept ahead another silent step.

A movement in the bush off to his right.

He crouched and peered through the leaves. Tightening his grip on the knife, he brushed a branch aside.

A white tail deer nibbled at the soft tips of a fir. The buck stiffened, alerting to Roman's presence. It lifted its head, adorned with a four-point rack of antlers, and the animal's dark-brown gaze settled on Roman.

Roman's breath gusted out with a loud whoosh.

The deer bounded into the trees, its white tail flashing like a flag.

He curled his lip in self-disgust. Folding the knife blade, he stuffed the knife back into his pocket and headed to where Hannah and Nathaniel waited.

Fear had drained the color from her face, and her eyes were wide, her pupils dilated to the size of quarters. "Was it him? Did you see Derek?"

He shook his head. "It was only a deer."

Her knees buckled, and she sagged.

He rushed to hold her. "It's okay. You're safe. I won't let him get close to you. Not again. I promise."

Time slipped away as he held her, their hearts beating in sync.

Nathaniel cleared his throat. "Can I talk to you for a moment, Roman?"

The expression on his grandfather's lined face unsettled Roman, and he released her, regretting the loss the second she stepped free of his arms. "What is it?"

Nathaniel moved several feet away and gestured for Roman to join him.

"I'll be right here. Okay?" Roman said.

She nodded but rubbed her arms as if she were cold.

He crossed to Nathaniel. "What is it you don't want her to hear?"

"Shas isn't afraid of deer."

The chill in Roman's bones deepened. He'd forgotten Shas's nervousness. Something had frightened the big dog, and it wasn't the deer. "Do you think it was Derek?"

Nathaniel's face hardened. "I think we need to be very careful."

Roman nodded and strode back to Hannah and clasped her hand again. "Let's get back to camp." He led her down the trail, moving fast.

As soon as they crossed the clearing and entered the crew camp, the buzz of nervous conversation died, and the group of young people swiveled as one and faced them.

"Hannah!" Peter rushed over and enfolded her in a tight embrace. "Thank God. I was so worried." He leaned back and studied her face. "What happened? Are you okay?"

"I-I—"

Roman stepped in. "She ran into Derek."

A loud gasp rose from the group of watching students.

"Derek? You saw him?" Peter hugged his sister again. He glanced over her shoulder, his anxious gaze on Roman. "What happened?"

"Derek left her a note outside her tent. The note was supposedly from me. It said she was to meet me at Nathaniel's camp. He confronted her, and she bear-sprayed him. He ran off when he heard me." Roman spat out the words and glared. "You were supposed to be watching her, but you fell asleep, and Derek waltzed into camp and left the note." His anger and fear took over, and he shouted, "What were you thinking? This jerk's dangerous. We're damn lucky that's all he did."

Peter stumbled back a step, his face ashen. "You're right." Tears shone in his blue eyes. "It's my fault." He staggered to a stump and collapsed on its surface, burying his face in his hands. "I'm sorry. I shouldn't have fallen asleep."

Guilt settled like a lump of lead in Roman's gut. His friend had messed up, but the man was exhausted, both mentally and physically. He was struggling with his marriage breakup, and now his sister was facing a malicious stalker. He'd been up searching the forest for Derek most of the previous night, refusing to quit even after everyone else had given up and gone to bed. Roman should apologize, but his anger burned too hot and heady.

"I'm sorry, Stick." Peter dropped his hands, revealing the anguish on his stricken face. "I'm so sorry."

The knot in Roman's stomach tightened tenfold.

Hannah knelt on the ground before her brother. "It's

okay. I'm fine. I was frightened, that's all."

"When I woke up, and saw you were gone, I-I was so worried. I thought Derek had taken you, and—"

"Didn't you see my note?"

Peter's brow furrowed. "I didn't see a note."

"I left you a note telling you where I was going so you wouldn't worry." She sprang to her feet and crossed to the table. "I set it right here." Her frown deepened. "Where is it?"

Roman found his voice and faced the students. "Did any of you see a note?"

They shook their heads.

"Maybe it blew away." Sam shrugged. "A gust of wind could've kicked up when we were working in the field."

An icy chill slipped like a witch's finger along Roman's spine. He peered under the picnic table.

No note.

He searched the kitchen area.

No note there either.

Moving farther afield, he traversed the grassy meadow, his gaze switching from the ground to the branches of the trees, and back again.

Still no note.

He couldn't shake the unease burning a hole in his gut. Derek must've snuck back into camp and taken Hannah's note so Peter wouldn't know where she'd gone. Then he followed her to the meadow. Hannah's stalker was escalating. Roman shouldn't have waited so long to call the police. That was a mistake. One he had to rectify.

He'd been reluctant to call for help for selfish reasons. Any issues that arose during the excavation were his responsibility. Calling in the police would guarantee the end of his career, but he couldn't delay the call any longer. Hannah's life was at stake.

Once the RCMP heard of the events at Keyoh, they'd send a helicopter with armed police officers. They'd track Derek down and haul his sorry ass out of there in handcuffs. He almost smiled at that image. Talk about a walk of shame. "I'm calling the RCMP." He wheeled around and headed to the camp's supply tent.

"Wait, Roman." Peter jumped to his feet. "You can't do that."

He stopped and faced Peter. "Why not?"

"When I couldn't find Hannah, I feared the worst and decided to call the police." He wiped the back of his hand over his face, scrubbing his beard. "The phone's destroyed. Someone smashed it to pieces."

Chapter 32

Roman's face hardened to stone, and he whipped around and charged into the supply tent.

Following on his heels, Hannah ducked through the tent flap and gasped. The satellite phone lay on the tent floor, a blunt-nosed hammer beside it—the same hammer she'd used to pound in her tent stakes on her first day. The phone case had been smashed. Black plastic pieces of phone were scattered across the floor.

Roman picked up the shattered phone, examined it, and tossed it across the tent where it landed with a thunk on a plastic tub.

She pressed a hand to her chest to slow her racing heart. "Derek did this?"

He nodded. "He doesn't want us contacting the police."

"There must be another way we can call for help." She searched the tent, hoping to see another satellite phone or a radio transmitter set, something…

"The budget for this project was tight, and I only leased one phone." He stuffed his hands into his pants pockets, cursed again, and stormed out of the tent.

As if in a daze, she trailed after him to the campfire and sank onto a chair.

He faced the group seated by the picnic table. His cheeks were flushed, the cords in his neck tight. "How the hell did this happen?"

No one spoke.

The students shuffled their feet, crossed and uncrossed their legs, coughed, but no one met Roman's fiery gaze.

He slapped his hand down on the picnic table.

She jolted at the loud smack.

"Come on. Spill." He narrowed his gaze. "Someone saw something. No way that bastard's creeping around this camp without someone seeing him."

Peter extended his hands in a placating manner. "Don't be angry at the crew, Roman. I'm the guy who let this happen. It's on me. I fell asleep. No one else is to blame."

Sam cleared his throat. "We were working on the new test pits on the far side of the site like you told us to." He shrugged his narrow shoulders. "That dude could've snuck in here and smashed the phone, and we wouldn't have heard."

"We would've told you if we saw anything unusual." Jillian tossed her long braids over her shoulder.

"Okay." Roman heaved a heavy breath as if fighting for control. "Let's stop the blame game and figure this out. What happened isn't just one person's fault. We all should've been more vigilant. Agreed?"

They nodded.

He paced across the hard-packed dirt. "The satellite phone's trashed, and we don't have a way to communicate with anyone outside of Keyoh."

Everyone nodded again.

"We know Derek's here, hiding in the forest."

More nodding.

"What if we're wrong?" Sam said.

Roman stopped pacing.

Everyone's gaze fixed on the red-haired young man.

The adrenaline that surged through Hannah's body when Derek accosted her in the meadow had left her drained, and it was all she could do to keep her eyes open, but the conversation was important, and she leaned forward in her seat and studied Sam.

"Think about it." Sam stood and looked at everyone, his gaze earnest. "This stalker dude got what he wanted. He confronted Hannah and scared her. Heck, he frightened all of us. Maybe he's accomplished what he came here to do, and now he'll leave."

"How would he leave without us knowing?" Roman asked.

Sam shrugged. "The same way he got here." He gestured at the group of students. "No one heard him arrive, did they? But we know he was here. Nathaniel and Hannah saw him, and someone's caused all the damage."

His speculation was met with silence. The expressions on the group's faces made clear they didn't buy his optimistic scenario.

She didn't believe it either. Derek came to Keyoh for a reason, and it wasn't just to vandalize the camp and say hello. He wanted something, and the thought of what he wanted—*her*—was terrifying. She bit back a mew of fear and sank into the depths of the chair.

"I don't think we can assume he's gone," Roman said. "He destroyed the satellite phone because he doesn't want us contacting the police." He rubbed the back of his neck as his gaze raked the group. "I'm going to set up a schedule for each of us to take turns keeping watch on the camp. No one is to be alone. Always be with a partner." He set his hands on his hips. "Is that clear?"

The students nodded.

"This guy's dangerous. He's shown he'll stop at nothing to get to Hannah." He pinned each crew member with a steely gaze. "We're not going to let that happen. Not again. Right?"

They murmured agreement.

"Good." Roman nodded. "Peter and I'll take the first shift. The rest of you head to bed. It's going to be another long night."

"But how are we going to contact the cops?" Zack asked.

"We're not. Not yet. We're packing up and leaving. We'll contact the police when we reach Fort Cutter."

Gasps filled the air.

"But the project's supposed to run two more weeks." Zack's face was pale against his all-black clothing.

Sam nodded. "Yeah. The new pits we dug today are really promising. We can't stop now."

"We don't have a choice." Roman cut off the protests. "Safety is our priority. I've made the decision. We'll backfill the excavations, pack up, and leave tomorrow. The sooner we get out of here, the better."

Hannah couldn't look at anyone, couldn't bear to see the disappointment on Roman's face. The excavation was a dream of a lifetime for him, a one-time opportunity to learn the secrets of the Dakelh people's precontact past buried beneath Keyoh's sandy soil.

He wasn't the only one invested in the project. The students worked hard every day under the hot sun and in the rain, surveying and excavating. Their passion for their work and their respect for the people who once inhabited Keyoh was something she'd planned to highlight in her article.

This disaster was her fault. She'd brought trouble to the excavation, trouble in the name of Derek Pasternak. It was up to her to fix the problem. She stood up. "You don't have to end the project. Not because of me. I'll go." She shot a glance at Peter. "Right, Peter? You and I'll pack up and leave this afternoon. If we're gone, there's no reason for Derek to stay."

Peter scrubbed his beard. "I'm sorry, Hannah. We can't leave right now. I need to catalogue the two artifacts I dug up yesterday, and with all the forms, that'll take most of the day." He patted her arm. "Tomorrow will be better. Okay?"

She grimaced at the delay, but Peter was right. He'd come to Keyoh to help Roman. He couldn't leave without finishing that job. She nodded. "I guess we can wait a day."

Approval shone in his eyes. "It's settled then. Hannah and I'll leave tomorrow. We'll paddle downriver to Fort Cutter like we planned, and as soon as we can, we'll let the authorities know what's been going on here."

Roman was shaking his head before Peter finished speaking. "The project's over. We don't have a satellite phone, and I refuse to continue the excavation without a connection to the outside. It's not safe."

She opened her mouth to object, but Roman held up his hand silencing her.

"No one's going off on their own. We'll all leave together." He nodded at the crew. "Now, if we're finished here, head off to your tents and start packing. We leave in the morning."

The students shuffled to their tents, their shoulders

slumped, strain and disappointment carving lines in their youthful faces.

She stayed where she was, too exhausted to move. A massive load of guilt weighed her down.

Roman motioned to Peter. "Look, man. I'm sorry about earlier. I shouldn't have said what I did. It wasn't your fault. I've been pushing you too hard. No wonder you fell asleep."

"Thanks, but this is on me. I was supposed to keep an eye on Hannah. I let her and everyone else down."

"No. I should've stayed at camp and kept watch," Roman said. "I'm in charge of this project. I—"

"Hey, guys." She stood and jammed her hands on her hips. "I'm right here, and I can hear you." Her anger flared hot and heavy, dissipating the tiredness. "I'm not a child."

The two men gaped.

"I don't need either of you to be my keeper."

They blinked but didn't respond.

"Is that clear?"

They both nodded.

Her anger fizzled at their quick compliance. "Well, okay then. That's good. We understand each other."

Roman cleared his throat. "Peter, will you take the east side of the camp along the river, and I'll check the western boundary?"

"Right. I'm on it." Peter grabbed a flashlight from the box on the table and headed toward the river. He waved. "See you later, Hannah. Try and get some sleep."

And then there were two.

Roman's gaze settled on her, a twinkle in his eye. "You should start packing. If you want to, that is. Of course, you don't have to do what I say. It's just a suggestion." He picked up a flashlight.

Now he was overdoing it, and she fought back another sharp retort. A more important issue weighed on her mind. "Please don't shut down the project. This excavation means a lot to you and the crew."

He threaded his fingers through his hair. "Why do you care about this project so much? You're just here to research your story."

The fire had died down to glowing coals, and she couldn't read his face in the dim light. "You don't know what else you'll find. It could be something exciting like the Chinese coin. You have to keep investigating."

A log shifted in the coals, and a spark shot onto the ground and landed at his feet. He stomped on the hot coal. "This is about your article, isn't it?" His eyes narrowed. "If the excavation ends early, your story won't get published. Is that what you're worried about?"

"I don't care about the article. Not anymore. Peter and I are leaving, but you and the crew don't have to." She brushed a strand of hair off her cheek. "This project's important, and I don't want to be the reason you quit."

"Your safety's more important than this excavation." He switched on the flashlight and stepped away from the table. "I'm going to check the perimeter. I'll see you in the morning." He disappeared into the dark.

She opened her mouth to call him back, but the words died on her tongue. He was a man bound by a strict code of honor and integrity. Keyoh was his project, and he'd do whatever was necessary to keep the people there safe, even though it meant the end of his lifelong dream.

She stuffed her hands in her sweater pockets. The

crew would shut down the project and pack up. They'd leave in a convoy and head down the river to the nearest settlement and call for help. Once the authorities arrived and secured the site, and Derek was arrested, Roman and his crew could return to Keyoh and continue their excavations.

Maybe.

She rubbed her temples, hoping to ease the dull ache. She needed to rest and wrap her mind around the recent frightening events and the terrifying reality that Derek was at Keyoh.

Chapter 33

She didn't sleep. Each time her eyes drifted closed, she jerked awake, her heart racing at the slightest sound. She kept reminding herself she was safe. She wasn't alone. People were nearby. Roman slept in his tent a meter away, and her brother and the rest of the crew were close by in their tents. One of them could get to her in a hurry if she needed.

She was up and pacing around the cooking area before the sun rose. She wanted to leave. Now. She didn't want to wait. If there was the slightest chance Derek was still at Keyoh, she didn't want to be there. If she could paddle the canoe on her own, she'd leave right then and go for help.

If she were honest with herself—and she was too exhausted to be anything but honest—she liked Roman. Liked him a lot. Maybe she was even falling in love with him. Sometime in the dark lonely hours of the night, the truth had struck her like a revelation and rocked her to her toes.

But she was living a lie. Like a coward, she still hadn't revealed where her article would be published. Not that it mattered anymore. She twisted her long braid through her fingers. Along with acknowledging her growing feelings for Roman, she'd reached a decision. She wasn't going to write the article. How could she, when she was responsible for the project's early conclusion?

Marilyn wouldn't be happy. She grimaced. That was a gross understatement. Her senior editor had been keen on the idea of an article highlighting an archaeological investigation in Northern British Columbia. She'd jump over the moon at the added intrigue of Derek pursuing Hannah to Keyoh and the mayhem he'd caused. The story was guaranteed a front-page placement.

Front page! The lead article.

That was a goal she'd worked hard to attain these past three years. But this story came with a price. If it were published, whatever Roman was hiding about his past would be exposed for the world to read. She couldn't do that, even if staying silent meant the end of her career.

Loud angry voices erupted, slicing through her turbulent thoughts.

Roman, Sam, and Zack strode into the camp.

Roman's face was carved in stone, his mouth drawn in a thin line. "Are you kidding?" His voice was strident. "Are you damn well kidding me?"

Zack shook his head. "I wish I was, man, but we saw the damage with our own eyes."

Her scalp prickled. "What's going on?"

They turned as one, but no one spoke.

"Something's happened. Tell me what it is."

Peter stumbled into the clearing, his blond hair hanging in his face, his eyes heavy-lidded with sleep. "What's all the yelling about?"

"Someone disabled the motorboats," Sam said, his voice shaky.

"What?" She and Peter spoke at the same time.

Sam nodded. "Zack and I were on watch, and we

decided to check down by the creek. Right away, we saw something was wrong. We—"

Zack jumped in. "The housing's smashed on both boat motors, and the fuel lines are cut. The motors are a mess. There's no way we'll be able to repair them."

"Derek!" Her gaze flew to Roman. "It was him. He did this." Her legs wobbled and the ground beneath her shifted. She staggered a few steps and collapsed onto a chair.

The furrow between Roman's dark brows deepened. "What about the boats themselves? Are they okay?"

Sam shook his head. "The plug in the aluminum boat's been removed, and it's been scuttled. The wooden boat has holes the size of my fist in the bottom of its hull."

Roman cursed under his breath.

She gasped. Hadn't Derek caused enough trouble? What did he want? What was his end game? A shudder rippled through her, and she rubbed the goose bumps on her arms.

Roman's gaze settled on her, and she flinched at the raw fear darkening his eyes to a deep, bottomless black.

He turned back to Sam and Zack. "What about my grandfather's canoe? Did you check that? Is it okay? It was pulled up on the creek bank farther upstream from the motorboats."

Zack nodded. "After we saw the damage done to the crew boats, we checked Nathaniel's canoe." If possible, his face paled even more. "It looks like someone smashed the hull with a large axe." He shook his head. "I'm sorry, Roman, but the canoe's destroyed too."

Other than a narrowing of his eyes, Roman's expression didn't alter, but Hannah wasn't fooled. The destruction of Nathaniel's canoe was a devastating blow.

Peter had shown her the beautiful cedar-strip canoe the day after they arrived. He'd told her Roman's grandfather had paddled the river on his own to Keyoh in the canoe he and Roman had made when Roman was a teenager. The project had taken them two years, and the finished canoe was stunning. Crafted from Alaska yellow-cedar strips, it was a rich glossy golden color.

"Damn!" Peter said. In the next moment, he took off running toward the cliff top.

"Peter? What's going on?" she called. "Where are you going?"

He didn't acknowledge he heard her and kept up his rapid trot.

Roman cursed and raced after him.

Her legs were rubbery as she followed. She had to find out what had her brother looking concerned and moving fast.

****

Roman's heart rate kicked into the stratosphere as he chased after Peter. He didn't know why his friend was upset, but whatever it was, it couldn't be good. Nothing positive had happened in the past forty-eight hours. The coin stolen, Derek confronting Hannah, the satellite phone destroyed, the boats vandalized, Nathaniel's canoe smashed... What the hell else could go wrong?

Peter halted on the riverbank and released a string of colorful curses.

Roman caught up. "What is it? What's wrong?"

Hannah stumbled across the rocky shore. "What's going on?"

Peter, his nostrils flaring, picked up a fist-sized rock and threw it into the river. It landed with a loud splash.

"That bastard stole our canoe."

Hannah wrapped her arms around her chest and shuddered.

"Are you sure the canoe was here?" Roman fought back his rage. "It didn't get washed down river when we had that storm?"

"I saw it yesterday," Peter said. "It couldn't have floated away. We hauled it high up on the shore."

"Derek took the canoe. He must have. That's the only explanation for why it's not here." Deep furrows carved into Hannah's smooth forehead.

Roman gritted his teeth. He was going to kill Derek when he tracked down his sorry ass. The jerk had left them stranded, and with no way to communicate with the outside world. The fifty-million-dollar questions were why, and what was Derek planning next?

"Maybe Sam's theory's right, and Derek's gone. He knows we'll find some way to contact the police, and he wouldn't want to be here when that happens. He took our canoe and paddled away," Hannah said.

Roman hated to burst her bubble, but he didn't want her to have false hopes. "I don't see a guy like that paddling downriver for two days. My gut tells me he isn't finished with us, and he's still here." He winced as her face fell, and the gleam of hope in her blue eyes vanished.

"I don't know. Hannah and Sam might be right." Peter rubbed a hand over his unruly beard. "We've been running our search grids, and we've covered every centimeter of this place. He knew we were closing in on him, and it was only a matter of time before we caught him. He had to escape, so he snuck down here and launched the canoe."

"Why didn't he take one of the motorboats before he destroyed them?" Roman asked. Someone had to be the voice of reason. "A motorboat's faster than a canoe."

"We would've heard the motor, and the creek's not easy to navigate. We'd have been on him before he reached the river," Peter said.

Hannah shuffled her feet and rubbed her hands together, nervous energy radiating off her. "Once he pushed the canoe into the river, the current would do the rest. He wouldn't have to paddle until he was downriver. No one would've heard him leave."

Peter's blond curls danced as he nodded his head. "That makes sense."

Roman bit his tongue, stopping the words bursting to escape. He didn't buy into their fantasy. His gut told him Derek had followed Hannah to Keyoh for a specific reason, and he wasn't leaving until he got what he came for. But he didn't want to frighten her. "I hope you're right." He shoved his hair back from his face. "Let's get back to camp. We should tell the others and figure out our next steps."

Next steps? What next steps?

Thanks to Derek, they were stranded, with no way to communicate. He stalked down the shoreline, kicking pebbles and driftwood out of his way.

Chapter 34

Roman studied the group of pale-faced dull-eyed students slumped on the picnic table bench seats. Over the past two days, they'd lost their youthful exuberance and looked years older than people just out of their teens.

Peter, his hand resting protectively on his sister's shoulder, stood behind the others.

Nathaniel sat in a lawn chair at the head of the table.

Another disaster, another crew meeting. His head throbbed. Everyone looked shell-shocked. No wonder, after the bomb he'd dropped.

"Oh man." Sam smoothed the palm of his hand over his frizzy red hair. "So, this is it. We're screwed. Our communications are cut off, the motorboats and Nathaniel's canoe are disabled, and Hannah and Peter's canoe's missing."

The beads woven into Jillian's braids rattled like dried bones. "We're stuck here, and there's a guy creeping around who's shown he's prepared to do anything to get what he wants." She shuddered. "It's like we're in one of those slasher movies."

"This is too gnarly for me," Rafferty said and shot to his feet. "I didn't sign up for this. I want out of here."

Zack stood. "Me too." His Adam's apple bobbed in his thin throat.

Jillian and Sam jumped up.

Roman held up his hand and raised his voice to be

heard over their nervous muttering. "Sit down. All of you." He stared at each of them until they sat back down. "There's a good possibility that Derek stole Peter and Hannah's canoe and paddled away from Keyoh." He eyed each student. "He's probably halfway to Fort Cutter by now." He gulped. And there he was—lying to them. He didn't for a hot minute believe Derek was gone. The bastard was hiding somewhere nearby, waiting to make his next move. But panic wouldn't help the situation. And he'd keep everyone safe, even if he had to stay on guard twenty-four hours a day.

Zack cleared his throat. "How are we going to contact the police and let them know what's happened?"

"I talk to the director at least twice a week. If he doesn't hear from us in the next few days, he'll know something's wrong and send help." Roman fought to keep his voice calm and level. He understood their fear. Hell, he was frightened too.

"We won't go hungry. We have plenty of supplies." He spread his hands as if smoothing turbulent water. "Until then, we'll carry on like business as usual. We'll continue excavating the new tests pits." He forced a smile to his stiff lips. "With any luck, we'll find another Chinese coin."

Nathaniel tapped on the table. Once he had the group's attention, he said, "I have an idea. One that might work."

Roman narrowed his eyes, afraid to ask the old man about his idea, but desperate for any solution.

Hannah beat him to the punch. "What is it, Nathaniel? What are you thinking?"

"Someone could walk out and find help."

"Walk out?" Sam threaded his fingers through his

long hair. "The closest town is Verity, and there's no trail. It would take someone days to walk out of here. If they even made it."

Nathaniel smiled. "There's an old Saik'uz trail that runs from here to the mountains in the west. It was used for thousands of years. My ancestors traded furs and obsidian with the tribes from the Coast for eulachon. The fish has a high oil content, its grease was valued for its healing properties, and they were dried and used as candles." He shook his head. "Sadly, industrial development has decimated the eulachon stocks, and there aren't many fish left. I—"

Roman cut him off. "That trail hasn't been used in years. With all the fallen dead pine trees, it would be impassable."

"I've been on the trail. I hiked part of it last week when I went picking berries."

"You have?" Frustration burned like an inferno deep in Roman's gut. "Why didn't you tell me?"

"You never asked."

Roman bit back a sharp retort. Now wasn't the time to vent his fear and frustration. His grandfather was just trying to help. He caught movement out of the corner of his eye.

Peter slipped away, disappearing into the shadows.

Where was he going? But he recalled what Nathaniel had announced, and he refocused. "Tell us more about this trail."

"We call it Duje Ti." Nathaniel glanced at the students, who were hanging on every word. "*Duje* is our word for huckleberries, and *ti* means trail. The trail passes through areas thick with huckleberry bushes."

"Could someone hike out on the trail all the way to

Verity?" Hannah asked.

"The mountain pine beetle devastated the forest, and most of the dead pine trees have fallen. The Duje Ti would be challenging." The lines grooving either side of Nathaniel's mouth deepened as he frowned. "But I believe it could be done."

"How long is the trail?" Hannah edged closer to Nathaniel, her blue eyes flashing with excitement.

"Hundreds of kilometers. It runs all the way to the coast."

"If someone were to follow the Duje Ti, they wouldn't have to walk all the way to Verity to find help, would they?" She studied the group, her eyes sparkling. "Lots of people live and camp in the backwoods, and there must be logging and mining operations. Right?"

Peter returned and laid a map on the table in front of Nathaniel. He smoothed the crinkled paper and pointed at a spot on the map. "This is Keyoh. Can you show us the trail?"

Nathaniel leaned closer, squinted, and rubbed his eyes.

Knowing the old man was blind without his readers, Roman hurried to his tent and rifled through his grandfather's sack. He grabbed the glasses and rushed back. "You might want to use these." He held out the readers.

"Thank you, Roman." Nathaniel settled the lenses on his nose and peered at the map.

Roman moved closer.

"Long ago, there were many trading trails, but this is the Duje Ti." Nathaniel's arthritic finger traced a line from the Sturgeon River at Keyoh, across the valley, past countless lakes and streams, to the Cohosh Mountains and beyond, to the Pacific Ocean.

Roman's heart rate kicked up. He knew that area. The trail passed through ranches, farms, and logging clearcuts. An old gravel logging road bisected the trail. His brain spun with possibilities. "If we were to follow the trail, we'd have a good chance of finding someone with access to a satellite phone or a vehicle."

The silence rang like a tuning fork.

"I'll go." Sam jumped up. "I'm an experienced hiker. My dad and I go on a two-week hike in the Rockies every summer."

Zack stood. "I'll go with you. The two of us will find help."

Roman slammed the palm of his hand on the table. When he had everyone's attention, he said, "I appreciate your enthusiasm, but you're not going. The trail's too arduous. There's lots of deadfall, and it'd be easy to get lost."

Sam opened his mouth to protest, but Roman stared him down, and the kid sank back onto the bench seat. "I'm in charge here, and I'm responsible for your safety. I'll go. The rest of you will stay and continue excavating."

Rafferty jammed his safari hat over his long dark hair. "If you go, who'll decide where we excavate next? And what if we find an artifact like the Chinese coin? Who'll ensure we treat it properly? We're just students."

Roman fisted his hands. Rafferty was right. Keyoh was Roman's project. He was responsible for the integrity of the site. If he left, he'd be blamed if something went wrong. He'd be like a captain deserting his sinking ship. He ground down on his teeth until his jaw ached. But if he sent someone else to find help, he'd be in major trouble if something happened to that person.

"I'll go."

Peter's voice cut through the turmoil in Roman's brain. He shook his head. "No."

"Hear me out, Roman."

He studied Peter's earnest gaze and reluctantly nodded.

"I should be the one to go for help. I've done lots of wilderness hiking, and I'm familiar with the back country." He straightened his shoulders and kept his gaze on Roman. "You know it's the right choice."

Roman jammed his hands into his pants pockets. As much as he didn't like the thought of his friend hiking across the challenging terrain, Peter was right. He was the best choice. "Okay."

"I'm going with you, Peter." Hannah stood and moved beside her brother.

"No." Both Peter and Roman spoke at the same time.

Roman scowled. "No way. You're not going. You're safer here." Though as soon as the words were out of his mouth, he wasn't sure they were true. If Derek was still at Keyoh, how could Roman guarantee her safety?

"I've been hiking since I was a little kid. I know my way around the forest." Her mouth set in a stubborn line. "Peter and I'll both go."

Roman winced, but he couldn't think of another argument to convince her to stay. "When are you leaving?"

Her gaze shifted around the group, looking anywhere but at him. "Right now. I'm packed and ready to go. Are you ready, Peter?"

"Give me a couple of hours. We need to organize the supplies we'll need, and I want to go over the trail details with Nathaniel." He looked at his watch. "How about we leave right after lunch?"

Hannah frowned, her displeasure at the delay obvious, but she nodded. "Okay."

That was it, then. The decision had been made. She was leaving. A heavy dose of loss struck Roman, and somewhere deep inside, a tiny flame of hope died. A part of him realized he was being unreasonable, that he'd known all along she wasn't staying, but the hurt cut deep.

He pushed back from the table and strode toward his tent. Let her leave. What did he care? She was a journalist. He didn't like reporters. He never had.

But she's not like other reporters. And you like her. You like her a lot.

He ignored the snide voice inside his head and thrust open his tent flap. He didn't have time to mope around like a sad, lonely lost puppy. He had a project to finish.

He scowled at the stack of papers on the desk— reports of the excavations, recordings of the artifacts they'd uncovered, the daily mundane record of the progress of the excavation…

Yeah. Real important work.

Chapter 35

Hannah double-checked her backpack, ensuring she had everything for the long hike. In a few hours, she and Peter were setting off on their rescue mission.

The second Nathaniel told them about the Duje Ti, she wanted to be the one to go for help. This nightmare was her fault, and she needed to make amends. Thanks to Derek, hiking out was their only option.

Nathaniel had warned her and Peter that the trek would be arduous. There'd be downed trees blocking the trail, and sections of the old path had washed away over the years. Even though they had a map with the Duje Ti marked by Nathaniel, the trail had fallen into disuse. Buried under deadfalls and thick, tangled brush, it would be challenging to find and stay on the trail.

She undid the elastic holding her braid in place and freed her long hair, running her fingers through the tangles. She had mixed feelings about leaving. So many frightening things had happened at Keyoh, but she didn't want to say goodbye to Roman. Her feelings for him were deepening. A vision of him holding the rainbow trout she'd caught and grinning like a boy, his dark eyes glowing, floated through her mind.

When he'd kissed her, she'd forgotten their differences and her worries about Derek, forgotten everything but the touch of his lips against hers. That was the moment *IT* happened—the moment she started falling for him. A bubble of happiness had risen from deep within, and she felt lighter, as if a weight had lifted.

Since then, there'd been one disaster after another, and there hadn't been time for a heart-to-heart, nor an opportunity for her to reveal the truth about her employer.

Now it was too late.

She shrugged into her sweatshirt and crawled out of the tent and headed to the kitchen area. Sam had made a batch of chocolate chip cookies on the camp stove for dinner the previous night. Maybe a few cookies were left. Eating was her way of coping with stress, and right now, she craved a truckload of chocolate.

The camp was quiet. The only sounds were the distant rushing of the river as it wended its way through the canyon below and the crackle of the fire. Everyone was busy with the new excavations. The project had only a few more days to run, and there was a sense of urgency to complete as much of the work as possible before the dig was shut down.

She halted.

Someone was sitting in a chair before the fire.

Her heart leaped. His back was to her, but she knew with a visceral certainty who it was.

Roman turned and faced her. He patted the chair beside him. "Join me."

She stared. *Join him*? No. She couldn't, not now, not when her feelings for him were so confusing. "I-I was going to grab a cookie and see if Peter needs any help." Her feet moved across the hard-packed ground, and before her mind caught up, she was sitting in the chair. She gulped. If she shifted her leg a centimeter to the left, she'd brush against his thigh.

Blue, orange, and yellow flames licked a burning log, and smoke billowed in a plume, rising into the clear blue sky.

"You missed your chance."

"Pardon me?" Her mouth opened in a gasp. Had he read her mind? Did he know how she regretted not telling him the truth before she left?

"The crew ate the last of the cookies before they headed to the excavations, but I can offer you a hot chocolate." A thin spiral of steam rose from the ceramic cup in his hand.

"Hot chocolate?" She arched her brows. "Not chamomile tea?" She pictured him as many things, but not a hot chocolate drinker. Tea, strong black coffee, maybe even scotch, but not hot cocoa.

"Chamomile tea's a favorite, but when I'm worried, nothing's better than a cup of hot cocoa." His mouth curved in a smile, and he leaned forward. Using a hot pad, he grabbed the handle of a pot set on a rock beside the fire. "I just made it, so it should still be hot." He poured a stream of steaming liquid into a mug. Reaching behind him to a small table, he opened a plastic bag and grabbed a handful of mini marshmallows. He added those to the drink and handed her the mug.

"Marshmallows? Yum." His hand brushed hers, and her skin tingled at the contact.

"It's not real hot cocoa without marshmallows. Not in my book." He raised his cup in a toast and sipped.

The flames flickered, casting intriguing light and shadows across his handsome face, and her heart melted like the mini marshmallows floating in her hot drink. She wrapped her hands around the mug, letting the warmth flow through her fingers.

"Are you going to try the cocoa, or sit there and stare at it?"

His teasing tone drew her out of her musings. She ducked her head, hoping her heavy fall of hair hid the heat flooding her face. Raising the cup to her lips, she sipped. "Mmmm."

He arched his dark eyebrows.

Her cheeks flamed hotter, scalding her skin, at her unbridled moan of pleasure. "Th-this is delicious."

"Glad you like it." He grinned. "It's my special recipe."

"Thank you." She sipped more hot chocolate. "This is way better than chocolate chip cookies."

He chuckled.

A comfortable silence settled between them, broken by the crackling of the fire and the cheeping of birds.

He cleared his throat. "So you and Peter are leaving."

It wasn't a question, but she answered anyway. "Yes. I'm all packed and ready to go."

"I hope Nathaniel's memory is sharp and the trail's where he says it is. You guys are going to have a tough trek."

"Hopefully, we won't have to hike far before we find someone who can help." She stared into her cup.

He set down his mug on a stump. "Did you get enough information to write your article?"

She fought not to flinch under his penetrating gaze. "I'm not going to write the article."

"What? Why not?"

"I don't think I should write the story after everything that's happened."

"But you took tons of photos, you researched

Keyoh's history, and interviewed everyone. Couldn't you write your article, but leave out any mention of Derek and the trouble he's caused?"

She was shaking her head before he finished. "I could, but once the police arrest Derek, everything that happened here will become public knowledge. My editor would fire me on the spot if I didn't reveal the whole sordid story."

He shook his head. "You're in a cutthroat business. Selling newspapers and corporate profit are more important than people's lives." He narrowed his eyes. "Wait a minute." His frown deepened. "I thought you were a freelance journalist. Isn't that what you and Peter told me? Why do you have an editor?"

The heat from the fire was closing in, suffocating her, and it felt as if she couldn't get enough air. "About that. I-I may have misled you."

His gaze gripped hers.

"I work for *Aspire*."

His eyes widened.

She soldiered on. "My editor assigned me the story on Keyoh. It was supposed to be published in November's edition."

An echoing silence settled between them.

The furrow between his dark brows deepened, and he lurched to his feet. "All this time, you've been lying—to me, to everyone."

She cringed under the force of his anger. "I-I'm sorry, I—"

He held up his hand stopping her. "I don't want to hear your excuses. You know full well what I think of that rag." He shook his head, his gaze scorching.

She searched for the words to cool his outrage. "I

don't know what you're afraid of. You're doing a great job. You're making a real difference. Your discoveries here will help your people."

"What about the valuable artifact that was stolen under my watch?" His voice cracked.

"That wasn't your fault." She shoved back a strand of hair. "*I'm* the reason Derek was here. *I'm* the reason the coin was taken."

"You don't get it, do you? Keyoh is *my* project. I'm responsible for everything that happens here." He shook his head and strode away.

"Roman, wait."

He didn't slow as he continued his determined march to his tent.

Tossing the remains of her hot chocolate on the ground, she stood. His reaction was what she'd feared. It was a good thing she and Peter were leaving. Blinking back tears, she set her cup on the stump and headed toward her brother's tent.

Chapter 36

Roman stepped through his tent flap and crossed the few meters of bare ground to her tent. He threaded his fingers through his hair, uncaring it was a tangled mess. Ever since he'd stormed off in a snit after Hannah's shocking confession, he'd been in turmoil. His stomach burned as if he'd eaten something rotten, and his head ached like someone was driving a stake into his brain.

She'd lied to everyone. Worse—she'd lied to *him*. That's what hurt the most. He'd trusted her. And now this. She worked for *Aspire*. All this time, she'd kept the truth hidden. He should've known. A small part of him had suspected she was hiding something, but he'd let his growing feelings take over, and he'd ignored his misgivings.

Peter was in on the lie too. He snorted. Some friend.

When his anger cooled and his brain function returned, he regretted his harsh words. She was a good journalist. He'd seen that from the start. Her questions were probing but insightful, she was respectful of the Indigenous culture, and she treated the crew with professionalism and kindness. Her easy charm had them eating out of her hand.

She'd even cracked Nathaniel's shell and convinced him to grant an interview. The old man liked her, and he was a good judge of character.

It wasn't her fault Derek followed her to Keyoh. She

was trying to rectify the situation by volunteering to hike out for help. That said a lot about the sort of person she was. She had principles. He'd messed up. Big time. Angry words and accusations weren't the way he wanted things to end.

And that was why he was standing outside her tent, his knees quaking like a teenage boy working up the courage to ask the popular girl on a date. Before she walked out of his life forever, he wanted to apologize for being a jerk. Even more, he wanted to come clean and confess his own secret and explain his hatred for *Aspire* and hope she would understand. He smoothed his hand over his wild hair and tapped on the tent wall. "Hannah?" He winced at the squeak in his voice. "Can I talk to you?"

He waited.

And waited.

His shoulders sagged, and a deep exhaustion wormed its way into his bones. She wasn't willing to talk. Not to him. He turned back to his tent, his shoulders drooping, and he lumbered away.

"What do you want?"

A spurt of joy flared, and his exhaustion vanished. He spun around. "Can we talk?"

Indecision was written across her face.

"Please, Hannah. Just hear me out."

Dressed for the hike, she wore a long-sleeved loose white T-shirt and baggy cargo pants that looked like she'd borrowed them from her brother. She'd never looked more beautiful. Her hair was free of its usual braid and hung in a golden cloud around her face. Her vibrant blue eyes were surrounded by thick eyelashes.

She nodded. "Go ahead."

He inhaled a deep breath. This was his chance. His

shot in the dark. "I'm sorry for how I reacted earlier. You didn't deserve that."

"I should've told you the truth from the start."

"I don't blame you for not telling me." He shrugged. "I made it pretty clear how I felt about your magazine."

"Okay. You've apologized, and I've accepted your apology. Are we done?"

He opened his mouth to speak, to explain the real reason he was standing there like a supplicant, but the words stuck in his throat, and he stared at her helplessly.

"If that's all, I'm leaving in a few minutes, and I have packing to finish." She ducked to crawl back into her tent.

"Wait. Please." His plea was like a cry ripped from his soul. This was one of those moments Nathaniel talked about—the seconds that changed a person's life. If he didn't speak up, he'd regret his cowardice for the rest of his life. "Please, Hannah."

She swung back to face him.

"Look, I-I like you. I *really* like you." Her eyes widened, but he kept speaking, throwing his heart on the ground. "I'd like to see you outside of Keyoh after this is all over." He paused a beat, trying to read her expression. "Wha-what do you think? Are you willing to give me—us—a second chance?"

Moisture filled her eyes.

She was crying. His heart sank. That couldn't be good.

"I'm sorry, but it would never work between us."

He felt as if the ground beneath him disappeared, and he was falling. "But—"

"Journalism is more than a job. It's my life, and I'm proud of the work I do." She sniffled and slipped a tissue from her front pocket and wiped her nose. "I want a man who respects my career." She shrugged. "I don't think you're that man."

Her voice reached him as if from a great distance, echoing hollowly. He opened his mouth to speak, to refute her painful words, but she shook her head, stopping him.

"Please. Let me finish."

He nodded, though he wanted to jam his hands over his ears so he couldn't hear any more. Hot tears pushed against his eyes.

"You despise journalists. Maybe you have a good reason for your disgust, but you haven't trusted me enough to share that. I don't know what happened, but you have walls around you I can't breach. You don't trust me. Not really. And because of that I can't trust you." Her voice hitched. "That won't change until you deal with your insecurities."

The finality in her voice was like a hook deep in his guts being ripped out. "Wait. Let me explain."

She shook her head. "I'm sorry." A sob broke free, and without another word, she turned and crawled into her tent.

He stood there, tears burning his eyes. He'd bared his heart, and she'd stomped on it and ground his hopes into the dirt. Served him right. He should've told her about his experience with *Aspire* when he ran into her on the road outside Renton Falls. Now it was too late.

He started at the sound of a foot scraping the dirt.

Nathaniel stood a few feet away. "I'm sorry, Roman."

"You heard?" Why was he surprised? His grandfather slipped through the forest like a ghost.

Nathaniel nodded. "You're in love with her."

He shook his head. What the hell was the old man talking about? He hadn't said anything about love.

"Don't lie to me, Roman. I've known you since you were a baby."

"I told her I liked her, but she's not interested." He blinked back tears. "I don't blame her. I've acted like a jerk since the moment I met her."

Nathaniel clamped his hand on Roman's shoulder. "You're my grandson, and I love you. I always will." He stared into Roman's eyes. "Believe me when I tell you this—that girl loves you."

Roman's lip curled. "Come on, Grandfather. Don't try and make me feel better. She made her feelings clear. The woman kicked me to the curb. It's over."

"When you were a young boy, you wanted to play basketball. Do you remember?"

Roman frowned. He didn't want to go down memory lane. Not now. Not when his heart was crushed.

Nathaniel tightened his grip on Roman's shoulder. "You tried out, but you didn't make the team. You were devastated, but you didn't give up. You practiced every day, bouncing basketballs and shooting hoops in the driveway until dark.

"When you tried out the next year, you made the first cut, and you were a team starter." He eased his grip on Roman's shoulder, but stayed close, his gaze fixed on Roman.

"You fought for years to get permission to run this excavation. You didn't give up, because you're not a quitter. Don't quit now." He turned and strode away, his footsteps silent as he vanished into the trees.

Roman scrubbed his hands over his face, stumbled

back to his tent, and flopped onto his cot. Squeezing his eyes closed, he fought to shut down his brain and stop the thoughts tumbling through in a wild frenzy.

Nathaniel said Roman wasn't a quitter. What was he supposed to do? Follow Hannah and force her to hear him out? That'd make him no different than Derek. If a woman said no, that was it. She'd said she wasn't interested, and so it was over. No matter how much he wished the situation were different.

He groaned and flipped over onto his stomach, burying his face in the pillow, trying to shut out the torrent of guilt and recriminations. Her cold words, playing on an endless rewind, cut like a knife to his gut.

Nathaniel was smart. He knew people and what made them tick. What if he was right? What if Hannah did care for him? A tiny coal of hope deep inside flickered to life.

What if?

Exhausted, he drifted off to sleep on that wondrous possibility.

Chapter 37

Hannah straightened the shoulder straps on her backpack and wiped the moisture from her face. The rain had started shortly after they left camp, and the storm hadn't let up all day. A steady drizzle dripped from the branches of the tall fir trees.

She grunted as she climbed over another downed log, shoving through the tangle of wet branches that tore at her hair and clothing, lathering her with rainwater. She and Peter had been hiking for six hours. They'd only stopped for a quick snack and a couple of water breaks. She was hungry, exhausted, soaked, and cold.

She'd expected the hike to be challenging, but not this difficult. Nathaniel had drawn the route on the map and indicated the distinguishing landmarks he remembered. He'd told them to look for culturally modified trees and circular depressions in the ground that would indicate ancient people had travelled there. In a nod to the modern world, he'd also given them a compass.

The crew had made them a special sendoff lunch, but she hadn't had an appetite.

Roman had sat there silent, his food untouched, his face set in rigid lines, avoiding her gaze. No wonder, after the tongue-lashing she'd subjected him to.

When lunch was finished and it was time to set off on the hike, he handed Peter a GPS and wished them luck. He didn't look her way or say anything, but as they hurried across the meadow, she felt his gaze burning into her back.

They hadn't traveled more than a kilometer along the trail when they realized they needed the GPS. The ancient pathway was visible only as a slight indentation in the ground from thousands of years of use by the local Indigenous people. Duje Ti was overgrown, and fallen pine trees lay crisscrossed on the ground in jumbled heaps.

She was physically and mentally shattered from fighting her way through the thick bush and the strain of the past days. The muscles in her body ached, and the soles of her feet throbbed. As she slogged over the muddy ground and waded across shallow streams, a steady reel of disturbing images flashed before her. Derek, and his destruction, featured in some of her visions, but the star of the show was Roman.

He'd confessed he liked her, and she'd thrown his words in his face. She had no excuse other than his dislike of her profession and *Aspire* magazine hurt, and she'd lashed out. A mistake. One she'd regret for a long time.

"What do you think?" Peter's voice broke through her recriminations. "This looks like a good place to camp for the night."

"Let's not stop yet." She was beat, and every step hurt, but the crew and Roman and Nathaniel were counting on them. "It's still light out. We should try and hike another few kilometers."

Peter's tangled hair hung in wet strands, dripping in his eyes. "I need a break. This trail's a nightmare." He smoothed back his hair, revealing the exhaustion lining his face. "I don't think I can go any farther today."

Guilt flooded her. Of course he was tired. He carried a heavier backpack than she did, and he'd walked ahead and cleared the trail. "Okay. Let's stop here." She shrugged out of her daypack and dropped it onto the soggy ground. "It'll be good to set up the tent and get out of this rain." Every centimeter of her body ached, and she'd kill for a soak in a hot bath.

"Help me with this tarp, Hannah." Peter had set up the small, three-person pup tent on a raised, mossy bench beside the creek.

She grabbed a corner of the nylon rain tarp, and together, they draped it over the tent's thin nylon roof. Staking down the corners, she snugged the pegs tight into the muddy ground. Grabbing their packs one at a time, she lugged them into the tent and untied her sodden boots and set them by the tent opening.

Peter crawled in beside her and rolled out the self-inflating bedrests and covered them with their sleeping bags.

It was cozy in the little tent and a relief to be off her tired feet and out of the rain. She removed her wet raincoat, shook off the raindrops, and spread the coat across the end of her sleeping bag to dry.

Peter stripped off his boots and coat and sat cross-legged on his sleeping mat. "I'm starving. What did you make for dinner, Sis?"

She bit back a smile. "Did you catch any fish?"

He smoothed his wet hair off his forehead. "You're the expert fisher. Roman told me about the big rainbow trout you caught...and released."

An image of Roman teaching her to fly-fish flashed before her, and her brief spurt of humor evaporated like a drop of water in the hot desert sun. She loosened the ties on her pack. Burrowing inside, she dug out four granola bars, two apples, and two plastic bottles of water. "Eat up."

"Yummy." He ripped off a wrapper and stuffed the entire bar into his mouth.

She eyed the granola bars and shuddered. The last thing she wanted was food. Her stomach had been tied in knots since they started the challenging trek. The rational part of her brain knew Derek had left Keyoh, and she no longer had to be afraid, but she couldn't shake the primal uneasiness that twisted her gut.

"You should eat. You're going to need your strength. We have a long way to hike tomorrow before we hit anything remotely like civilization." He bit off a large chunk of his second bar and chewed.

"How much farther, do you think?"

He shrugged and tugged out the map, unfolded it, and spread it on the tent floor. Picking up a headlamp, he shone the light on the map. "According to Nathaniel, we follow this creek—" He traced a thin blue line with his finger. "—across the valley and over these hills. It's a long trek, but—" He pointed at a blue oval. "—if we can reach Maddow Lake, there's supposed to be a forestry campsite there. Nathaniel said there's a logging operation in the area too. Maybe we'll be lucky and find a camper or a logger with a radiophone in his truck."

"Yeah. Maybe." She wasn't counting on luck. The only luck she'd had for the past three months was bad luck. She opened a granola bar and munched on the crunchy peanut butter-covered nut bar. The bar was stale and tasted like cardboard. She grabbed a water bottle, twisted off the cap, and gulped.

The steady beat of rain on the nylon tent over her head was soothing, and she yawned and replaced the cap on the water bottle and set the granola bar aside. Snuggling into her sleeping bag, she yawned again. Her eyes drifted closed.

"If you're not eating your last granola bar, can I have it?"

She forced open her heavy eyelids. "What?"

"Sorry. I didn't know you were sleeping already. Can I have your granola bar?"

"Sure. Go ahead." She envied him his appetite. "There's some nut mix in my pack if you want. Zack gave it to me."

"This'll be good. We're going to need food for tomorrow and maybe the next day too. If Nathaniel's wrong, and we don't find anyone at Maddow Lake, we're going to have to walk a lot farther."

"He only hiked a few kilometers of the trail. Everything else is based on what he heard as a young man." She rubbed her grit-filled eyes. "But he's been right so far."

"Yeah. He's pretty incredible." Peter munched on a bar, swallowed, and wiped the back of his hand over his bearded chin. "So is his grandson."

She blinked, and her tiredness vanished. "What?"

"You heard me."

"We weren't talking about Roman."

His eyes gleamed. "Maybe not, but don't tell me you aren't thinking of him."

Heat flared up her neck, and she flipped onto her side so he wouldn't see her flushed cheeks.

"I was right. I knew it." He chuckled. "You do have a thing for him."

250

She bit down on her bottom lip. She should've known she couldn't hide anything from her brother, but she'd be damned if she'd reveal her feelings for Roman. How could she, when she didn't understand them herself? "I'm going to sleep. See you in the morning." She tugged the down bag over her head and closed her eyes.

"You can ignore your feelings, Stick, but that doesn't mean they're not real."

She jammed her hands over her ears, but his voice still penetrated.

"Roman's a great guy. I know he has this thing about reporters, but you two hit it off. He likes you, and not in a friend-zone way." A loud crackling of plastic wrappers and rustling of bedding. "I know you. You like him, whether you admit it or not."

"Go. To. Sleep."

"Sure thing, Sis."

More rustling and heavy sighs as he settled into his sleeping bag.

At long last, there was silence.

She rubbed her aching temples. Roman *had* liked her. He'd liked her enough to kiss her. An incredible, bone-melting kiss. But she'd ruined everything with her harsh words, and she doubted he liked her much now.

Shoving that upsetting thought to the back of her mind, she snuggled deeper into her bag, closed her eyes, and ordered her mind to shut down.

Chapter 38

Her eyes flew open. Her heart raced, and adrenaline flooded her body. The muscles in her arms and legs flexed, preparing for battle. She lurched up. Faint light filtered through the thin walls of the tent. Other than the distant gurgling of the creek and a hoot of a saw-whet owl, the dawn was quiet.

She'd had the dream again. The one where Derek attacked her with a knife. She inhaled a cleansing breath.

"What's wrong, Hannah?"

Peter's soft voice reached her through the near darkness.

"Nothing." The lie slid off her lips.

"Yeah, right." He shifted in his sleeping bag and lay on his side facing her. "You were having that nightmare, weren't you? The one starring Derek." A click sounded, and light filled the pup tent as he shone the beam of a headlamp on the ceiling, so as not to blind her.

She rubbed her eyes, erasing the remnants of the dream, and shoved her tangled hair out of her face. "What time is it?"

He shrugged. "I don't know. Early."

The sides of the tent billowed in a breeze, but the rain had stopped.

He yawned. "You know Derek's probably halfway to Fort Cutter by now. Once we contact the authorities, the police'll pick him up. You don't have to worry anymore. He'll be spending the next year locked in a cell."

She prayed he was right, but a deep foreboding lurked in the back of her mind. What if the missing canoe was another deception? What if Derek wanted them to believe he'd left Keyoh so they'd stop looking for him and let down their guard? Her stomach twisted. Were Roman and the crew in danger? She shuddered and shot a glance at her brother. "Did you get any sleep last night?"

His face was pale, and the headlamp illuminated the hollows in his gaunt cheeks. Dark circles rimmed his eyes. "Not much."

"What's wrong? Are you sick?"

Again, he shook his head.

"Well, then, what is it? You look like hell."

"Thanks a lot. I can always count on you to boost my ego." A grin flashed across his hairy face, but just as quickly, his smile faded. He flopped onto his back and rested his head on the rolled-up hoodie he was using as a pillow.

"Peter, come on. Tell me, please. What's bothering you?"

"I guess everything's getting to me. You know, all that stuff with Derek, the constant worry about what he'd do next. It was intense." A sad smile twisted his lips. "I'm glad he left Keyoh and you're safe."

"Bullshit." She didn't buy it. Sure, the past few days had been stressful, and he *was* concerned about her, but something else was going on. She leaned up on her elbow. "This is about Marissa, isn't it?"

He toyed with the silver chain around his neck, but he didn't meet her gaze. "I thought I was handling the breakup pretty well, but now—" He shrugged. "—I don't know. After everything's that's happened… I-I guess it's made me realize what's important, and I—"

"You still love her, don't you?"

"Yeah. I guess I do. But it's over." His eyes filled with tears. "She made that clear when she walked out."

A lump thickened her throat. "I'm so sorry. I liked Marissa. You guys were good together."

"*Were* being the key word." He sniffed and rubbed the back of his hand over his eyes. "It's kind of funny, isn't it?"

"What is?"

"Us." His mouth twisted in a parody of a smile. "We're the unlucky-in-love Marchands. We both suck at relationships." He flipped onto his side. "I'm going to try and get a bit more sleep. We're heading back out on the trail in a couple of hours."

Unlucky in love.

Was it true? Her parents had divorced when Peter and Hannah were kids.

That was bad luck.

Peter and Marissa were deeply in love when they married four years ago. But then trouble started, and Marissa left.

More bad luck.

She blinked back tears. Her own dating history was another sad tale. She'd never been in love, never found that special someone. Look at Derek. She couldn't have had worse luck than meeting and dating that monster.

But then you met Roman, and your luck changed.

She snorted. What was she thinking? She wasn't in love with him. Was she? Was it possible that her feelings for him ran deep, and she did sort of love him? Squeezing her eyes shut, blocking out the astounding thought, she started counting sheep, breathing in and out in slow, measured breaths, focusing on the flapping of the tent walls in the breeze, anything other than thinking of the tall, dark, and handsome archaeologist.

****

Roman knelt on the muddy ground, and using the pointed-tip trowel, he dug into the wet sandy soil. Unable to concentrate after Hannah and Peter left, he'd started laying out the new test grids in the rain. He needed to focus on work and take his mind off the events of the past days and the overwhelming certainty that he'd failed.

The rain had eased in the late afternoon, but dark clouds hovered, and the day was gloomy. A light breeze ruffled his hair, adding to his chill. He sat back and studied the meadow.

The crew was hard at work. He'd assigned each person a test pit. Their job was to excavate the square of ground to a depth of one meter, sift through the piles of displaced soil, and recover any artifacts or charred bone. He was pushing them, but time was running out. As soon as Hannah and Peter contacted the police, help would arrive, and the project would be shut down.

He should've known from the start that Derek was at the site, and Roman should've stopped him and his malicious vandalism before the situation spiraled out of control. He should've protected the Chinese coin better. And he definitely shouldn't have allowed Hannah and Peter to head off into the wilderness searching for help.

It didn't sit right that they'd gone for rescue, and he'd remained at camp. But Peter's logic was irrefutable. He was the best choice to make the trek. Roman understood that, but he didn't like that Hannah had joined her brother. Watching her walk out of camp and his life eviscerated him. There was so much he hadn't said, so many unresolved feelings.

His knees throbbed from kneeling for hours on the hard ground without a break. The muscles in his arm burned, and his wrist ached. Rubbing his muddy hands on his pants, he resumed scraping layers of earth, digging deeper into the past with each centimeter.

As he dug, the soil transitioned from the O horizon of decomposing grass and leaves, to the A horizon of topsoil, and the thin eluviated layer beneath. The dark subsoil stratum of clay mixed with flakes of charcoal and charred bone fragments was the level where any artifacts deposited more than two hundred seventy years ago would be found.

His gaze zeroed in on an obsidian chip jutting out of the clay. Obsidian didn't naturally occur in the area. The Dakelh had traded furs and salmon with Indigenous groups from the northwest for the deep-black translucent volcanic rock. Because of its glassy hardness, obsidian was used to fashion arrowheads and knife blades.

He rifled through his kit bag and retrieved a fine dental pick, and then he scraped soil, a millimeter at a time, from around the chip, revealing the top half of a large knife. He leaned closer, admiring the striations created by a long-ago skilled artisan.

"Roman, I need a word."

He didn't remove his gaze from the stunning obsidian blade. "I'm busy, Grandfather. Can we talk later?"

"This is important."

Something in the old man's voice made Roman's

heart skitter, and he dropped the dental pick and stood.

Nathaniel's face was pale, the lines carved deep into his leathery skin.

"What is it?"

His mouth tightened. "Our intruder's still here."

Chapter 39

Roman stilled, and his mind blanked.

Our intruder's still here.

His grandfather's words blazed like an edict from Hell. "Show me."

Nathaniel turned and trudged through the long wet summer grass.

Roman followed, a thousand thoughts swirling in his brain. Was it possible? Was Derek still at Keyoh? Had he tricked them into thinking he'd left? Was the jerk that devious?

Shas barked and raced ahead.

They passed through a dense stand of giant cottonwood trees to the grassy bank overlooking the creek.

Nathaniel clambered down the sandy bank like a mountain goat, even though Roman knew the old man suffered from arthritis.

Roman slid down the bank to the gravel shore. The motorboats lay half-submerged in the water, their engines smashed and useless. The once-beautiful cedar-strip canoe lay on the rocks, gaping holes gashed in its hull. A flash of rage roared through him like a wildfire, and he tightened his hands into fists as he studied Derek's handiwork.

"Over here, Roman."

He shook off his anger and strode to Nathaniel.

His grandfather was crouched over a soot-blackened ring of rocks. A pile of coals and partially burned chunks of wood marked the remains of a campfire. Lying amidst the ashes was a half-melted plastic bag. A label was visible through the blackened soot, almost as if someone had displayed the package.

Another blast of anger rushed through his veins as he recognized the packaging. Someone—probably Derek—had found Roman's stash of chamomile tea and burned the package and tea leaves in the fire.

He gripped his hands until his they ached, fighting for control. "This may not mean what we think. Hannah and Peter's canoe's gone, and we haven't seen any sign of Derek in the past twenty-four hours. He's probably paddling down the river to Fort Cutter like we thought." But he knew he was blowing air. He didn't believe what he was saying any more than Nathaniel did.

Nathaniel jerked his thumb at the campfire ring. "The coals are still warm. And that's your special tea, isn't it? That stuff you get shipped in from Egypt?"

Unable to stand still a second longer, Roman stomped down the shoreline, kicking rocks out of his way, fighting to think through the storm raging in his brain. Derek had stolen his tea and burned the package where he knew the fire and remains of the tea packaging would be discovered. He was thumbing his nose at Roman, letting him know he was still there and still a threat.

Shas, his tail wagging, galloped ahead, sniffing bushes and boulders. He stopped, his body stiffened, and he barked and pawed at a haphazard stack of fir branches and river rocks.

The bark cut through Roman's fury. Something in

that pile of brush had caught Shas's attention. An animal den? Maybe an otter? Roman crossed the creek bed. Please don't let it be a skunk. Not now. Not when there was so much to consider.

Shas barked again and dug at the stack of branches.

A flash of orange glimmered beneath the tangled heap.

Roman ripped off the branches and tossed them aside, revealing the brilliant orange of a life vest. Blood pounded in his ears, and his chest tightened. Another life jacket, this one yellow, lay buried beneath a pile of shrubbery a meter away. Partially hidden beneath the life vest were two wooden canoe paddles.

Nathaniel hurried along the bank, scattering pebbles with each step. He stopped and stared at Roman's discovery. "Life jackets? And paddles? What are they doing here?"

"They're from Hannah and Peter's canoe."

"Are you sure?"

Roman nodded. "Peter told me he borrowed the canoe and gear for his trip to Keyoh from a friend." He pointed at a name written in black ink on the orange lifejacket. "That's his friend's name."

The lines in Nathaniel's weathered face deepened. "Derek did this. That's obvious, but why? What's his plan?"

Roman gritted his teeth. Hard. "He wanted us to find this. Just like he wanted us to find the campfire."

"Why would he want that? Once we found the canoe gear and remains of the fire, we'd know he didn't leave in the canoe. We'd know he's still here."

Roman kicked a branch, sending it sailing. "The jerk's toying with us. He planned the campfire scene and knew we'd find the lifejackets and paddles. It's all a cruel game." The shocking implications of the discoveries settled over him like a suffocating weight. There was only one reason for Derek's subterfuge. "I'm going to kill that jerk when I find him."

Fury raged through him like a category-five hurricane, overshadowed by the foul taste of self-disgust filling his mouth. He should have listened to his gut and kept up the watches, but he was more concerned about his reputation and the success of the project than Hannah's safety. He wanted to go back in time and do things differently. Maybe if he'd been more vigilant from the first day, Derek wouldn't have been able to sneak into the site and wreak fear and havoc.

There were many things he should've done better, but wallowing in regret and self-pity wouldn't help. Right now, his focus was Hannah. Unaware of the danger, she and Peter were out there in the wilderness alone without any weapons other than a can of bear spray and a bear banger.

"That man's evil. He won't stop until he punishes Hannah for rejecting him. And you too." Nathaniel's penetrating gaze drilled into Roman.

"Me?"

"He sees the attraction between you and Hannah and—"

Roman was shaking his head before Nathaniel finished, but his grandfather cut off his protests.

"No, Roman. Now's not the time to deny your feelings. Hannah's in danger. You are as well." His gaze bore into Roman with a fervent intensity. "Derek has shown he'll stop at nothing to destroy you and your career. Find her and Peter and warn them, but be wary of a trap."

As if voicing his agreement, Shas barked.

Roman's mind buzzed, a thousand thoughts fighting for attention—what he should do, what he shouldn't do… Impossible to think through the maelstrom. He inhaled to the count of four, held the breath for seven beats, exhaled for eight.

Again.

And again. Until the rage and fear abated, and his mind cleared.

Derek had followed Peter and Hannah. That was a certainty. His grandfather was right. Derek wouldn't stop until he made Hannah pay. The bastard had already shown he was prepared to do anything, commit any crime, to achieve his evil goal. Would frightening her be enough? Or were his intentions more sinister?

A shudder rippled along Roman's spine, and the hairs on the back of his neck prickled. He couldn't…*wouldn't* let anything happen. He loved her. Damn right he did. He raced for the bank, calling over his shoulder, "Keep Shas here. I'm going to find them."

He tore up the hill and sprinted across the meadow. His chest was heaving when he burst into camp.

"What's going on, Roman?" Sam asked. He was chopping green peppers and onions as he prepared supper.

Roman didn't answer as he flew past him to his tent. Shoving the flap aside, he rushed inside and scrabbled under the wooden work bench and grabbed the shotgun. He rummaged in a plastic tub and withdrew a box of bullets.

He wasn't a hunter, but Nathaniel had taught him how to use a shotgun when he was a boy. He'd brought the old short-barrel pump-action shotgun to Keyoh in case bear spray didn't work, and he had to shoot a marauding bear. Now the gun would be used against a far more vicious predator.

Cracking open the shotgun, he used his thumb to push in the shell until he heard a click. He stuffed in two more bullets until the magazine was full. Depressing the release button, he pumped the slide backward and forward and loaded the chamber.

All set.

He grabbed a headlamp and a bottle of water, but he didn't bother packing food. He wasn't planning on stopping to eat or rest until he found Hannah and her brother. They'd left hours ago, but with all the dead pine trees clogging the trail, their progress would've been slow. They'd stop for the night somewhere. If he ran fast and pushed hard, he could catch up with them.

He burst out of the tent and took off in a sprint, ignoring the curious looks of the students. He didn't have time to explain. Nathaniel would tell them what was going on. With the shotgun resting on his shoulder, he burst into the forest at a run, shoving aside branches and leaping over downed trees.

One thought blazed through his brain on constant repeat—find her before Derek did.

Find her.

Chapter 40

Hannah helped Peter take down the tent. The rain had stopped, but gray ominous clouds hung low over the forested hills. A chill hung in the air, and she shivered. She fished in her day pack and grabbed two granola bars and handed Peter one. "Eat up."

"What? No scrambled eggs and bacon?" He thrust out his bottom lip in a fake pout. "What sort of camp cook are you?"

"The sort who wants to get moving before she freezes to death." She opened the package and nibbled on the bar. The rich taste of chocolate and peanut butter filled her mouth. "These aren't bad."

"I know, right? You get used to them. I live on them when I'm working on a project." He finished his breakfast and stuffed the tent and their sleeping bags into his backpack. "Ready to go?"

"Do you think we'll find someone to help us today?" She lifted her pack and settled it over her shoulders.

"According to Nathaniel's map, we should come across a logging road in about three kilometers. With luck, a logging operation will be working in the area."

"I hope so." She swallowed the last bite of her granola bar and shoved the wrapper into her pocket. "I don't know how much more I can take. Yesterday was brutal."

He hefted his backpack over his shoulders and

clipped the chest strap. "Don't worry. We'll find help. I know we will."

A smile tugged at the corners of her mouth. He was always so optimistic. At least, he had been until his split with Marissa. "Let's get started. What's that old Chinese saying? The longest journey begins with a single step."

He studied the GPS and pointed west. "There's the trail. Come on. Let's take that first step." He crossed the clearing, shoved raspberry and thorny wild rose bushes aside, and penetrated the forest.

Three meters in, they encountered the first dead tree blocking the trail.

She clambered over the trunk, snapping off pointy stubs of branches that threatened to poke out her eyes. Ahead lay more downed trees, jumbled together in a twisted nightmare. She fought her way through that mess and the next one and the one after that in an unending obstacle course. She couldn't see her feet, let alone the furrowed depression in the ground that was the Duje Ti. Sweat beaded her forehead and dampened her shirt, but she slogged on, setting one foot in front of the other.

The trail wound through a valley and climbed a steep hill to a ridge. Her lungs burned, and she was out of breath by the time she reached the top. She paused and studied the view. A river sparkled in the distance as it flowed through the canyon below. The sun peeked out of the clouds and lit the forested hills in a soft golden light.

Peter dropped his pack onto the ground and tugged out the map. Opening the crinkled paper, he held the map out and pointed at a thin blue line and then at the river below. "That's the Parsko River."

She tapped the map, and her heart sank. "Is that where we stayed last night?"

He nodded. "We haven't made much progress this morning."

Rubbing the scratches on her arms and face from her too-close encounters with sharp branches, she pointed to the trail ahead. "It doesn't look like there are as many dead pine trees ahead. We should be able to move quicker."

"I hope so." He peered at the map again. "The trail follows this ridge for a bit and then we descend to Maddow Lake. That's where we should find the forestry campsite and the logging road Nathaniel mentioned." Grunting with the effort, he lifted his pack and settled it on his back. "Okay. Let's get this done."

"I have to—" She gestured to the trees. "—use the ladies' room. Don't wait for me. I'll catch up."

"Okay." He set off at a slow pace.

She fought through a tangle of willows and slid down her pants and crouched behind a tree. A mosquito buzzed her ear, and she swatted the pesky insect before it could land and bite. She already had red itchy bumps all over her exposed skin from the swarms of mosquitoes and biting black flies. The bugs hadn't been as bad the previous day, probably because of the constant drizzle, but with the drier weather and the sun coming out, the hungry insects had returned in full force.

She stood, yanked up her pants, and fastened the snap at the waist. Digging in her pack, she drew out a wet wipe and rubbed her hands. She slipped the used wipe into her pocket and shoved her way through the brush to the trail.

She froze at a furtive scuttling sound. Her stomach tightened, and she studied the surrounding forest.

The branches of a thimbleberry bush ten meters

distant rustled, and a rabbit burst across the ground and disappeared into the dense undergrowth.

She released the breath she'd been holding and turned back to the trail.

The crunch of footsteps on pine needles sounded somewhere in the forest behind.

She stopped.

The crunching stopped.

She stood still and listened. Slipping the can of bear spray from the holster belted around her waist, she flipped off the safety guard.

Another crunch, this time light and furtive, as if the maker of the noise was trying to be quiet.

The fine hairs on her arms rose, and she wheeled around and fled along the trail. Puffing, she caught up to Peter. Relief washed over her, and she slowed her steps.

A line furrowed between his dark-blond brows. "What's wrong?"

"Nothing." But she couldn't help casting a look over her shoulder.

"Nothing, huh?" He nodded at the bear spray clenched in her hand. "So, why's that out? Did you see a bear?"

"I…I thought I heard something." She pasted a smile on her face. "But it was probably just another rabbit. Let's keep going."

His gaze fixed on her, his blue eyes delving deep. "Okay." He scanned the forest and turned and led the way along the ridge.

She stayed close and kept the bear spray handy. Her back prickled with the unsettling sensation they were being watched, the same feeling she'd had at Keyoh. She checked the trail behind so often, she stumbled over exposed roots and rocks.

The trail wound down the hill at an angle through a dense grove of aspens. At the bottom of the hill, they passed a pretty marsh rimmed by cattails and reeds. The clouds had vanished, and the sun shone from a brilliant blue sky.

Dragonflies swooped and darted, their iridescent-blue bodies flashing. Ducks quacked and flapped across the water of the still pond, unhappy at the human intrusion. Red-winged blackbirds flitted amid the bullrushes, their musical trills adding to the melody of the wetland.

She paused to admire the serenity of the beautiful marsh, but swarms of biting insects attacked, and, swatting and slapping her arms, she hurried her steps.

The trail followed a narrow winding creek that flowed out of the marsh. Her feet ached, and she was tired and hungry. How much further until they reached the logging road? Even then, there was no guarantee they'd encounter anyone, but walking on a road would be easier than fighting their way through the impenetrable forest.

"Yes!"

Peter's excited shout broke through her thoughts. She tightened her grip on the bear spray and hurried to catch up.

"We made it." He pointed through the stand of trees. "That's the forestry campsite indicated on the map. Come on." He skipped ahead.

Breaking through the trees, she entered a grassy clearing fronting a small lake with a narrow gravel beach.

Maddow Lake.

A wooden picnic table painted dark brown was set in the center of the clearing. Nearby, a metal fire ring enclosed burned chunks of wood and gray coals. A haphazard stack of firewood lay scattered beside the fire pit. A well-trodden trail led into the trees to an outhouse.

A wide grin wreathed Peter's bearded face. "We did it!" He held up his hand and high-fived her. Shrugging off his pack, he tossed it on the picnic table.

"That must be the logging road." She gestured toward a rutted one-lane gravel road that led from the rustic campsite. Excitement bubbled in her stomach. Her exhaustion and the aches and pains vanished.

He held out a plastic water bottle. "Drink up, and then let's have something to eat. I'm starving."

She smiled what felt like her first real smile in days. "Sure. I have more granola bars."

He recoiled, his face a rictus of disgust. "That's what I was afraid of."

Grabbing a handful of bars out of the pack, she handed him two and settled onto the picnic table bench seat. "How long do you think we'll have to wait until someone drives by?"

He chewed a mouthful and swallowed. "No idea, but this site looks like it's well used." He pointed at a crushed beer can lying on the ground. Old bottle caps and broken glass littered the worn grass. A partially melted aluminum beer can was half buried in the mound of gray ash in the fire pit.

Nibbling on her bar, she rested against the tabletop.

A loon's haunting cry echoed from somewhere out on the lake.

Overhead, an osprey soared on the afternoon air currents.

The scenery was serene and beautiful, but she couldn't shake off her apprehension.

Swatting at a fly, she bit off another mouthful of granola bar. Her thoughts, as they had a zillion times over the past hours, returned to Roman. What was he doing at that moment? Was he waist-deep in an excavation pit, scraping layers of soil? Or was he working in his tent, focused on paperwork?

Did he miss her? She grimaced. As if. He was probably relieved she'd left. She couldn't blame him. She'd brought nothing but trouble. Because of her, the Chinese coin was missing, and the crew was left without any way to communicate with the outside world.

To top it off, she'd rejected him. She hadn't meant to be cruel, but her bruised pride took over, and the next thing she knew, she was attacking him. She couldn't take back her words, but she could apologize. When? She probably wouldn't see him again.

She swallowed the last bite of her bar. Maybe a vehicle would show up soon, and they'd be able to contact the authorities. That would redeem her in Roman's eyes. Maybe.

"Want one?" Peter held out a chocolate bar.

"Where'd you get that?"

He grinned, looking like the young boy she remembered. "My secret stash."

"You've been holding out on me." She accepted the chocolate-covered wafer bar…her favorite. Why was she surprised? He probably had a bottle of rum hidden in his backpack. *Just in case*. That was her brother's motto.

"I've been saving these for a celebration." Unwrapping his own bar, he stuffed half of it in his mouth.

"Let's hold off on the celebrations until a vehicle shows up." She finished her bar, savoring the creamy milk chocolate, and stood.

A rustling sound.

She stiffened.

A pine branch creaked and swayed as if moved by a strong breeze. But there wasn't a wind. The surface of the lake was smooth and unruffled.

"What's wrong?" Peter's voice cut through her focus.

She motioned him to be quiet and studied the tree line. Nothing moved. No other branches shifted, but she couldn't shake the certainty that someone was there, watching.

"Hannah? What's going on? You're shaking." Peter's voice was hushed. "Did you see something?"

She shook her head. "I don't know. I-I thought I heard something." She pointed to the dense stand of trees. "In the forest."

He followed her gaze. "I don't see anything. It was probably a squirrel or rabbit. Do you want me to check?"

Yes. Please. But she didn't say that, didn't want her brother to worry. "No, it's okay. It was probably nothing."

"I know you, Stick. You won't relax until I check. Wait here." He opened the flap of the bear spray holster on his belt and crossed the small clearing and headed into the trees.

She wrapped her arms across her chest and waited, her breath held.

Time slowed. Where was he? What was taking so long?

Peter strolled out of the bush. "All clear. I didn't see

anything."

Her breath rushed out.

He patted her arm. "I know you're nervous, but Derek's long gone. We don't have to worry about him. Not anymore. Okay?"

His earnest gaze met hers and she nodded. He was right. There was nothing to fear. Derek was paddling down the Sturgeon River. "I guess I'm on edge. Thanks for looking though." She forced a smile. "I'm going to the outhouse, and then we should get moving. If we walk down the road toward Verity, we might find someone who can help."

"Sure thing, Sis."

Her legs had stiffened from sitting, and her muscles throbbed as she followed the trail to the tiny outhouse.

Painted a dark green, the cement-sided building topped with a clear corrugated plastic roof blended into the forest. An outline of a half-moon was cut into the wooden door.

She stepped inside, closed the door, and wrinkled her nose. A plastic air freshener was stuck to the cement wall, but it didn't mask the unpleasant odor.

Light filtered through the transparent plastic roof. Pine needles and leaf litter were scattered across the wooden floor, and scorch marks from cigarettes scarred the white plastic toilet seat. A spiderweb hung in a corner by the ceiling, its sticky filaments dotted with silk-wrapped dead flies.

Nice.

Undoing her pants, she perched on the toilet seat. When she was finished, she stood and pulled her pants over her hips. Grabbing the bottle of hand sanitizer from the narrow bench, she squirted a few drops into her palm and rubbed her hands.

A loud boom thundered, followed by a piercing crack that shook the outhouse.

She screamed and dropped to her knees, crouching, her hands covering her head.

A chunk of the cement wall crumbled and fell to the floor.

Another explosion. And another.

The noise was deafening. Her ears rang, and she slammed her hands over them.

More pieces of concrete broke away.

Her heart pounded, threatening to burst through her ribcage. Terror iced her veins.

Someone was shooting at the outhouse!

Chapter 41

A loud explosion followed by a woman's scream rent the air.

Hannah!

Roman's breath caught in his throat.

Another cracking boom.

His heart leaped into his throat, and he took off, sprinting through the woods, his fear intensifying with each ear-piercing blast. He swung around a large root ball and stumbled over a beaver-chewed stump hidden in a clump of Oregon grape shrubs, landing hard on a half-buried rock.

Agony stabbed through his right knee. Ignoring the painful throbbing, he sprang to his feet and raced on, shoving aside fir branches, and thrusting through tangles of willows and brambles.

Another shot fractured the air, echoing off the surrounding hills.

He was too late! Derek had found Peter and Hannah. Sweat beaded his brow and soaked his shirt. He uttered a fervent prayer that they were still alive and uninjured.

A branch snapped, followed by loud rustling as something or someone crashed through the forest.

He froze, his chest heaving, his heart thudding like the bass at a heavy metal rock concert.

Scuffling footsteps on the forest floor. The snap of a twig, the rattle of dislodged rocks, the swish of bushes.

No forest animal would be that noisy, no matter how panicked.

A human, then, and he or she was running in his direction.

Pursuer or pursued?

He slid behind a tree trunk, gripped the shotgun, and flicked off the safety catch.

Peter burst through the bush, stumbled over a root, and crashed to the ground.

Roman reset the safety, leaned the gun against a tree trunk, and hurried to help his friend to his feet. "What's going on? Where's Hannah? Who's shooting? Is it Derek?" The questions spewed, one after the other, as if fired from a machine gun.

Peter's eyes were wild, his hair a tangled mess. "Roman! Thank God." He grabbed the other man's shirt in his hands, and his hot breath blasted Roman's face. "We have to help her. We have to save my sister."

"Where is she?"

"She went to the outhouse, and then the shooting started. I-I tried to get to her, but I—"

Roman pried Peter's fingers free of his shirt and gripped him by the shoulders. "Okay. Calm down. Where were you running to?"

Peter's Adam's apple bobbed in his throat. "I-I don't know. I thought if I could work my way around to the far side of the campsite, I could reach the outhouse without the shooter seeing me, but—"

"I need you to get help." Roman pointed to the east. "Head in that direction. You should find a homestead not too far from here. I passed it on my way."

Peter shook his head. "I'm not leaving Hannah. I won't."

Roman gripped his shoulders and shook him, forcing him to meet his gaze. "Listen to me. You're not armed. The best thing you can do for your sister is find help." He released his hold. "I'll get her."

Peter didn't move. "I-I can't leave." Tears streamed down his bearded cheeks. "She needs my help. Together, we—"

Roman cut him off. "There's no *we*. *You're* going for help." He hefted the gun. "I'll find Hannah."

The distraught man still didn't move, indecision written across his bearded face.

"Go. Now. Find help." Roman pointed into the woods. "That's how you're going to help your sister."

Peter's blue eyes, so like those of his sister's, welled with tears. "Please. Save her."

"I promise." He winced. There he was again, making promises. But this was one he vowed to keep.

No matter what.

Peter nodded and raced off, vanishing into the thick stand of trees.

****

A blast rocked the outhouse, and she cowered on the floor and bit back a scream. The wall cracked, and another piece of cement crumbled and fell. Dust filled the air. Her breath rushed in and out, and spots flickered before her eyes.

The ear-splitting noise and all-consuming terror made it impossible to think. Peter was out there in the open. She had to find him, and together they'd run for help. But how was she planning to do that? Should she call out and let whoever was shooting know someone was in the outhouse?

Who was she kidding? The shooter—it had to be

Derek—knew she was there. He must have followed her and Peter and waited until she was alone to take his revenge.

It was only a matter of time before one of his shots struck her, or he charged the outhouse. She couldn't stay where she was. She had to escape.

Sweat beaded her brow and dampened her shirt. Every cell in her body urged her to flee, but a tiny part of her brain was operating and cautioned against bursting through the door and running into the woods where she'd be an easy target. The bullets couldn't pierce the five-centimeter-thick cement walls. She was safe for the moment. But she had to clear her mind of everything but the necessity of escape. She prayed Peter had managed to get away, and he wasn't attempting a rescue. Bad enough her life was in danger, she couldn't bear if her brother was wounded…or worse.

This mess was her fault. Her hand trembled as she wiped cement dust from her eyes. Derek had tricked them. He'd let them think he'd taken the canoe and left Keyoh, but he'd hidden near the camp and waited until she and Peter left and then followed them.

Why was he shooting? Did he want to kill her? Was that his plan all along? Disabling fear stole over her like a smothering blanket, and her mind went blank. She sagged against the reeking toilet and hung her head. Tears filled her eyes and slid down her cheeks, dripping in wet splotches onto her shirt.

Another bullet smashed into the tiny building, and she jammed her fist in her mouth to smother a scream. Time was running out. She had to get out of there. The impacts of the bullets were centered on one wall of the outhouse. Derek had to be standing in the forest near the road. That was the opposite side from the outhouse door. If she raced out the door and sprinted for the trees, would she make it before the sniper figured out what she was doing and took aim?

Maybe.

A big maybe, but she couldn't sit there waiting to die.

She crawled to the door, pushed it open a tiny bit, and peeked out. The afternoon sun shone on the trees and surrounding forest.

Nothing. No dark shadow lurking in the forest.

Inhaling a fortifying breath, she rose to her feet and edged the door open a little more.

Still no sign of the shooter.

She opened the door another ten centimeters and burst through the opening. Crouching and swerving, she raced for the trees. Her body tensed, a painful tickle of panic on her back as if Derek was rubbing the muzzle of his rifle along her spine.

Six meters to the dense stand of trees…four meters…

She pumped her arms and legs, willing herself to safety.

Faster! The command blasted through her.

Almost there.

Another two meters.

Now!

She dove into the dense bush, ignoring the sting of nettles abrading the exposed skin on her arms and face. Landing on her knees with a bone-jarring thud, she was up in a flash, running even before her mind ordered her body to move.

A tree trunk, less than a meter away, exploded in a

shower of splintered wood.

She screamed and ducked, covering her head with her hands, but she ran on, too terrified to stop, to breathe, to think of anything other than her immediate survival. Her lungs hurt, and the muscles in her legs burned, but still she ran, dodging thick fir branches and leaping over rocks and fallen logs.

She raced through the forest, praying the shadowy depths hid her progress. Dodging a haystack of fallen trees, she caught her foot on a root. She yelped and stumbled, losing her footing.

A hand grabbed her arm, stopping her fall, and she was hauled against a muscular male chest.

Chapter 42

An intense wave of relief washed through Roman, and he grabbed Hannah's arm, halting her mad rush. Pressing her to his side, he slipped the palm of his hand over her mouth, silencing her scream.

She punched and kicked, fighting to break free.

"Shhh. It's okay." He tightened his hold and grunted in pain when her booted foot struck his shin. "It's me. Roman."

She stopped struggling.

He removed his hand.

Her chest heaved, her warm breath gusting his face. "Roman? How—"

"Don't talk. We have to be quiet, or he'll hear us." He fought to gentle his voice despite the adrenaline pulsing through him. "Do you understand?"

Her chin trembled, and tears pooled in her eyes, but she nodded.

"Good girl." He stepped back and scanned her body. Thank the Lord she was uninjured. "Let's keep moving." He gestured for her to follow, and holding her hand in his, he led her deeper into the forest. They pushed through the tangle of trees, careful not to step on dry branches or dislodge rocks.

The forest was hushed, the wind still, the animal inhabitants hunkered down. Even the relentless mosquitoes had vanished.

"Wait." Hannah pulled to a stop. "Peter's back at the campsite. He's in danger. I can't leave him."

"Peter's okay. Now, come on." They didn't have time to chat. Derek could show up at any second. Explanations could come later when she was safe.

"How do you know he's okay?"

"I saw him." He tugged her hand. "Look, we have to move. We need to find somewhere to hide."

"I'm not going anywhere." She jerked her hand free. "Not until I know Peter's safe."

He huffed out a breath. "I found Peter in the forest."

"Is he okay?"

"He's fine. He's gone for help." He held up the shotgun. "I persuaded him to let me handle Derek." He made it sound simple, but convincing Peter to leave his sister hadn't been easy. If Roman hadn't stopped him, the fool would have rushed back into the campsite and attacked Derek with only his bare hands for weapons. No question how that action-hero move would have turned out.

He grasped her hand again. "We can't stay here. Let's go." Relief surged through him when she didn't pull away and ran with him.

They'd only covered fifty meters when she halted again. "Did you see the shooter? Is it Derek?"

He gritted his jaw. At any second a bullet could strike its target, but the stubborn set of her chin told him she wouldn't budge until he answered. "Nathaniel found the remains of a recent campfire. Your lifejackets and canoe paddles were buried nearby. Derek hid them, so we'd think he stole the canoe and left Keyoh."

Her eyes widened, but she still refused to move. "Why are you here? Why did you come?"

"I figured Derek wasn't finished with you, and I followed. I had to warn you."

Her lower lip trembled, and she blinked back tears. "Thank you. I don't know what I would've done if you hadn't found me."

The terror in her blue eyes unmanned him, and it was all he could do not to take her in his arms and tell her everything would be okay, and there was nothing to be afraid of. But this wasn't a movie. The danger was real. The man after her would stop at nothing to get what he wanted. And right now, the jerk wanted her dead, and—

A quiet rustling sounded in a thick stand of trees to his right.

His body stiffened, and he released her hand and gestured for her to hide behind a tree trunk. He waited until she ducked out of sight, and then he widened his stance, feet apart, body braced, and lodged the gun butt against his shoulder. Sighting along the top of the barrel, he adjusted his grip. His finger brushed the trigger. He breathed in, holding steady, and waited.

More rustling.

The shuffle of furtive footsteps.

The pounding of his heart was so loud he feared their pursuer would hear. Sweat dampened his shirt and trickled into his eyes. The sensation that Derek was close was overwhelming, and it was all he could do to remain motionless.

A tree branch creaked, but there wasn't a breeze.

Another quiet shuffle further away. A branch swished and then silence.

He waited another ten minutes. Ten minutes that lasted an eternity. Finally, he lowered the gun. Derek had moved on. He hoped. Unless he was lying low and waiting for them to show themselves.

They couldn't stand there forever. They had to find shelter. He crept through the bush and slipped behind the giant fir.

Hannah was sitting on the ground, her back pressed against the base of the tree, her eyes closed and her knees drawn up, resting her head on her knees.

He crouched before her. "I think he's gone."

She opened her eyes. "Thank God you're safe. I-I was so worried."

He helped her stand. "I know you're scared, but I promise I'll get you out of here. Okay?" She'd told him back at Keyoh she didn't trust him. Would she trust him now when her life was at stake?

She studied him, her blue-eyed gaze penetrating deep into his soul. After what seemed an eon, she nodded. "I know you will."

He wanted to kiss her. It didn't make sense. A dangerous lunatic was after them, and he was fantasizing about tasting her sweet lips. He'd lost his mind. But... Before he could stop himself, he leaned closer and planted a kiss on her mouth. Heat shot through him like a bolt of lightning.

Her lips softened beneath his, and he ached to take the kiss deeper, but an iota of sanity remained, and he jerked back. "We need to get going."

She nodded and tucked her hand into his. "Let's find a safer place."

They raced along the narrow deer trail.

His knee throbbed from his earlier fall, each step an agony, but he pushed the shooting pain out of his mind. A crazed man was chasing them, and they had to keep moving.

He'd promised Peter he'd protect Hannah. Now he had to figure out how he was planning on doing that. He wasn't familiar with the area, and he didn't know any caves they could hide in or convenient bolt-holes. There had to be somewhere they could shelter until help arrived.

For the moment, all they could do was keep moving, and pray Derek didn't find them.

Chapter 43

Hannah stumbled after him, her chest heaving, her lungs on fire. How much longer could she keep this up? She was fit and ran three times a week when she was at home, but the past days of sleeplessness and worry had taken a toll.

Roman halted so suddenly she bumped into his back. She opened her mouth to ask what was going on, but he gestured for her to be silent, and the words died on her tongue.

Indicating she should stay where she was, he released his grip on her hand and slipped into the bush.

Her heart skittered. She wasn't waiting there alone. No way. Not again. She followed, pushing through the still-moving branches, and caught up. "Where are you going?" She kept her voice at a low whisper.

He grasped her upper arms, pulling her close. "Do you trust me?"

There it was again. Trust. "I already told you I did."

"I know. I just like hearing you say it." A smile flickered across his sweat-streaked face. "Wait here while I check something out." He looked deep into her eyes. "Okay?"

She nodded.

His eyes darkened, his fingers on her arms tightened, and for a heartbeat, she thought he was going to kiss her again.

Instead, he released her, turned and shoved through a tangle of wild rose bushes, and disappeared.

She shivered. This was crunch time. She either trusted him or she didn't. Wherever he'd gone, whatever he was doing, he was doing it for her, to keep her safe. She missed his calm, reassuring presence. When he was beside her, she felt hope they'd make it out of there, that somehow, they'd survive the nightmare.

But alone…she was terrified.

Roman slipped back through the bushes and motioned for her to follow. He held a thick curtain of leaves and intertwined branches to the side, and she ducked under his arm and broke through the dense undergrowth into a small clearing surrounded by tall fir trees, their thick trunks cratered and scarred, the bases scorched black from a long-ago forest fire.

Yellow and white wildflowers dotted the vegetation under the shade of the heavy, drooping branches.

He looked pleased with himself, as if he'd discovered something exciting.

She raised her hands, palms up, and arched her brows in a *what's up* gesture. The little glade was pretty, but they were in the open. There wasn't anywhere to hide that she could see.

He pointed into the treetops.

She peered up. Branches, lots of branches. Shaking her head, she frowned.

The flicker on his lips transformed into a grin. He moved to the base of a massive Douglas fir and beckoned.

She crossed to his side.

He cupped the back of her head and directed her to look up. Way up.

Her eyes bugged and she stared. Camouflaged by branches, and hidden in the tree canopy, was a structure. "What is it?"

"A deer stand."

She wrinkled her brow.

Removing his hand from the back of her head, he tangled his fingers in her braid, the movement transforming to a gentle caress. He pointed again at the weathered slats of wood. "That's a deer stand built to conceal a hunter while he waits for a deer to wander by." He gestured at a series of rusted spikes that had been driven into the trunk of the tree. "These nails work like a ladder. We can use them to climb."

"You want to climb up there?" She shuddered. The stand was dizzyingly high in the tree. "Do you think it's safe?"

"It's our best option." He frowned. "Hell, it's our only option. Once we're up there, we'll be able to spot Derek before he sees us." He strapped the shotgun over his shoulder, gripped the tree, and stepped onto the first spike. "I'll go first, and if it's safe, you come up. Okay?"

She nodded and held her breath as he scampered up the tree with speed and agility like he climbed trees every day.

Partway up the tree, he disappeared, lost in the thick branches.

She studied the silent forest and shivered. She wanted to call, to beg him not to leave her, not even for a second. But he was right. If the deer stand was solid, they could hide up there, and they'd be able to spot Derek's approach. She knew with a visceral certainty he'd show up. In his single-minded determination to punish her, he'd gone to incredible lengths to follow her.

He wouldn't stop. Not until he was forced to.

A broken branch landed at her feet, and she craned her head back and looked up…way up.

Roman's head poked out between the branches, and he motioned with his chin toward the tree trunk.

His meaning was clear. He wanted her to climb the tree.

Yeah, right. She didn't like cramped spaces, but she really didn't like heights. Not at all. But she didn't have a choice. A madman was after her. It was either conquer her fear and climb, or stay on the ground and die.

Her stomach quivered, and her heart skipped a beat, but she grabbed onto the tree trunk, placed her foot on the rusty nail, and muttering a fervent prayer under her breath, she hefted herself up to the next spike, and the next.

Beads of sweat popped out on her brow, and she paused, drawing in ragged breaths. She didn't look down. If she saw how high she was, she'd freeze. She shifted her grip on the trunk and stepped up and onto the next nail.

"You're almost there. Grab my hand." Roman leaned over, grasped her hand, and hauled her up onto a rickety-looking wooden platform.

She leaned against him, clutching his solidness, fighting to catch her breath.

"You did it!"

His low husky voice washed over her like a soft summer breeze. She released her death grip and edged back a step. She was standing on a set of warped wooden planks built into the fork of the fir tree. The structure was secured to the tree by rusted metal spikes. She gulped. "Is this thing safe?"

He stomped his booted foot on the planks. The structure creaked and swayed. "It's old, but it's sturdy."

Biting hard on her bottom lip to stop her yelp of fear, she grabbed onto a thick hanging branch with two hands and held on. "We're pretty high up."

"I'm guessing seven meters."

A gasp escaped. "That high?"

"Look out there." He pointed over the edge of the platform. "We can see a long way."

Shaking her head, she clung to the branch. No way was she looking down or letting go. No way.

The lines on his face softened. "It's okay. You don't have to look, but this stand is our best option. Derek'll be tracking you on the ground. He won't expect you to be up here, and we have a great field of vision. We'll spot him before he comes anywhere near us."

Sitting, he laid the shotgun on the floor and rested his back against the tree trunk. He patted the space beside him. "Come on. Sit here. It's safe."

She shook her head. The branch was her security. She wasn't letting go.

"We could be up here for hours. You can't stand there forever."

She could. Oh yes, she could. "I'm not moving."

"Okay." He scratched a welt on his arm, and stretched out his legs, and crossed his feet, clasping his hands on his lap. Considering the circumstances, he looked comfortable.

Her legs wobbled, and she shuffled her feet. A drip of sweat stung her eyes, but she refused to free a hand to wipe her face. Her fingers cramped, and she shifted her grip on the branch. The small of her back ached from standing.

"Are you sure you won't sit?" One dark eyebrow arched a fraction higher. "You'll be safe. I promise." He held out his hand. "Come on. Take my hand, and I'll help you."

She stared at his hand—broad and strong, tiny black hairs sprinkling the back. "Okay."

His mouth curved in a smile. "Atta girl."

Freeing one hand from the branch, she grabbed onto his hand like she was drowning, and he was a life preserver.

"It's okay. You can let go of the branch. I have you."

Easing her grip on the branch, she took a leap of faith, and let go.

He held her tight, his hand warm and solid around hers.

She inched a step toward him. One of the planks creaked under her weight, and she froze. Her knees locked.

In the next breath, strong arms surrounded her, and she was lifted off her feet and set on her bottom on the planks beside him.

He laid his arm across her shoulders and drew her close.

The thick tree trunk wedged against her back, and her shoulder brushed his. His long muscular thigh was warm against her quivering leg. She snuggled closer, seeking the comfort and safety he offered.

Chapter 44

The nerves in Roman's arm were numb, but no way
was he moving. He liked having her close, liked the
softness of her body nestled against his, liked inhaling
her scent. The silky wisps of her golden hair caught in
his beard stubble, and despite the stress of their current
circumstances, he smiled.

They'd been sitting on the deer stand, their backs
against the rough bark of the stately fir tree, for over
three hours. He tore his gaze from keeping watch on the
forest below and studied the woman in his arms.

Her eyes were closed in sleep, her chest rising and
falling, slow and steady. Her face was pale, and dark
circles rimmed her eyes. A scratch from a too-close
encounter with a branch marred the soft skin of her
cheek. Two inflamed, red bumps from mosquito bites
spotted her graceful neck.

For the first hour, they'd sat side by side, the silence
heavy with a thousand unspoken words hanging in the
air. He wanted to reassure her everything would be okay,
but he couldn't lie. She was being stalked by a crazed
madman who was armed and determined to kill her.
Nothing Roman said, no matter how eloquent his words,
would ease her fear.

He jerked his gaze from her mesmerizing beauty and
scanned the forest. There'd been no sign of their pursuer,
but he wasn't fooled. Derek was out there somewhere in

the forest searching, stalking his prey. The bastard wouldn't give up.

Roman thanked the spirits of his Dakelh ancestors for helping him spot the deer stand. When he'd found Hannah fleeing from Derek, he didn't have a plan. He'd heard the rifle shots, and he'd panicked. One thought and one thought alone stabbed through his brain—Hannah was in danger. He had to save her. And like a hero in one of the action movies he liked to watch, he raced to the rescue to save the pretty girl. The problem was that once he found her, there wasn't a script, and he didn't have a plan for the next scene, the one where he saves the girl.

But then he spotted the deer stand, and their hopes of surviving the twisted game Derek was playing rose from near zero to a solid fifty percent. They were safe in their elevated hiding spot.

For now.

Derek wouldn't think to look up in the trees. At least, he wouldn't right away. The longer his prey remained at large, the closer he'd look. Eventually, he'd spot them.

Hopefully, Peter found help. That was their best bet of getting out of there unscathed.

Roman hated sitting like a lame duck. He ached to track Derek down and stop him before he attacked again, but when he'd suggested he go look for Derek, Hannah hung on tight, tears filling her blue eyes, and begged him to stay.

After his second attempt to leave was met with the same reaction, he gave up. He couldn't bear to witness her unbridled fear. She'd been through a lot in the past week. Being stalked by a psychopath and shot at would terrify anyone.

A raven's raucous croak broke the late-afternoon quiet.

She started, and her eyes fluttered open. "What was that?"

Their gazes met, and for a nanosecond, there was a connection, something deep and visceral that shook him to his core. "Just a raven. It's okay. Go back to sleep."

"How long was I sleeping?" She rubbed her eyes, and a shiny strand of blonde hair slipped from her braid and fell across her face.

"Not long. A couple of hours or so." His hand twitched with the desire to smooth back the curl, and let his fingers linger on her soft skin.

She sat up, and his arm dropped from around her shoulders. "Have you seen him?"

He rubbed his arm, wincing at the pins and needles as the circulation returned. "Nothing's moved down there. Not even a squirrel."

"That's good, really good." She brushed the curl behind her ear.

Darn. He'd wanted to do that. He started to speak, but the words died in his throat. The slanting golden rays of the lowering sun streamed through the branches, shining on her heart-shaped face, illuminating her upturned nose, stubborn chin, and full, pink lips.

"How soon do you think Peter'll find help?"

He snapped out of his daze. Their hopes of rescue rested on Peter's broad shoulders. *If* his friend found his way through the thick vegetation and downed trees to the remote homestead Roman had seen in the distance. *If* someone was home, and *if* that someone had access to a satellite phone or other means of communicating with the outside world, this story would have a happy ending.

The world would have to align with all the planets in the universe for that scenario to play out. But he didn't tell her any of that. Instead, he plastered a confident smile on his face. "Shouldn't be too long. Your brother's resourceful. He'll find help." He could tell by her face she didn't believe him, but she didn't call him on it.

Another heavy silence settled over them.

Birds flitted through the veil of leaves, the raven croaked again, and a branch creaked in the rising breeze.

This was his chance to come clean. Maybe the only opportunity he'd get, because once this shitstorm was over, he'd probably never see her again. Maybe if she understood the reason behind his distrust of journalists, and especially *Aspire* magazine, she'd forgive him and give him another chance.

Maybe.

His heart pounded in his chest, and the moisture in his mouth dried.

"I'm sorry." They both spoke at the same time.

Her eyes widened, and she laughed.

A strangled chuckle squeaked through his lips.

Their gazes met and locked, and then hers slid away. He cleared his throat. "You go first."

"Are you sure?"

He nodded, but the voice inside his head called him out for the coward he was.

"Okay." She fussed with her braid, drawing the thick plait through her fingers. "I'm sorry for what I said." She rubbed her hands together. "You know, yesterday at camp when we talked outside my tent?"

He nodded again. Her words were branded into his soul and replayed endlessly through his brain.

I want a man who respects what I do for a living.

And the most painful of all… *You don't trust me, and because of that I can't trust you.*

His heart skipped a beat. "Wait a minute. You're *sorry*?"

"I-I was angry and upset." Tears filmed her eyes. "I didn't mean what I said."

"You didn't?" Was this another of his fantasies? Was he dreaming? A rush of something resembling joy flooded him.

"I-I hope you'll forgive me."

Forgive her? Was she kidding? Of course he forgave her. The urge to wrap her in his arms and kiss her bowled him over, but he resisted. One of the hardest things he'd ever done. He had to come clean, and then he'd kiss her.

You bet he would.

A flicker of movement in the trees below caught his eye, and he froze, the words of contrition congealing in his mouth.

Derek, clad in army-green camouflage pants and jacket and carrying a hunting rifle, crept through the shrubs and willows, heading their way. His head was down, and his gaze was fixed on the ground, following tracks.

Their tracks.

Chapter 45

Roman's body stiffened, the muscles in his arms tightening as he reached for the shotgun.

"What—"

Shaking his head, he held his forefinger in front of his mouth, motioning her to be quiet. He pointed to the forest below.

She followed his gaze and bit back a gasp.

Derek!

Her bowels turned to liquid.

Even from her perch seven meters up in the tree, the intense concentration on his face as he skulked through the trees was evident. He looked different, and it was like she was seeing the real man for the first time.

The Derek she knew, the man she'd dated for three months, dressed in made-to-order suits, Egyptian-cotton shirts, and leather shoes buffed to a mirrored shine. His auburn hair was gelled and swept back from his high forehead, and the beard stubble on his chin was a contrived scruff. Even on weekends, he wore chinos and collared golf shirts.

The man creeping below was dressed in loose-fitting, dirt-stained camo clothes. His hair was rumpled, and his beard thick and scruffy. Dark-green rubberized boots reached his knees, and he carried a long menacing-looking rifle with a scope mounted on the top.

She tightened her lips, muting the sounds of her

breathing. Any noise would catch his attention and cause him to look up. She slid a glance at Roman.

He remained as still as a statue, his steely-eyed gaze fixed on the man below.

Derek edged closer to the deer stand, his steps slow, careful, and soundless. He kept his gaze on the ground, as if he were following something, as if—

She bit hard on her bottom lip to stop a whimper of fear escaping.

Mere hours earlier, she and Roman had walked that same deer trail.

Derek was stalking! He was hunting her, and she was his prey.

The horror struck her, and it was all she could do to stifle her scream. But she didn't make a sound, didn't move, barely inhaled or exhaled.

Derek walked under the deer stand.

Don't look up. Don't look up. The fervent prayer ran through her like a mantra.

Silence. Not a whisper of sound. The wind had calmed, and even the birds and insects were quiet.

The pounding of her heart was so loud she was terrified he'd hear.

Roman slid her a glance and laid his hand on her leg, and his warm reassuring touch eased her trembling. He switched his gaze back to the man stalking them.

The brief contact lent her the courage to remain motionless and silent as the man who wanted to kill her strode beneath their shelter.

She lost track of time. Her bottom hurt from sitting on the hard wooden planks. The mosquito bites on her arms and neck itched, begging to be scratched. A tickle started in her nose, and she closed her eyes and fought the overwhelming urge to sneeze.

The sun was sinking behind the distant hills, its rays casting long shadows across the ground, and a pale hint of orange streaked the sky.

"He's gone. We're safe for now." Roman's husky whisper broke the strained silence.

"Are you sure?"

Roman nodded. "It looked like he's retracing our tracks back to where I first found you."

Unable to sit motionless another second, she scratched her itching bug bites. Instant relief flooded her. "I hardly recognized him. I've never seen him dressed like that. And that rifle? I didn't know he had one."

"He seems to know his way around the forest. Not something you'd expect from a guy who lives in a big city." His gaze fixed on her. "That's a high-end hunting rifle he's packing. Is he a hunter?"

"I don't think so." A memory flickered. "But on our first date, he took me to a club, some sort of posh sporting venue. There were all sorts of animal heads mounted on the walls." She shuddered. "I couldn't stand the glassy eyes of the dead animals staring at me, and I guess I didn't hide my revulsion because we didn't stay long. We didn't talk about it, but we never went back."

Another memory popped into her brain. "He told me that a few years ago he and some friends went on safari in Tanzania. I remember because I've always wanted to go to Africa." She shrugged. "I assumed the trip was a photo safari, but maybe not. He knew how I felt about trophy hunting, and he never brought up the subject."

"So we can assume he knows how to use that rifle."

She digested the terrifying thought, but an even more frightening notion reared over her like a monster.

"Oh my God. When he shot the wall of the outhouse, he knew the bullets wouldn't penetrate the cement walls, didn't he? He was toying with me." She rubbed the goose bumps riddling her arms. "It was terrifying. There's nowhere to hide in an outhouse. Believe me, I tried." The last words broke on a sob.

Anger radiated off him in waves visible even in the dying light. "He wants to frighten you." His hands fisted. "That's your punishment for rejecting him."

"What did I ever see in him?" Sobs shook her body, and she covered her face with her hands. "He's a monster."

Roman wrapped his arms around her and held her close.

She burrowed into his embrace, seeking the strength and security of his muscular body. Tears streamed down her face, dampening his shirt.

His arms tightened, his heart beating in sync with hers.

The sun set behind the hills, and it was that in-between time where the sky was dusty purple, and the light was leaving the land, when her sobs finally eased, and her tears dried. She raised her head and met his gaze. "Sorry for losing it."

He smiled, his teeth a flash of white in the growing darkness. "Don't be sorry. Not ever. Not with me."

The air between them heated, charged with possibilities.

"I hope you're okay with this, because I can't wait a second longer." He lowered his head and pressed his mouth to hers.

His lips were warm and soft.

Her eyes drifted closed, and she breathed him in as

if he were the essence of life. Time stopped in a collision of senses…his taste, his smell, the rasp of his whiskered chin… Her body melted, and liquid fire filled her veins. A warm fuzziness settled over her, and she nestled her body against his. She stroked the soft skin on the back of his neck and slipped her fingers through his long silky hair.

A pleading moan slipped from her mouth, and she parted her lips, but instead of deepening the kiss like she so desperately wanted, he eased his mouth from hers.

"There's something I have to tell you."

She flinched as if he'd doused her with a pail of icy water. "Wha-what are you talking about?"

He clasped her hand and rubbed his thumb over her skin. "I don't feel right doing this when I haven't cleared the air. I need to apologize."

"For what?" *Really? The man wanted to apologize? Now?*

"I wasn't fair, and I'm sorry. I judged you before I gave you a chance." He squeezed her hand. "There's a reason I don't trust journalists. It's a long story, and I don't like to talk about it, but you deserve to know."

She licked her lips tasting him. Her body hummed from the passionate kiss, but she fought to focus. "I'm listening."

"A few years ago, after I earned my PhD, I was assigned the position of expedition chief on a major archaeological excavation on the coast. The job was a dream come true." His voice was rough with emotion. "Word leaked that we'd discovered an unusual ancient artifact, and a reporter from *Aspire* magazine requested an interview." He rubbed the back of his neck.

She waited, but the silence dragged on, and she

could see how hard this was for him. "It's okay. You don't have to tell me." She meant it. He didn't have to bare his soul. His past didn't matter. Not anymore. What mattered was the man he was today. The man he was at that moment. The man who'd kissed her so passionately. The man with whom she was falling in love.

He shook his head. "You deserve to know."

She listened as he told her the sad tale of how a priceless artifact was damaged and he was blamed. The reporter from *Aspire* wrote an exposé based more on gossip and conjecture than truth. The author broke every journalistic ethic and didn't do any fact-checking or research. As a result of that reporter's negligence, Roman's career was destroyed, his reputation shattered.

When he finished, he sat back and watched her.

Her heart bled for him. No wonder he didn't trust journalists and hated *Aspire*. "If I were to write the article on your project at Keyoh, it would be fair and honest. You know that, right?" She had to ask, had to know.

And there it was.

A chill rattled through her. The truth was in his eyes, and the way his gaze shifted. The guilty flush on his face was visible even in the last rays of the setting sun.

He didn't trust her. Not fully.

He wanted to, that was clear, but deep down he was afraid she'd betray him, and once again, he'd look the fool. He feared she'd lay the blame for the damage Derek caused, for the theft of the Chinese coin, for the early end of the project on him. His walls were up, his demons guarding them.

A deep sadness, and an even heavier sense of loss, crept over her. She tasted tears in her mouth, but she refused to break down again, and she swallowed them back. Edging away until their bodies were separated by cold night air, she drew her legs up and wrapped her arms around her knees, careful not to brush against him.

"Hannah? Please. Hear me out."

The raw anguish in his voice struck like a knife to her chest. "I think you've said enough. I don't want to talk anymore."

The branches swayed, and the deer stand creaked and groaned in a sudden gust of wind.

She bit back a scream but refused to reach for him. Whatever was between them, was over. He couldn't get over his mistrust, and she couldn't forgive him for that.

Another freezing blast of wind struck, and she shivered. Despite her determination not to cry, tears leaked from her eyes. It was going to be a long night. If she survived her heartbreak, the frigid temperature, and Derek, she was going on a trip somewhere warm where she could heal.

If she survived.

Derek was out there in the darkness, searching, hunting his prey. He'd proven his determination. He wouldn't give up.

She buried her face in her hands and let the tears flow.

Chapter 46

The night was filled with sounds—the cold wind rustling through the branches, an owl's mournful hoot, the high-pitched chirping of crickets, and a menacing low growl below, followed by a grunt as an animal snagged its prey.

Roman yawned and sagged against the rough corrugated tree trunk. He was cold, exhausted, and thirsty, but none of that discomfort compared to the ache in his heart. For the thousandth time, he slid a glance at the woman huddled beside him.

Shivers wracked her slight body, but she was asleep. Her legs had slipped to the side, and her head rested on his shoulder. That's how he knew she was sleeping. If she were awake, she'd never get that close. Over the past long unendurable hours, he'd tried to convince her to let him hold her so they could share their body heat, but she refused.

He shouldn't have kissed her. That was his first mistake. But he was weak, and he couldn't help himself. The desperate desire to taste her lips was powerful, and it was all he could think of. She'd enjoyed kissing him. Her moan of pleasure had fired his blood, and the touch of her fingers slipping through his hair left him breathless.

But then his conscience burst to life, and he stopped fantasizing about taking the kiss to a deeper level and made his second mistake—he spilled his guts.

Now she wouldn't talk to him or listen to his explanations. Hell, she wouldn't even look his way. He understood her anger, but that didn't ease his agony. Why couldn't he have told her he trusted her and knew her article would be truthful and well written, and she wouldn't throw him under the bus?

The wounds of the past ran too deep, and she'd seen through him, seen the inkling of doubt deep in his soul, and she shut him out.

He'd spent the past hours struggling to think of something he could do—an act so selfless, so perfect— she'd forgive him and all his flaws. He knifed his fingers through his tangled hair, ripping at the snarls, relishing the stabs of pain. What was the point? Happy endings only happened in the movies.

He rubbed at the chill on his bare arms. Despite the cold wind, it was a beautiful night.

The stars sparkled in the clear sky, and the moon's cold light lit the small clearing below.

How long could they stay on the stand? They didn't have food, and they'd drunk the water he'd brought. He shivered and rubbed his cold hands together. How long before hypothermia set in? If the police didn't arrive by first light, they'd be forced to leave the security of their hidden perch and seek help on their own. It was only a matter of time before Derek found them.

Roman had kept watch all night, studying the forest, searching for movement, a sound, any sign of the man hunting them. Had the creep given up and left? He had to assume help would arrive at some point, and if he stuck around, he'd be caught.

Had Peter found someone at the homestead or was

he still following the logging road searching for help? Or—Roman shuddered, not from the cold air, but from a deeper chill that settled into his bones—had Derek found Peter? He refused to consider that terrifying scenario. They hadn't heard any rifle blasts. That was a good sign.

He patted the shotgun resting across his lap. The old pump-action gun wasn't a match against Derek's high-powered hunting rifle, but it could do some serious damage. *If* he managed to get off a shot before Derek, and *if* he hit his target, and *if* the old gun didn't blow up in his face.

A hell of a lot of ifs.

His eyes drifted closed, but he jerked awake. He couldn't sleep. He had to stay alert and keep watch. He yawned and rubbed his gritty eyes. His eyelids were so heavy…

A low rumble filled the air, and he started.

The sun was peeking over the hills, the sky streaked with pinks and yellows.

Despite his best intentions, he'd slept. He shot a glance at Hannah.

She was still asleep, curled on her side on the hard plank floor, her head resting on her hands.

The rumble increased to a roar.

It was a minute before his exhausted brain started to work, but when his thought processes kicked into gear, his heart leaped.

A helicopter! Help had arrived at last.

The roar grew louder, and he nudged Hannah. "Hey, princess, time to wake up." The second the words exited his mouth, he wished he could take them back. Princess? Really? And he was—what?—the charming prince in a fairy tale? Was he supposed to kiss her awake? He

C. B. Clark

wished. If he tried something like that, she'd probably shove him off the deer stand.

She sat up, blinking and rubbing her eyes. "What's going on?"

He stood and pointed over the treetops. "I think it's an RCMP helicopter."

In the distance, a white helicopter with red, yellow, and blue stripes and a blue tail swooped low over the horizon and disappeared behind the trees. The roaring reached a high-pitched crescendo, and then the chopping *whup whup whup* faded into silence.

"He did it! Peter found help." Beaming, her eyes sparkling, she jumped up and hugged him. "I knew he would."

He hugged her back. Of course he did. He wasn't a complete fool.

But then she realized she was touching him, and she leaped back as if he'd scalded her.

His heart cracked…again.

"Come on. Let's go." She inched to the edge of the platform.

"Wait. We can't leave yet."

A frown puckered her brow. "Why not?"

"If Derek's still out there, he would've heard the chopper come in." He scratched a bug bite on his neck. "The jerk's probably waiting for us to come out into the open."

The excited gleam in her eyes dimmed, and she sank back onto the boards. "You're right. We have to be careful." She smoothed her hand over her rumpled hair. "I guess we'll hang out here awhile longer."

He winced. She made the thought of being with him sound like it was as distasteful as if she were sentenced to a life term in a prison cell with a serial killer.

That hurt. It hurt a lot.

He'd better get used to the pain. Once the police took care of Derek, Roman wouldn't see her again. Their relationship—if you could call it that—would be over. He settled back onto the platform, careful to keep to his side of the tiny stand.

"What do you think's happening?" She clasped her hands in her lap. "Will they capture Derek?"

He nodded. "Peter would've told the cops Derek's armed and dangerous, and they'd send an assault team. They'll find him." *Hopefully before he kills one of them.* The horrific thought floated through his brain, but he didn't speak the words aloud. She'd been through a lot these past days, especially the past twenty-four hours. She didn't need him telling her how perilous the situation still was.

The RCMP were the best at what they did, but Derek was devious. He'd have found a place to hide, somewhere he had an advantage while he waited to ambush an unwary cop. The guy wasn't the type to give up easily, and he wouldn't go down without a fight.

"Why haven't we heard anything?" She shifted, jiggling her foot, bouncing her legs, scratching her arm. "It's been over an hour."

"These things take time. The cops won't want to escalate the situation." He winced. He sounded like he was an expert on police procedure. The only arrests he'd witnessed were on television shows.

She chewed on her bottom lip, and once again, he focused on her mouth. It felt like a lifetime since he'd kissed her, but he remembered. Damn right he did. She'd tasted sweet like cherries in July, her mouth soft and welcoming. Just thinking of that kiss had his blood heating. And his heart breaking. He—

Three loud blasts of a horn rent the air, jolting him out of his fantasy.

"What's that?"

"I think it's a signal that it's safe for us to come out of hiding."

"Really?"

She looked at him with such hope, he wanted to hug her, but he didn't. Of course, he didn't. One rejection a day was enough. He pasted a smile on his face. "Are you ready to leave?"

She beamed. "I can't wait." Scrambling across the stand, she peered over the edge.

I can't wait.

She couldn't get away from him quick enough. Once again, her words gutted him.

"Um, Roman."

He blinked. "What is it?"

She quivered, looking sheepish. "How do we get down?"

He'd forgotten she was afraid of heights. She hadn't liked climbing up to the high perch, but she was going to hate climbing down. He'd done some rock climbing. Ascending was far easier than descending. "Let me go first, and then I'll help you."

"Th-thank you." Her voice was a thin squeak.

He edged past her and stepped onto the first spike. Gripping the tree trunk, he lowered himself to the next nail, and the next. He stopped and studied her. "Are you ready?"

Her face was pale, her eyes wide. "I-I don't know if I can do this."

"The secret's not to look down." He softened his voice and stretched out his hand. "Hold onto my hand, turn around, and step onto the first nail."

She shook her head. "I can't. I can't do it."

"I won't let you fall. Now, come on. Grab my hand."

She licked her lips, then clenched and unclenched her hands.

He waited.

Her body shook and beads of perspiration popped out on her smooth brow, but she reached for his hand.

He gripped her tight and steadied her while she set her shaking foot on the spike. "Good girl. Now, step onto the next one. Don't look down."

She inched down, one spike at a time, with him holding her hand and bracing her body with his until they reached the final nail.

He released her and jumped to the ground.

She landed beside him.

"You did it!" He high-fived her. Really? A high five? What was he—eight?

She met his gaze. "There's something I have to say, something I should've said earlier."

He nodded. "Okay." His heart sped up, and—fool that he was—hope flared.

"I—"

"Hannah!"

They turned.

Peter charged through the bush, a wide grin wreathing his bearded face.

Chapter 47

Peter hugged Hannah so tight she feared he'd crack her ribs, but she was thrilled to see him, and she ignored the pain and hugged him back. Tears streamed from her eyes, blinding her.

"Thank God you're okay, Stick." He squeezed her harder.

"Um, Peter?" She fought to draw in a breath.

"What?"

"I-I can't breathe."

"Sorry. It's just great to see you're okay." He dropped his arms and stepped back and clapped Roman on the shoulder. "You too, Roman. I can't tell you how worried I was."

Roman's smile was strained. "You did good, bro."

Using the tail of her shirt, she mopped her wet face. "Where's Derek? Is he—" She shuddered. "Did the police capture him?"

Peter wiped the back of his hand over his damp eyes. "That's a long story. I can't wait to tell you all about it, but—" He jerked his thumb over his shoulder. "—the cops want to talk to you two first."

She followed the direction of his gaze.

A man and a woman wearing dark-green uniforms, body armor, and helmets and carrying assault rifles strode into the clearing. They nodded at her and Roman.

The tall red-haired female officer spoke. "Glad you

both are okay."

Even though dark sunglasses hid her eyes, Hannah felt the weight of the woman's assessing gaze. "What about Derek? Where is he? Did you arrest him?"

"I'm Constable Teller, and—" The tall RCMP officer nodded at her partner. "—this is Constable Desaulniers. We're members of the RCMP's Emergency Response Team stationed out of Fort Cutter." She held out her hand. "I'll take the shotgun, if you don't mind. You won't be needing it anymore."

Roman handed her the gun. "I hope I can get it back. It's my grandfather's."

Constable Teller nodded. "Once the investigation's complete, you can pick it up in Fort Cutter."

"When I called for help, they told me they were sending a chopper with an ERT tactical unit," Peter said. "I couldn't believe it when the helicopter landed, and six heavily armed officers piled out. It was a scene right out of a movie."

Hannah smiled at his boyish enthusiasm. Her brother loved watching cop shows. When he was younger, before he was bitten by the anthropology bug, he'd wanted to join the RCMP. "Thank you for calling for help. I-I was so afraid that Derek—" She broke off and looked at the two constables. "Where is he? Did you find him?"

"The suspect's been apprehended, and he's in our custody," said Constable Desaulniers in a voice tinged with a French Canadian accent.

"You caught Derek? You have him?" She couldn't believe the nightmare was over, and she no longer had to live in fear.

"We have him, ma'am."

"Thank you so much."

"How did you capture him?" Roman asked. "Derek isn't the sort of guy who'd surrender."

"It was so cool," Peter said. "I waited in the helicopter while the ERT dudes did their thing, but I saw everything. These cops know how to take down a perp."

The corners of Constable Teller's mouth twitched as if she were suppressing a grin. "We like to think we know what we're doing."

Constable Desaulniers coughed into his hand. "We ran an area search grid and located the suspect hiding in a tree-root hole. We surrounded him, drew arms, and called him out. He surrendered a short time later. No shots were fired, and no one was injured."

"I saw the monster rifle Derek was packing, and the police told me about the bullet holes in the outhouse." Peter shuddered. "That creep meant business. How did you guys stay safe?"

She pointed to the deer stand high in the tree.

Peter and the two constables glanced up.

"What is that?" asked Constable Desaulniers.

"A deer stand. Hunters use them in hunting season," Roman said, his voice wooden.

Peter's eyes widened. "Are you kidding me?" His gaze settled on Hannah. "You climbed up there? You're afraid of heights."

"It's surprising what you can do when you're terrified." She touched Roman's arm and frowned when he flinched. "I couldn't have done it without Roman. He saved my life. He found the stand, and he helped me climb up and come back down." She shuddered. "Derek was hunting us like we were a couple of deer. He tracked us to below the stand, but thank God he didn't look up."

"You must have been terrified." Tears shone in Peter's blue eyes. "I-I'm sorry I left you, Stick. I didn't want to, but Roman convinced me I'd be more useful going for help."

She hugged him. "You did the right thing. If you hadn't called the police, I don't know what would have happened." But she did know. Derek would've found them. The sting of impending tears burned her eyes.

Constable Teller cleared her throat. "Your brother's a hero."

"He saved the day," said Constable Desaulniers. "He hiked three kilometers through dense forest to a cattle ranch where he called 911."

Peter's face flushed red. "It wasn't that difficult. I was lucky the Simonsons were home, and they had a satellite phone." Dark circles rimmed his eyes, and his hands and face were scratched, his hair tangled. A dark swelling of a bruise puffed his right eye. His clothes were muddy and torn, evidence of his treacherous hike through the woods.

"I'll never be able to thank you enough." Hannah shifted her gaze. "And you too, Roman. You're a hero too. If you hadn't come after us, I-I—" Her voice broke.

Their gazes met and held, and the familiar zing of awareness—as if they were the only two people in the universe—flared. But then he looked away, and the connection fizzled.

"What happens next?" Roman asked the two RCMP officers.

"We'll fly you to Fort Cutter, and you'll be debriefed."

He nodded. "My crew and my grandfather are back at Keyoh. We should let them know we're safe."

"We sent a helicopter there early this morning. They're all fine," Constable Desaulniers said. "We'll radio the chopper and tell them the good news."

"Thank you," Roman said.

"All part of the job." Constable Desaulniers nodded. "Now, let's wrap this up. Come on." He and Constable Teller led the way through the trees to the recreation site.

Hannah walked beside Peter, while Roman forged ahead, his face set in stone, the walls he'd erected almost visible.

They broke through the trees and into the clearing.

The sun was high in the sky, and dazzling sunshine lit the picnic table with a warm glow. The lake sparkled. Farther out, whitecaps whipped up by the wind crested.

Her gaze lit on the trail that led to the outhouse, and all the moisture in her mouth evaporated. Images reared over her, each one more frightening than the previous one—the terrifying boom of bullets pounding the cement wall, cowering on the floor in the foul-smelling outhouse, her overpowering panic and fear, zigzagging through the woods petrified that at any moment a bullet would smash into her spine, fleeing the monster…

"You okay, Hannah?"

Peter's voice, thick with concern, nudged her from her thoughts. She nodded, though she wasn't sure if she was okay. How could she be, after everything she'd been through? Her stalker was in custody, and she was safe. She should be elated. But she wasn't. She took one glance at Roman's closed face, and her heart clamped tight.

A helicopter sat in the middle of the campsite, its white-striped body and blue tail gleaming in the morning sunshine. Two armed RCMP officers stood by the chopper's open door.

"Hannah! There you are. I've been looking all over for you." Derek, his hands secured in handcuffs behind his back, was flanked by two armed officers as they escorted him to the waiting helicopter. "Tell them this is a mistake. Tell them you love me, and you want to be with me."

His eyes were wild, his hair a disheveled mess, his clothes filthy. He didn't look anything like the suave handsome well-dressed man she'd met three short months ago. "Hannah. I love you. You know that. I did this for you, to prove my love."

A chill of fear bubbled up her spine. Her knees wobbled, and she staggered and would have fallen if Roman hadn't caught her and steadied her. "You did this for *me*? You tried to kill me! That's not love."

As if a switch had been flicked, his eyes blazed hatred. "What? You think you're too good for me? Well, I showed you—" He glared at Roman. "—and your *boyfriend*, didn't I?" Spittle sprayed from his mouth with each vile word, and he cackled. "I had you running like a couple of scared rabbits."

She reeled back.

He nodded, as if satisfied. "This isn't over, sweetheart. I'm not finished with you. You can count on that."

Roman stepped in front of her, his hands on his hips, his face set in stone. He glared at Derek. "If you ever touch her or speak to her again, you'll answer to me. Do you hear me? Stay away from her!"

Derek's mouth opened in a rictus of a grin, and he snickered. "*You*? I'm not afraid of you. You're a loser. I was hanging around your stupid archaeological site for a week, and you didn't have a clue."

Roman's hands clenched into fists. If looks could kill, Derek would be a heap of smoldering ash. "Looks like you're the one who's the loser. You'll be spending the next ten years in a prison cell. I hope you enjoy your stay." He stepped aside and nodded at the two officers.

The ERT officers gripped Derek by the arms and frog-marched him past.

Struggling and fighting, mouthing profanities, blaming Hannah and Roman for his present circumstances, he was dragged into the belly of the helicopter.

A wave of exhaustion flooded her, leaving her drained, and she sagged.

Roman helped her to the picnic table, and she collapsed onto the hard wooden bench seat.

He sat beside her and cradled her hand between his warm strong hands. "Don't give him the pleasure of seeing you're afraid. That's what he wants. Your fear's where he gets his power."

She blinked back tears. What had she ever seen in Derek? How could she have been attracted to such a monster?

"What a jerk! I hope they throw the book at him," Peter said.

The roar of a powerful motor shook the air.

She turned.

A four-wheel drive pickup, trailing a thick cloud of dust, sped into the campsite, and skidded to a stop.

"Who's that?" Peter asked.

The driver's door flew open, and a short balding man with a ferocious scowl on his heavily lined face burst out.

Roman's face lost all color, and he surged to his feet. "What's he doing here?"

Chapter 48

"Dr. Martens!" Roman's insides quivered.

The little man stormed toward them. He kicked an empty beer can out of his way, sending it flying into the lake, where it landed with a plop. Stopping in front of Roman, he slammed his hands on his hips. His furious gaze swept Roman, Peter, and Hannah, and then settled on Constable Desaulniers. "Is everything okay here, Officer? Did you find the artifact?"

Constable Desaulniers nodded. "The suspect's in our custody, and the artifact you were concerned about has been recovered."

"I don't understand. Why are you here, Dr. Martens?" Roman rubbed his throbbing temples. How on God's green earth did Frederick Martens, chair of the archaeology department at the university, end up there? Since he'd completed his last archaeology project ten years ago, the man hadn't left his well-appointed office with the large corner window facing onto the university common and ventured into the field. It was a campus joke.

"The police called and informed me they were deploying an emergency response team to rescue you and—" He leveled his gaze on Hannah and Peter and wrinkled his nose as if he smelled something unpleasant. "—some friends from a deranged killer. You can imagine my concern. I flew to Fort Cutter, rented a truck, and drove here as fast as I could."

Constable Desaulniers cleared his throat. "We informed Dr. Martens about the situation here as part of standard protocol. His name's on the permit for the excavation at Keyoh."

"I wanted to personally ensure the Chinese coin's treated in a proper fashion and arrives at the university in one piece."

Heat flamed up Roman's neck and his face. Dr. Martens's not-so-subtle reference to the shattered bone fishhook from the disaster of the excavation that destroyed Roman's career nearly drove him to his knees.

Hannah jumped up, her blue eyes flashing. "None of what happened at Keyoh is Roman's fault."

Dr. Martens's pale eyebrows arched. "Really? Pray tell, why is that?"

"Because *I'm* the one responsible. Derek Pasternak followed me to Keyoh. He stole the coin and destroyed the crew's boats and their satellite phone. All to get back at me for rejecting him. If it weren't for me, none of those events would have happened. Roman had nothing to do with any of it."

A warm tingling filled Roman's body from the tips of his toes to the top of his head. He didn't need her to defend him, but it felt good. Darn good.

Dr. Martens sniffed. "I'm sorry for everything that happened, and of course, I'm pleased the incident was resolved without any harm coming to anyone. My priority is the integrity of the excavation at Keyoh, and the preservation of the Indigenous artifacts recovered." He turned back to Roman. "Word of this fiasco has already leaked, and the media's been calling my office asking for comments."

"That's not possible." Roman gestured at Peter and Hannah. "No one outside of these people and my crew know anything. Derek destroyed the project's satellite phone, and no one can call out."

"Well—" Martens's mouth pursed. "—someone's talked."

Roman eyed Peter and arched his brows, asking an unspoken question.

"It's not me," Peter said. "When I called for help, I only talked to the 911 operator. I didn't even tell the people whose phone I used all the details. All they know is that some guy was shooting at my friends at the forestry campsite. I didn't mention Keyoh."

Dr. Martens heaved an aggrieved sigh. "Keyoh's a sensitive project. Some of the local Indigenous elders are against the excavation. The last thing we want is the media reporting on this debacle."

Roman glanced at the heavily armed police constable who was closely following the conversation. "Constable Desaulniers, you said you recovered the coin. Is that correct?"

"Yes, the suspect had it in his possession, along with another artifact and a diamond ring."

Roman blew out a breath he hadn't realized he'd been holding. The coin was safe. That was something positive, at least.

The furious *whap, whap, whap* of an approaching helicopter filled the air.

He squinted into the clear blue sky.

A white helicopter appeared over the treetops, its rotors whirring. The roaring increased to a deafening rumble. The birch trees lining the lakeshore bent over. Leaves, pebbles, pinecones, and dust were caught up in a whirlwind as the chopper lowered onto the ground.

"Why is another helicopter landing?" Holding her unbound hair back with her hand as the helicopter rotors kicked up a wind, Hannah shouted over the noise.

"That's your transport to Fort Cutter," Constable Desaulniers said. "We didn't want you to have to fly back with the suspect."

"Thank you for your consideration." She shuddered and rubbed her arms as if she were chilled. "That would've been horrible."

The pilot shut down the engine, the rotors slowed, the backdraft died, and silence returned.

Dr. Martens removed his glasses and wiped the thick lenses with a tissue. He set the glasses back on his nose and pinned a sharp gaze on the ERT officer. "Show me the coin. Now, if you please."

The constable eyed the arrogant little man for a long minute and then nodded. "Follow me."

Martens started after the policeman, but after a few steps, he stopped and scowled back at Roman. "Aren't you coming?"

Roman shook his head. "Not yet." Derek was in custody and the danger was over, but Roman wasn't ready to say goodbye. Like Nathaniel had said—he wasn't a quitter. He'd give it one more shot. If Hannah rejected him again, his heart would be shattered, but he'd walk away. For good this time.

"I suggest you come and examine this artifact your team found." Martens's steely-eyed gaze stabbed into Roman. "For the *moment*, you're in charge of the Keyoh project. You should act like it." With those cutting words, and the implied threat hanging in the air, he marched to the helicopter where Constable Desaulniers waited.

Roman watched him go. The department head was considering firing him. He didn't blame Martens. Keyoh was Roman's project. He was the excavation director. As such, he was responsible for everything that happened on his watch. He should've suspected Derek was lurking in the woods, and he should've taken the appropriate measures to stop the maniac before the situation careened out of control.

He glanced at Hannah. She'd defended him and taken the blame, and he was grateful for her support, but it wasn't her responsibility to protect the artifacts the crew dug up. That was his job, and he'd dropped the ball.

"Roman, come on." Dr. Martens shouted from across the campsite. "Let's get going."

He was torn. He wanted—no, he needed—to stay with Hannah. But if he didn't leave with Martens, he could kiss his job goodbye. He jammed his hands into his front pockets and glanced at Hannah.

"You'd better go." She nodded in the direction of the impatient department head.

"But—"

"I'll be fine. Peter's here."

His gaze shifted to his friend.

Peter nodded. "It's okay, bro. Go with him. I'll look after Hannah."

Roman shuffled his feet, hoping…praying…she'd beg him to stay.

"Go on." Her soft voice urged. "You don't want to lose your job. Besides, the crew's counting on you. You can't let them down."

He swore he heard the crack as his heart fractured. He nodded. All right. If that's what she wanted.

He walked toward the massive truck, each plodding step feeling like he was slogging through thick mud. A desperate desire to look back, to see her one last time, fired through him, but he didn't stop. His control was hanging by a thread. If he turned and saw her, he'd race back and take her into his arms. And then where would he be? He'd already lost her. She'd made that clear. Did he want to lose the girl *and* his job?

Dr. Martens held out a small wooden case. "Here, take this, and see if you can hold onto it this time." He climbed into the truck, settled behind the wheel, and slammed the door shut.

Roman stared at the package. His fingers trembled as he lifted the lid. The copper coin, with the distinctive flower hole in the middle and the incised Chinese characters rested on a cushion of soft muslin. It was old, beautiful, and unique.

The truck horn tooted, and he tore his gaze from the coin.

Dr. Martens motioned from inside the truck, his meaning clear.

Roman rewrapped the coin and set it in the wooden box. Unable to resist, he looked back to where he'd left Hannah and Peter.

They were nowhere in sight.

The helicopter that had just arrived rumbled to life, its rotors spinning.

Hannah's pale face peeked out of the window, and she waved.

His gut clenched, but he lifted his hand and returned her gesture.

In minutes, the chopper rose from the ground and lifted into the air, arced over the clearing, and swooped away.

That was it then. It was over.

He'd hit bottom before and clawed his way out. He'd do it this time too, but it just might take him a lifetime to recover.

He patted the box, and with a heavy sigh, he headed to the passenger side of the idling pickup.

Chapter 49

Hannah twisted the key, opened the door, and stepped inside. Breathing deep, she inhaled the comforting smells of home. The apartment was musty from being closed up for the past three weeks, but there was an underlying hint of the rose shampoo and conditioner she favored and lemon furniture polish.

She shrugged off her jacket and hung it on the hook by the door. Kicking off her shoes, she shuffled in her socks to the living room and collapsed onto the couch. The muscles in her body ached, and her eyes were scratchy as if filled with sand. She couldn't remember the last time she'd slept more than a few hours.

Stretching her legs out, she laid her head on a pillow and fought back a yawn. The helicopter flight to Fort Cutter had lasted two long hours—hours with nothing to do but stare out the window at the clearcut scars hundreds of meters below and think of everything she should've said to Roman, what she had said, and what she regretted saying.

The engine noise inside the chopper was too loud for conversation, and she didn't have to listen to Peter tell her what she already knew—she'd made a mistake. The frown on his bearded face made his opinion more than clear.

Once the RCMP helicopter landed in Fort Cutter, the ERT officers escorted her and Peter to their headquarters, where they were separated and questioned for what seemed like hours. By the time the investigating officer was finished, she was drained.

She met up with Peter, and they called a rideshare to take them to the airport where they caught the last plane of the day to Vancouver. The flight was only an hour, but that gave her sixty long minutes to brood.

They separated at the Vancouver airport.

She wanted to go home, close her door, and shut out the world.

He had a meeting the following day at the university and was spending the night with friends.

She promised she'd be in touch in the morning, and they'd talk before he flew back to his project near Renton Falls.

An image of Roman standing by his boss's truck looking up at the helicopter as it rose into the sky was branded on her brain. She rubbed her eyes, fighting to dispel the guilt that flooded her when she thought of how he'd tried to explain, but she'd brushed him off. Not only that—she'd practically pushed him away.

Encouraging him to go with Dr. Martens was one of the hardest things she'd ever done. But it was the right thing to do. She'd seen the indecision in Roman's dark eyes. He wanted to stay, but if he had, the officious little man would've fired him on the spot. She refused to allow that to happen. His career was too important. Archaeology was his life.

Her cell phone rang, shattering the silence of her apartment and startling her out of her thoughts. She let the call go to voicemail.

The ringing stopped for a blessed few seconds and then started again.

And continued.

She expelled a resigned breath. The call must be important. Maybe Peter was locked out of his friend's place, or he'd been in an accident, or… She grabbed the vibrating phone off the coffee table, and without looking at the call display, she punched the answer button. "Hello?"

"Hannah! Finally. Where've you been?" Marilyn's voice blasted from the speaker. "You were supposed to have finished your research last week."

She hadn't checked her phone since the morning she and Peter had left for Keyoh. She'd planned to call the managing editor in a day or two, once she had a chance to recover and prepare herself for the difficult conversation. "Hey, Marilyn."

"Are you back in Vancouver? How'd the trip go? Was I right? Is the article a good one? Did you take lots of pictures?" Marilyn blasted one question after the other.

Hannah's tired brain shut down. "Look, Marilyn. I'm sorry, but I just returned home an hour ago, and I'm exhausted. Can we do this tomorrow?"

"I've been trying to reach you for days." Accusation was ripe in the older woman's voice.

"My research took longer than I expected, and there wasn't cell service at the site." She crossed her fingers, hoping Marilyn hadn't heard of the events at Keyoh. Hannah wasn't ready to talk about what happened. Not yet. Maybe not ever.

"What was the name of that guy you dated a while back?"

Ice cubes filled her stomach. "Why—" She swallowed. "—why are you asking?"

"The weirdest thing happened, and I thought you should know. That's why I've been trying to reach you."

Her fingers tightened on the phone, and she feared she'd crack the plastic case. "What was it? What happened?"

"A few weeks ago, I was out for dinner with friends, and I ran into that guy you're dating—"

"Derek." His name tasted sour in her mouth. "His name's Derek."

"Yes, that's the guy. Anyway, he stopped, and we chatted. He's quite charming, and he really seems to like you. He—"

"What happened?"

Marilyn laughed a nervous laugh. "I may have had a few too many glasses of wine, but he seemed sincere, and he was so concerned about you." More tinny laughter. "I let it slip you were heading out of town on assignment." The phone line filled with the sounds of distant music and laughter.

Marilyn was in a restaurant or a bar. Not a surprise. She was a talented journalist and had earned dozens of awards, but years of life in the trenches, plus too much alcohol had softened her edge. Rumor had it she was retiring soon.

"Hannah? Are you there?"

Hannah jerked out of her thoughts and focused. Marilyn had run into Derek. A coincidence? Or a planned encounter? "Did you tell Derek where I was going?"

"I did. I hope that was okay. I'm usually more discreet, but like I said, he was worried about you. He seems like such a nice young man, and I thought you would have told him. I mean, from what he said, you two are pretty serious."

She sagged back on the couch. Derek hadn't needed to follow her. He'd known she was going to Renton Falls. Once he was in the small northern town, it would've been easy for him to figure out what archaeological excavations were operating in the area. Peter had told his friend that he and his sister were going to Keyoh. People knew and people talked. They always did.

Derek could've paid someone to take him downriver by motorboat and landed at Keyoh before she and Peter arrived. He'd have had plenty of time to check out the site and set up camp in the cave.

She shuddered. He'd waited for her like a spider sitting in his web.

"Hannah? Are you listening?"

She shook off her disturbing thoughts. "Why are you telling me this now?"

"I don't know. After I got home that night, I started thinking, and something didn't feel right. Maybe it's my reporter's instincts, but I think I made a mistake. I shouldn't have told him where you were." Marilyn huffed a breath. "I called you the next morning, but you'd already left on your trip. I've been trying to reach you ever since, but I guess it was okay, because you're home now. How'd the story go? Is it ready for me?"

"I'm not going to write the article."

A heavy silence settled over the line.

"Why not?"

"There's—" She chewed on her bottom lip as she struggled to form the words. "—there's a lot you don't know. My experience at Keyoh wasn't what I expected." She smoothed back her hair and proceeded to tell her editor all the disturbing events that happened.

Her voice was raw, and she was drained by the time she finished.

"How horrible! Are you okay?" Marilyn asked.

"To be honest, I don't know."

The distinctive sound of ice cubes clinking in a glass filled the line. "I feel like this is my fault. If I hadn't told that man where you were going, none of this would have happened."

"Derek would've tracked me down somehow. He was determined to get his revenge."

"This is your story to tell, Hannah. Why won't you write it?"

There were lots of reasons she shouldn't write the article, but only one that mattered—Roman. "I don't know if I can be impartial. I'm a big part of the story."

"That's what makes it so compelling." Excitement lightened Marilyn's voice. "Don't you see? The story has everything…rejected love, theft of an invaluable artifact, mystery, and danger. Readers will eat it up. Your insight will add the secret sauce to the story, a story only you can write."

Hannah winced. For the first time, she had an insight into how Roman saw journalists. Marilyn's sole concern was magazine sales. She didn't care that people had been terrorized, or Roman's career could be ruined by the tragic events, or even that her junior journalist had been hunted like a wild animal. The story was all that mattered. She opened her mouth to inform Marilyn once again that she had no intention of writing the article, but the editor cut her off before she could speak.

"If you don't write this piece, someone else will. You know that, right? This story's hot. By tomorrow morning, every reporter in the country will be on it."

Marilyn was right. The events at Keyoh would be front-page news, even if Hannah chose not to write the story. Roman's boss had mentioned he'd already been getting calls from reporters. She'd been there and lived through the nightmare. She knew and cared about the people involved. If she wrote the article, she'd control the narrative. She could ensure Roman was treated fairly. She made a snap decision. "Okay. I'll do it."

"That's my star journalist. I'll expect the article on my desk first thing tomorrow morning."

"Tomorrow morning?" She was dead tired. "I don't think I can do that."

"Look, Hannah. This is a breaking story. It's big, and it's going to get bigger. You've always wanted to be a top-notch journalist. This is your chance. I'll expect your story in my inbox in the morning." She hung up.

Hannah dropped the phone onto her lap and shook her head. What had she agreed to?

Chapter 50

Roman stared out the office window. Rain streaked the glass, smearing the view of the red-brick building across the quad. A gloomy day to match his mood. The loud *rat-a-tat* of someone knocking on his office door startled him out of his lethargy.

He glanced at his watch, and his stomach dropped. The university ethics committee hadn't wasted any time reaching a decision. That couldn't be good.

The office chair squeaked as he shoved back from his desk and slowly stood. His legs were heavy, his steps sluggish as if he were slogging through deep snow rather than the two meters of worn carpet. Wiping his damp palms on his pants, he braced as if preparing for the firing squad. He gripped the handle and opened the door.

"Hey, buddy. How's it hanging?"

Relief swamped him. "Peter!" He extended his hand to shake Peter's, but his friend leaned in for a man hug, thumping him on the back.

"Good to see you, man."

"Come on in." Roman gestured to the sole visitor chair jammed into his cramped office. He lifted a teetering stack of books from the chair and set them on the floor. "Sit down."

Peter reached behind him and grabbed two take-out cups from a shelf in the corridor. He handed one cup to Roman and shuffled into the office and sank onto the hard metal chair.

The nutty, smoky aroma of dark-roast coffee filled the small room.

"Thanks for the coffee."

"I figured you could use it." Shoving aside loose papers and books, Peter set his cup on the scarred wooden desk. "I heard the ethics committee was meeting today."

Roman wasn't surprised. There were no secrets at the university. Gossip was the fodder that kept the place running. "I'm waiting to hear the verdict."

"That sucks, man. You don't need me to tell you that you did a great job at Keyoh." He threaded his fingers through his tangled mop of blond curls. "I don't get why Dr. Martens reported you. If you ask me, that arrogant little prick has a stick up his butt."

Roman's mouth twitched at Peter's vivid but accurate description. But he didn't laugh. He hadn't cracked a smile in forever. Now wasn't the time to start. "What are you doing here? I thought you had to get back to your project."

"I'm leaving on the evening flight, but I wanted to talk to you before I left. I heard about Sam. That was a shock." Peter slurped coffee. "Who would've thought he was working with Derek?"

Roman sucked back half the coffee, wincing at the burn as the hot liquid flowed down his throat. When an RCMP inspector had called early that morning and told Roman that Sam had been helping Derek, Roman was floored. The stalker had met Sam in Renton Falls at the Zoo. As they sat in the popular bar, he'd spun a sad tale of unrequited love and offered the archaeology student a hefty amount of cash if he helped him win back Hannah, the love of his life.

Sam's betrayal hurt. Roman had liked and trusted the student, but hiring him was a mistake. One more blunder in a long line of mistakes. "I guess you never know what someone's capable of."

"I heard that after the cops arrested him, Sam spilled everything." Peter, his eyes bright with curiosity, leaned forward. "Is it true he stole food and equipment from the crew and gave it to Derek?"

Roman nodded. Sam had done that and so much more. He'd left the note that was supposedly from Roman outside Hannah's tent. He burned the note she left for Peter, and he kept Derek informed on what Roman and the crew were planning. That was how Derek avoided being discovered for so long. A sour taste filled his mouth, and he drained the last of the coffee, and then tossed the empty cup into the overflowing trash can. When he thought of Sam and the student's lies and deceit his gut roiled.

Peter set his coffee cup on the desk. "Did Sam admit to taking my journal?"

"Nathaniel found your journal hidden in Derek's gear in the cave." Roman looked away, unable to meet his friend's gaze. He couldn't tell the man about his sister's underwear secreted in Derek's sleeping bag beside Peter's journal. He couldn't risk that Peter would tell Hannah. She didn't need the image of Derek drooling over her intimate clothing weighing her down. Shoving a stack of file folders aside, he picked up a small package wrapped in brown paper and handed it over. "I was going to mail this to you this afternoon."

Peter stared at the package and up at Roman. "Why am I getting the feeling you're not telling me everything?"

Heat flooded Roman's face. "I don't know what you're talking about."

Their gazes locked.

Peter shook his head. "Never mind. It's probably better that I don't know." He ripped off the brown wrapping, revealing a red notebook. Smoothing his hands over the faux leather cover, he frowned. "I'm glad they caught him. Sam too. I heard the kid's being charged with aiding and abetting." His lip curled in a sneer. "I hope the money Derek paid him was worth ruining his life."

Roman opened his desk drawer and fumbled through the tangle of pens, paper clips, and sticky notes, and grabbed a plastic bottle of antacids. Fighting with the childproof cap, he finally managed to pry off the lid, tipped out two bright-pink pills, and tossed them into his mouth.

"That bad, huh?" Peter nodded at the pill bottle.

"It's been a rough few weeks." He chewed the tablets, grimacing as the chalky, over-sweet paste coated his tongue. He eyed his friend. "Why are you here? You didn't come all this way to rehash gossip."

Peter grabbed the strap of his cross-shoulder leather bag and flipped open the flap. He tugged out a magazine and tossed it onto the pile of papers before Roman. "Take a look at this. Hot off the press. It's a special early edition, and it's only been out a few hours."

Roman stared at the glossy magazine with its all-too-familiar gold logo.

Aspire.

He opened his mouth to ask Peter why he'd brought the magazine, but then he saw the cover photo. His skin tingled, and his chest felt tight.

A beautiful color photograph of the Sturgeon River Rapids taken from the bluff at Keyoh filled the cover. The headline screamed, *Excavation Excitement Exceeds Expectations.*

He winced at the alliteration and glanced at Peter. "This is Hannah's article."

Even though Roman hadn't asked a question, Peter nodded. "Don't judge the story by the headline. Hannah's editor chose that." He tapped the cover. "The magazine published a special edition so they could get the story out before anyone else." He smiled, pride evident in his voice. "The article's good, really good. Hannah's already getting lots of acclaim. It's trending on social media."

Roman looked at the magazine. So, she wrote the story after all. He rubbed a sharp crushing pain in his chest. A panic attack? Or was he having a heart attack? He'd been a fool to cling to the hope she'd have second thoughts, that deep down she cared for him, and wouldn't participate in the feeding frenzy that had ensued since word leaked, thanks to Sam and the secret satellite phone he had stashed in his tent, about the terrifying events at Keyoh.

Reporters called Roman day and night and waited outside his office at the university and at his condo. He couldn't cross campus without being harassed by people shouting and begging for a statement.

"You should read the article." Peter's calm voice broke through the riot of noise filling Roman's head.

Read the article.

He stared at the headline as if he were facing down a poisonous viper. He felt like Adam when the snake tempted him with the apple. He didn't want to read what she'd written. At the same time, he wanted to. More than anything.

"I never took you for a coward."

He rubbed his hands over his face. "Okay. I'll read it."

"Good." Peter heaved himself out of his chair. "I'll leave you to it." He paused at the door. "I'll come back in an hour." The door shut behind him.

Roman stared at the closed door, looked out the rain-streaked window, and studied the glossy magazine cover. His hand trembled as he opened the cover, flipped through three pages of advertising—expensive perfumes and skin creams promising eternal youth—and stopped at the article.

Hannah's byline was beneath the title, along with a small color photograph of her smiling into the camera. He tore his gaze from her captivating blue eyes and flipped more pages. The six-page article contained photographs of Keyoh, the crew, the excavations, and the Chinese coin. There was even a picture of Nathaniel looking every inch the respected Dakelh elder.

He went back to the beginning of the article and started reading. He didn't look up until the door opened and Peter poked his head in.

"All finished?"

Roman nodded and closed the magazine. He sat back, ignoring the loud squeak as the old chair protested the movement. "Come on in."

Peter sat in the chair across from the desk. "Well, what did you think?"

"You were right. It's good."

Peter's face broke into a grin. "I figured you'd

approve. Hannah has some serious writing skills. She nailed it."

Roman smoothed his hand over the glossy magazine cover. He was still digesting what she'd written. The article was an impartial, honest portrayal of the shocking events at Keyoh and the remote forestry campsite. The story wasn't sensationalized. She'd even managed to present him in a positive light. Like Peter said, his sister was a talented writer.

Peter mumbled under his breath.

Roman gaped at the other man. "What did you say?"

"I said, you're in love with her. You are, aren't you?"

Roman's mouth dropped open and closed, and opened again, as he struggled to find the words to refute his friend's ridiculous statement.

Peter's eyes lit with a knowing gleam. "Don't try to deny it, man. The truth's written all over your face."

"You've spent too much time working in the bush. You don't know what you're talking about. She doesn't even like me. You were there. You heard her. She told me to leave." He scowled at his grinning friend, but Peter's words swirled around him like a cloud of persistent flies.

You're in love with her.

Denial pulsed through him with each beat of his heart. He didn't love her.

Did he?

Okay. Maybe he loved her a little, tiny bit.

The inner voice scoffed. Okay, okay. Maybe he loved her a lot. But what did that matter? She didn't love him.

"Whatever you say." Peter nodded agreeably. "If

you're afraid to admit the truth, it's fine with me." His grin faded, and his gaze turned solemn. "But you should know she's unhappy. Her article's going to be a great success, and she did an awesome job. Her editor couldn't be happier. She offered Hannah a promotion to senior journalist." His mouth twisted in a sad smile. "But she's so far down in the dumps she can't see daylight, and nothing I say helps."

Roman glanced out the window. Raindrops pelted the window, sounding like someone was throwing pebbles at the glass. Hannah was depressed. Maybe the weather was getting her down, or she was upset about Derek, or… There could be a hundred reasons she was despondent, none of which had to do with him. But a tiny flame of hope deep in his soul flickered to life.

"What do you want me to do?" He spread his hands on the desktop. "She told me she knew I'd never believe in her, that I'd never trust her as a journalist. I-I tried to talk to her, to explain, but I missed my chance."

"It's not too late."

His head jerked up, and he met Peter's gaze. "What?"

"You heard me. Before you head back to Keyoh to wrap up the project, go and talk to her. Be honest. Tell her how you're feeling." Peter rose, and strode to the door, dodging the stacks of books teetering on the floor. "She'll understand."

Roman stared at his friend, his mind churning with possibilities. "I'll think about it."

"Don't think too long." Peter opened the door. "One more thing. Whatever you decide to do, don't hurt her. She's my sister, and if you break her heart, you'll answer to me." He stepped through the open doorway and closed the door behind him with a decisive thud.

Roman's heart skipped a beat, and his stomach flipped over.

Talk to her.

It sounded so easy. Talk. A conversation between two people. Such a simple thing. But not for him. And not with her. He was too emotionally invested.

But what if Peter was right? What if she did love him? He'd be a fool not to fight for that.

He thumped his palms on the desk, stood, crossed to the closed door, swung it open, and charged through before he chickened out.

Chapter 51

Hannah tossed the damp dishcloth into the sink, slammed her hands on her hips, and glared. "This is my life. I don't want you interfering."

Holding his hands in front of him, Peter backed up a step. "I'm sorry, but I can't stand by and watch you ruin your life." He tugged on the silver chain hanging around his neck. "You and Roman are acting like you're in high school. I was just trying to help."

"Help?" She shot him a sharp look. "You call going to Roman and showing him my article helping?"

He nodded.

"He left. Don't you remember? He left *me* at the forestry rec site."

"You told him to."

She heaved a sigh. "I know, but I didn't mean it. He should've known that." Another sigh escaped her mouth, and she sagged against the kitchen counter. "He made his feelings clear when he chose his job over me. Over us."

"Give the guy a chance, will you?" His features softened, his light-blue eyes turning the color of an alpine lake. "If he comes over here and wants to talk, hear him out. Please? Will you do that for me? Will you listen to him?"

Would she?

Maybe. Maybe not.

Besides, it was a moot point. Roman wasn't going

to show up at her door. He was too concerned about preserving his precious job. An image of his soulful gaze watching as the helicopter she was in soared into the sky flickered before her, and a kernel of doubt arose. What if she was wrong? What if she'd misjudged him? "If—and that's a big if—*if* he comes here and wants to talk, I *might* be prepared to listen."

"Thanks, Sis." He grabbed his coat off the back of the chair where he'd dropped it when he arrived two hours earlier for an early supper of baked chicken breasts, wild rice, and green salad. Shrugging into the distressed leather jacket, he smiled. "Well, I'm off. My plane leaves in a couple of hours. I'll call you when I land in Fort Cutter." He strode down the short hall to the apartment door.

"Not so fast, brother."

He stopped and turned back, a frown furrowing his brow. "What is it?"

"Why are you acting like a bearded Cupid? What's it to you if Roman and I work this out or not? I would've thought that after what happened between you and Marissa, you'd be jaded about love and romance."

His face flamed red.

"Come on." She pinned him with a sharp gaze. "Spill."

"After…er…um…after we returned to Fort Cutter, I checked my cell phone. There were a dozen texts from Marissa."

"What did she want?" She frowned. The breakup of his marriage had gutted him, and she couldn't bear to watch him suffer through that pain again.

"She—" His Adam's apple bobbed in his throat as he swallowed. "—she wants to talk." More swallowing.

"She wants to try and work things out."

"Marissa wants to get back together?" She moved closer and peered into his eyes. "What are you thinking?"

"I don't know."

She opened her mouth to tell him that Marissa had walked away from *him*, and she was the one who'd ended the marriage. But the hope in his eyes curbed her tongue. "You want this, don't you? You want to be with her."

He nodded. "I'd like to give it a shot. We were good together once. Maybe we can be that way again."

She enfolded him in her arms and squeezed. "I hope it works out. You deserve to be happy."

He stepped back. "You do too, Stick. Remember that." He opened the door and smiled. "I'll catch you on the flip side."

He closed the door, and she stood there, listening to the heavy clomp of his boots as he strode down the hall. The ping of the elevator, and then he was gone. She said a silent prayer, hoping he and Marissa were able to work things out.

Her step was lighter as she strode into the kitchen. At least one Marchand sibling's love life was picking up. She grabbed the wet dishcloth and wiped the top of the stove. She'd already cleaned the kitchen after their meal, but she needed to do something mindless, something to keep her busy while her brain buzzed.

Thirty minutes later, she tossed the cloth into the sink. The kitchen gleamed, but she wasn't any closer to resolving her feelings. Peter had told her Roman read the magazine article. The story on Keyoh was the most challenging article she'd ever tackled, but also the easiest to write.

Once she started writing, her exhaustion faded, and the words flowed. She'd worked through the night, finishing in the early hours of the morning. Usually the first draft was rough and required hours of editing and revising. Not this time. She'd read the finished article through once, and before she could second-guess herself, she hit Send, and the article was on its way to Marilyn's inbox.

Purged, feeling as if she'd wrung the last drop of blood from her body, she'd collapsed and hadn't come up for air until late the following afternoon when the persistent ringing of her cell phone drove her out of bed.

It was Marilyn. The managing editor was thrilled with Hannah's article, so thrilled she wanted to publish a special early edition and feature the article on the cover.

Hannah should've been ecstatic. Making the cover was her dream, but she couldn't get excited. The story was too personal, the hurt too real.

The magazine had hit the stands earlier that morning, and the phone started ringing. She wasn't only the author of the article; she was part of the story. Reporters from all the major media outlets wanted a comment. Television talk shows called, desperate for in-depth interviews. She even had an offer of a book deal.

She turned everyone down. She'd said what she wanted to say and didn't have any interest in discussing the story.

The police had called and informed her of Sam's involvement. Her deranged stalker had offered the archaeology student a great deal of money if he helped him hide out at Keyoh. Sam confessed to his crimes, but he swore he didn't know what Derek planned, and he wasn't involved with the vandalism of Roman's tent, or the destruction of the boats and the satellite phone. He thought Derek was in love with Hannah and was making a grand gesture to win her back.

Grand gesture.

Her lip curled. Following someone and spying on them was real romantic. An even truer sign of love was shooting at the object of your affection. Now that was love.

She wasn't angry with Sam. He was just a kid, another of Derek's victims. When things went south, Sam realized he'd been duped, but by then he was in too deep. He was terrified that if he confessed, Derek would harm him.

Standing on her tiptoes, she opened the cupboard over the fridge and grabbed a bottle of red wine. She needed something stronger than tea tonight, something that would take the edge off her pain and slow the cacophony of thoughts tumbling through her brain. She twisted off the lid, snatched a wine glass from another cupboard, and poured the wine into the glass.

The rich fruity flavor of blueberries filled the small kitchen. She lifted the glass and sipped, closing her eyes, savoring the sweet, dark flavor. The wine slipped like silk down her throat, warming her belly. Her toes and fingers tingled.

She gripped the glass in one hand and the bottle in the other and walked into the living room and sank onto her recliner. She drew her feet up under her, settled back against the soft cushions, and sampled more wine. Grabbing the television remote control, she flicked on the TV. Wine and watching a mindless television show—escape, in every sense of the word.

She refilled her glass and glanced back at the reality show portraying beautiful young people, dressed in skimpy bathing suits that revealed their perfect bodies, on a hot beach in Mexico as they searched for love. A ridiculous concept, but the shenanigans and fake tears of the cast members kept her mind off her own problems.

The doorbell rang, and she startled, slopping a splash of wine onto the arm of the chair. Cursing, she grabbed a tissue from her pocket and swiped the red blotch.

Another long peal rattled her nerves. She checked the time. Damn reporters wouldn't leave her alone. Calling wasn't enough? They had to track her down at home? Pushing to her feet, she marched over to the intercom on the wall by the door. "Who is it?"

Static crackled, mixed with the sound of cars swishing by on the wet street. "Hannah? It's me. Roman. May I come up? We need to talk."

She stumbled back from the door. Flattening her hand over her stomach, she drew in deep shaky breaths.

Roman.

Peter must have given him her address.

Her hand trembled as she hit the buzzer that unlocked the lobby door.

Chapter 52

She scratched her arm and her neck, though the bug bites had long faded. Her stomach fluttered and her legs wobbled, her knees jelly. She stumbled to the wall and leaned against its cool hard surface. What did he want to say that was so urgent? Was it the article? Was he angry about her story and her portrayal of Keyoh and his role in the excavation?

The urge to flee was overpowering. But where would she go? The fire escape? A collapsible metal ladder hung outside her bedroom window in case of a fire. She laughed, the nervous titter grating on her nerves. She could picture the expression on his face if he entered her apartment and found her, three floors above the hard ground, hanging by her hands and feet from a rickety ladder. Besides, she hated heights.

She jolted and bit back a yelp at a soft knock on the door. Smoothing her hand over her hair, she tucked in stray curls, pushed away from the wall, slid the security chain off, twisted the deadbolt, and opened the door.

His tall frame and lean, muscular body filled the doorway. "Thanks for letting me come up."

He smelled like rain, fresh air, and him. She crossed her arms over her chest, trying not to breathe. "What do you want?"

"May I come in?"

No. Go away. Leave me alone. You've hurt me

enough. The biting responses trembled on the tip of her tongue, but she didn't speak the words aloud. Instead, she nodded and walked into the living room, praying her wobbly legs would support her.

She sank onto the recliner, perching on the edge of the seat, and folded her hands on her lap. The half-full glass of wine on the table beckoned, and she fought the urge to grab the glass and drain the contents.

He shrugged out of his jean jacket, laid the faded denim coat across the arm of the couch, and sat on the couch facing her.

"Don't you have an excavation to run? I thought you'd be back at Keyoh." She couldn't keep the hurt out of her voice.

"I booked a flight for tomorrow afternoon. The project's over, but the crew and I need to pack up our equipment and backfill the excavation pits."

"You're ending the excavation early?"

"After everything that happened, I thought it was best."

"The police told me about Sam." She smoothed her palms on her thighs. "I couldn't believe it. He was such a nice young man."

"Derek's an expert manipulator, and Sam's just a kid." His mouth curved in that sad smile again. "He thought helping Derek was an adventure. I guess it was, until the whole sorry scheme blazed out of control, but then it was too late. Sam was in too deep. When he was released on bail on his parents' recognizance, he called me and apologized." He rubbed the back of his neck. "I'm not going to press charges. I think he's learned his lesson."

"That's nice of you. He deserves a second chance."

The silence lengthened, broken only by the soft ticking of the clock in the kitchen and the rumble of a large vehicle on the street outside.

"I read your article."

Her heart skipped a beat. So, he *was* there about the story. "Peter told me he gave you a copy."

"You talked to Peter?"

"I had him over for supper. He just left to catch his plane to Fort Cutter. He has to be back at work tomorrow morning."

"I see *Aspire* published a special edition of your story."

"Is that why you're here? You're unhappy with the article?"

His brow furrowed. "No. Not at all. I thought the story was great. You did an excellent job."

"Really?" She sank back on the chair, struggling to take in his unexpected words of praise. *He liked the article!* Until that second, she hadn't realized how important his opinion was. She wanted to jump up and pump her fist in the air.

"Really." He smiled, and the dimples in his cheeks flashed.

"That's great. Really great." A matching smile filled her face.

"Because of your article, the archaeology board chairman at the university has agreed to issue me a permit to run an extended excavation at Keyoh next season." His smile widened. "I'll be in charge of ten post-graduate students, and our budget is triple what I had this year." Happiness radiated off him in visible waves. "I owe you a big thank you."

The happier he was, the heavier her heart.

Excavating Keyoh was his dream. But her hopes faded at the realization he'd come to see her, not to express his undying devotion, but to thank her for doing her job, for writing an unbiased article on the Keyoh project and all the events that happened. "That's great." Her voice was wooden and stilted. "What does Nathaniel think?"

"He's still at Keyoh. I left Shas with him." He threaded his fingers through his silky black hair. "I talked to Dr. Martens, and I've convinced him the excavation should change its focus. I plan on hiring local Indigenous youth to assist with the project. That way, they'll see firsthand what an archaeology excavation entails and be right there when artifacts are uncovered." His dark eyes sparked. "Nathaniel and other Saik'uz elders will be housed at the site. They'll meet daily with Dakelh youth and share Indigenous oral history and traditions."

"It's a wonderful idea. You'll get to continue your excavation, and your grandfather will have an opportunity to pass on his knowledge of Dakelh culture. It sounds like a win-win."

"Do you think so?"

"I do." Once again, silence settled over the room, expanding with each second, sucking out the oxygen, until she felt like she was suffocating.

He cleared his throat. "I didn't come here to discuss your article—though it's terrific—or next year's project or Nathaniel."

"Okay." She rubbed at the red-wine stain on the recliner's upholstery.

"I-I wanted to apologize."

She stopped rubbing.

"I'm sorry for being such a jerk. I should've trusted you from the beginning." He stared at his hands on his lap. When he glanced up, his eyes were fathomless dark pools. "I don't deserve your forgiveness, and I won't blame you if you don't accept my apology. I-I wanted you to know how much—" He swallowed, his Adam's apple working in his tanned throat. "—how much you mean to me. I respect you as a journalist and as a woman." He met her gaze. "I love you, Hannah."

She gaped. Her mouth literally dropped open. The hot coal in her soul flickered to a tiny flame and flared into a raging fire.

He loved her!

The rustle of clothing cut through her riotous thoughts, and she focused. He was zipping up his coat. "Where are you going?"

"Home."

"Wait. What? You're leaving *now*? After the bomb you just detonated?"

"I wouldn't call telling you I love you a bomb." He fished in his coat pocket and tugged out a small jewelry box. "I have something for you."

She stood, her knees shaking, and crept closer, one careful step at a time. "What's that?"

He placed the small blue box in her hand. "Open it and see."

She stared at the box and back at him. "Are-are you sure?"

He smiled. "Go on. Open it."

Fingers trembling, she lifted the lid. Her breath rushed out in a blast of air. Resting on a white satin pad was the teardrop amber agate. A delicate gold chain was looped around the narrow tip of the glossy stone. "I don't understand."

He grinned, the dimples dancing. "Turns out it's not

an artifact. It's what we call a geofact, a stone shaped by thousands of years of erosion and glacial action. I thought you'd like it."

"Like it? I love it." She held up the necklace. The agate's translucent amber surface glowed in the lamplight. "Help me put it on."

He plucked the necklace from her fingers and moved behind her.

Centimeters separated his body from hers, and unable to help herself, she leaned back against his muscular chest.

His fingers brushed the sensitive skin on her neck as he draped the thin gold chain over her head and set the lock on the clasp.

He stepped away, and she sighed at the loss of the physical connection. She ran her fingers over the satiny stone. "Did you mean what you said?"

"About the agate being a geofact?" The corners of his eyes crinkled.

"No. Not that. The other thing you said."

"I did. I do. I love you."

Her heart swelled, and with a joyous cry, she leaped into his arms. "I love you too, Roman."

He lowered his head and claimed her lips in a kiss that seared her to the soles of her feet. She moaned, opening her mouth, welcoming him in.

She was breathless when he lifted his head, his eyes heavy with desire, a loving smile wreathing his rugged face.

"I love you, Hannah. I really do."

Joy filled her, and for the first time in her life, she felt complete.

She loved him. He loved her.

Her luck had changed. The Marchands were batting a thousand in the romance department.

His dark eyes, no longer shadowed, glowed with love and promise. He kissed her again, and her heart soared with happiness.

The teardrop agate pulsed warmly, nestled in the darkness between her breasts.

Lucky in love indeed.

Author Afterword

Hunting Hannah takes place at an historic location I called Keyoh (the Dakelh word for village) in the story, but it's based on an actual Dakelh site. Nestled at the confluence of the Nechako and Stuart Rivers in the heart of the traditional territory of the Saik'uz First Nations in North West British Columbia, Chinlac is the site of a once-thriving Dakelh village that was destroyed in 1745 in a bloody massacre.

There are no written records of the village, and information is gained through the oral history of the local Indigenous people, who tell that a Tsilhqot'in war party traveled hundreds of kilometers north and attacked the village while the chief (Khadintal) was away hunting. The invaders brutally murdered most of the inhabitants and burned the lodges. When Khadintal returned, he and the few remaining survivors piled the bodies of their loved ones in heaps and cremated them according to Dakelh tradition.

Over the centuries, the site became overgrown and lost to history. Father Adrian Morice, a Roman Catholic missionary traveling through the area in 1890, heard the story and recorded the tragic event in his journal, but it wasn't until 1951 that Charles Edward Borden and a team of archaeologists excavated part of the site. They found traces of thirteen burned lodges, hundreds of cache pits used to store food, porcelain and glass beads, iron and stone projectile points, awls, and an iron blade.

The most astounding discovery was a copper Chinese coin, dating from the Song Dynasty (960-1125 CE). This artifact proves that precontact Indigenous people traveled hundreds of kilometers along forest trails that connected the Interior of British Columbia with the Pacific Coast and traded with foreign visitors. Chinlac is one of the richest archaeological sites in B.C.

As an archaeology major, the story of Chinlac has long fascinated me, and as part of researching this novel, I paddled in a canoe for two days down the remote and beautiful Stuart River from Fort St. James to Chinlac.

The site sits atop a steep cliff overlooking the Chinlac Rapids. The remains of an ancient weir used by the inhabitants to catch salmon is visible in low water. Today, the site, set in a clearing amidst towering fir trees, remains deserted, with only depressions in the ground to indicate the existence of the once-thriving village. The haunting beauty and stillness called to me, and I knew Chinlac would be the perfect setting for the story of Hannah and Roman.

Roman, Hannah, Nathaniel, and the other characters, and the things they say and do in this book, are entirely the product of the author's imagination.

A word about the author...

C.B. Clark has always loved reading, especially romances, but it wasn't until she lost her voice for a year that she considered writing her own romantic suspense stories. She grew up in Canada's Northwest Territories and Yukon. Graduating with a degree in anthropology and archaeology, she has worked as an archaeologist and an educator, teaching students from the primary grades through the first year of college. She enjoys hiking, canoeing, and snowshoeing with her husband and dog near her home in the wilderness of central British Columbia.

Thank you for purchasing
this publication of The Wild Rose Press, Inc.

For questions or more information
contact us at
info@thewildrosepress.com.

The Wild Rose Press, Inc.
www.thewildrosepress.com